Lucifer's Guide

Book One of the Cowboys and Angels Saga

Deborah Riley-Magnus

Lucifer's Guide

Book 1
Cowboys and Angels Saga

by

Deborah Riley-Magnus

ISBN – Paperback: 978-0-9980273-0-2
ISBN – ebook: 978-0-9980273-3-3

Dedication

Dedicated to all my fanfiction loving friends.
You know who you are.

CHAPTER 1

The essence of love is not bestowed upon humans alone. It was spread among all God's creatures of thought and choice and free will, including those far above who carry the staggering responsibilities of watching over the frail beings of blood and bone below. Mr. Paul was among the best of His forces, an accomplished Elite Guardian destined to sit on the Celestial Judgment Committee before the end of the millennium. But time, fluid as air, moves in many directions in the heavens and brutally affects all who work in critical departments, from the Elite Guardians of the Earthbound Saints, to the mere simplicity of the Angel Traffic Division.

Those who toil in Traffic are fine, well meaning angels who began their careers in sacrifice as volunteers. Those who remain tenacious in their efforts find ways to advance their careers in order to do more exciting and interesting work. Most, but not all.

The Traffic Division is the heavenly unit dedicated to the uncomplicated challenges of human life. Traffic Angels watch over simple souls like homemakers, husbands, shopkeepers, and children with the sole purpose of protecting them from harm. Tough work, but nothing like the big leagues. Traffic Angels never cross paths with the superstars of humanity, seldom see the complexities of watching over those who shape the world and lead mankind. Traffic Angels are the average Guardian Angels everyone knows exist. The angels that make sure you stop at the red light, just miss the bad weather, or suddenly remember your mother's birthday. It could be boring, mundane work, or it could be fun, as Vibrant Light, the Traffic Angel also known as Vivi, had learned long ago.

"And that is the issue, Vivi. You seem to feel this is all a game for your entertainment," Mr. Paul said calmly and leaned back to eye his one-woman repeat catastrophe. Vivi stood at his desk, her brilliant golden eyes ahead but the shadow of a grin on her lips. For over a thousand years he had managed the rag-tag collection of Traffic Angels, some extraordinary, some fulfilling their limited potential, and some, like Vivi, not actually getting it. She had what it took to go far, but unfortunately, just didn't seem to know how to get there. For the hundredth time he mentally questioned his own ability to guide her, but alas, it was now out of his hands. He had one last shot at helping this lost angel. It was an important but simple case. He already knew where it would lead and why, but he couldn't help wondering how she would handle the challenge.

"I'm prepared to give you one more chance."

"Oh goodie, another last chance." She sighed and rolled her eyes. "What's it to be this time?"

He ignored her disrespectful mannerism, knowing full well it was simply her personality and not intended to insult, but Vibrant Light had a rude awakening ahead. He secretly grinned, choosing to hold that bit of information for just a little longer.

"I am giving you an exclusive case. This will not be easy for you, Vivi. You absolutely must follow the rules. You will watch over this particular Charge until his death. Watch over him and protect him no matter what he does." Mr. Paul's voice became stronger as he spoke, watching her expression change with every word. "You are not to interfere with his free will or attempt to redirect his choices in any way. There are valuable outcomes to be benefited by what he is destined to become and the deeds he will perform."

"So, I'm just to watch him? What about his soul?"

"That is not your concern. Repeat the responsibilities, please."

"I understand them, I really do." Her brow knotted. "I just don't understand why. What good am I if I can't make this man better?"

"He's not clay for you to mold." Mr. Paul stood and paced before her. "We have had this conversation over and over again. Vivi, listen to me. This is your last chance. You must follow orders to the letter this time."

"All right, all right. Let me get it all straight. Just watch over him and protect him from harm … nothing else. I get it."

"Do you? This is the most important case this division has on the books right now. Say something, anything to convince me you are not the wrong choice of guardian for this Charge."

"I'm not! I am the perfect choice. Holy crap, sir! I've been waiting so long for an opportunity to shine! I won't fail you."

He winced then nodded and returned to his chair. "You will be given a few powers you've never had before in order to carry out this assignment."

"Shoot. I'm ready. Whatever it is I can do it."

"No, you can't just yet. You will need training before you begin. The first power will be that of making your Charge hear your words and understand them. The second power is that of making yourself visible to him."

"That's amazing! So I probably need to think about clothes and things like that. Where am I going?"

"There's more, a few critical things you must understand. You may never, ever, permit this man to touch you physically and most especially emotionally, for there will be swift and severe repercussions should that occur."

"Swift repercussions. Got it. When do you start training me?"

Her excitement was obvious but there was a little bit of the devil in Mr. Paul where Vivi was concerned. "I won't be training you. I am leaving the Division this very day."

"A promotion?" she said with a gasp. "Well hell, everyone gets promoted but me! Where are you going?"

"That isn't your concern. You will be trained by—"

"Forgive my tardiness."

His eyes rose with pleasure, but Vivi's crunched tight.

"You have got to be kidding," the Traffic Angel hissed under her breath. It was no surprise that his replacement would displease Vivi. After all, her long ago training days nightmare just walked in the door, and it appeared the bad dreams were about to get worse. She turned, sweeping her wild dark hair over her shoulder with a swing. Her smile resembled a pained grimace. "Madam Miriam."

Miriam settled into Paul's chair and scowled. "You speak my name as though I were the keeper of a whorehouse, Vibrant Light. It smacks of disrespect."

"I meant no disrespect, ma'am. I swear."

"Yes, I understand you do that often too. Where are we, Mr. Paul?"

"The assignment has been outlined and I have explained the powers you will teach her to master. Vibrant Light seems to grasp the importance of this assignment ... to the Charge and to her own career."

"Very well. They await you in the gardens Mr. Paul."

As he left his office in the Traffic Division for the last time, his fingers grazed Miriam's and he felt the spark of love. Paul and Miriam were together in the deepest sort of way, a rarity in heaven. Hopefully Vivi didn't notice. Such knowledge would give her an edge, if not with her new boss lady, at least with her colleagues.

* * *

Mama was crying again. He could hear her soft sobs through his door. She wasn't crying because Daddy was dead. She was crying because she didn't know what to do next. She planned to go back east. He didn't want to leave.

Eight-year-old Raphael Bennett didn't necessarily like the dried-up Texas Territory town or his life, but he went to school religiously and was a good student, even though the old spinster teacher didn't like him. She said his mother was a whore. Rafe knew nothing about his mother before, cared even less. She was his mother and all he had left.

His daddy wasn't a good man, but he was the only father he knew. The sheriff came by the day before and Rafe listened at the door. Prosser Bennett was shot dead in the saloon by a man called Boston Shark, another gambler who made all kinds of ruckus in town. He accused Bennett of cheating, of killing his kid brother ten years ago, and stealing his horse last month in Tulsa.

Prosser Bennett was a smug bastard, said he didn't know nothing about no dead brother and he was never in Tulsa. Everyone, even young Rafe, knew Bennett went to Tulsa often to visit a loose lady friend named Goldie. Then Rafe's daddy did something real stupid. He reached over, took Shark's whisky and downed it right in front of the man. Got himself killed for it.

They'd buried Daddy that very day and Mama had already started packing up their meager possessions. Since he couldn't convince her they'd be fine staying in Texas, Rafe decided to help her. As he left his small room, he saw the door fly open. His mother stood straight from her packing and carefully gripped Daddy's pistol, hidden in her trembling hand behind her back.

"What do you want, Shark? Ain't you caused enough damage?" she shouted and Rafe moved closer, sidling near his mother's skirts.

The man was big and shiny, even his teeth glowed. His vest looked like spun gold and his mustache was trimmed to perfection. "Evenin' Mrs. Bennett. Maybe I come to offer my condolences?"

"You killed my husband. Get outta here!" Garland Bennett was usually a brave woman. She was a tough woman living a tough life, but her hand had begun to shake so hard Rafe feared she'd drop the pistol.

The boy slowly put his arm behind her and took the gun, held it firmly in his hidden hand and growled. "You heard her, mister. Get outta here."

"Well see, your daddy, he owed me a lot of money. I'm here to collect my winnings."

"We got nothing, Shark." Garland's voice trembled.

"Oh, you got somethin' that'll fulfill my needs and pay off your dead husband's debts too. Ain't like a whore ever forgets how to whore, Garland. And it ain't like it'll be our first time, either. You gonna send your boy outta the room, or we gonna show him how it's done?"

Rafe gripped the hidden gun tighter, pulled back the hammer and shouted. "I said get outta here!"

"Maybe I should tie you up and make you watch, kid." He stepped closer and Rafe swung a full circle, quickly pushed the barrel forward and squeezed the trigger, just like his daddy taught him. Boston Shark dropped hard onto his back with a splattering thud. Already his dead eyes looked empty.

Rafe tumbled to his behind with a gasp. The spray of still warm blood soaked his shirt and he struggled to stand and catch his breath. Garland simply blinked.

It took several moments, but she finally spoke. "Boy, go get the shovel then help me pull up these floorboards."

"Why?" his voice sounded like a baby still at the teat. "Why?" he repeated stronger and look down at the dead man.

"Just do as I say. Quickly."

It took hours but together they buried Boston Shark under the floor. The boards were replaced and Garland scrubbed the wood raw to clean away the blood. "We're leavin', Rafe. We're leavin' right now."

She lifted her bag, swallowed hard then turned to fully face him. "Rafe, what we did ain't right. You understand?"

The boy thought for a moment. "Yeah, it was."

"No, Rafe. It wasn't right and we can't never say nothing about it again. It wasn't right." She turned and left the shabby cabin.

Rafe followed, his head shaking. "Yeah, it was," he said under his breath

Garland mumbled low and quiet as they walked. "So many things I done wrong, so many chances to make it right, and here I am, doing wrong again." She turned a glare at him but continued to walk briskly. "It's you that worries me. It's you that can be my redemption, boy. If I can grow you into a good man, maybe it'd make up for my mistakes."

At the crumbling train station, she put down her bag and opened it. "Here," she said and handed the Bible to her son. "You sit here and you read this. You gotta learn. Some things just can't be done, or you pay. Pay forever."

His crystal blue eyes rose from beneath a curtain of wild dark chestnut waves. "You want me to think like the preachers? Start believing in hellfire and brimstone? Mama, he was gonna hurt you. What I did wasn't wrong. It had to be done."

Anger brewed in her eyes. She reached down and grasped his collar tight in her balled fist, leaned her nose close to his and hissed. "You read this. You learn somethin' me and your worthless daddy didn't never teach you."

She released her grip and tenderly kissed his brow, but only after he opened the bible to the first page. "Good. You're a good boy, Raphael Bennett. Now I'm gonna go get our tickets. Might take a while but I'll be back. You just keep studying that bible."

"Yes, Mama."

* * *

6

Outside the station Garland looked right and she looked left. She had some options. She could go to the sheriff and say that she shot Shark dead, lie to protect her son from ever facing it all, but that would just get her hanged. Her other choice was to get money for the train tickets. More money than she had. In her pocket was a pair of diamond earbobs she'd kept hidden from Prosser. If she could sell them, they'd ride to Philadelphia in style. If she couldn't, she could just go to the saloon and offer herself. A few men would earn her enough to get them some tickets. The dead man under her house was right, it ain't like a whore ever forgets how to whore.

Garland Bennett couldn't sell the earbobs, no one in town had what they were worth and she was afraid to let them go for too little. In Philadelphia she could get a fair price for them, get a good start for her and her boy.

With a quick rip, she removed the fabric covering her cleavage, tucked it back provocatively then she pinched pinkness into her cheeks. She tugged the right side of her skirt to her waist and tied it to her belt. She smoothed her hair and walked into the saloon. Not too late to get a good price for her body. She was still young, still pretty, and not too work-worn or skinny. There were several gamblers and steer drivers there, even a few rich ranchers she knew for a fact weren't faithful to their wives. She got several offers but held out for the best one. He was a man who looked a lot like Prosser Bennett and dressed a lot like Boston Shark.

He took her to his hotel room.

No one found her body for three days.

* * *

Vivi wasn't the patient sort. She'd never been good at practicing anything until she had it right, but there was something about going head to head with Madam Miriam that made her determined beyond reason. Unlike her normal banter with Mr. Paul, when Miriam demanded that she repeat something, she recited like a trained parakeet. She even remembered what she repeated. That amazed her. Could it have really been that easy to move herself ahead? Or was she just hell bent on proving to the grand Madam that she was the perfect angel for the job?

And what was the job, exactly? It wasn't until she had perfected her new powers and could state the appropriated situations in which to use them that it occurred to her to ask for a few more details about her new Charge.

"Must be someone important for me to get all this training, right?"

"Well, Vibrant Light," Miriam mused and gazed off into the distance. "There is important, and there is important. Naturally, every human is watched over by an angel, this Charge is no different. You must keep one thing in mind. Never forget that this assignment is as much a learning process for you as it will be for him. If you hold to the simple rules and always remember that this is all a test, you will succeed."

"That simple, huh?" Vivi fluffed her mass of wild dark curls and leveled a golden gaze onto the grand Madam. "May I ask you a question?"

"That's what I'm here for."

"Why bother? I mean, why me? If you all think I'll never be more than a mediocre Traffic Angel, why are you doing all this? Why the five-hundredth last chance?"

Miriam sighed. "Vivi, Mr. Paul believes in you, and I believe in you. This just might be the case to help you break through. Now, repeat the rules, please."

"Arghhh! Fine. I'm to watch over this Charge until his death. Watch over him and protect him no matter what he does. I'm not to interfere with his free will or attempt to redirect his choices in any way." She took a deep breath and continued. "This assignment is important to the Charge and important to my career."

"And?"

"And ... oh right. And I can make him hear me and see me, but I may never let him touch me, physically or emotionally." Vivi grinned with pride.

"Or?"

"Oh yeah. Or there will be swift and severe consequences ... repercussions ... ah, just don't do it. Right?"

"Correct," Miriam stood and settled her hand on Vivi's head. "And now, it's time to begin. Be careful, Vibrant Light. Be careful."

8

In the blink of an eye Vivi found herself standing in the dark corner of a train station. The place smelled of dry dust and urine and oil from a flickering lamp. Outside it was quiet. Inside, she was practically alone. She carefully eyed the few people there.

An old Indian man with long grey braids looked her square in the eye then shifted his vision across the room. She followed his focus but there was no one there except a young boy reading a book in the failing light. She must have imagined that the old man seemed to be guiding her to her Charge. That was just a kid, not an important assignment.

Several feet away and cramped tightly in the far corner of the bench sat a young woman in buckskin, drunk, snoring and grumbling at her dreams. She looked interesting, but Vivi knew that her change was a man. Vivi sat on the bench between the woman and the boy and she waited.

And waited.

And waited.

Travelers came and left and when the wrinkled Indian stood to board the train, he gave her a direct glare and insistently pointed to the little boy. Odd, thought Vivi. Was she misusing her powers and could the old man actually see her?

No, it couldn't be. So she waited longer. Two days passed before she realized her assignment had to be the boy, he was the only one still sitting in the ugly train station. She was to watch over a child?

Well hell. This isn't what I expected at all. She gazed at the ceiling and wondered if Madam Miriam was up there having a good laugh.

CHAPTER 2

Vivi was bored near tears. Another night passed and again the boy curled up on the bench and snuggled his head on the large carpetbag beside him. He's been sparingly eating hardtack from a linen bundle and reading, reading, reading. People came, and people went. Once or twice, she had nudged a waiting traveler into a kindness toward the child, but either he refused the offering of food, or ignored it.

On the third day she watched him read the last page of his book then flip to the front and begin to read it all over again. She'd walk behind to see what he was reading, to pace the small space, or simply grit her teeth. What kind of assignment was this? If her Charge was a child, where were his parents? Why was he alone? But asking those questions didn't create enough curiosity in her to really watch and attempt to understand. They only served to irritate her further.

The day blazed, hot but heavy with clouds that made the small station even darker. She sat in her strange garments and tugged at the tight corset. Her research of appropriate clothing was minimal and mainly out of curiosity, an inquisitiveness drawn from her newly acquired skills and the thrill of using them at some point. If she decided to be seen, she intended to appear correct but the garments were unbearable. They were heavy, hot, and uncomfortable. Her shoes pinched her feet, and her body itched with perspiration. Imitating human, and being human, were two different things, and what she experienced gave her a whole new respect for those coming and going around her.

Another train arrived and chugged off and again she was alone with the boy. A man swaggered in, looked around then chuckled and sat next to the child.

Madame Miriam was on the ball up in the heavens, and knowledge of this particular man flooded Vivi's mind. Cole Eddings was a gun for hire. He and his brother Spenser traveled light and moved fast, but that afternoon they had stopped to smell the roses that scented a whore's flesh and drifted in the air close to her neck. Rose water was nothing but a perfume for covering up the Texas sweat stench, but a major attraction to men like Cole and Spenser all the same.

Vivi took in the man, his brutish dark form, stocky, sturdy. He was nearly bald, but not so old he couldn't move at a brisk pace, or demand the attention of anyone he wanted. His legs were bowed and his arms were thick, his knuckles speckled with coarse dark hair.

"What's that?" Cole grunted and reached for the book. The boy said nothing but pulled it away, turned his back and continued to read. Cole chuckled and took it roughly, slamming it closed and reading the cover aloud. "King James Bible. Now, what kinda entertainment is that for a young man like you?"

The boy pulled at it firmly but could not retrieve it. "I'm reading it, Mister."

"No you ain't. You're just pretendin'." He flipped the cover and eyed a drawing the boy had scratched there with a piece of charcoal. "Who drew this pretty picture? You?"

"Leave me alone," spat the boy and Vivi sat at attention.

"Let's just take a closer look at what you been drawin'. Who's this?" He turned the book and the boy shrugged. "Well, she's a purty one, that's sure. But you drew some strange eyes."

"They're gold. Now, gimme back my book."

Spenser stomped his dusty boots at the open doorway then leaned casually against the jamb. Unlike Cole, Spenser Eddings was a handsome man. Tall with hair the color of summer wheat, corn flower blue eyes, broad shoulders and a charming smile. "Cole, I thought we were goin' to the saloon."

"Yeah, yeah, just came in here to see what I could see … and look what I see." He grinned and held up the drawing.

12

"Whee ha, I'd like to see the rest of that lady. You draw that, kid?"

Vivi suddenly felt what she'd never expected. Aside from a desperate desire to protect the child, she felt the need to see how he would protect himself. Holding herself in check, she watched him nonchalantly reach into the carpetbag and calmly lift out a pistol

"What the fuck? Cole, you see what he got?" Spenser straightened.

"I see it, but he don't know what to do with that gun. Do ya boy?"

The kid said nothing, simply gripped the handle and glared at Cole.

"What's your name, kid?"

"Rafe Bennett," he snarled and fingered the trigger.

Spenser snorted nervously. "Bet you can't even shoot that thing."

"I already killed a man, mister."

"Have ya now?" Cole stood abruptly and snapped a tight grasp on the boy's shoulder. "What say we go outside and you show us you really can shoot that pistol?"

Vivi was on her feet and swiftly on their heels. Was this when she was supposed to step in? Every case scenario slid through her mind. Every one but what actually happened. She expected them to take the gun, shoot the kid, wound him or worse yet, kill him. She listened as they walked ahead.

"What're you doin' all alone in that station, Rafe Bennett?" Spenser growled as he took long strides, following Cole and the kid around a corner and behind the livery stable.

"My mother told me to wait there."

"When'd she leave?" Cole set a rusted can atop a log and dragged the boy, gun in his small hand, back fifteen feet.

"Three days ago," the kid said, carefully raised the pistol and aimed. "She ain't comin' back." He squeezed the trigger and the can clanged loud then flipped into the air.

"Fuckin' Christ," gasped Spenser. "Do that again."

Cole replaced the can and the kid sprung it into the air again. "Who taught you to shoot like that?"

"My daddy. He taught me. Now can I go?"

Cole laughed, took the pistol, tossed it to Spenser then heaved the boy like a sack of dried beans.

Oh shit! Oh shit! Oh shit! Vivi ran to follow as the men headed for their horses. When they mounted, flopping the child over the saddle in front of Cole, she panicked. She pursed her lips, blew then spit. The rain

13

immediately obeyed, pouring a deluge over them. The men seemed completely impervious, but Vivi was perilously affected.

She tried to run after the horses but her skirts became so heavily soaked and twisted around her ankles that she dropped onto her face, a full sprawl into a puddle of mud and horseshit.

"No! No, no, no! Dammit!" Her hands slapped soft wet soil once, then twice, but the third time it was different. That time it was obvious that her palm was no longer splattering water, but hitting solid, cool marble. "Ah damn," she groaned and looked up, spitting mud. Her eyes trailing from the gilded sandals to Madam Miriam's very angry face.

"Well," Miriam growled.

"Well," repeated Vivi as she straightened her soaked skirts and stood at attention. "What did I do wrong?" Her fear was that it was over, that she'd failed miserably and would never get another chance. Not this time.

"What do you think you did wrong?" Miriam walked a circle around the mud soaked angel. "You were supposed to protect him. Watch over him. You were not instructed in any way to redirect his destiny."

"How was I to know if those men were part of his destiny or part of his demise?" Vivi said, frustration raising her voice.

"Pay attention! Watch him! See what's going on around him! Think, girl, I expect you to think!"

A sickening sense of ineffectiveness washed over Vibrant. A feeling of neglect on her part that was inexcusable. Madam Miriam was correct. Recalling the three silent days alone with the boy in the station, there were in fact several clues as to what was to come. Why hadn't she looked for them, digested them, understood them? She groaned and her shoulders drooped with disappointment.

"What would you have done, Madam?"

Miriam sat and crossed her legs casually. "First of all, I'd have done what I could to discover my Charge's situation. Investigated, did a little moving around that town. Someone knew about him, someone might have said something about that boy that could have given you valuable clues. Even in that station there were signs. Signs as clear as a bell."

Vivi nodded agreement but made no excuses. What excuses were there? She'd been careless.

"Second, I would not have called the weather. Vivi, you must know your limitations, and know them precisely. Calling nature, and controlling nature, are two very special skill sets. You didn't think ahead, you didn't see the ramifications. All you did was create an obstacle for yourself.

"An angel walking the earth is highly affected by the elements. Did you think that storm would be easy for you to navigate? It was destined to be a major difficulty. You put yourself at a great disadvantage."

Again Vivi nodded and listened carefully. She would keep the lessons learned sharp in her mind should she ever get another last chance.

"And finally, I'd have rethought the clothing. Chosen something I could move more easily in, less encumbering. Yes, yes, I understand the attraction of being seen pretty and prim and proper, but Vivi, the priority is the performance of your duties. When, and if you ever chose to be seen, it would not be a situation where the clothes on your back hold any importance. Common sense, Angel. Common sense."

Vivi shrugged belligerently and rolled her eyes in an attempt to hide her mounting tears. She had hoped so much that she'd succeed. "Now what?"

Miriam tapped a finger on her desk. "Now we go back to the beginning. I must tell you, this is most disappointing and certainly not the best time to be absent from young Bennett's life. But we have no choice. Go immediately to the training grounds and prepare for a crash course. I expect you to be up to your top skills level as soon as possible."

Vivi blinked and a tear rolled down her cheek. "I'm still on the case?"

"Go, Vibrant Light. I suggest you not press me, I am already doubtful of my decision."

Miriam leaned back as the soaked angel strode purposely toward her and took her into a dirty, wet embrace.

"Thank you! Thank you! I won't let you down, I promise!" Vivi called as she rushed down the shimmering, brilliant marble hallway. "I swear!"

"No swearing!" shouted Miriam and turned to hide her smile.

* * *

15

Vivi put herself wholeheartedly to the test, punctuating her efforts with constant mental reviews of what she'd experienced and what she had observed during her brief few days on earth. She considered everything, from how she should see the situations, to how she should react to them. When Miriam called, Vivi knew she was as prepared as any angel should be, maybe even more.

"What did you learn from all this?" the Madam asked.

Not the question Vivi expected but her mind was always quick. Only this time, it was quick with an appropriate answer rather than a glib retort.

"I learned to watch fully, plan carefully, and respond. Not just react, and never overreact."

Did the grand Madam respond with surprise? No, she simply accepted and somehow in Vivi's heart, she knew it was the best reaction she could have hoped for.

In retraining, she had learned the extent of her responsibilities, the complexities of the assignment and respect for the importance of the case. Even though she still didn't understand why it was so important, she would treat it as paramount. She'd learned to respect what she didn't know and deal with what she would be unable to manage. She'd learned to sharpen her proficiency, most especially her observation skills, honing them to receive every speck of information readily available at any given moment. Most especially, Vivi learned to value the dichotomy of human nature, the unpredictability of man, and to never assume anything.

She had chosen her clothing well this time, a mixture of fabrics and textures that not only reflected the period, but would perfectly blend in with her surroundings. She wore a soft tan homespun shirt, a warmer tan vest and pale brown velvet jacket over doeskin britches and brown boots. Vivi's shining black hair was bound in a long braid down her back. In her leather gloved hand, a pale white hat. Her eyes blazed with the color of polished gold and the brilliance of her sharpened, determined mind.

Miriam nodded approval. Vivi had found herself and discovered how to reflect it perfectly. Reflected in the Madam's eyes, she looked flawlessly dressed for the practicality of her mission, but she felt mysteriously beautiful at the same time. If this went well, heaven would not see her again until it was finished

Miriam reached out and straightened Vivi's collar like a loving mother. "Remember … never let him reach you, Vivi. Never let him touch your heart, or your body. Restrain him from your soul. Keep him as your professional responsibility and all will be well. Now," she smoothed the soft pale velvet shoulder. "It is time to go to work."

* * *

Rafe sat with his legs stretched long and his head tilted. He lounged at the back of the one room cabin they'd taken over. The place had been deserted by squatters some time ago, and the winter wind whistled through bug infested logs that made up the walls. He observed everything around him, the crackling fire in the hearth, the steamy breath floating from his lips, the smell of unwashed men, and his own growing distaste for the company he kept.

For almost eight years he'd ridden with Cole and Spenser Eddings. A quiet, thoughtful boy, he'd grown strong and sturdy giving the appearance of a man. Around him was the gang, a ragged collection of stupid assholes Spenser had gathered together a few months earlier. The conversation was a gruff, enthusiastic review of the train robbery they planned to pull in less than three hours. Rafe's mind clinked and crackled. He was never one to fall into the mad, frenetic energy during such times. He liked to watch and listen and think things through his own way.

Spenser led, and Rafe thought it was just plain wrong. He glanced around the cabin. Whittier had potential, was a good sharp shot and treated his rifle like it was something holy. Rafe appreciated that. As for the remaining three, he saw nothing but drunks and imbeciles. They were Spenser's boyhood buddies. Facing the challenge ahead alongside men he didn't trust or care about, Rafe felt the loss of Cole deeply.

The man he actually saw as his father was not Prosser Bennett, but Cole Eddings. Not a gentle or kind man, Cole was a man of intent. He was precise and direct and rough as the Rockies. He'd taught Rafe everything he knew before he got himself into a gunfight he had no chance of winning. Cole was faster than most, but a gun for hire had to

17

choose his opponents carefully. Cole wanted the money, his opponent wanted to live.

Whatever Cole taught Rafe had never been learned by Spenser. What began as a small enterprise comprised of three men with better than average pistol skills, had changed drastically after Cole's death. Spenser no longer wanted to earn his money, he wanted to take it.

Rafe rolled the concept around and around his mind. He liked it. It made sense to him. Men were men and would always take what they wanted, whether it was women, money, land, or lives. But following Spenser wasn't the way to get what he wanted. Short of a shootout, there were few ways to make the outfit his own, and oh yes, even at the tender age of sixteen, he already knew he would have his own gang.

He chuckled quietly and looked down at the sketch he'd scribbled. She was a woman he'd dreamed about a hundred times, a woman with eyes so golden they lit up the whole world. A woman who didn't exist, but in his mind she was his. He drew her often, her perfect face, her form, her softness and her edges. Someday, Rafe though, I gotta give her a name.

"You payin' attention boy?" shouted Spenser, glaring like it would scare Rafe but it got him nothing but a grin.

"Yeah, I hear you. I'll sit this one out, Spens."

"The fucking hell you will! You come or you get nothin'!"

"Well," Rafe stood and moved closer to the hearth, rubbing his chilled hands together and eyeing them over his shoulder. "The way I see it, no one's getting nothin' today. I ain't about to get myself dead out in that blizzard waitin' for a train that most likely ain't comin'. The pass is snowed in, Spenser. Think about it."

Spenser blinked, looked around and saw the others clearly nodding agreement.

"Second, I ain't interested in this plan, it can't work. Why would I push my horse in four feet of snow to chase a fuckin' train we got no chance of catching?"

"Like you got a better idea?" Spenser shouted. "No, ya don't, you ungrateful little shit!"

Wittier tossed another log onto the fire and hissed. "Let the kid talk."

"I thank you, Mr. Wittier." Rafe turned a glare to Spenser but waited for the nod.

18

* * *

Three days later they were in position, ahead of the coming train. The chugging behemoth approached through a cleared pass, loaded with even more railroad money than it would have carried before the raging storm. Rafe squinted against the sun blazing off the snow and looked up into the hills. Whittier was tucked up there, hidden behind the rocks and aiming for the nearing engine. Too bad the conductor had to die, but it had to be done. Rafe had plans for his take. Big plans.

CRACKKKKK!

It was a perfect shot that catapulted the conductor right out of the other side of the car. The engine slowed enough for Spenser and the rest to board, rob the passengers, empty the safe and leap off for their horses, safely reined in Rafe's hand. Now that was how to do it.

But before they could turn and ride away in a flurry of laughter and hoots, Rafe's eye caught something. Up in the hills someone sat astride a palomino, white hat tipped back, and even though it wasn't possible, Rafe Bennett could have sworn it was a woman with golden eyes.

CHAPTER 3

Vivi watched, and she learned. For three long years she galloped close behind after a robbery, or sat a fair distance away to observe them, their faces alight from the campfire, their voices gruff and wild. Except for Bennett. He was always quiet, always thinking, always listening and ready.

Vivi discovered early why those men followed a young buck like Bennett. There was a critical surety in his mannerisms and confidence in his plans. Even Spenser, who presumed to be the leader of the crew, often looked to the kid for direction and advice. He called the boy Professor, and often spewed jokes about his voracious reading habits. But more than once Spenser Eddings crossed the line, insulting or berating the kid just for the pleasure of it. Vivi could feel the pot begin to boil and knew it would blow just like the steam that blasted from the billowing stacks atop the trains they robbed. She could see the men around Spenser tighten, and their energy slowly, surely, flow toward Rafe Bennett.

It concerned her even more that the law was catching on to the gang, beginning to predict where and when they'd hit, and more prepared each time. What had grown to a gang of nine outlaws had quickly whittled down to six.

On a fateful late August day in the Arizona desert, Vivi listened while Bennett stated he didn't like the plan Spenser had laid out for their next job The government guns were getting too close, and he had no interest in spending time in prison if he didn't have to. Spenser, still a bigger and meaner man than Bennett, beat the young man senseless and left him to perish on the burning sand as the men road off for the take.

Vivi sat vigil. It was the first time she'd seen him closely since those days in the train station so long ago. His face was bloodied, but painfully beautiful. Long dark lashes lay silent on his cheek and his soft mouth lay slack, opened and crusted with blood and gritty dirt. She squinted against the relentless sun and analyzed the situation.

Her Charge was not meant to die from the brutal beating, but would remain unconscious and unmoving for several hours, hours when the heat could easily steal the life from him. She made an important decision. Spenser and the others had left, most likely never to return. She had no other choice.

She closed her eyes and felt herself alter, sensed the pressure of the earth's gravitational pull drag against her acquired mass, fought the weight of it then accepted. When she could move, she planted herself at his head, slid her arms under his and grunted, dragging him inch by inch into the shaded protection of a rock formation. Vivi dropped to the ground, panted then ran an arm across her sweaty brow. He was safe from the sun, but what else could threaten him? She stood and took a dried mesquite twig then poked it into the stone crevasses. Satisfied that no rattlers hid there, she went to her horse and retrieved her canteen as the coming sunset painted the desert sky. Feeding water in dribbles across his lips she wondered what was next for them. In the distance, a cloud of dust. Someone was coming, but who?

"Thank ya, ma'am," Rafe's raspy voice rumbled and she startled. His eyes were still closed, his breath still even, calm as a sleeping babe. "You got golden eyes?"

"You're hallucinating," she whispered then stepped away. The riders approached quickly and Vivi melted into oblivion, again safely unseen as Rafe struggled to open his eyes and sit.

"Where are ya?" He looked around and rubbed his temple.

She remained silent and unseen, held her angelic breath and prayed.

* * *

22

He shook his aching head, struggled to rise on an elbow and watched the men leap from their horses. "What happened?"

Whittier handed over his canteen and squatted. "Looked like you'd be dead 'fore we could get back to ya. How'd ya get in the shade?"

Rafe shrugged and gulped hungrily then dragged his sleeve across his mouth. "Crawled I guess. What happened?" He eyed Wittier and the two riders who'd returned. Mouse and Petie were brothers, just like Cole and Spenser, only they were dumb as doornails, and less than good guns to boot.

"Start a fucking fire, boys. Gonna be dark and freezin' cold in less than an hour!" Having sufficiently occupied them, Whittier turned to talk quietly with Rafe. "Went just like ya said. Bad. Real bad. We were outnumbered. Rooker and Butch, dead. They took Milton."

Rafe nodded, grunting as he shifted on the cooling ground. "Spens?" he asked.

"I killed him."

He eyed Whittier with serious consideration then nodded. "Good."

"So, what now?" Mouse asked, feeding twigs to the flames.

"I'm leadin'," Rafe stated and shuffled closer to the warmth.

Petie stood straight and glared. "We was thinking Wittier should lead, seeing as how he got more experience and all. I'll follow Whittier."

"Me, too," Mouse chimed.

Rafe stood, stretched his aching legs, rolled his shoulders and twisted his back. "I'm leadin'. You men don't like it, there's the road." His smile was calm, congenial, almost inviting, but Petie bristled.

"No, you ain't. I ain't following no fucking kid, Wittier. You lead!"

"There's the road, Petie," Whittier said with a snorting chuckle.

Petie kicked the dirt and stomped to his horse. He swung up onto it and turned to his brother, but the shot slammed him clean off the saddle before he could say a word.

"I said, I'm leadin'," Rafe twirled his smoking pistol.

"Why'd ya do that?" shouted Mouse, staring down at his dead brother.

"I need his horse. Ya wanna join him? Or ya wanna join me, Mouse? Your choice. Can always use an extra horse."

"I'll fuckin' kill you for this, Bennett!"

But Whittier killed Mouse quick as a snake strike then kicked out the fire. "Let's get outta here, Rafe."

"Fine by me."

* * *

Dodge City. Another year had passed. Bennett and Whittier had gathered five gunslingers looking for the excitement of robbing the railroad. Two were cattle rustlers familiar with the progress of the Central Line, but Rafe had other plans. Strangely enough, they followed where ever he led.

A bank in Abilene and three stagecoach robberies in Northern Texas had set them pretty, and they were laying low in Dodge City just for the fun of it. Rafe Bennett had rules and no man dared break them. One set of rules during a job, and another set to protect them all between jobs. They were more than rules, they were law. No one wanted to die breaking one of Bennett's laws.

They associated with each other sparingly while in Dodge, dressed impeccably, were never too drunk, or too distracted. All stood ready to jump and leave at a moment's notice, and none spread their take too thick in any one establishment except the whorehouse. There, they were treated like kings and none of Bennett's men ever wanted for a clean whore or a decent meal. But Rafe bored quickly of easy women.

"I like that, Mister," sighed the pretty mercantile owner's daughter as she smoothed her hand down the soft velvet sleeve of the dark blue jacket he'd donned.

"Do ya now?" his eyes sparkled. Rafe Bennett always liked the soft sound of a woman's voice saying nice things to him.

"It makes you look like a grand gentleman, mister. This jacket was made for an important man."

"Or a man with the money to buy it," he teased. "So, I'm grand and important and I need a new hat. What've ya got from that wonderful Sears and Robuck Company back east that'll look as good as this jacket?"

To his surprise, she leaned close and whispered in his ear. "I have a hat I fancy that would make you even more handsome than you already are. But it's not here in the mercantile, mister. I'll be happy to bring it to your room … late tonight."

"Sold," he groaned a purr of delight, paid for the well tailored coat and left.

* * *

Vivi shot a glare at the girl. She would never understand the reasoning of humans that caused them to show one face and be another. The girl was petite and fairly plain, extremely proper and appropriate with customers, until Rafe walked in looking to purchase the new coat.

Vivi had seen him with all sorts of women, some painted and round, and some with kind smiles. These women never stayed with him, even though he'd asked several. They knew what he was. Women were smarter than men. They could see that their chance of creating happiness and a family were slim with a man like Rafe Bennett. Even when they didn't know what he was, they practiced superior observation skills and understood. So they took his body and enjoyed him. He was always gentle, always tender, and always looking, watching, thinking. Could they read his mind? Did they know he understood himself more than anyone? That he believed he had little to offer? That his longing for something solid and loving was a temporary wisp of an idea that would dissolve the moment an opportunity for a big take drifted his way?

Most times, Vivi wondered off when he was with these ladies, uncomfortable watching and struggling with odd sensations that pummeled her mind and thoughts. What was that like? Touch? Passion? Climax? How did it feel to receive a man's seed? Rafe Bennett's seed? Once when she listened closely, she actually heard the bond, the creation of a new life, and in her heart she mourned for the woman who would raise that child alone, shunned and unwanted. Rafe never knew that he had two children already. How would he? He left long before knowledge reached the mother, and was a hundred miles away before she could attempt to find him. His mind was somewhere else, lost in its own tangle of want, and desire, and passion.

That night she settled into a chair in the far corner of Rafe's fancy hotel room. She watched him bathe and dress, then wait patiently for the girl and the hat to arrive. She sensed that night would be important and change something in Rafe forever.

There was a tap at the door. Rafe was sitting across from Vivi, drawing. He grinned, continued and waited for the knock to sound once more before standing to answer. The girl stood there, a beautiful sleek black hat in her outstretched hands and her eyes shyly lowered.

He took the hat and set it aside, grasped the girl's hand and tugged her in then closed the door. His mouth lowered slowly, sweetly to hers and she sighed, melted back against the wood and cupped his face tenderly.

There was no rhyme or reason to lovemaking that Vivi could understand. It seemed animal, detached, as though each partner became lost within themselves and knew nothing of the rest of the world. They were asleep in a frantic dream, pressing and pushing, crying out, and grunting. Rafe moved a bit differently that night with that girl. He was slow, easy, smooth.

He undressed her as though she was something special, a gift to be cherished. His mouth worshiped every part of that small body and his hands slid over her terrain, committing it to memory, a drawing he would do some day. When he entered her he was especially gentle, pressing with controlled movement, his expression reflecting the strain of holding himself in check.

Twice Vivi stood and moved closer to watch. Perhaps Rafe was changing? The last time she witnessed such activity, he was with a seasoned whore who had little time or patience with a young man. That was years earlier. He was a different man now, a different lover, and Vivi was captivated.

* * *

The girl was a virgin. Rafe knew it the moment he touched her, felt that unique emotional mix of excitement and terror, only this time more intense than he'd ever sensed from a woman before. He did what he could to make it easier for her. He wanted it to be a pleasant memory, a good one, something that might make her smile in her old age. She trembled and whimpered and, breaking his heart, actually cried out as he moved into her. Slow. Aching. Painful. He was patient. The results would be the same and Rafe liked the idea of holding a satisfied woman after, hearing her delighted sighs and feeling her grasp onto him. Something about those moments felt right to him.

Restraint. Persistence. Control over himself, and her, would make it good and he did just that. When it was over he soothed her, whispered to her and ran a warm palm over her trembling flesh to comfort her.

"Lordy, lordy, lordy," she gasped and he chuckled, rolled to his back and grinned at the ceiling.

"What's your name?" he asked as she shuffled on the mattress and reached for blankets to cover her chilling flesh. She shifted, propped her head in hand and watched him. He could see her smile from the corner of his eye. Yeah, it pleased him right well and his grin widened.

"My name's Kathy Ann Fisher. And you're Rafe Bennett, right?"

His head rolled on the pillow to look at her. "Yeah, I am. Damn, you're pretty, Kathy Ann Fisher. Real pretty."

"Am I?"

His thumb trailed her chin and he nodded. Then he felt it, her hand had moved and there was the cold press of a pistol barrel deep into his belly. He swallowed, but tenderly slid his thumb to her lips. "Real pretty." Rafe remained still, relaxed. "You don't wanna do this, Kathy Ann Fisher."

She ground the hard metal deeper into his flesh. "Yes I do, Mr. Bennett. See, my brothers used to ride with you. Peter and Michael Fisher. You remember them?"

Rafe nodded, clearly seeing Petie and Mouse's faces in his mind. "I remember them."

"You killed them, and knowing they were dead killed my mama. I loved my brothers, and I'm all that's left to take revenge for what you done. Daddy don't care about nothing but the mercantile." She swallowed and drew in a breath. "Somebody's gotta take revenge."

Her hand shook, but Rafe controlled his mind and nerves carefully. "You don't wanna do this, Kathy Ann. Trust me."

"Shut up!" Her voice trembled, her shoulders shuddered and Rafe just kept talking, holding her eyes with the intensity and sincerity in his own.

"When I was eight-years-old, I killed a man who was gonna rape my mama. You don't wanna do this, it'll change you, break you. Break you in ways that'll never get fixed." His voice was smooth, hypnotizing, and she blinked and loosened her tight muscles for just one split second.

27

Just long enough for Rafe to act. With a snap he had the gun in his fist and rolled over her. He set the weapon aside and held her hands tight above her head and looked down into her terrified face.

"There are a hundred paths in life to take. You got a chance I never had, Kathy Ann. You can have what you need. A pretty girl like you don't even have to fight for it or steal it, all you gotta do is smile and it'll all come to you. But you take this road and we're both dead. You'll be dead, Kathy Ann, dead from your soul out. Revenge," he kissed her hard, "just," another kiss, his tongue driving into her mouth, "ain't worth it."

She didn't fight him so he took her hard and fast, took her with passion and abandon until she was weak and sobbing, holding him tight and whispering her thanks.

"I won't kill you, Rafe Bennett."

He pushed his sweaty hair back, looking down at the simple girl beneath him. "Kathy Ann Fisher, I'm already damned, but you got a chance." He kissed her one more time, softly, slowly, and with gratitude. She never moved for the pistol or left the bed as he dressed and propped the new hat on his head with a grin. "It's a real good hat," he chuckled, winked then left her alone, used and naked on the soiled sheets.

Rafe Bennett and his gang were gone from Dodge City within minutes, a cloud of dust heading north.

* * *

Vivi climbed onto her horse and sighed. She had just witnessed one of those moments, the worrisome, dangerous kind of moment, where anything could happen and a clear course of action on her part could not be defined. But somehow she knew Rafe would manage his way out of it, she just wasn't sure how he'd pull it off. It appeared everyone in that room had a lesson to learn that night.

CHAPTER 4

Bennett knew what he wanted, and he knew what he needed. Three days on the rough trail, avoiding towns and roads and laying low in the gullies, his gang began to itch for action. Torn from the comforts of spending their take, they grumbled and groaned and Rafe ignored them, one and all.

It was a moonless night, the sky speckled with the pinpoint lights of a million stars. He sat at the campfire, quiet, thinking. His eyes narrowed and he critically watched each man. Someone had broken a cardinal rule and put them all in danger. Someone got a little too drunk and said a little too much. His gaze slid from one to the other. They were all oblivious to his thoughts, all occupied with whittling, or cleaning pistols, telling stories of whores, or the food they ate. One would have thought they were all friends, but it would take little for those men to turn on each other, or all turn on Rafe. He quickly tired of speculation. There was no speculation. Only one man knew the Fisher boys were dead. Only one man gunned one brother down as Rafe killed the other. Only one man.

He stood smoothly and walked away from the fire, over to his horse and he ran a hand along its neck.

Vivi watched him with horror, as she had been for days, seeing his mind move toward a rationalization only Rafe could devise. She wondered at how his logic worked, far from those around him, isolated in his intellect, managing and manipulating a universe all his own. She stepped close and brought her thoughts to verbal power.

"I know what you're thinking," she said softly.

Rafe didn't start or slow his soothing movements over the animal. He glanced up at the star sparked sky as one shot in a blaze across the expanse.

"You … again," he purred and fingered the horse's velvety ear.

"Don't do this, Rafe."

He sighed and checked the set of his saddle.

Vivi huffed and shuffled her feet. "Do not do this."

She knew he could not see her, but everything in his mannerisms indicated he knew exactly where she stood, less than a stride from him, close enough to feel his heat.

"Ever read the Bible?" His drawl was smooth and elegant.

Vivi's brow curled and she scratched her temple. "No."

"Ya should. Lots to learn about human nature in the Bible. Lots to use if a man wants to survive."

"Rafe," she groaned. "Are you bound and determined to break every law you claim to understand?"

"Am I?"

"Don't do this. Whittier is a good man. He's covered your back more than once, and you know it."

"Not this time." His face eerily turned and his eyes focused exactly where she stood. Vivi stepped back and pressed a hand against her chest. "Not this time," he repeated with a growl.

"Who the fuck ya talkin' to, Bennett?"

Whittier had strolled out and turned his back to Rafe, opened his britches and pissed, humming a soulful moan.

"My horse." Rafe sighed and watched him, his urine hissing a splatter against the dry ground.

Stupid.

Whittier rolled his shoulders and shuddered, both hands grasping his working cock.

Stupid.

The man's fingers tightening as he felt the press of a pistol barrel against the back of his head and heard the click of the hammer.

"Good bye, Whittier."

Blammm!

The man seemed to drop slower than possible, his hands still vice tight on his cock, his cock still spewing piss. Rafe shook his head, calmly tucked his heated barrel in the holster, swung his leg wide to mount his horse then slowly rode away. No one dared follow.

* * *

As the sun rose he stilled the animal, sighed and leaned forward against the saddle horn. He gazed to his sides and behind and he chewed on what he'd heard the night before. It was a woman, he could feel it. The same woman he felt watching him more than once in his life. The same voice he heard alone in the desert when he could've died, the same woman who had pulled him into safety from the brutal sun that day. The same woman he tried to thank. He could feel her, but he couldn't see her.

Another man might have been shaken, but Rafe didn't question his intellect. He was sure of his mind, and sure of his ears. Whatever she was, wherever she was, she'd moved something other than his steady constitution last night. With a quiet click of his tongue, the horse sauntered ahead.

"I know you're there," he said quietly. "I just don't know what ya want. Probably nothin' I got to give anyway. So maybe you should just move on."

But he swore he could smell her, still at his back, still watching, and he chuckled.

* * *

San Francisco. Bustling. Sprawling. Wild with gamblers and gunslingers, money and hopeful prospectors.

While in such a city, Rafe dressed impeccably, spoke like an educated man, and vigilantly hid his identity. It was his unique opportunity to be something other than an outlaw, and he always

31

savored the experience. Those times would carry him through the long rough rides and dangerous men he rode with.

He walked down the steps from his hotel room to the luxurious lobby crowded with ferns and fancy sitting areas, the smell of cigar smoke, and perfume, and wealth. His eyes quickly fell on a dignified gentleman, wrinkled and bald, and rotten with that cocky, rich attitude the hotel was famous for attracting.

"Interesting city, San Francisco," Rafe said and the man nodded.

"Most interesting. My home," he boasted. "I'm Fredrick Bickerstaff. Welcome to my town."

Rafe grinned, bobbed his head respectfully and shook the man's robust hand. Then he did something he didn't know he was going to do. He introduced himself as Rafael Whittier, fully enjoying the private irony of it all.

"Well, Mr. Whittier. Whatever you've came to San Francisco for, you're sure to find it, my man. You look like an intelligent sort. May I ask, sir … what are you looking for?"

Rafe's mind was clear. He wanted a good fuck, a good card game, and anything he could learn about the bank across the street, but his answer was something else completely. "Mr. Bickerstaff, I'm an investor. I'm here to take a good look around. Perhaps there's something that can make me very, very wealthy."

"Oh, by all means, Mr. Whittier." The round face beamed and all the old man's wrinkles vanished, along with his small eyes that quickly became buried in his fleshy smile. "I'm a shipping mogul, sir. Entrepreneurial efforts are my specialty. In fact, I know nothing about ships. I know how to become richer," his laugh was ugly but made Rafe grin wider. "It's my dear wife who knows ships and shipping, her daddy being a sea captain and all. Ah, here she is. Finally, my love."

Rafe turned, fully expecting an ugly old crone but he nearly stepped back with shock. The woman was striking, young and beautiful with thick shining black hair and eyes he'd only seen in his imagination. They were golden eyes, changeable, vacillating from a rich brass to the hues of a brilliant sunrise and back again.

"Let me introduce my lovely wife, Janine," Bickerstaff beamed. "This is Mr. Whittier, in town to explore investment opportunities. Do join us for dinner, Mr. Whittier. Janine will be honored to inform you about the prosperous avenues of the shipping business."

Enthralled, Rafe took her outreached hand in his. It was delicate, small, and as fragile as her form. Her eyes lowered as he agreed to join them, fully forgetting his original intention of visiting the saloon and finding a card game. She was endearing in her demure presence, and well worth the distraction. But as the evening wore on, Rafe knew in his gut that Janine was far more than a mere diversion.

They dined well at Fredrick Bickerstaff's expense and talked casually of the weather and San Francisco's healthy financial climate. Janine had just arrived from a holiday in Paris and mildly complained of exhaustion, suggesting that she hire a carriage to take her home while her husband and Mr. Whittier discussed business.

But before she could leave, Fredrick smiled nervously and spoke. "Mr. Whittier, we have not talked of the most lucrative investment option available to you as yet. Perhaps you would agree to dine with us at the house? Tomorrow evening?"

"Unfortunately," Rafe groaned, his eyes focused on the lovely Janine. "I'm otherwise engaged tomorrow evening. But I wonder if you and your wife would join me here at noon?"

"Ah, I have meetings all day tomorrow, as I may, or may not, have mentioned."

Of course he had mentioned such, and of course, Rafe hadn't forgotten. "Well," he stood with a pleasant, yet knowing, smile. "Investment opportunities are everywhere here in San Francisco, as you've said." He reached out his hand. "It was a pleasure to meet you. Good evening, Mr. and Mrs. Bickerstaff." He took less than three steps and got exactly what he wanted.

"No, no, wait," Bickerstaff nearly shouted, his tremendous greed flashing speckling sweat across his brow and bald head. His lovely wife trembled and closed her eyes. "One moment, Mr. Whittier. We have not explained the advantages of a shipping venture with my growing and extremely profitable company." He reached into his pocket and mopped dripping perspiration with a fancy monogrammed handkerchief. "My wife will be honored to dine with you at noon tomorrow. She is truly the expert in this area, as her poor departed father taught her well and educated her at great expense. She surly knows more than all of my business associates combined and can fully inform you … before you consider other options. Will you concede to discussing business with a woman?"

Janine shot a pointedly shocked glare at her husband, but Rafe simply fingered his hat. "If that's okay with you ma'am, I'd be honored."

* * *

As Franklin Bickerstaff drew back his lovely wife's chair, Vivi stepped closer to the woman and marveled. Janine lifted her parasol and turned to leave, but the old man recognized several business associates and left her standing alone to greet them. Vivi walked around her.

Am I looking into a mirror? This is remarkable? If Vivi dressed in the same gown and hat, pinned her hair high on her head and was willing to humble herself for a frog like Bickerstaff, she could have passed for Janine! It was astounding that Rafe was so completely drawn to the woman. She could hear his heart running wild with need, and want, and how to get it.

Oh damn! This is not good. This is so not good! Not good multiplied by infinity! And she braced herself for what was to come.

CHAPTER 5

Vivi nervously stayed close to young Mrs. Bickerstaff and watched, praying something would push the woman far from Rafe's reach.

Janine spent the morning pacing alone in her room, or standing near the window, taking in the view of her departed father's beautiful ships bobbing in the sparkling bay. Those ships were now her husband's property, as she was. Vivi listened carefully to the woman's thoughts as Janine quietly practiced explaining her displeasure about meeting Mr. Whittier, then finally resigned to the fact that her words would be fruitless. Her avaricious husband was determined beyond reason for her to talk with the man alone. She considered lying that the man did not show up to meet her, but she was not well versed at such deceptions and feared discovery that could make her sad life even more unbearable.

The young wife wondered what would come of Mr. Whittier's investment in Fredrick's enterprise. How often would she have to see him? Would she be able to avoid the temptations he presented, the intense feelings that welled up in her like the surf against the rocks? She would not. Vivi pitied the girl.

Poor Janine had only one option left to her. She determined to convince Mr. Whittier that his investment would be unwise and strongly suggest that he seek better opportunities on the east coast, far from her.

This decision seemed the best of her choices and Vivi took joy in the woman's resolution, although she knew Rafe would not be pleased.

She watched Janine dress her hair carefully in an attractive yet complicated coif. She donned a plain dark green taffeta skirt and proper crisp white blouse, layering it beneath a matching green jacket. The small gold cross on a delicate chain from her Catholic, Irish father snuggled warm and deep against the hollow of her neck. Her mother's brooch. Her simple white gloves. She studied herself in the mirror, curious what Rafe Whittier would think of her demure attire. Would it sufficiently deter him? But what, pray tell, would deter her?

Me, I hope, Vivi prayed.

Before Janine could lose her nerve, she left for the fateful luncheon.

When she neared the table, Rafe rose, pulling out the chair next to him for her, but Janine chose to sit across the table, her hands tight in a locked knot on her knees and her eyes lowered. He grinned and settled in then ordered their lunch. Vivi took the empty chair between them to watch, holding her breath.

"You look beautiful this afternoon," Rafe's voice was a low, soft growl.

The lovely Janine braced herself. "Thank you ... I ... I think we should begin. Mr. Whittier, regarding your considered investment—"

"That color makes your eyes look extraordinary."

She blinked and wrung her small hands. "As a person well versed in this kind of shipping investment I must—"

"Your hair's real pretty too. Never saw hair fixed up like that. You learn that in Paris?" His eyes twinkled.

"Mr. Whittier," she sighed nervously. "We are here to discuss—"

"Janine," he said softly.

"... to ... to discuss your investment. But I fear ... Mr. Whittier ... that ..."

"Janine."

"... that ... that an investment of this nature may not be as lucrative as my husband has indicated ... that ..."

"Janine."

She blinked, looked directly into his eyes and Vivi sat at attention. Oh-oh.

Leaning closer across the table, Rafe sighed softly. "We're not here to discuss an investment. We both know we're here to discuss you ... and me."

* * *

There. He'd made his move and now it was her turn to either play or walk away. It wasn't common for Rafe to put so much thought and strategy into bedding a woman, even a beautiful one like Bickerstaff's wife, but that afternoon, he was ready, primed, and fired up to get what he came for.

"Mr. Whittier," her face had blushed painfully red and her fingers shook even harder. He longed to reach over and touch her lovely cheek but instead, he simply repeated her name yet again.

"Janine." Slow as a cactus flower blooms, she finally brought all of her attention to him. His head tilted and his expression grew soft. "I can see you've never been loved the way you should be."

"Please, don't say these things."

"I can see you're not happy with that old man."

"He is my husband."

"And you, beautiful Janine, are wasted on him." Rafe shuffled in his chair and whispered, thrilled to see her lean closer to hear him clearly. "Fredrick Bickerstaff gives you everything but he has nothing you want, Janine. I have what you want ... what you need.

"No. No. I must leave now." But she did not stand.

"I can bring you everything, Janine. Joys and pleasures you never even dreamed about. All you have to do is let me. That's all."

"I can't. Please. Can we talk of the investment?"

"Have you ever cried out with ecstasy at the touch of a man?"

She pressed a trembling hand against the crown of her hat and cleared her throat. "I truly feel that your money would best be invested elsewhere, Mr. Whittier."

Rafe's brow curled. "Why? So that you can hide from what you need? What I can give you?" He leaned back and watched her, realizing for the first time how much he wanted this woman for his own, or how far he'd go to have her. "You don't wanna walk away from this. You gotta do this, Janine. You need this."

She visibly melted, her shoulders slumped at not only his words but the gravelly depth of his voice, just like he intended.

"Where are you to be after our meeting?" Rafe fought a grin, sensing success.

37

"I ... I ... told Fredrick I would see ... someone ..."

"Another possible investor?" he teased.

"No, no."

He again leaned forward, his eyes scanned the restaurant to assure that no one noticed them. "Then he won't know where you are. Here's what we're gonna do. We'll say our proper farewells and leave this place. Then you," he slid his folded linen napkin toward her fingers, lifting the corner slightly to expose the flash of a polished brass key. "You walk right through the lobby and up to my room. And me," he grinned reassuringly. "I'll make a quick comment to the desk clerk and leave through the front door. Take a walk. When I come back, I'll tap on the door."

"I can not do this, Rafe," she whispered.

"Yes, you can."

"It's not right."

"Yes, it is."

He watched her take the key laden napkin and set it on her lap.

"Now," he sighed calmly. "Right through the lobby and upstairs. Room eight."

"What if I'm seen?" Her voice was small and choked.

"By who? A hotel lobby is full of travelers and strangers. There's no better place to hide than in a crowd."

She looked down into her lap. "I ... I can't do this."

"You can do this," he whispered.

Rafe stood as she did and they shook hands. He signed for the lunch they never ate and left the restaurant. From the corner of his eye, he spied the soft flow of green taffeta move through the lobby and up the steps. He stopped at the front desk and stated that he'd be gone a while, should anyone call for him. Rafe walked out into the street and calmly strolled down and around the corner. He checked on his horse in the stables then walked until he was between the bank he wanted to rob, and the hotel where the lovely Janine waited. The space was dim and quiet. His eyes scaled the building to the second floor window. Wouldn't be difficult at all to reach her.

* * *

38

Vivi stood in the hall and watched poor Janine struggle with conscience and desire. The battle raged in the woman's mind and heart, but longing for Rafe won. Janine took a deep breath, slid the key into the lock and disappeared behind the door.

"Well hell's bells, I really thought she'd make a better choice," Vivi whispered then stood aside to wait for Rafe.

Rafe Bennett was no stranger to sin, but she had never seen him commit this particular sin. He was a calculated soul, complex and well practiced in the art of self-preservation. The good Mrs. Bickerstaff was not the only one taking a grave risk that afternoon. Rafe was hiding in a crowd, but hiding on borrowed time. His thoughts repeatedly expounded on how he needed to take that bank and get the hell out of San Francisco. What was making him stay far too long?

She startled at the shushing sound of a man smoothly climbing into the hall window. Rafe never ceased to surprise her but as Vivi watched him brush off his jacket and run a hand through his hair before settling the hat on his head, she was caught by the look in his eyes.

Oh damn! This is not good. Not good multiplied by infinity!

There, floating in the sea of his crystal blue eyes, Vivi saw all the reasons. Her heart jerked and panic set in. This was something she had no clue how to protect him from. Rafe Bennett was helplessly, hopelessly in love, and this could easily be his demise.

She stepped from the door and he quietly tapped. It swung opened. She felt his heart lurch as he entered, already gathering the lovely Janine into his arms.

Vivi could not watch this one. She sat in the hall with her back to the door to wait it out and be watchful for her Charge. She considered leaving to locate Fredrick Bickerstaff and make sure he wasn't looking for his wife, but she couldn't tear herself from her vigil.

More than concern tore at Vivi. Something else, something she couldn't put her finger on. An ache grew in her heart, a sudden sensation of loss. What the hell did that mean? She dropped her head in hands and prayed.

Two hours passed and she felt the strong need to listen, so she pressed her ear against the wood. What she heard terrified her even more.

"Wake up, darlin'. It's time to get ready."

"Ready?" Janine's voice was strained, her words horrified. "Oh God, what have I done?"

"Nothin' sweetheart. I did it and we've changed everything. Here's what we're gonna do—"

There came a desperate shuffle of bodies and clothing. "This was wrong. Oh God, Rafe. This was wrong."

"No it wasn't, now all you need to do is trust me. We're gonna leave together and we're gonna do it tonight."

"Stop!" Janine gasped. "Please, stop. Don't say these things. I can't leave with you. I just can't."

She suddenly became quiet, her voice a whisper and Vivi pressed her ear harder against the door.

"It isn't that I don't want you. Rafe, I want you more than breath. I just can't do this."

"Yes, you can. Here's how we're gonna do it."

Tears welled in Vivi's eyes and her ears strained to catch every word aloft his deep, resonant voice.

"You go home now," Rafe said softly. "Spend the evening with your husband and after he's asleep, you meet me at the stables across the road. I'll have horses ready, everything we need. We'll head north to Canada. Do you understand?"

Silence, then came a pained, "yes."

"Don't let on anything's different. Do it just like you did when you came up to this room, Janine. Nice and easy and we'll be gone and safe and together."

"The stables," she whispered.

"Yes."

"Canada."

"Yes, darlin' You need to leave now. Right down and through the lobby. No one will notice. I'll be waiting for you tonight."

Vivi followed Janine down the steps and through the lobby. She rode beside her in the carriage to Fredrick Bickerstaff's elegant house. She noticed the dark man following at a distance, and how he left right after Janine disappeared inside the heavy beveled glass front door.

Oh damn! Oh lord, Madam Miriam! I think I need some help down here!

CHAPTER 6

Rafe returned to the bed with a swagger. He thumped down, flopped his ankles crossed and grinned a deep, satisfying grin that thrilled his flesh and made him feel alive. It wasn't that he felt cocky, he felt happy. He should've taken the bank, but he didn't need the money. What he needed was Janine. He had more than enough stashed in his saddlebags. He had even more buried south near the Mexican border. Probably more money than old Frank Bickerstaff. The travel would be hard and rough at first, but he'd care for Janine well when they reached safety. Give her everything he'd promised and more.

Five o'clock and he strolled casually out of the hotel. He went to the saloon, played a few lucky hands of poker then collected his winnings and left, promising them all a chance to recoup their losses another night. They were lucky hands, lucky enough to buy a horse for Janine, a good saddle, and another gun just in case she needed it.

His brow knotted. Was he doing the right thing? Was Janine ready for what lay ahead? He hadn't even confessed his real name to her. Would it matter? Leaving with him made her nearly as much an outlaw. A little time was all she'd need to see how it would all go. A little time for him, too.

There was no reason to worry or rush. He purchased a fine horse then stopped at the mercantile to buy a small gun, one perfect for her delicate hand but his eyes trailed the glass case to something else. It was a cameo, a match for the one she wore. A man's face was carved there, facing left. Her cameo was a woman facing right. He grinned and purchased the silly pin instead of a pistol, just to make her smile. She wouldn't need a gun. He'd protect her with his life. After all, he wasn't wanted in San Francisco. There wasn't even a wanted poster with his face on it north of the New Mexico territory.

They'd be safe after the initial escape. His only concern was the wrinkled, brokenhearted old husband, and it wasn't much of a concern. Rafe shook his head. What was wrong with that asshole? What kind of man sent his beautiful wife to do his business dealings? He was asking for it, plain and simple, and his loss was Rafe's gain.

He saddled the horses at eight and returned to his room, washed, shaved, and brushed down his jacket. By nine he decided to check one more time on the provisions he'd packed in the saddlebags then he tucked the delicate cameo pin into his pocket.

As he trotted down the steps to the lobby, Rafe stilled and held his breath. He heard a voice booming below, laughing and boasting with several others. Fucking bounty hunter. He recognized the man before he even turned to look. Charlie Silver. Rafe turned and climbed the stairs, not hurrying even though he could hear the man coming up right behind him. He went into his room and listened. Damned if that bastard wasn't standing and conversing right outside his door.

"I ain't here for no frivolity, Fulton. I'm here for Bennett," roared the idiot.

"What the hell would he be doing up here in San Francisco?"

"Damned if I know, but I'm on his trail. He's here, been seen, and I'm taking him in." Silver grunted a dry chuckle.

"That's tomorrow, Charlie. Tonight let's have us a few drinks at the saloon. Maybe some soft flesh? They got one hell of a stable of whores in this town."

"Fuck, no. I'm getting some sleep. Gonna be sharp as a knife tomorrow. Bennett's worth a fortune and that fortune is mine."

Charlie Silver's laugh was a hiss that burned down Rafe's spine. He listened carefully, his eyes closed. Silver's room was right across the hall. The door closed and locked with a tinny clank then Rafe released a held breath. He went to his window and looked down. Not a good way out, facing the front street. It wouldn't be possible to get down unseen. He paced quietly, his mind calculating, shifting, manipulating. Janine would be meeting him soon. He wasn't sure how soon, but he wasn't about to miss her and have her run back to Bickerstaff. The lobby was out of the question. Silver had been shouting Rafe's name down there, probably started passing around wanted posters too. Those were never a good likeness, but he might be recognized. The only way out was the hall window. He pulled his pocket watch. Nine-twenty. He growled with frustration. At least another hour, it'd be safe then. The asshole would be asleep. Rafe tried to wait, but he just couldn't. He envisioned Janine, scared and alone, running away from the life she could have with him. No. He couldn't wait another minute.

He tucked his watch into his vest pocket, tenderly fingered the cameo there, then groaned and shook back his hair. Hat snug in place, he opened his door. No better place to hide than in a crowd, he'd told Janine. Unless you're Rafe Bennett and a damn bounty hunter was on your ass. Time to hightail it out of San Francisco, but first he had to meet Janine. He wasn't leaving without her, wouldn't even consider the thought.

Silent as a whisper, he moved down the hall and slipped out the window. His feet were sure, even in the darkness and a mere minute later, he was on the street, heading to the stables. He hunkered down near the horses, hidden in the quiet blackness and waited, his heart pounding in his ears.

Time passed but he had no clue how much, it was too dark to read his pocket watch so he didn't even try. When all was totally silent, he stood, sure something was wrong. She said she'd come. Where the hell was she?

He mounted and held the reigns, leading the second horse out. With a click of his tongue, the animals moved docilely. He knew where Bickerstaff's big house was, had been looking at it from his hotel window since Janine left his room. Watching it. Knowing he'd see her that night. Anticipating what lay ahead, his mouth watering.

He rode at a calm gait, past the gas streetlamps, further from the city, to the large place on the hill, isolated and pompous. Not a neighbor to hear if he had to shoot Bickerstaff dead. And he knew he would. He even wondered if he'd need to kill the man right beside her in bed. Maybe it would go down easy. Maybe she'd be pleased and run into his arms, maybe not. No matter. She was his and he'd have her. Kicking and screaming, or ready and willing, she'd be his forever, damn it.

Charlie Silver was a distant thought tucked in the back of his mind as he tied the horses not far from the big front porch. Soft light flowed from the front parlor window, but every other room was dark. He skirted the house, rounded to the back between the cook house and a door near a rose garden. He'd have smiled and taken a rose for Janine, if he didn't have so much to think about. He wasn't about to make a bad move, not for love, or fear, or even survival. A window was open and his hand quietly slid it high enough to slip inside.

Rafe waited for his heart to steady then listened. Nothing. Not a sound or creak of the sturdy polished floorboards beneath his feet. Even the night seemed to have stilled. Silent and holding his breath, he inched his way toward the parlor. Yellow lamplight poured onto the expensive Persian hall carpet. He slid closer along the wall and finally tilted a turn of his head to peek into the room.

The first thing he noticed was Bickerstaff's polished shoes. Rafe leaned further to see more. The man was lying, his body prone on the floor, the barrel of the pistol that had blown off the back of his head, still lodged deep in his mouth. Rafe stepped into the parlor, holstered his gun and eyed the surroundings. Had Janine done it for him? Killed the bastard to make it all easier?

But before he could begin to grin, his eye caught a slip of green taffeta. Everything inside him slammed tight like a prison cell. Cold. Alone. He stepped around the fancy settee, stood and just looked.

Her face had already gone ashen. Her amazing golden eyes, wide in terror, no longer held the magic, no longer alive. He knelt, watched her stillness, then reached out and roughly tore at her blouse.

"What're you doing?" came the strange disembodied voice he'd heard before. "What are you doing?" she repeated. "Rafe, stop."

"Shut up," he said coldly then grasped the small gold cross clasped around Janine's neck, broke the delicate chain and held it in his palm. He took the pretty cameo from his vest pocket and arranged Janine's destroyed blouse modestly before pinning it to the white fabric. There was no blood, he could tell the bastard had strangled her by the ugly marks on her face and neck. He could feel the loss of the revenge he wanted so badly he could taste it. Rafe stood, swallowed hard. There was himself to save, himself to protect. It was well past time to get the hell out of San Francisco.

Vivi scrambled to keep up as he stormed from the house, mounted his horse and spurred it to a gallop. South. South to Mexico. A day passed and another. His pace was relentless, unyielding and when he could go no further, the frozen chill of snowcapped mountains watching solemnly from the east, Rafe finally collapsed. He slid like water from his horse and thudded to the hard ground. In his open palm lay the small gold cross, catching the dull twilight and softly shooting a sad ray to the heavens. Vivi knelt beside him and prayed silently.

Rafe was more than broken, he was gutted. Nothing remained but his own desire to survive, and she wondered how long it would take for him to relinquish even that. He stirred, curled to his side and cried out, the sound of a wounded animal, torn, bloodied, destroyed. It didn't last long before he again weakened and dropped into a bottomless sleep that held him safe for hours.

Vivi paced and cried, she begged for assistance that seemed would never come. Finally, at the deep darkness just before dawn, she noticed him stir. Rafe groaned and got up, then gathered loose twigs and started a fire. She looked around, fearful that his flame would be spotted, but then even more fear trembled in her soul.

"Rafe? What are you doing?"

"You again," he said, his voice raw but smooth as satin. "Leave me alone."

He pulled his beloved Bible from his saddle bag and squatted near the small fire. One by one, he ripped away page after page from the binding and fed the thin paper to the flames, his face blank, his heart so empty it shouted a hollow cry to her. Then he fingered the tiny gold cross he'd taken from Janine's dead neck and tossed it too into the fire.

He stood, sighed, then climbed onto his horse and slowly rode away, leaving the dying blaze to smolder in the coming dawn.

* * *

He rode calmly, slowly, zigzagging down the dry rough terrain, silent and alone. Day turned to night then day again. Occasionally he'd camp, but mostly he moved on. He worked his mind empty, thought out a plan, where and how he'd gather a crew, what they should be, and how he'd use them. What he'd rob, and when. He grinned, an ugly expression of satisfaction. The railroad. He'd go after the railroad. If Charlie Silver wanted a crusade, he'd give him the challenge of a lifetime and he'd enjoy it all the way.

Janine had been returned to his imagination, a storybook character that never existed and had never touched him. How the hell could she have touched him? There was nothing to touch. He was a dead man from the heart out and he knew it, probably always had been, and he vowed never to let another woman reach him like that. Oh, women were a good, comforting diversion, and he had no intention of passing on a fine opportunity. They were soft and sweet and completed something that always got lost during the tough times. He'd never be cruel to them, never disrespect or hurt them. He just had no place inside himself for them. Touching a woman had it benefits, but letting one touch him, really touch him with that searing power that burns from their souls? No. No woman would ever get that far with him again.

He glanced behind, squinted at the sunlight and swore that there, floating in the rising heat waves, trailed a set of horse tracks right beside his. He shook his head.

"You're there, ain't you," he said.

Silence.

"Don't wanna talk?"

Still she said nothing.

"S'okay. You don't gotta talk. I can do the talkin'." He cleared his throat and began a one sided conversation that lasted from the north edge of the New Mexico Territory all the way across the border and into Mexico. It started with one question.

"You ever been to Abilene? No? Well, let me tell you about Abilene."

46

CHAPTER 7

It had been a difficult two years, tougher than Vivi ever expected, or experienced, since coming to watch over Rafe. Her assignment had been to watch over and protect him, but to be careful never to redirect the path he was on. Her mind often blasted into frustration. She'd stood beside him since childhood, knew the tender human heart deep in his corrupt chest and understood where his logic came from. Was she wasting her time, or his? She often took Madam Miriam's name in vain, swearing to get even, for never once in all those years had her prayers been answered. Or had they?

Each time it seemed impossible for Rafe to get away or survive, he had. Was that her doing, or was it because of help from above? Was it Rafe's own instinct for survival? Did he need her, or God, or anyone? Twenty years she'd ridden beside the outlaw. Twenty years of sin and killing, robbing and fornicating. Twenty God-forsaken years, and what had she learned? What had he learned?

Was she meant to learn anything? Vivi wasn't even sure if she was doing her job well. Perhaps she'd been forgotten, left on earth without anyone watching at all. There had been good times and bad times. This was most definitely one of the bad times.

She sat on the bunk and watched him play with a deck of cards, laying them out in a straight line. He'd been locked in that cell for three days and had yet to show any sign of fear or remorse. Maybe he thought it would all work out like the last time he was caught and thrown into prison? At least that time he was so afraid, Vivi felt the rolling of his gut in her own aching belly. He had almost resigned to the fact that he'd hang, but somehow, like always, Rafe managed to escape.

This was his second time at the Wyoming Territory Prison near Laramie and the guards were a lot more careful. They knew he was a crafty sort and had kept him as far from the other prisoners as possible, at least the prisoners who had a chance to survive their incarceration. In another tight cell across from Rafe's sat a young man of nineteen. He too had the look and swagger of a king in control of his destiny. He wriggled down on his bunk and drifted off to sleep, his quiet snores like the sound of waves on a shore.

Two cells down, a Mexican, and across from him, an Apache. Those men made Vivi shiver, they were ugly from the soul out, moved and thought like dogs in a pack just sniffing for an alpha male to lead them. Her eyes moved to Rafe. The alpha male? But she'd been at his side since he was captured, watched over everything he did and said. Her head slowly moved to take in those three others. Something was up, but what? Nothing could have been planned. They hadn't even spoken and Rafe had been uncharacteristically quiet. They had never met one another before. This she knew as fact.

The reason they were together at the far end of the complex was simple. All four would be hung the very next morning. Vivi feared all was lost. It terrified her to have to watch Rafe struggle and suffer at the end of a noose, but perhaps there was no need for concern. Perhaps her prayers were going to be answered.

She grinned. Why would they be? When she thought about it all, there was a good reason her prayers weren't being answered. She watched over and protected a damned outlaw. A murderer, although truth be told, she could count on one hand how many fell at the business end of his pistol. Rafe wasn't one to hurt or murder without reason. Granted, he had a few more reasons than a simple man, but perhaps thinking of him as a murderer was unfair. Most were killed in self-defense, after a robbery, which made him an outlaw. She paced, irritation tingling her every nerve. What the hell kind of assignment was this, anyway? But when she calmed she could see it more clearly, even comprehend the whys and wherefores of it all.

Rafe Bennett was accomplishing something only those far above her understood. Fine, she could handle that. She was obviously doing her job well, he was still alive and she was still with him, right? She slid to sit in the corner of the cell, her back against the cold bars and her mind racing. Now there were three different men snoring, making an irritating sound and she rolled her eyes. Rafe sat silent, shuffling cards and laying them out.

"Wanna play a hand with me?" he said softly and her head shot up. No, he couldn't see her, she knew that. Besides, she hadn't spoken to him since Janine's death. She'd been silent for years. That was a record for Vivi but now, in that prison cell, less than twelve hours before he would face the noose, she figured it was time to speak.

"No, thanks."

His hand stopped moving but his face remained calm. "I'd let you win, ya know."

"No, you wouldn't. Rafe, what are you doing? You are going to hang when the sun comes up."

"No, I ain't."

"Damn it! Stop playing cards! You should be praying, preparing to meet your maker!"

"No, I shouldn't." His face rose and he looked directly into her face even though she knew he could not see it.

"You are fucking hopeless!"

He chuckled then gathered the cards to shuffle again. "Least I know you ain't no angel now. You have the mouth of a devil. No need to be worrying for me. It'll work out, but whatever you are, if you can arrange to have my horse near by, I'd be much obliged."

Vivi blinked back a tear. "I'm afraid for you."

"That's very kind of you, ma'am, but no need." He set the cards aside and leaned back, his hands locked behind his head. "You sound like a pretty thing. I can feel you. Sometimes I can smell you. I know you're there. When are you gonna let me see you?"

"Never."

"I once knew a woman, she'd argue with me all the time, but she could … sorry ma'am … not a story for your ears."

"You think I don't know who you're talking about? Rafe Bennett, I've watched you fuck woman after woman, I've seen—"

"So, you like watching?"

49

"No!"

He sat up and leaned forward, glaring into the empty corner, into her eyes and he whispered. "Maybe you should try doing instead of watching. It's far more pleasant. What's your name?"

She'd gone silent, her heart throbbing with a strange desire to think about his suggestion. What was happening to her? Perhaps, she was just so afraid for him she'd lost control. It was time to regain the upper hand. She stood and left the cell, turned back as his eyes drifted closed.

"It's okay, don't gotta tell me your name. But since you're leavin' may I ask again that you—"

"I'm going for your horse."

* * *

A smile lightened his heart, and he knew he was suddenly alone. There were so few times in his life he'd really been alone. He knew she was there at the station when his mama left him. Felt her with him when he bled and burned in the dessert. She was almost always with him, and yes, she was an angel. Had to be. Pure and simple. He'd suspected such for years. Why she was bothering with him was a curiosity, but there was a strange responsibility that came with knowing she was there, an odd need to protect her from what he really was. It redirected his actions, sharpened his survival, made him think. No matter she might just be his imagination, no matter she might be the woman he'd been drawing his whole life. No matter if she was just a fitful dream fostered in a lonely man's fevered brain. She was still there, and he wanted to protect her, even if it meant sending her away when he died.

Rafe Bennett wasn't going to die that day, or the next, or even the next. Something was coming. Something was going to change things. What? He didn't know. He could only be sharp and prepared for it. Not ten minutes later, it arrived.

"Trial time, Bennett," shouted the guard and instantly Rafe's eye fell on the pistol in the man's holster. The man casually leaned against the bars and grinned, looking around at all four killers. "You all swing today, but you Bennett, that's gonna be the most fun I seen in years." He chuckled and lounged like he was talking to a whore at a saloon.

50

Even his cock was hard, pressing against his britches and he pushed a palm against it. So this was how it would all come down.

"Well sir, I can see how excited you are," Rafe drawled and grinned, but never moved from the bunk.

The kid across from him stirred, eyed Rafe, and nodded. The Apache stood, grunted and growled like a coyote, and the Mexican swung into action so fast it surprised Rafe. Before he could blink, the guard's pistol was grasped and fired, and the man was down in a growing pool of blood. Rafe slowly stood, nodded to the Mexican who fished the keys from the dead man and proceeded to free them all.

Not a word was spoken. They were far enough from the other guards and prisoners that no one even heard the muffled shot against the man's soft belly. Rafe reached for his hat and stepped out as the bars swung opened. The Mexican handed over the pistol and they all waited. A jerk of his chin and they followed Rafe. Two more guards died, one strangled viciously, and the other's neck broken in the strong hands of the Mexican. They slipped out of the building unnoticed and right to the main gate.

The kid fumbled with the keys until he found the correct one and they were free. Less than fifty yards away, Rafe's horse and three more waited. He gave a grin and they were gone, racing in the dust through the predawn dessert, and he knew she was there, knew she was riding hard right at his side.

"Thanks, ma'am," he whispered then turned to the men. Slowing to a stop, the breathless men suspiciously eyed each other then looked to him. "Split, go as far as you can. Meet me right … there." Rafe pointed to a small sad excuse for a town sitting at the base of the hills. "Two weeks. If you're not there?" He shrugged and grinned then turned to ride but shot a shout over his shoulder at the Indian. "If you got any Injun prayers to protect me, say 'em. I'm goin' through Apache country."

"I'll pray for you." The big man's laugh was ugly but he nodded and repeated. "I'll pray for you."

They split and rode hard. Three full days later, and Rafe was still moving at a fast pace and planning some rest in Mexico. Finally, sure of his safety, he slowed to a calm amble and sighed.

"You keeping up?" he asked but she didn't answer. "You know, maybe you remember that woman I had in that little town back there," he jerked his chin. "Her name was Lizzy. Pretty thing from back east.

51

Got herself in a bad way with a saloon owner who beat her. You know, that man deserved to die. He was a real bastard, hurting her like that."

His companion remained silent but he felt her approval.

They rode, Rafe talking on and on for several miles until he stopped dead. From the rise he could see the devastation, hear the cries of terrified women, and observe the mutilated bloodied bodies of children and wrinkled old men. Rafe's eyes trained on one man, Charlie Silver. Silver walked along a deep ravine, kicking small bodies, some wailing, squirming, still alive into the hole and laughing loud enough to be heard on the hot desert breeze. Rafe remained still until the gunmen had all left and Silver's laughter disappeared in the distance.

He heeled his horse and slowly descended the rise. At the edge of the ravine he dismounted with a growling moan. At his boot, a small child's eyes went dark, extinguished, dead. His foot tenderly pushed the baby into the open grave and shook his head. Apache, all. Old men and women, children. Too many children. His stomach turned and he spit bile that crawled up his throat. Then he heard it.

A cry, a gasp. His eyes scanned the still, twisted bodies until he spied the one still alive. Crawling into the mass grave he picked his way closer and closer. It was a boy, probably two years old, bloody and broken, but still alive.

He tugged to free him from the corpses covering most of his lower body and heaved the child over his shoulder to climb out. He rode with the now unconscious boy over the horse and snug against him. "Don't be thinking I gone soft," he said to the ever present, silent rider at his side. "This boy just may be the bargaining chip I need to get through this pass alive."

His hand often soothed the small body, checking to see if it still breathed, or if its flesh was still warm, or too hot. The child was holding his own and Rafe shifted the blanket under the sleeping face to make it a bit more comfortable. "Just a bargaining chip."

CHAPTER 8

"Just a bargaining chip," Rafe Bennett had said and in the heavens, Miriam rolled her neck. She turned to Paul and sighed.

"What are we to do?"

"Nothing," Paul said, his voice maddeningly calm, his expression stoic, the face of a leader, a Master Guardian. It was a knowing expression that forced her to stand and stomp into a frustrated pace.

"What do you know?" Miriam demanded.

"I know that you must release this overprotective human quality you seem to have developed where Vibrant Light is concerned. It is all written, Miriam. We are to do nothing but play our parts. You know that. You can not change this, I can not change this, even poor Vivi who is right at his side can not change it. Come, sit."

"I can't sit! Paul, she is about to fail! We can't just sit and watch her do it. She … will … fail!"

"Will she?" Paul snagged Miriam's hand as she passed and tugged her to sit beside him on the sofa. "Listen to me, there is failure, and there is failure. What will come of all this will reveal the reason behind it all. What we see as her failure may have a larger role we can not determine. I have watched her closely, Miriam—"

"You are monitoring my work?" She glared up at him but remained tight in his embrace as he chuckled.

His brow bobbed. "You've read my job description. Of course, I've been monitoring. I will concede that both you and I have taken a far too personal interest in this case, but I will tell you a few things. You need not worry, Miriam. Vivi has been doing her job with extraordinary proficiency, and little help from us."

"I don't like this. We've set her up to face the worst alone. She is being tested with situations no angel of her level should be forced to handle. She has not been trained or prepared for this, Paul. We are failing her."

He snuggled Miriam closer. "My dear, I must ask that you trust me. There is a reason Vibrant Light was chosen for this case, a reason she has faced the challenges untrained, and unprepared. This will all work out as it should but it will not be easy to watch. It will follow God's plan, not ours. It may not seem so but I can tell you this, my love. Vivi will not fail."

* * *

I'm failing! I just know it! Vivi shuddered as they slowed to a stop and prepared to camp for the night. Her eyes scanned the area. Open, desolate. Far from the treacherous canyons infested with wild Apache, but they had no choice, and she understood that. If Rafe was to use the child to get himself safely through the pass, he had to keep the little boy alive.

She sat vigil as he cradled the baby against his chest, fed it drops of water from the canteen then finally groaned resignation.

"Gotta get that bullet out," he said with a sigh, laid the child on a blanket close to the firelight and held his blade in a shaking hand. "Gonna need your help, if ya don't mind, ma'am. The bullet is deep in this little boy's thigh. Say a few prayers I don't fuck this up and kill this poor kid."

"You won't fuck up. It's not as deep as you think," Vivi spoke in a whisper close at his shoulder and he nodded, all his attention on the silent, feverish child. "Press your finger just above his knee, push, and you'll feel it. Did you clean the knife?"

54

She grinned as he swiftly pulled it away, wiped it off on his shirt then shrugged.

"Hold it over the flame a bit. You'll have to do just a small slice, nice and easy, not deep and the bullet will slide right out."

He curled his brow, did as he was told. The blade sizzled as it touched the tender golden flesh and the child cried out. Vivi pressed her ethereal hands on the small body, holding it still as Rafe followed her directions perfectly. The bullet moved then slithered from the soft skin in a bloody spurt. It had missed the artery and now removed, the boy was sure to recover. He took the child to his chest and pressed a piece of the blanket hard against the wound. To his amazement, the bleeding slowed and stopped. Rafe grinned.

"Thank ya, ma'am," he mumbled as he drifted off to sleep with the babe in his arms. Vivi sighed relief. Their bargaining chip would live, and hopefully, so would Rafe as he made his way through to Mexico.

The child would slow the travel but just until Rafe could pass him off into the right hands. If no one bothered him going through the pass, he intended to leave it at the little church just over the border. He believed someone there would care for it.

High noon the next day, searing, blinding. Rafe whispered to the moaning child. He looked down, grinned at the frightened expression and pushed wild black hair from the boy's eyes. "You're gonna be fine son. Hush now." When his face rose his heart jerked.

Blocking the path, nine armed warriors stood ten feet behind a man so old and twisted, Rafe couldn't even guess at his age.

His mind raced. The Apache were a calculated, strong people, and something sure as hell wasn't right about this. The warriors were young and untried, probably fourteen or fifteen-years-old and looking as afraid as could be expected. What happened here? Rafe saw no able-bodied men in that ugly pit of dead Indians. Most likely the real warriors were out hunting when Silver showed up and attacked. The old man might have been off somewhere working with the young boys when it all happened. Now he was standing, bold as could be and trying to look in control. Rafe's eyes quickly scanned the rocks above. It was possible there were a few dangerous warriors up there, hiding and waiting for the perfect moment to cut him down. His next thought was of the strange unseen companion who traveled, silent and unseen at his side.

"Time for you to leave, ma'am. I can handle this alone." To his frustration, he did not feel her ebb away, but instead, he felt her become stronger. He turned to the old man but before he could offer the child in exchange for safe passage, the ancient Indian spoke in a language that was not Apache, and Rafe knew it. It was no Injun language he ever heard, and he'd heard a lot. The young warriors puzzled expressions reflecting his own. To his left, Rafe clearly heard an equally obscure response from his unseen companion.

"What the hell are ya doing?"

* * *

Vivi ignored him. The old man wanted to know what they wanted and after swallowing back her amazement that he could see her, she realized that he had spoken a language of the heavens. She smiled, straightened and responded.

"We have a child who belongs to you. Many have died thirty miles east of this place. Women, children, elders. Killed at the hands of terrible men."

"And the man beside you?" grumbled the ancient holy man.

Vivi bowed her head humbly. "He took no hand in those murders. He has saved this child at great risk to himself. He brings it into your care."

"And he wishes safe passage?" The old man's eyes twinkled. "I cannot promise I can control these strong warriors, sacred one."

Vivi chuckled. "I'm not a sacred one, old man. I am simply here to watch over this man. He deserves safe passage, he has saved this child's life."

The holy man grunted a nasal sound and his young warriors turn a bemused glare at each other. The old man's eyes rose, the angry glint of a once warrior in them. "Bring that child to me."

"I cannot. You know this. But this man will bring him to you. He will come unarmed and place this child into your arms."

"No. You."

Vivi tilted her head. "Will you push me, old man?"

56

He chuckled and shrugged. "I will come and take the child." His pleasant demeanor abruptly changed as he stomped toward Rafe and reached up.

"This is … this is …" the holy man babbled.

"The child is important, is he not?" Vivi said. "Does he not warrant safe passage for this man?"

The old man turned, shouted for the warriors to allow Rafe to pass and looked up into Vivi's eyes. "Thank you," he whispered.

* * *

Twenty miles and not a word was spoken. Rafe knew nothing of what was said in the pass, and cared little. He was busy rethinking his plan. That night he would camp a safe distance from the pass and remain there for the time being. He would not take the comfort of pretty senoritas and protected refuge in Mexico, but instead think quietly and develop his strategy until it was solidly carved into his mind. And he would learn what he could from the strange being at his side.

He shot a rabbit, a skinny, sinewy creature with long ears and little meat on its bones. It crackled over the campfire, drifting a wonderful aroma that made his stomach growl and his mouth water. "Are you hungry, or don't you eat?"

The ever present unseen being remained silent, sitting close at his side, so close he could swear he could smell her sweetness. He imagined her arms wrapped around her knees, eyes scanning the emptiness for any possible danger. Afraid. But that couldn't be true, she seemed to fear nothing.

Rafe shrugged, savored the stringy meat and smacked his lips with a mellow hum. He was always vocal with his pleasure, far more than with the turmoil and frustrations he kept well hidden from the world; irritations, aggravations and uncertainties no one knew. His life was a complex maze of compartments, all well disguised, all buried deep, all secret, some even from himself, but he knew his pains, those things that ached unbearably. It was the true reason for his care of the child. He chose to believe it was done for personal gain, but was wise enough to wonder if it meant more.

Another whiff of her scent drifted to him on the desert night breeze. Now, he wanted to talk. Would she oblige and permit him to hear her lovely voice again? He was a bit cocky about knowing she was there and particularly enjoyed the idea that it annoyed her.

"So you don't eat. No problem," he said, smearing grease from his lips. "Ain't much here anyway. I'll enjoy it without you ... but someday..." He shifted and turned a look in her direction. "Someday ... you and me, we'll enjoy something together. Might be my demise, 'cause I know God's vengeance ain't far behind you. I do know I'll burn in hell, I just ain't scared." He pulled another piece of the roasted meat from the bone and chewed thoughtfully.

* * *

Vivi held her breath. His statement was far too cavalier, and it terrified her. He could never know the agonies of hell, and he never would. This, she was sure of. It seemed written in her soul.

"Rafe," she said softly. "It's not that you haven't earned it, but I will tell you something you probably shouldn't know. You will never burn in hell."

He grinned, lounged back and fingered his pistol. "Got me a reprieve from hell, do I? Don't seem fair. Seems I been working my whole life to earn it. That slow burn that just might ..." The words choked in his throat.

Vivi finished for him. "What? Cleanse you? Purify you of sin? That's not how it works, but that doesn't matter. You'll never go there. I want to talk about your plans."

"Do you now? Funny, suddenly you got lots to say." He slid down and closed his eyes. "Too bad, 'cause I don't feel much like talking anymore. Good night, ma'am."

She was infuriated, who was he to deny her? She already knew his intentions and knew she must deter him from them. Going after the railroad in the aggressive manner he intended resonated from him. He knew Silver would be on that train. The bounty hunter had gotten his fill of bloodshed during the massacre of those innocent Indian woman and children and would leave Rafe alone for a while, at least until the hunger

58

for killing and bounty burned in his belly again. It was Silver's pattern, and if there was one thing Rafe was very good at, it was discovering a man's patterns. The memory of those bloodied, frail bodies had built a blaze in his gut and she understood he wanted revenge. He'd take it out on Charlie Silver, traveling on the only train east, to Kansas where the man owned a thriving saloon and whore house. Rafe's men would take all they could from the passengers and the railroad safe too. If it went well, they'd take Charlie Silver's life in the process. He had the right men for the job, all ready, willing, and waiting for him to lead them, but it was only going to make things tougher for Vivi. She wanted to shout, to push him hard with hands solid and human to get his attention, but she knew better. Perhaps she would never truly show herself to him, but somehow she had to get her point across. Vivi readied to shout loud and hardy; to demand that he listen and change his mind.

With an angry huff she leaned close to his face, suddenly startled by the overwhelming desire to touch her lips to his, to taste the lingering flavor of broiled meat on his mouth, to feel the heat of him. With a jerk she retreated and Rafe Bennett, his eyes still closed, chuckled quietly.

"Someday. Someday soon, you and me …" And he dropped into a sound asleep.

CHAPTER 9

Vivi sat across from Rafe and young Hoyt Cawfield. She sneered dislike at the kid and turned to take in the activity around them. The deserted cabin was dark but for the bright moonlight flowing in, and the new crew looked to their boss for guidance. Rafe Bennett was a master. He'd pulled together twelve men who would die for what he could bring them, but not for him. They followed unquestionably, knowing that he would make them rich enough to disappear if they wanted, but Vivi could see inside their diseased souls. They didn't really want wealth. They wanted the thrill of the take, the charge of the kill, the excitement of spurting blood and shattered bones and exhilarating escape. It was what drove them, animals all. Then, there was Rafe. Calculated. Brilliant. Flawed.

They served him well, permitted him the safety of distance between him and the crimes. Controlling them was an issue in the beginning. He'd watched their every move during a robbery and between jobs, spending far more time around them than he liked to decipher the distinct, imbedded weakness within each man. It was his ace in the hole, his power. Knowing their value and knowing their corrupt core gave him the ability to use them to his best advantage. To Vivi's horror, he soon identified the disposable and the valuable among them.

Among his first concerns was Hoyt. The young man was too bold, too arrogant, and too brave for his own good, a prideful little bastard who had latched onto Rafe with a tenacity that could not be shaken. Hoyt could be his demise, so he manipulated the kid carefully, letting him feel the illusion of power yet never truly letting him have it. He cultivated an unnatural loyalty from Hoyt that both irritated and satisfied him but never gave him comfort. The kid was so intrinsically evil, it gave Vivi the willies.

Rafe glanced around the silent room and right at Vivi's unseen form for a moment. Not one man spoke or even breathed heavily and Rafe hid a secret grin behind a cough. He had them, one and all, in his tight fist. Vivi knew that they'd kill him in the blink of an eye if he released his commanding mastery over them. If they loved the thrill of the robbery, Rafe truly loved the thrill of having his dogs in line. It all made her job so much more difficult.

The afternoon had gone well, exactly as planned. His fourth direct robbery of the railroad payroll, this gained from a disguised coal car heading west on the Southern Pacific Line. It was messy, but as usual, Rafe watched from a distance. He lost no men but the one he killed himself. There was no call for Cuthbert to rape that poor lady passenger. No call to slit her throat first either, and Vivi could read in the ebb of his energy that it still sickened Rafe, even though he showed no sign of disgust or remorse. Those feelings had a special pit hidden deep in his soul, and no one but Vivi knew it was there.

Hoyt dispersed the take, dropping bundled wads of cash before each man, an unheard of equal amount to their boss, and that was Rafe's intent. If they saw he got no more than them, they felt an unjustified equality. He didn't need more than they got, and he didn't want it. He wanted them to see the value of what they got from the arrangement, forget that he took few risks and faced almost no danger, always just far enough out of sight to simply ride away if things went bad.

Rafe cleared his throat and all eyes turned to him. "We're ready. Everything we do from here on is focused on the railroad. We'll all be richer than fucking God when it's over."

Vivi gasped. She'd hoped this would be the last train robbery, that the closeness of the advancing posse would shake his determination to ride his plan to the end of the line. Every sign pointed to disaster, tearing at her heart. "Rafe, don't do this," Vivi hissed and he ignored her.

"Until the tracks are all laid, there's payroll money to be gotten. Between every job, we split, fucking disappear somewhere. Hoyt'll get word to you when we're ready to go again. This is gonna be fast and hard and …"

Vivi paced and spat. "Jesus, Rafe! Do not do this! Not with these men! They'll …"

" … and the Pinks," he said with a grin, still disregarded her, "they'll have fucking hard-ons for us." The men snorted laughs, their eyes gleaming with excitement and admiration for his boldness. Not one of them thought Rafe's plan was impossible or even difficult. Idiots, one and all.

"Please Rafe. Please, at least get rid of Hoyt!" Vivi had leaned close to his ear and shouted, but he was indifferent. Had she lost her power to communicate with him? Or had rational thought finally escaped him?

"Blackard," Rafe grunted and the man raised his face.

Vivi shivered. Blackard was the most vicious of them all, now with Cuthbert dead. The man, was a half breed originally called Black Herd whose white mother left him with startling blue eyes and skin so pale most never suspected his Indian blood. He grunted and squared his shoulders. Blackard had never been singled out before. He wasn't the best shot or most agile on a horse, but Rafe had kept him around for his fierce brutality. His face reflected a mix of pride and fear.

"Yeah, Boss?"

"You're leaving. I want you to go to Wichita—"

"Kansas?" Blackard boldly interrupted then blinked.

Rafe eyed the men, Hoyt sniggered and slid back a few inches, the others took a cautious step further from Blackard, fully expecting a quick shot to obliterate the man.

"Yeah," Rafe said kindly, as though he was speaking to a child. "Wichita, Kansas. Get yourself a nice respectable job there, lay low and listen hard. You're gonna watch Charlie Silver and learn everything you can about that bastard. How he lives, what he does before he rides out for bounty, what he does when he comes back. I'll be sending someone—"

"I'll do it," Hoyt announced.

"All right, I'll be sending Hoyt to gather what you learn. After that you just keep on doing the same. You're my ears and eyes, Blackard. Don't fucking fail me. You'll be getting an equal share for it."

The men bellowed but silenced at Rafe's scowl, garish in the brilliant white slice of moonlight cutting through the deserted cabin's missing door.

Vivi was shocked. "This is insane! You have to abandon this stupidity! Blackard? He'd kill you in your sleep if he could get close enough!"

"He won't," he sighed and the men's brows curled. Rafe cleared his throat. "Blackard won't ever stop watching out for us, not with an equal share. What he's gonna do is gonna make it all easier. But..." He tilted a glare at Blackard. "You let me down, you know you're a dead man."

The man's blue eyes widened and he nodded. "I ain't gonna let you down."

* * *

Within moments they were all out of his sight, leaving clouds of sparkling moonlit dust and going in several directions, sure to befuddle the coming posse. Rafe tucked his take in the saddlebag and swung his leg wide to mount. Deep into the night and far from danger, he slowed and rode quietly, proud to have been able to ignore the rambling woman's voice still prattling in his head, ignore it for the most part at least.

"You keep your mouth shut when I'm talking with them," he said, veered the horse west and enjoyed the blessed silence that followed.

It wasn't until he reached his hiding place, a crevasse near the Mexico border known for its infestation of rattlers, that he spoke again. The snakes never bothered him but he heard them and observed them slither, sometimes close to his hand as he buried his cash. "I ain't here to hurt you snakes." He sighed, steadied and finished, the serpents still and watching but never striking. "Thank ya, ma'am."

"It's not me saving you from those snakes," Vivi's voice groaned and he chuckled.

"Still mad at me?" He mounted and crossed the border. "No reason to be. Women talk all the time and I'm usually real good at ignoring them." He turned to his left, somehow sure that's exactly where she rode, not three feet away by his guess. "See, the problem with you is that sometimes you say something worth hearing. So, I listen. But you keep your pretty mouth shut when I'm plannin', you hear?"

"And what can you do if I don't?"

He reveled in the emotion rattling her voice. "Them's fightin' words." He laughed. "One of these days, I'm gonna get to see the fire in your eyes when you try fighting with me."

"You will never see me. For all you know, I don't even exist."

"Oh, you're there. I can smell you. Did you know when you're mad like this you smell different, musky, like a woman in heat."

"Fuck you."

He laughed and heeled his horse ahead just to feel her rush to catch up.

"You will fail," she said and it sounded like she would cry. "Do you want to die, Rafe?"

"Dying ain't so bad, living is better, but at least I know I ain't going to hell."

She growled, her voice burning with anger. "I can't do this! I can't do it anymore! You are fighting me all the way and I just can't save you!"

"Maybe I don't wanna be saved."

"You are an idiot!"

He suddenly shifted in the saddle and glared with fury. Maybe it was he who'd had enough. "Why don't you get away from me? Goddamn it! I never asked for you! Get the hell away from me and leave me alone!" His shout was loud, rustling a distant rattler to hiss and a red tail hawk far above cried out, but then, all was unnaturally silent.

And Rafe Bennett knew for the first time in his life that he was fully and utterly alone.

* * *

Rafe's plan worked flawlessly. Eight robberies in four short months but there was an end in sight, the railroad had made its way from coast to coast and was nearly complete. Life was changing, people would be coming in droves to stake out the promise of land and prosperity, but he knew better. He knew they'd find nothing but hardship. Most of them would end up going back east where they belonged and hopefully leave the wild simplicity of the west for men like him.

Something about the last take cut deep in his gut. Hoyt, gone, all of them, dead or captured. Rafe had barely made it away unseen, but he knew they were looking for him. The Pinkertons, Charlie Silver, the Devil, they were all looking for him. It wasn't the loss of those men that bothered him. Men like that were easy enough to find, simple to train and never important enough to mourn. It was something else he missed.

Knowing he was alone ate at Rafe, made him sharper, more careful. He'd said he wasn't afraid of dying or even hell, but it was a lie. It was his nature to take what he wanted, but what Rafe took didn't satisfy the needs inside him. A massive stash was buried, silent in the snake infested crevasse near the border, but not being a frivolous man and determined to lay low between takes, he seldom spent any of it. Now, he needed a new plan. Not to gather men and do the same thing, it was time to move on, try something different. It was time to get some of his money and live a little.

"Miss you, ma'am. Miss talking with you. Miss your scent." He stilled the horse, closed his eyes and listened. No response.

A little over a day's ride and he was there near the border. The sun kissed the horizon as Rafe climbed down like a tired old man. He tossed the saddlebag over his shoulder then thumbed the animal's velvety ear. "You stay here, hear me?"

The horse's head rose then fell and Rafe grinned sadly. "Least you listen to me." He turned and walked the quarter mile alone. The crevasse was in sight and he stepped gently, nearing as close as he dared then slowly sat and watched. Several rattlers circled near the opening, basking in the cooling desert evening air. Several times the hissing sound of the rattle reached him but he simply grinned. He remained alert all night, watching and waiting until finally dawn brightened the sky and heat speckled sweat on his brow. Soon the snakes stirred, lazily slithered then moved into the shadows.

He was patient, wanting to assure their distance before approaching. He stood silently and smoothly reached for the money. Slow, calculated, careful. An occasional rattle sounded. Rafe's hands slid cautiously, pushing dirt from the cash and finally exposing far more than he realized was there. He leaned back on his knees and brushed away his sweat-slicked hair.

As he loaded the saddlebags, the head of a snake slid from a small crack and Rafe's hand stilled. Their eyes met and he quietly spoke. "We got us a deal, don't we? Not gonna hurt you and you're not gonna hurt me."

More of the shiny body exposed and coiled, the echo of the rattle from deep within the rocks, and still he didn't move away. "Not gonna hurt you and you're not gonna hurt me." He drew a deep breath and simply continued his slow, calm movements until the saddlebags were loaded.

The rattler didn't strike while he covered the remaining money with sand, and he slowly stepped backward until well out of the snake's reach. When Rafe turned he released a heavy breath he'd been holding. Every time he came to his money, he faced the Devil again. Each time, he was less sure that he'd survive, especially now that she was gone.

* * *

Vivi wasn't gone, in fact, she wasn't far. She watched and worked from a distance, safe from his ability to confuse and baffle her. She begged and prayed for guidance during the most difficult times, and hoped for compassion from the heavens when all seemed lost. Even though Rafe always managed to survive, she felt helpless so far away. She tried to imagine herself like him, watching crimes from afar, safe from danger and sure to gain profit in the end, but she knew that it wasn't the best way to watch over a man like Rafe. Maybe she should be more hands-on with her protection and steel herself against his ability to reach inside her.

Heaven had seen fit to give her additional powers just for this case, but now she was reduced to taking on human form only when she was alone, hidden from him, so that she could cry and feel heated salty tears run down her face. Madam Miriam must be infuriated with her. In fact, that night while Vivi sobbed pitifully, she was sure heaven had washed its hands of her. She'd been watching over Rafe since his childhood, witnessed his sins and startling kindnesses, learning his depth and capacity for evil and still, still, she loved him. But wasn't that as it should be? She was an angel charged with the care of a frail human being. Wasn't she supposed to love him? But even as she thought these things she knew it was wrong.

Far from him, she longed to see the color of his eyes, the turn of his lips when he grinned, the way his hair fell over his eyes. She longed to hear his voice right at her side, and she clearly understood that feeling that way broke the rules.

"This is bad. So bad. Take me back," she prayed softly. "Take me from this case, from this man. Don't let me fail so miserably. Please, take me back."

A star shot across the sky, sliced the heavens then fizzled out. It wasn't an answer she hoped for, just a shooting star and she cried more. She'd heard Rafe say that he missed her, and she missed him terribly. Vibrant Light, like Rafe Bennett, was sure that she was truly, fully and utterly alone.

CHAPTER 10

He thought to head to Mexico, thought to go north, maybe even east. Maybe he'd slip through Wichita just for the thrill of it, just to take a look at Charlie Silver who still, no matter his efforts, was alive. He'd have Blackard to deal with. The man had to know by now that the whole gang was done. He might be running scared, or waiting to kill Rafe the moment he showed his face. Then, of course, there was Rafe's face. It wasn't like there was a man, woman, or child, in that town who wouldn't recognize him at a hundred paces. The artist's likeness had vastly improved on the wanted posters over time. No, Wichita was no place for Rafe to go.

Was there a place to go? He sat tall in the saddle then shifted to look behind, to look around. The craggy hills called to him. The possibility of running into a few of those Apache renegades in the pass got his blood rushing. He wondered if saving that little boy a while back would protect him. He wondered if the little boy survived, if maybe the Apache remembered that he saved one of their own, and maybe Rafe could cash out that chit one more time. No matter, it was the quickest way north so Rafe turned the horse with a quiet click of his tongue and headed into the shadows. He grinned. Might see nothing at all. All the renegades might've been caught. Less than two weeks earlier, his men killed four of them. There were few left but his gut told him they were still there. Where were those Injun warriors and their people hiding? Someplace safe, no doubt. Someplace perfect. The kind of place Rafe needed right now.

He crossed through untouched, even remained for two nights knowing few posses were brave enough to face the Apache, but it was time to move on. He kicked out his meager fire and scanned the surrounding rocky hills. "Where are you?" he whispered. She was gone. Were the Apache too gone? He mounted as dawn brightened the eastern sky with pale pinks and blues and the promise of searing heat to come.

Just as he passed through the last protected turn they charged him, a posse just sitting in wait, like they knew he was there. He raced and fingered his pistol, but never drew. Was it because he figured it was over? That death was near and maybe he really was going to hell? Low to his horse, bullets soaring past, he growled like an angry wolf, heeled the animal that was determined to save them both, but they were overcome.

Rafe was yanked from the saddle, dropped to the ground and mercilessly beaten and kicked. Blood spurted from mouth, eye, and nose. His arm was broken, the bone protruding from the skin just below his elbow and still he didn't fight. They weren't going to shoot him, had no intention of killing him. They wanted him to stand trial and be hanged, and in that moment, he too wanted to hang. Wondered how it felt to have the last breath strangled from his body. Would he fight it, or would he willingly drop all the way to the fires of hell?

He grinned, spat a garish, blood splattering chuckle and looked up at his tormentors, but suddenly, one dropped with a thud, right across his chest and he desperately pushed the dead weight off. He was unable to sit up or even crawl away. The sound of gunshot and wild Apache hoots drifted to him and the remaining men of the posse turned and scattered like rabbits. Not one made it alive. The flat desert was littered with bleeding bodies and less than four Apache warriors were already kicking and counting coup on the corpses. Rafe remained silent then slowly shifted his hand to reach for his pistol but it was suddenly, painfully jerked away and tossed. Sunlight flashed and flared off the weapon until it landed far from his reach. A face blocked the blazing sun and he blinked through pain and a terror he couldn't recall ever experiencing before. Hanging is one thing, but what the Apache did to a man was unthinkable.

Another warrior walked over and swung a swift kick into already broken ribs and Rafe let loose with an agonized howl.

"Enough!" the first Apache bellowed in perfect English. "Enough. Leave." And to Rafe's surprise, the man's renegade crew mounted, gathered the free horses and rode calmly back into the hills.

His mind spun. Had they taken his horse? He gave a soft whistle and heard the whinny only feet away.

"What are you gonna do with me?" he grunted to the warrior glaring down at him and the man gave a wicked grin.

"I would leave you here to burn on the sand, Rafe Bennett, but I owe you. That boy you saved … he is my son. So now we are even." He stood and Rafe watched the moccasin feet turn to leave.

"Thought you weren't gonna let me die here?" He felt like he was already dying, piece by piece as numbness slid over him like hot water.

"She's coming. You won't die today, Rafe Bennett." The man laughed, mounted and rode away.

"She's coming?" He achingly twisted his neck in the direction the crazy Apache had pointed. Did he hear the man right? And if she was coming, how did the Indian see her?

But Rafe could see her too. She walked slowly, silhouetted against the soft morning light, holding the reigns of her white horse, wearing buckskin britches and vest, her hair flowing long and dark beneath a pale hat. It wasn't until she knelt at his side, a tear glistening in her eye that he was sure. It was the woman he'd dreamed of, the woman with eyes the color of polished gold, the woman he'd felt at his side his whole life.

"You're here." He gasped at the paralyzing pain, at her beauty, at the intense compassion in her eyes.

* * *

Her hands trembled as they hovered over his beaten body. "I'm here, Rafe." She cried, wet tears slid down her face and dropped onto his chest. "Oh God. Your arm." Vivi was desperate, trying to see inside his skin to determine how to repair the damage, but all she saw was blood and bone and ragged, torn flesh. Her eyes rose to the skies. "Help me," she begged.

"Ain't no one to help us." He groaned long and pitifully. "You're here," he whispered. "You're really here. I love you and … you're here."

Vivi's fingers pushed back his hair and everything in her body shuddered. "I love you, Rafe." Her hand shot to her chest and pressed against the strange agony there, she felt the pumping of blood and the searing heat of it soared beneath her flesh. She stood and raced to the horse for her canteen, but tripped, stumbled and fell. The rocks pressed painfully into her knee and she scrambled to stand. Dizziness washed over her, but all she wanted to do was help Rafe. She gathered her bedroll and canteen and ran back. Ripping her homespun shirt, she pulled a piece free and wet it, tenderly wiping the area around the broken, protruding bone.

"You're here," he gasped then raised his good arm, slid his hand beneath her thick hair and pulled her face to his. He kissed her deeply, with passion and thankfulness. Vivi returned that kiss as though she had known her whole life how to do such a thing.

* * *

Miriam ran through the marble halls. She rushed into Paul's office, panting, tears streaming down her face. "What do we do? How do we fix this?" she gasped as Paul sat still as stone at his desk, his eyes on his monitor screen and his head slowly shook.

"We can't fix this, Miriam. It is done. It's over."

"No! No, we have to get her back. This isn't how it's supposed to happen, Paul. All these years, all her work! Wasted? There has to be a way!"

Paul stood and pressed Miriam into a chair. He knelt at her feet and held her hands, waited for her to catch her breath then spoke quietly. "Miriam, Vibrant Light knew the rules. She knew them clearly and she has broken them. She was to never permit Rafe Bennett touch her, emotionally or physically. My dear, Vivi has made her choice. There is no returning for her now."

"But you've been watching! You can see that she didn't realize. He reached for her and she was preoccupied with helping him. It wasn't her choice, Paul! There has to be a way to—"

"And her words before he reached for her?"

Miriam blinked.

"She had already let him touch her heart before he ever reached for her. She had already chosen. She told him of her love. Human love, Miriam. She crossed the line and then she permitted him to cross the line. This is over."

It took several moments, but finally Miriam was able to accept. "And this was all for nothing," she said with a sniffle.

"It was not, my dear. She had preserved him far longer than we expected. Now, she will continue to try to do the same at his side, that's all. All we can do is pray, Miriam. We pray, and we hope."

"But now she is human. Who will protect her?"

Paul smiled sadly. "Already there is a minor guardian assigned, but Miriam, you do realize that she is not alone down there, right?"

Miriam shivered and clearly understood. "Yes."

* * *

Rafe moved in and out of consciousness, his fever burning and pain unbearable, but as darkness fell, he became oddly alert. "You gotta fix my arm … name?" he panted, sweat stinging his eyes. "What's your name?"

"Vivi. I don't know how to fix your arm." She desperately soothed his brow with the wet cloth and sighed. "I just don't know how."

He shifted, shouted in pain then calmed. "Take my wrist and pull, Vivi. Plant your heels and pull until it sets. It'll slide back in the skin and find its place."

"I can't! Oh Rafe, I'll hurt you more. I can't do this!"

"Did I say that when you told me how to get the bullet from that Injun baby?" His eyes were wild with frustration and misery. "Just do it!" he shouted and she blinked in terror. Drawing in a deep breath Vivi did as he asked, gripped his wrist and sunk the heels of her boots deep into the hard, gritty earth. She slowly pulled. "Harder!" He yelled and she pulled more, slowly, further, as sweat poured into her eyes. "More!"

Vivi gasped in another deep breath and braced herself better. As she pulled the arm, she noticed the bone move, it slid, and she panicked.

Rafe cried out in pain but again he shouted. "Don't fucking stop!"

She pulled with all her strength, tugged the break apart then watched the bone recede beneath the flesh and smoothly plant itself. How correct it was set, she would never know, but blessedly Rafe was unconscious. She quickly tied the repaired arm tight between two sturdy mesquite branches then washed and wrapped the wound.

Vibrant Light sat and cried, loud sobs toward the heavens. What had she done? Every part of her body ached and itched, it twitched and throbbed and her shoulders trembled from the weight of human existence. Her belly growled and rumbled and her head thumped. She slithered away from Rafe, not wanting to disturb his rest and she cried even harder.

"That's quite enough," a mellow voice drifted over her shoulder and she sharply turned, terror in her heart.

"You!"

"Yes, me. Who did you expect, Vibrant Light? An army of His winged soldiers to come and rescue you? Take you home? Well, pretty Vivi … you can't go home. Not anymore."

Lucifer stood in his astounding glory, beautiful beyond words, amazing and pleasing to look upon, and as horrifying as though he were a filthy beast. Vivi scrambled back, away from him, and a smile lit his entire face. His massive wings shuffled then calmly tucked behind his shoulders. "Where are you going?"

"Why are you here?" she gasped.

"It's where I work little angel … well, little human now," he chuckled. "What pompous shits they are, sending you down here like that, expecting you to figure it all out yourself. Of course, you were bound to fail. The entire mission was doomed from inception."

"Are you here to try to take me?" Vivi whispered, terror streaking through her veins.

"Of course not. You're of no use to me. I'm a volume broker, sweetheart. I'm here for him," his perfectly chiseled cleft chin jerked toward Rafe's silent form. "I've been working on that one for eons, life

after life, since long before you came along, and he brings me volume."
Lucifer chuckled.

"You won't get him." She stood, eye to eye with the Devil, her shoulders squared and eyes blazing but his laugh resounded across the desert.

"Oh yes, I will. But not tonight, Vibrant Light. He can still do a lot for my cause." Lucifer blinked his brilliant eyes and suddenly they were standing in the Apache pass. Rafe, still unconscious, was comfortable beneath a blanket and shielded between two massive rocks. A large rattler slithered near the sleeping man's face but Lucifer clicked his tongue.

"Now, now there. We have a deal, don't we? He won't hurt you and you won't hurt him." The snake turned and moved to Lucifer's leg, coiled its way to his knee where it raised its head and the Devil petted it tenderly. "Off with you now, let him rest."

Vivi watched the serpent disappear into the darkness and turned to survey the camp. A small fire crackled and fresh meat sent a delicious scent that tickled her senses. Both horses were tethered nearby, watered, cared for. "Why?" she asked suspiciously.

"Why? I told you why. Rafe Bennett brings me volume." Lucifer paced the space, knelt close to Rafe's peaceful body and she restrained herself from pulling him away. "This arm will heal, very nice job, Vivi. There are two, no three, cracked ribs. Wrap them tightly and don't ride for another few days, give him a chance to rest." He stood, pointed to the fire. "Food, he'll need to eat and so will you. You need to sleep now too, little human, but try to do it in the daytime. This canyon, like the pass, is still infested with Apache, but I'll venture a guess they won't bother you. Unless you provoke them, that is."

"Why are you helping me?"

"I'm not helping you, I'm protecting him. You're just here to help me now, that's all."

"You won't get his soul," she said with a hissed.

"I already have his soul. Now, look at you, not even grateful. In five minutes I've given you more assistance than they," his eyes raised to the heavens, "have in over twenty years. A 'thank you' would be nice."

"You will never get his soul."

Lucifer laughed, gave an elegant bow then simply vanished.

CHAPTER 11

Rafe slept deeply and Vivi struggled with the things of human life. She tasted the fire seared meat, chewed, reveled in the texture and flavor then swallowed. She guzzled water from the canteen then decided that it should be preserved and set it aside. The night became cold and she shivered, moved closer to the fire for warmth and tucked blankets tight around Rafe. And finally, for the first time ever, Vivi fell asleep.

The sensations of floating and sinking, of warmth and chill washed over her as strange images tormented her and she woke with a start. Sweat soaked her shirt and the soft, pale dawn whispered its greeting. The earth was different through human eyes and Vivi found herself mourning the vision of it she once had and never truly appreciated.

Now, the world was solid, hard, and difficult, but that's not the way of it. Vibrant Light had seen the truth of all existence, the fragility, flexibility, and translucent qualities of it. She understood the living, vibrating elements that created the forms and shape humans saw only as obstacles, and she sadly accepted that now they were her obstacles too. No wonder man lived so precariously. He had no way to recognize how fully malleable the world could be because humans were unable to use it. But for years she had used it to protect and preserve Rafe Bennett's life.

A shudder traveled up her spine. Who was she saving Rafe for? Heaven had never given her a reason for her assignment; they had no cause to do so. It was for them to know and for her to carry through but she'd failed miserably. Lucifer now assumed she was helping him, but looking down into Rafe's sleeping face, watching his chest rise and fall with his sleep breath, Vivi was only sure of one thing. She would be protecting Rafe Bennett for herself, not for heaven, and not for hell, for herself, for she loved him with an overpowering intensity that was bound to put her solidly on the ground. A fallen angel. A failure in heaven, but her heart would succeed on earth or she would die trying. The man beside her was all that mattered.

Her bladder pressed and she gasped quietly. She'd watched men and women relieve themselves in many places and situations. It was a mundane necessity and she should have treated it as such, but her face burned with sudden embarrassment and she skirted a large bolder for privacy. The sensation of steaming urine flowing from her body was excruciating, strange, unfamiliar and a small cry escaped her lips.

"You okay?" Rafe had struggled to stand and lean against the rock, concern in his eyes and a small grin pulling at the edge of his damaged face.

"Go away!" she gasped and he chuckled.

"What say I just turn my back, darlin'?" And he did, hissing an aching rumble as the embarrassing splatter sounded against hard packed rock and sand. Finally finished, Vivi slid her arm under his and he permitted her to lead him back to the fire. Rafe looked around. "How'd we get here?"

Vivi shrugged and hung thin slices of meat over the stoked fire. "You don't want to know, trust me."

"You hunt this meat?" he questioned as he watched it sputter and sizzle. She didn't answer so he waited, accepted the food and ate then ran his sleeve across his mouth. He sighed and leaned back, eyed her carefully. "You're here. You're with me. What I wanna know is, are you gonna leave again?"

"No." A tear frustratingly distorted her vision.

"Don't be scared, Vivi."

She squared her shoulders and laid a glare on him. "I'm not scared. I can't protect you like I used to anymore, but I am not scared at all."

The tear dripped down her cheek and he tenderly caught it with his finger. "Yes, you are, but don't worry your pretty head, I'll be protecting you. Hush now."

Vivi pushed her long dark hair back, carefully avoiding his eyes and sure he'd see through her façade. Yes, she was afraid, terribly afraid for them both. "Now what?"

"We ride today."

"No!" she stood, attempting to look bigger and braver than she was. They were alone in the middle of renegade Apache territory. He was hurt and she was nothing more than human. She was more than afraid, Vibrant Light was terrified. "You're too weak to ride yet. We can't go anywhere until you're stronger."

"I'm strong enough."

Agitated, she paced in the growing daylight. "And where would we go anyway?"

Rafe watched her and chewed on his lip a moment. "Texas."

"But you've never been to Texas, not since you were a boy."

"Exactly. No one's gonna recognize me there."

She dropped to her knees. "Rafe you can not do what you've been doing, not in Texas. Why don't we go to Mexico?"

"Mexico's no place for you, darlin'. Besides, I'm tired of running. Texas will do just fine."

"But you can't rob—"

"I ain't gonna rob nothing. Not until I need to. For now, I got enough in that saddle bag to last us a while, just 'til I get me another plan." He beamed his casual smile, his eyes twinkling as though nothing could go wrong. "In the meantime you and me, we're gonna travel like husband and wife."

"Rafe! I can't lie."

He stood with a miserable grunt, looked down at her and tilted his head. "Yes, you can. You been lyin' to me for years. It'll work out just fine. Now, we ride soon. Get yourself ready."

She reluctantly gathered the canteens and saddlebags then reached for the blanket and squealed. A rattler hissed and slithered from under it then backed into the darkness again.

"Leave it."

Rafe gripped her elbow and tugged her to safety. Stepping back she glared at the blanket, writhing from the serpents beneath, realizing that moments earlier Rafe had been sleeping on it.

"Let's go."

* * *

They rode, slow and easy, stopping often for Rafe to rest. As he settled in the shade of a tree, Vivi strolled casually around, watching for danger and spying the blazing form of Lucifer in the distance. "You'll never get his soul," she whispered.

"I already have his soul," Lucifer's voice hissed in the darkness.

She did not start or worry, simply shrugged and tucked the canteens into the loaded saddlebag. "You've never been up against me before, buddy."

"Who you talking to?" Rafe stood at her shoulder, a concerned curl in his brow.

She smiled up at him, a sudden feeling of love and protection washing over her. "Myself."

They rode without haste for days until Rafe no longer grunted and groaned with every movement. Entering El Paso, Vivi's eyes widened with excitement. The city churned with people, and noise, and new construction everywhere. It had a frenetic energy even San Francisco lacked, a sizzling power of promise and future. Surely the railroad made a major impact on a town, but this one seemed incredible to her. She'd heard people talk of New York or St. Louis, but El Paso looked and smelled more massive than anything they'd described and Vivi imagined she had witnessed a vision of what man and ideas could accomplish.

Rafe slid from his horse and tossed the reins over a post so she did the same. Without asking, she followed him into a saloon and right up to the bar, and that's when her new reality slammed Vivi smack in the face.

Hoots and whistles rose from the men all around as a pretty young girl danced on a table, swinging her skirts high and kicking her feet far above her shoulders. Vivi blinked. "What are they doing?"

Rafe turned, obviously shocked that she'd followed him into the place. Before he could take her wrist and pull her out, another man gripped Vivi around the waist.

"Hey, look at what I found!" he slurred, smelling of rot gut and wobbling precariously on his feet.

The men turned and all their attention focused on her. Vivi drew in a sharp breath. "Rafe?" she squeaked and he calmly moved between her and the men.

"Now, isn't there a lot more to see on that table?" he smiled, real friendly-like.

"Yeah, but we seen it already. This one's covered up and we wanna see what's under all that buckskin."

Rafe grinned wider. "Well, it's gonna cost ya."

Vivi gasped and glared at him, then at the men reaching into their pockets.

"How much you want for this filly?"

"Well, see that's just it, mister. See, she ain't for sale." Rafe spoke in a congenial manner, his charisma working flawlessly as the men listened like he was a preacher quoting the Bible on Sunday morning. Their eyes glazed over with lust and whisky and Rafe took clear advantage. "It'll cost you what you ain't about to give up to get at this one."

"What's she doin' in here if she ain't offering?"

Vivi didn't wait to hear another word, she ducked and turned and slithered her way through the laughing crowd, receiving several fondles and brusque slaps across her behind along the way. As she exited the swinging door, she heard Rafe's voice bellow a laugh.

"Drinks on me, gentlemen!"

She looked up and down the dusty street, panting and curious at how her knees shook from the experience, at just how dangerous human life could be. She was at the mercy of those men, at Rafe's mercy too, but before her anger took full control she walked to their horses and thought. Running a hand along her mare's neck, she realized that Rafe was protecting her the only way he could. They were in a new city for him, one where he was not recognized, one where he needed to lay low to be safe. She knew better than to walk into the saloon, but her energy was so tied to his, she'd simply followed.

"I'm a fool," she sighed to the animal.

"No, I'm the fool," Rafe stood behind her and lowered his face close to her ear. "I wasn't using my head … and I always use my head. Having you around is new. Different. Gonna take some time to figure out."

"Being around is just as new to me."

81

"Tell me where you were, Vivi?"

She stepped away, her eyes scanning the crowded street. "I can't."

He sighed, nodded and laid his warm palm at the small of her back. "Come with me."

"Where?"

"Look around you, darlin'. Don't you want to feel pretty like those ladies over there?"

She watched two women carefully walk on heeled, tight shoes, sway heavy skirts that limited their movement and hold their heads straight and proper in order to keep their hats balanced. She wanted to say hell no, but wondered how Rafe might like to see her dressed that way. "So, what if I do?"

He laughed and led her to a fancy dress store. Hours later she strolled the street on his arm. He'd bought himself a new velvet jacket, his healing arm still held in a sling beneath the soft fabric. He'd bought Vivi a beautiful dress with voluminous petticoats, a hat from New York, lovely white gloves, and high heeled boots that pinched her feet.

"How on earth will I ride like this?" she smiled then nodded a sweet salute to a passing couple.

"You ain't riding right now," he stated.

"And what will we do now?"

"Now, we go to the hotel. Now, we get us a fancy room. And now I make love to you until the sun comes up." He steered her across the street, walking slowly to accommodate her shorter stride and her obvious nervousness.

"But—"

"Darlin', I waited my whole life for you, did everything to make my way to you and it's time. Don't be scared, Vivi. I ain't never gonna hurt you."

* * *

Charlie Silver was in one hell of a pickle. He stood in the telegraph office and rubbed his temples red. Things had not gone well. He came to El Paso for bounty, but it didn't pay much. He tried his hand at gambling, but the others cheated better than he did. His Wichita life had gone sour since he let that harpy of a whore convince him to marry her. Now she ran his saloon and whorehouse into the ground and he needed refuge and funding to rebuild it.

He looked for new bounty among the wanted posters hung on the wall, but there was nothing juicy enough for his tastes. He longed for the old days and the real outlaws that gave him a run for his money, outlaws like Rafe Bennett, who was presumed dead in Arizona after his last attempt at the Southern Pacific Railroad. The bounty well had run dry, Silver wasn't as young as he used to be and the outlaws had all gotten younger. With so many people around, bounty was being sucked up by chance encounters, amateurs and a new breed of hunter who wanted glory more than cash. It was time to change his life.

He bought a ticket for home, decided to kill his stupid wife and start new in Wichita. Maybe he'd build a nice respectable hotel and sap his earnings from the wealthy businessmen passing through town.

"So, now what?"

He turned to his traveling companion, Frank Blackard, the man who cared for his business while Silver hunted down outlaws. He too had tired of the harpy wife's meddling and demanded that traveling with Silver was the only way he'd remain in his employ. Blackard was a good bartender, a tough ruffian when the saloon got too rowdy, and a loyal man Silver didn't trust as far as he could throw. Best to have him where he could see him.

"We're goin' back to Wichita to get what's mine back from that bitch."

"Good," Blackard grunted then strangely stilled for a moment.

A wiry man, Blackard seldom became so silent and Silver blinked. "What?"

"Nothin'. When we leavin', boss?"

"In the morning. Not even gonna send her a telegram to warn her. You wanna strangle her?"

"Yeah, I do. I gotta go do something. See you later." Blackard walked off.

Charlie Silver shrugged. Maybe the half-breed spotted a relative. There were lots of Injuns on the streets in El Paso.

CHAPTER 12

Oh, he saw the man. Saw him as he walked toward the hotel with Vivi. Saw him inside that telegraph office, talking with Charlie Silver. Rafe knew Blackard was there, and Blackard knew he was there. The exciting part was wondering what Blackard would do about it. Did he want his share of the take they never got? Then, there was that other question. Did Hoyt ever deliver Blackard's share after any job? It ate at Rafe's gut every time he sent the kid to Wichita. Soon he'd need to deal with it, because Blackard was watching from across the street, pacing.

None of those worries were worth a second thought at that moment. Rafe already knew how, and when, to handle Blackard. He had something more important to deal with first. He had Vivi.

He settled her comfortably on a lobby settee and spoke to the man at the desk. He took a room and fingered the key with a knowing grin then escorted his woman upstairs. Inside the door he and Vivi stood and simply watched each other. Were they wild dogs circling each other? Was she as afraid as he was feeling? No woman ever brought out his worry like Vivi. His intentions were noble, but his heart thumped like a terrified kid at his first gunfight. Was it insecurity? Or was it something else? That one thing he refused to think about? That she'd disappear from his life again, and what would become of him then?

Vivi would never guess at his thoughts or fear. She'd never see it or know it. He reached a finger and slid it over the rise of her satin covered breast. Vivi stepped back.

"Don't be afraid, Vivi. I ain't gonna hurt you."

"I'm not afraid. But Rafe … are you … curious?"

His eye twinkled and his finger reached again. He allowed her one more step back, one last time to think she was in control. "Yeah, I'm curious." His eyes slithered over her form and he groaned softly.

"Not about that. It's just a woman's body. They're all the same."

He grinned and tilted his head, his hair falling across his eye. "No, they're not. Every one's different. Every kiss, every taste, every touch, is different. Every time." He stepped closer and again reached but this time pulled back in response to her next words.

"Aren't you curious about me?"

He swallowed, focused on her eyes. "No. I don't wanna know. Don't care. You're here and you're mine. Don't need to know nothing else."

"You're afraid, aren't you?"

"No." His hand snaked around her corseted waist and pulled her tight against him. "I ain't afraid. I'm taking what I want, that's all."

She struggled and broke free, stepped further back. "If you want it, marry me, Rafe."

"Oh, I'll marry you tomorrow. I'll have you tonight."

Vivi had been with him his whole life and probably knew everything about him, but what did he know about her? As he methodically removed bits of her new clothing, his mind calculated what he understood and what he hoped was true.

She wanted marriage and strangely, so did he. The lovely skirt was draped over the chair.

She loved him and he loved her. He'd always wanted love but never quite found it. Was that Vivi's fault? Did he know she was coming? He untied the satin laces of her corset and laid it next to the skirt.

Soft breasts moved gently beneath the chemise and his hands cupped them. A rush of heat shot through him. She was real, and really his. He tore the fabric from her chest and licked his lips. What else did he know? What else?

He'd heard her claim to have protected him. Bullshit. He took care of himself, but he liked the idea of someone like Vivi loving him enough she thought she was protecting him. Pantaloons billowed at her ankles and he beckoned her to step out of them.

She sighed, and Rafe was again drawn to her breasts. He suckled deeply, his hand strong and large against her back.

"Oh, oh God!" Vivi cried softly and he grinned, released the nipple with a snap, unwilling to tell her that God had nothing to do with what he intended to give her that night.

He stepped back and sat calmly on the divan. There he looked her over from head to toe. Vivi stood, naked except for the voluminous, pristine petticoats that covered her from waist to ankles. He watched her tremble, her eyes fearful, her shaking hands nervously bunching the crisp fabric. Oh yes, she'd be his wife, be his forever, but how he'd keep her was changing, not as simple as he'd hoped. His plans shifted the moment he spotted Blackard. Was there any place safe he could take her? Even Mexico was questionable. There, she'd be a prize to be taken from him. He'd thought to take her up to Abilene, to buy some land and be a rancher. Raise a family. Live well and comfortable on all the money he still had hidden at the border. But could he do it? Keep her safe there? In his heart he wondered, with Vivi at his side, was there anything he couldn't do?

She was afraid of him, shaking hard now, a tear rolling down her beautiful face but she defiantly ignored it, shook her long, shiny dark hair behind her shoulders. Was she afraid he wasn't pleased with what he saw? Rafe reached out a hand.

"Come here, darlin'." He patted his knee and she slowly sat on his lap. His bad arm braced behind her shoulders and he leaned her back until he could suck a painful mark on her pale neck. Then he lowered his attention to her breast and suckled there, nursed as she sighed and finally her knees relaxed. His hand slowly shifted the voluminous petticoats until it was buried beneath, seeking her heat. "Let me in, Vivi," he whispered against her breast and she opened her knees.

Sliding fingers along the tender, soaked flesh Rafe groaned with delight, sucked tight at a nipple and a plan formed. He'd take her to heaven first then he'd take her to the bed. There he'd seal the deal with heaven and hell. There, whether he married her right and proper or not, Vivi would be his wife. His fingers trembled as he slid them tenderly over the hardening pebble hidden beneath the petticoats. Vivi softened to his touch, permitted him more and more and he tightened his grip around her shoulders. Without pause, his mouth nursing at a nipple and fingers moving fast, he waited, held his breath and she fully opened, bloomed like a flower at his touch before curling in on herself and exploding with a climax that soaked his hand.

He pushed her thighs wide and pressed a finger deep. Tight. So tight, and there it was. The barrier. Just what he was looking for. Virgin. He took her virginity fast and hard with the thrust of two thick fingers then rocked her in his arms, his hand still buried deep. "Hush now, the hard part's over, darlin'. The hard part's all over."

On the bed he did as he pleased. He loved her with passion and lust, took what he wanted most and listened carefully for her pleasures. She was weak and satiated when he finished, filling her not once, but three times before the moon had reached its height in the sky. He allowed himself a brief rest then quietly rose and dressed. Vivi lay snuggled against the pillow and he smiled before turning to leave the room.

"Where are you going?"

He didn't look at her, simply reached for his hat. "Going down to the saloon for a drink, darlin'. I'll be back real soon."

"Will you take another woman?"

He turned to see her sitting up, terror in her eyes. His head tilted and he smiled. "No, Vivi. I got no need for another woman. You're all I want. Now sleep. Just going for some whisky. When I come back, I'll love you again." He kissed her back onto the pillow and tugged the blankets to cover her. "Sleep, darlin'."

* * *

Rafe didn't want whisky; he didn't go to the saloon. He reached into his pocket for the key he'd paid the desk clerk a large sum of money for. Slipping silently into the room, he waited until the occupant rolled over then cleared his throat.

"Blackard," he said and the man leapt from his mattress, reached for his clothes but stopped when hearing the click as Rafe cocked his pistol. "What are you doing in El Paso? And," Rafe chuckled casually. "Why were you following me earlier?"

Blackard lit the oil lamp with shaking fingers, pulled his jacket over his near nakedness and cleared his throat. He eyed Rafe then rubbed his nose. "You want the truth, Bennett?"

"Yeah, I want the truth, then you can tell me any lies you want. Final outcome's likely to be the same though, but you already know that, don't you?"

Blackard nodded. "Bennett, I swear, I thought you was dead."

"What are you doing in El Paso?"

"I been watching Charlie Silver, just like you told me," the man's voice rattled. "I sent reports! All of them! Every time Hoyt came, I told him what I knew."

"Yeah? So you saying you're still watching him for a man you thought was dead?"

Blackard moved his dry lips but not a word came out.

"No. You're telling me that you're now working for Silver, ain't you." Rafe shifted in the chair and continued to finger his gun, his eyes never leaving the man's face.

"I been working for him the whole damn time. How did you think I knew so much? I was just doing what you told me to do."

"And why are you here?"

Again, nervous silence.

"I knew you were here. I went to Wichita, you know." Rafe lied.

"No! You wouldn't! What if Silver saw you? You ain't stupid enough to do that."

"Well," Rafe pulled his handkerchief and polished the barrel of his pistol. "See, I went to check up on you."

"I was doing what you told me!" Blackard was on his feet, pacing the room like a caged animal.

"Yeah, I know. Just wanted to have a talk. See if you got the money I sent."

"I did! All of it!"

"Good, good. So now you're working for the Devil himself and you want more, maybe a piece of the bounty on my head?"

"No! I owe you Rafe! You kept me away from the danger—"

"I put you right in Silver's hands." Rafe grinned wickedly.

"You kept me from the robberies and sent me money for information! I owe you!" Blackard suddenly stopped pacing and ran a hand across his sweaty face. "Listen, you can still get outta this. Me and

Silver, were taking the train back to Wichita in the morning. Just lay low with your pretty lady friend and you'll be fine! He'll never know you're here." His eyes bore deep into Rafe's and for a moment, he believed him.

"You'd do that for me? Why?"

"Like I said, I owe you. When I get to Wichita, I'll hightail it away from that bastard. Meet up with you wherever you say."

"Won't have to. You're gonna kill him before you even reach Wichita."

"Yeah, yeah, I can do that, too! That's what I'll do. Push his dead body off the moving train."

Rafe remained silent.

"I owe you, boss. I got all the money you sent, and I owe you." Perspiration glittered off Blackard's brow in the lamplight. "I owe you. And ... and ... if you don't trust me, just ..." the man swallowed hard then squared himself to Rafe and the loaded pistol, "just kill me right now."

"No. Too messy, too much noise. I ain't gonna kill you in this fancy hotel, Blackard. But I will kill you if Silver lives. Consider it your last job for me."

Blackard nodded frantically. "Ain't nothing more pleasing than to kill that bastard."

"Yeah." Rafe turned off the oil lamp and slipped silently from the room, leaving Blackard to choose. None of it mattered. He and Vivi would be long gone before Silver's train left the station.

Rafe slithered quietly into the bed beside her, ran his hands softly over her flesh then glanced out the dark window. There was some time but he chose to let Vivi sleep. They'd both need rest if they were to get out of town before dawn. He still had time.

He drifted into a deep sleep, even his arm didn't ache enough to keep him awake that night.

CHAPTER 13

Eight sharp, Blackard knocked on Charlie Silver's door. "Time to get to the station, boss." He waited. "Boss?"

"There you are," Silver called from the far end of the hall. He rushed to the room, pushed Blackard inside and slammed him against the wall.

"What the fuck are ya doing?" Blackard struggled against the man almost twice his age.

"So, you know Rafe Bennett?"

Blackard gulped hard. "Yeah, you never asked."

"No, no, I didn't. You think I'm an idiot? You think I never saw you ride with him? Don't you know that all these years I knew you were spying on me?" His fist slammed so hard into Blackard's belly, bloody spit flew out with his grunt.

"I been working for you!"

"I knew you'd eventually lead me to Bennett. It was just a matter of time. Fuck, you're probably the only man in the territory who knew he wasn't dead." Another slam crushed into Blackard's gut and the man crumbled to his knees.

"I been working for you, Silver! Just you."

"Okay, you get a chance to prove it."

Blackard's face rose and his eyes met Silver's.

"I already got Bennett. They're taking him for a quick trial right now, then to the gallows. I been waiting years to watch that man dangle at the end of a rope, and now I'm finally gonna see it. Thanks to you, Blackard. Thanks to you."

Blackard struggled to his feet and leaned back against the wall. "So what do you need, boss?"

"Who's that pretty lady with Bennett?"

Blackard shrugged. "Some whore."

"Nah, I'm thinking she'd make me a good wife. So here's what you're gonna do. You're gonna get that woman and stay with her until this whole hanging ordeal's over. Make sure she watches, I ain't having no silliness about her thinking he's coming to rescue her or nothing. You bring her here to me when it's over. I expect she'll have a few bruises, she'll most likely try to fight you. Should've seen the fight she gave when we took Bennett." Silver gave an ugly laugh. "Yeah, that one's got some spunk. I expect a few bruises, but don't you rape her, you hear me? After you kill my old wife, this one's gonna be my new wife. It's bad enough Bennett has soiled her, I won't have your filth clinging to her, too."

Blackard calmed his breathing. "Where is she?"

"Still in their room. Twenty three. Sheriff's got a deputy guarding her, but I told them you'd be coming to get her."

He nodded.

"What are you waiting for?" Silver pushed him out of the room and brushed past him. There was a bounty to collect before the main event.

* * *

Before the sheriff dragged Rafe through the lobby in chains, his face was bloodied and swollen. He hadn't fought against them, didn't even drawn his pistol. He sat in the cell, thinking of Vivi and the time in her flesh, deep and throbbing, and he thanked God he'd had those hours. The trial was laughable and he grinned throughout the speedy proceedings. As he walked to the gallows, he saw her, his Vivi, the woman he fully loved. Beside her, that bastard Blackard gripped her elbow firmly.

As the rope looped over his neck and pulled snug, his eyes sought hers. "I'm sorry," he whispered, watching her tear streaked face.

A preacher stood at his side and opened a bible.

"I love you, Rafe," Vivi cried. A woman beside her spat, saliva splattered and slid down Vivi's lovely face but she didn't move or waver her focus from him, and he was grateful.

"And I love you," he mouthed.

That's when he noticed Blackard release his hold on Vivi and nod. What the hell was the man up to? Did he really have his loyalty after all? Did Blackard think he could change this? Rafe's mind spun with possibilities. Blackard wasn't a good enough shot to snap the rope, but he was a good enough shot to end Rafe's misery quickly.

* * *

How could this have happened? For years she'd carefully protected him from such situations, but as a human distraction, she had surely brought about the worst. Agony pressed in her heart. Vivi knew she would watch him die a horrible death, and she knew she was fully responsible. Then, like the coming of a dense, black mist behind her she felt the searing hot breath and cringed.

"And now, he is mine. Thank you, Vibrant Light," Lucifer laughed softly. "Thanks for making this so easy for me."

"No! No!" she cried. "You will never have him."

The preacher began his verse but Rafe spoke loud and strong, booming over the man's words to a crowd of people who strangely listened intensely.

"Remember now thy Creator in the days of thy youth, while the evil days come not, nor the years draw nigh, when thou shalt say, I have no pleasure in them; While the sun, or the light, or the moon, or the stars, be not darkened, nor the clouds return after the rain: because man goeth to his long home, and the mourners go about the streets: Or ever the silver cord be loosed, or the golden bowl be broken, or the pitcher be broken at the fountain, or the wheel broken at the cistern."

Vivi's eyes locked on Rafe's and her heart cried to God but Rafe continued, and finished the Ecclesiastes verse without fear.

"Then shall the dust return to the earth as it was: and the spirit shall return unto God who gave it."

Rafe gagged as the floor dropped from beneath is feet. She watched him drag in the deepest breath he could, his hands tied before him and his feet kicking. If he could gain purchase at the ledge he could save himself before his neck snapped or he choked to death.

Vivi cried out but someone gripped her hand tight, dragged her away and she struggled to retain her visual contact with Rafe. "Leave me alone!' she shouted and a young boy's voice shouted right back.

"Lady, that man said to make you come with me." She tried to free herself, but he pulled desperately. "He said you have to come with me!" A shot rang out and the crowd shouted, ducked. When Vivi turned she was at the edge of the crowd and looking into Blackard's concentrated focus. He was aiming a rifle, right at Rafe.

"No! No!" Another shot rang and people scattered. Again he aimed.

"There!" he pointed without looking at her. "Get those horses closer!"

She turned and saw Rafe struggle, the coiling fray of rope that had not been severed only inches above his straining face. Blackard wasn't trying to kill Rafe, he was trying to save him.

When the next shot rang, Vivi raced for the horses, looked again to the gallows. Rafe had fought to get his boot onto the ledge and failed. The rope snapped and swung wild as he dropped to the ground with a loud grunting thud. Blackard was less than four feet away. He swiftly turned and shot two nearing guards. The minister cowered back and Rafe scrambled from beneath the platform. The people screamed, and Blackard blasted several more shots above their heads, and one directly into Charlie Silver's heart. He reached Vivi and the horses, racing them as Rafe slithered from beneath the gallows then leapt into the saddle behind her. Rafe pressed her low, covering her body with his and slammed his heels into the animal's sides.

* * *

94

They cleared the town and rode hard, rode into the Texas nothingness and beyond, finally finding a stand of trees and disappearing inside.

Rafe dropped to the ground, pulled Vivi down and held her close before pushing her away to confirm she was unharmed. He turned to Blackard and nodded.

"Not too bad. For a bad shot you did real good," he said with a grinning grimace and wiped sweat from his face. "Now, you hightail it outta here. Go west, get as far as you can"

Blackard tossed a pistol to Rafe, spun the horse and sped off, heading straight into the coming riders before veering west.

At a vantage point a mile away and on a rise, Rafe watched the posse overtake Blackard and leave his dead body on the ground, then stop at the trees where they'd hidden. Riders split and headed to the south and west. Three men were coming toward him and Vivi. He leaned his elbow against a boulder, aimed and waited.

"Don't kill them," Vivi gasped and he said nothing.

It was a critical time. The ambush position was perfect. But he needed to wait. He could only take them down if his pistol blasts were well out of ear shot, otherwise the rest of the posse would regroup and come at them.

"Please Rafe," she sobbed. "Don't kill them."

"Got no choice. Sit quiet, woman."

"Rafe ... please."

"Quiet!" he hissed and waited. She had no way of knowing how impossible it was going be to get away if he let those men live. No idea how hard it would all get, and no idea how that noose had affected him. Hanging was not the way Rafe Bennett intended to die, and letting that posse reach them would take him too close to the gallows again for his liking.

Then there was Vivi. She was an outlaw too just by riding with him. The El Paso circuit judge had no problem hanging her right beside him. He'd have none of that. His finger twitched on the trigger. The men were fifteen feet below him, inching their way up to the rocky ridge. His sight was perfect, and his eye flickered south and west. The others were gone, not even a billow of dust was visible from either party. He slowly squeezed the trigger.

The first man dropped like a rock. The second had no chance to turn and run before the next blast bloodied his chest. The third fought his rearing horse and Rafe carefully aimed, but when the pistol jerked in his palm, he knew he'd only wounded the man. "Stay here!" he hissed to Vivi, stood and slithered down the rocky rise.

He stood over the man whose eyes were begging and for a brief moment he thought to spare him, but again, the vision of he and Vivi standing before a cheering crowd and dangling from nooses tight blazed bright. Rafe put the bullet through the man's head, gathered the horse and climbed back to Vivi. He gripped her elbow tight and ignored the terror in her eyes. "S'go, darlin'."

They rode hard to the north for days before he slowed their pace. They camped in hidden places, ate what they could kill, butcher, and sizzle, over the small fire. They spoke little. As the nights grew cold and Rafe forced his mind to decipher where they were, he smiled. It was November and those dark forms looming against the star speckled sky were the Rockies.

"Might snow tonight, Vivi."

She lay silent at his side and he assumed she was sleeping. He kissed her neck tenderly and draped his coat over her then snuggled close on the hard ground.

CHAPTER 14

Vibrant Light was not sleeping. She lay awake as tears soaked her face. An accounting of all she'd lost since her fall from the heavens weighed heavy on her heart. She no longer possessed powers that could help her see everything. She no longer had the ability to push and prod humans to help her to protect Rafe. Nothing that happened in El Paso was clear to her. She saw none of it coming, could do nothing to stop it. She had never suspected that Blackard would step up. The facts were the facts, Vibrant Light was now human, soft and weak, blind, and of no use to Rafe, or God. She had failed. Vivi was more alone than she'd ever felt in her existence.

* * *

"No, little one. You are most certainly not alone," Paul sighed, watching from the heavens, and pleased that Vivi and Rafe had survived the escape.

* * *

"No, little one. You are most certainly not alone," Lucifer grinned and watched from the darkness.

* * *

They woke under a thin blanket of snow and the new sun flashed off the crystals and bounced to the skies. Vivi sat in wonder, watching Rafe prepare for them to move on. She sighed and stood, walked toward her horse.

"You have to teach me to shoot," she said and he turned to glare at her. Vivi shrugged. "I'm useless if I can't help. Teach me to shoot."

"There's no need to be teaching you to kill, Vivi. I'll protect you."

"And what if this happens again?"

He swept her into his arms, held her tight against his heart and kissed her freezing nose. "It won't. We're slowing things down a bit. Taking this a little easier. Besides, I still gotta keep that promise to marry you, right?" His eyes twinkled.

"No! What if the preacher recognizes you? No. No need to take that risk." She freed herself and struggled with the saddle. Rafe lifted it from her hands, settled it on the animal's back and sighed.

"Vivi, we can't stop living. We're gonna find someplace quiet and do fine. We got the money in my saddlebag and I got thousands more buried down at the border when we need it. We'll be fine. And I'll be protecting you."

She climbed into the saddle, pressing a palm against her aching belly and his brow curled. "Something wrong?"

"No. Nothing." The blush on her cheek revealed the truth and Rafe chuckled.

"No need to be embarrassed about your monthly blood, Vivi. We'll ride easy today, find someplace warm for you to sleep tonight. It'll be fine."

The blush burned hotter on her face. It had happened during their travel to El Paso. But since then, they had become lovers and spent one astounding night in each other's embrace. To speak of her monthly blood seemed wrong, as though it were her only privacy, but as lovers, how could he not know? Rafe could count as well as she could and the

98

moon was once again full. As much as she wished for strength and endurance, Vivi's female, human body hoped he could keep the promise of warmth and a bed. Another part of human femininity came to the foreground as she watched him climb into the saddle and rub his healing arm. The break had never fully repaired and it concerned her.

"Where are we going?"

His eyes trailed to the mountains and he grinned. "Mountain men up there. Some stay all year, but most abandon their cabins for the bad months. We'll find something. Might even be well stocked."

"We'll just steal their food? Live in their cabins?"

"Oh, I'll pay for it. Done it before. Ain't no one complained yet, darlin'. The hearths are warm, blankets are thick and the food is edible. Unless you'd rather sleep outside again?" His brows bobbed teasingly and he clicked his tongue and together they rode into the mountains.

* * *

He knew of a cabin, prayed they would reach it that night, but the snow fell heavier and the passes became treacherous. He had promised Vivi warmth and was unable to deliver. The cabin he hoped to use had burned to the ground, most likely months earlier. They rode the slow, slippery path higher into the mountains before spotting the next hopeful place. If the owner was present, Rafe would kindly ask for a place for his wife to rest and be warm a while. If the man was not hospitable, there were ways to deal with that too. If he was lucky and the mountain man had gone to the flatlands for the winter, he knew this particular cabin to be real comfortable.

They dismounted. Smoke rose from the chimney and Rafe fingered his pistol. "Wait here, Vivi." He walked the fifteen feet across thick snow and pounded his fist against the sheared log door.

Nothing, so he turned the latch and pushed it open then quickly slipped behind the wall as he heard the shotgun cock.

"Who are ya and what the hell do ya want?"

He looked inside. There was an old man in a chair, his foot was swollen and green, and his eyes were clouded with a white film Rafe could see in the cabin's dimness.

"Just looking for a place where my wife can get warm a bit, mister. That's all." As he spoke he walked silently inside, reached for the rifle and tugged it easily from the old codger's gnarled hands. "Not lookin' for no trouble. Just some heat from your fire."

The old man grunted. "Well, get her on in here."

Rafe waved an arm to Vivi and she scurried inside, closed the door behind her and eyed the man suspiciously while she stood at the fire. She brushed snow from her skirts, looked to Rafe and he shrugged.

"Name's Rafe Bennett," he grunted and set the rifle aside, well out of the old man's reach.

"You're the man stole my food three winters ago while I was out hunting."

"I didn't steal nothing from you, old man. I paid and left a real polite note of thanks."

"Yeah, you left money I can't spend up here, you scoundrel." He chuckled.

"That foot looks pretty bad," Rafe commented, noting the oozing puss and twisted shape.

"Hurts pretty bad, too. Broke it running from a griz the other day."

Rafe looked around. The cabin was still neat but dark and more cluttered than the last time he saw it. "What happened to your eyes?"

"I'm old. Woke one day and found out I'm damn blind. God's kinda funny that way, ain't he?"

"What's your name?" He moved to the fire beside Vivi and rubbed his hands.

"Pennywalker. Franklin Pennywalker."

"Pennywalker?" Rafe's brow curled. "Frank Pennywalker. I know that name."

"You should, Rafael Bennett. I used to play cards with your daddy. The day Boston Shark shot your daddy dead, I came up here. Ain't left his mountain once since."

"Fucking Frank Pennywalker," he mused.

"Yeah." The old man grinned. "Kinda serendipitous, ain't it?"

"Serendipitous? Now that's a ten dollar word for the likes of you, Frank. Where'd you learn a word like that?"

"Preacher ladies come up here every summer trying to bring my soul to the Lord. Some of them'll fuck ya, some of them just leave books, and all them books ain't the Bible." The old man shifted in the chair. "Missy, if you're hungry there's some hot stew on that stove."

"Thank you, Mr. Pennywalker." Vivi again looked to Rafe but his expression was a mix of confusion and concern. She led him to the table and scooped stew from the big pot then served the old man and Rafe before sitting to eat. Pennywalker snorted and grunted as he chewed then his head dropped and he began to snore softly.

Rafe took Vivi's hand and led her just outside the door. "He's old, he's blind, and that infected foot is gonna kill him."

"So," Vivi sighed, feeling herself tense against the blast of cold wind. "We'll take care of him. Maybe he'll let us stay. Ask nicely, Rafe. Please. He needs our care."

But when they returned the man was still asleep in the chair. Rafe gently shook his shoulder. "Frank, let me help you to the bed."

"Stupid fool. Take her to the bed, asshole. I'm just fine here. But remember … I'm blind, not deaf. You fuck her quiet unless you plan on sharing." And the man chuckled himself back to sleep.

CHAPTER 15

It was still dark when Vivi woke to the sound of the old man's painful groans. She rose, lit a lamp and sat close to him. He startled to her gentle touch as she carefully removed the soiled bandage. The smell made her nauseous, but she swallowed back bile and tenderly washed the wound, gently around the exposed bone then sighed.

"Don't be worrying 'bout me, woman. Go back to bed."

"Mr. Pennywalker, this ankle needs to be set. Your foot will probably never be good, but this open wound has to be taken care of."

"Why you fussing? The sooner I die, the sooner you and your man can have my place to yourselves."

"I won't let you die, old man." She stood and shook Rafe's shoulder. "Wake up. I need your help to set this man's ankle."

He rubbed his eyes, yawned and sat at the edge of the lumpy mattress while Vivi cleared space on the wood slat floor and lay skins and blankets for Pennywalker's comfort. Rafe helped settle the old man on the nest of fur and wool then positioned himself at the man's mangled foot. Taking a deep breath, he gripped firmly around the ankle and foot then looked to Vivi. She'd soothed the grumbling old coot and placed a rolled piece of hide between his teeth then nodded. Pennywalker struggled, howled and squealed like a swine but finally dropped into unconsciousness, and blessedly that permitted them to do as much repair as possible.

"Still don't look right, Viv," Rafe said as he lay the limp old man on the bed.

She shrugged and washed sweat from Pennywalker's brow. "I think it's the best we're going to manage. Do you think he has anything around here to make him more comfortable?"

"Like what?"

"I don't know. There are herbs that kill pain."

Rafe grunted, sat in the old man's chair and yawned again. "Best we got to kill his pain is my fists, darlin'."

"You will not use your fists." She grinned and settled on his lap, then trailed her soft fingers along the still raw redness at his neck. His hand covered hers, slid the warmth of her palm to his heart. The fire had died and he knew he should be tending to it but his own exhaustion was heavy. His eyes drooped and when they opened, Vivi was bustling around the dark cabin, there was the scent of frying bacon and heat from the crackling fire. Women were astounding, formidable creatures, small and frail, and hard as steel rails. But this woman? What had he found in this woman?

After a few days, the old man finally rested comfortably. Rafe fashioned a crutch for him, padded it nicely with rabbit pelts and strips of hide and leaned it close to the bed. The old man was no longer burning with fever and had insisted on sitting in his chair, his shotgun at his knee. His head tilted and he listened to every sound around him. When a grin brightened his face, Rafe chuckled.

"What're you grinning at, you bind old coot?"

"Elk. Right outside. Right now, Bennett."

They ate fresh meat that night and Vivi made a stew and soup with root vegetables she found in a storage box outside the heavy door. She'd found many things that made her respect and admire the mountain man. A lonely existence, Frank Pennywalker had obviously mastered and enjoyed the life. There was a small chicken coop behind the cabin and she daily sought fresh eggs. With the pummeling cold, she worried for the birds and Pennywalker explained that the chickens were like family and usually brought inside for the winter. He'd never had guests to entertain before, never a woman who might find the feathered creatures unwelcome, but she had already begun to seriously consider sharing the cabin with them. The fresh eggs were a delight and she selfishly imagined a roasted chicken dinner on the near horizon. The rooster was a bold one, the eggs plentiful and with good planning, the sacrificed chicken would be replaced soon enough. Yes, Frank Pennywalker had made a good life, even for a woman.

Rafe remained inside the cabin for nearly a week, slipping outside to relieve himself and nothing more. He watched the heaviness of the descending winter and ticked off time. There had been no sign of a posse for weeks and he knew in his gut that they were safe.

"Need more fire wood," he announced and shrugged into his jacket. He checked his pistol and the old man's head tilted. "That ain't no good. Won't slow down a mountain lion or griz. Take the rifle."

"Is there really a grizzly bear out there?" Vivi gasped, holding out Pennywalker's heavy blanket coat for Rafe and as he slid his arms into it, both men chuckled.

"'Course there are grizzly bears, darlin'," Rafe kissed her nose, his eyes glinting with playfulness. "Big ass bears, griz. They like to dance."

"Sure do." The old man cackled. "They dance a good two step, but when they're done, they like to eat their partner."

Vivi shivered. "I'm going with you." She quickly reached for a blanket to wrap around herself but Rafe held her shoulders tight and looked into her eyes.

"You ain't comin' with me. You stay here, take care of this old man and do women stuff. Cook, do whatever women do. I'm just gonna get some wood, Vivi. Got an axe, old man?"

"'Course I got a damn axe. Out near the coop." Pennywalker heard Vivi move to the far corner of the cabin, rustling blankets as she straightened the bed. He reached out, grasped Rafe's arm and tugged him close. "Listen. Take down the dead tree west of the clearing. Usually, I go deeper, try to keep the protection for the cabin but you ain't got enough experience up here, boy. Stay close, listen good, don't look like no posse's stupid enough to come up here now, but the griz are fast."

"How many?"

"One female, got two cubs. Killed her male last summer. This big momma is what tried to eat my damn foot, so you be fucking careful!" the old man hissed.

* * *

105

Vivi fruitlessly fussed about the cabin, attempted to organize things and considered which vegetables to use for their dinner.

"What kinda woman are you, Vivi?" Pennywalker said and she turned.

"Pardon?"

He chuckled. "This ain't the life you're used to, is it? I can hear it in the way you move, how you talk, in the sound of your sighs. What kinda woman are you that you don't know the basic things other women know?

She didn't answer, simply sat near the hearth and listened.

"My guess is you're the kinda woman who's been pampered her whole life. A rich, sheltered gal who met a nice looking outlaw and ran off with him. Am I right?"

She gave another mournful sigh.

"Ah, don't worry none, I ain't judging. It's a hard life you chose, girly. That's all I'm gonna say about that." He nestled deeper in his chair and closed his clouded blind eyes.

What kind of woman was she? Vivi thought long and hard on that. It was true that she had no idea how to master all the womanly things Rafe mentioned, but she did the best she could. She'd learn. She was a new human, a new woman, a blank slate. It was strange and terrifying, exhilarating and exhausting, but often she longed for her days before the fall, the life she knew in the heavens.

Sometimes in dreams she felt the cool marble under her feet, the brilliance of light and the mellowness of the air. Once she dreamed of walking through the courtyard, she could actually hear the tinkling of crystal water splashing in the fountain. All around her was the friendly banter of her heavenly companions. She felt whole, right, home. In one such dream she saw Mr. Paul and Madam Miriam in the distance. She called out and raced to catch them and her heart soared with pleasure, but she couldn't reach them. They never turned to see her. They were lost to her. It was all forever lost to her.

But as a human, there were blessed times when she felt closest to heaven. Only in Rafe's arms, deep in the grip of his extraordinary passion, it was heaven. As close to heaven as any living human could have.

The tree was tall and dry, long dead and perfect for burning. Rafe looked around, sniffed, and set the rifle nearby. He hefted the axe. As he swung again and again, angling his cuts and occasionally pushing on the giant, dead pine, his mind wandered. Life had its complexities, but his life was fairly simple. Both of his lives. No one really knew what Rafe Bennett did when he wasn't robbing the railroad, but he had a whole life someplace else.

In St. Louis he was known as Rafael Forrester. He was a gambler. Damn good one, too. Skilled. Lucky. When there, he carried a polished, pearl-handled pistol in his holster and the best gamblers knew that where that shiny pistol handle was, there would be high stakes games. That prize pistol sat hidden near the Mexico border with his stolen stash.

Rafe loved St. Louis. There, he lived comfortably in fancy hotel rooms. He ate well, bought his replacement velvet jackets and took as many whores as he fancied. Once, he stayed with a woman for nearly a month. He thought about marrying her and forgetting the outlaw's life but his gut rolled and ached for the excitement of a crew and the smell of gun powder. He glanced back at the cabin and wondered if it was going to be that way again.

The slow drama of the planning, the take, the blood and wild escapes drifted in his mind and he suddenly shivered, washed over with desperation, longing and starvation for that life again. Already? Odd. Usually it took a while for that hunger to return and never before did he have something like Vivi to pin his whole existence upon.

Memories thicker than molasses seemed to cover him, sticky, disabling. He could leave, just get on his horse and ride off. Away from Vivi and the heavy responsibilities he'd taken on. The old man. A woman. Was that what he was meant for?

His arm froze. The axe stilled. Wind pushed against the weakened tree and it creaked but Rafe was paralyzed. He could go. He could. Maybe he should.

* * *

As Vivi handed a bowl of hot soup to the old man, a powerful awareness struck her like lightening. Her head swung toward the door. Without reaching for a blanket to protect her against the bitter cold, she left and ran through the clearing, following the deep footprints Rafe left behind. Her heart stuttered, ached, throbbed. When she neared, she saw him. Still as stone, his hat dusted with snow, the axe at his feet and looking to the south, directly at something she was sure he couldn't see, but she could.

Lucifer paced, his arms waving and his voice booming in Vivi's ears, his words maniacal, manipulative, threatening. Rafe heard them, just not the same way Vivi did. He imagined those were his thoughts and his ideas, but they weren't. It's how the Devil worked, his unique power over man. Vivi stilled against the wind and snow and watched. She could see Rafe's fists clasp and loosen. He was fighting it, rationalizing, choosing. She said nothing, stepped no closer. If Rafe did not choose her, she would lose him forever. If he chose the other path, he'd be lost to heaven forever. He would truly belong to Lucifer. It was the blackened crossroads of his soul and she, a mere human, had no power to sway him, no ability to help or guide him. A tear slid, hot and steaming down her freezing cheek and she held her breath. Slowly, Rafe's head swiveled and turned her way.

* * *

The pain had subsided, but Frank Pennywalker knew his days were numbered. He had a lot to offer the young couple. Not money, hell, not even wisdom, but he could impart a bit of his experience. If Rafe survived the threat of grizzly and frigid hellish winter, he could live a good life in the mountains with his woman.

Rafe Bennett. Now that was one hell of a curiosity. Young Rafael was a good kid, always good to his mama, always well behaved and polite. When Prosser Bennett got himself shot dead, he even thought to step in, offer to take care of the widow and little boy, but seeing his best friend die like that changed him, sent him off as far as he could get.

Pennywalker wasn't a bad man, though he never went to church or listened much to the preacher, he surely believed in God, especially since coming to the mountain. What man could live up there and not see there was a God? It was a good life, better than down in the flatlands. High and close to heaven, he had things. A nice, solid cabin. A warm hearth. Food. It was lonely too, but it was just as lonely before he lived in the mountains. Pennywalker never had a wife and nothing more than a ranch that never amounted to much. Leaving after Prosser's murder was perfect. And serendipitous, too.

He'd often thought about the kid, Rafe Bennett. Wondered if the stories he heard about the outlaw were true. His senses said it was all fact, but even blind he could see exactly how Rafe had held on to his goodness. Now he had the woman to show it to, to use it on, to help it grow, but only if he stuck it out with her. If Rafe was the outlaw he'd been hearing about, there was always the possibility he was just using her.

He heard Vivi leave the cabin suddenly and sighed. Serendipitous, indeed. He always wanted to help Prosser Bennett's kid. This was his chance. Right now, Rafe and the woman were temporary guests, but what if he changed that?

Frank set aside the hot soup and reached for the crutch. He tucked it under his arm and inched toward the table. Darkness wasn't his blindness, it was an ugly vision of cloudy grey, no form or structure, but he knew his cabin even in the stark blackness of a Rocky Mountain moonless night, and he had distinctly heard Rafe set that pistol on the old table.

He reached, slid his palm across the cool wood and grasped the gun. It was a perfect fit in his hand, weighted and balanced, and of course like any outlaw's pistol, loaded and ready. As he sat and fingered the trigger, a strange vision came in his blindness. A form, tall and lithe, glowing with yellow light and warm as the sun. He could feel the tenderness embracing him and he grinned.

"Why God would send an angel to take me home makes no sense," he said with a sigh as sad as Vivi's. "I ain't a good man, but I guess I ain't a bad man either."

The brilliant figure reached out a hand and Frank chuckled nervously. "All right, hold your horses, will ya? I'm doing this for Bennett you know, so I expect someone up there will take care of him. All I can do is give him this cabin to shelter himself and his woman. You gotta do the rest. Okay?"

The hand still reached and Frank smiled. "Okay." He set the barrel into his mouth.

* * *

Rafe heard it all, heard his heart shout for freedom, heard the sound of the rattlers down at the Mexican border, and heard the howl of the icy wind that didn't chill him. All he had to do was mount up and ride away. Ride away. Ride away. But to what? Wants and desires taunted, teased, tempted him, but he also heard his heart. Ride away to what? Vivi won't be there.

His eyes fell on her, standing several yards away and waiting in the freezing cold. He walked to her, a smile growing with every step. Vivi wouldn't be with him if he left, and without Vivi, he didn't want anything. He reached out and wrapped her tight in his arms, laughing with joy as he spun them in a circle. Rafe kissed her long and deep.

"Get your pretty behind inside. It's cold out here and I still got a tree to—"

They turned to the sharp sound of the gunshot and ran. Together they stood at the opened door as Frank Pennywalker's blood dripped from the table to the floor in a lake of crimson around his feet.

The angel turned to Vivi, nodded acknowledgement then joyfully escorted the soul of the smiling old man away. Frank Pennywalker's final words to Vibrant Light?

"You take good care of him, will ya?"

CHAPTER 16

It was a sadness Rafe couldn't recall before in his life. He'd seen men die at his hand and at the hands of his crew. Men who deserved to die if only because they intended to kill him. Somehow, the sight of old man Pennywalker, slumped near the table like that threatened to turn his stomach. He remembered Frank Pennywalker from when he was a kid, a friendly man who was always kind to his mother, always a friend to his father and always nice to him, just a boy who barely deserved attention. Often Pennywalker would bring candy from the mercantile, licorice or sweet hard tack, handing it to him in private and sending him away to enjoy it on his own. Now, he was a mass of bone and blood, his blind eyes staring off into nothingness.

Vivi sniffled then reached for the pistol lying in the puddle of blood. When she lifted it, Rafe quickly snatched it from her.

"Don't touch that! Still loaded." He set it aside, pulled a blanket from the bed and wrapped it around the dead body. "Stupid asshole. Why'd he go and do this?" He heaved Pennywalker over his shoulder and walked outside, Vivi at his heel. "Don't know if the ground's too frozen to bury him, darlin'. We might need to just cover him with snow and hope the animals don't get to him."

She nodded, her nose red from the cold, her eyes overflowing with tears. "I'll find a shovel so we can try."

He looked down at the covered bundle. "Stupid asshole," he hissed again and glanced toward the tree he tried to bring down. The rifle was still out there, the axe still leaning against a stump. Knowing women, Vivi wouldn't be comforted until he at least attempted to bury the dead man, but she was freezing. When she returned with a shovel, shivering, her hands had gone red and nearly numb. Rafe shook his head, took her cold fingers and led her inside.

"Viv," he said softly as his tossed the last of the quartered wood onto the dying fire. "Gotta take care of first things first. You get warm, maybe try to clean this mess. I'll get wood then start working on a grave."

"But …"

"No, darlin'. Gotta take care of the living first. Pennywalker's dead, he don't care when we get to burying his body. Maybe he'll be happier knowing you're warm and taken care of." Rafe didn't believe that for a minute, but he knew it would reach her. She nodded acceptance and inched closer to the fire, rubbed her hands and didn't even turn back as he left for his axe and the swaying pine.

Outside the door he quickly covered the bloody bundle with snow then trotted out to the tree. Darkness would be coming soon and he had a lot to do but as he neared the axe, he glanced around suspiciously. One of his senses had kicked in, the one that told him there was some kind of danger out there. He eyed the area carefully, brought the rifle closer and returned to the chore at hand.

* * *

Rafe held Vivi close and watched the fire crackle and pop. It had begun to snow hard again just as he brought wood inside to find her on her hands and knees, scrubbing blood from the floorboards. Visions of his mother raced at him from the past, but no one had killed Pennywalker but himself, leaving behind a bloody mess and a cabin full of noisy chickens.

He dragged the lumpy old mattress close to the hearth and cradled Vivi against his chest, watched the elusive forms in the fire and wondered about what to do next. Settling at the cabin was never his intention, but the winter grew more brutal and with each passing day, there was less and less chance of leaving before the thaw. It was time to hunker down and enjoy his wealth. He had his woman, plenty of firewood, more than enough game, stored berries and vegetables. If nothing else, they'd be warm and fed, and thankfully, together. All the blessings of a dead man.

He kissed the top of Vivi's head and slowly lay back on the mattress. "Vivi," he said. "We'll be fine here 'til spring. I can hunt and there's not much we'll need."

"Spring? April?"

He chuckled softly. "Spring up here might not come 'til June, darlin'. We'll be here probably that long."

"Oh," she snuggled closer and looked up into his eyes. "Then what will we do?"

Ah, the question even he didn't want to think about, but already the seed of a plan was catching, germinating, taking root in his mind. "Well, I got me another life, darlin'. A different life. A different name. See, I'm a gambler in St. Louis. A good one, too. I figure to take us there and get me a few nice, high stake games. Build up our money. You want a marriage paper and a house, maybe babies and stuff like that, and Vivi, I wanna give it all to you."

She sighed, sat up, cross legged near his chest and looked down into his eyes. "And?"

His heart skipped a beat. Vivi was no silly woman. She had a sense about him that sometimes scared him, sometimes worried him, and sometimes amused him. At that moment it did all three. He swallowed hard, sat with his knees touching hers then reached out a finger to trail it along the length of her arm. Like always, she sighed, trembled, and he wondered if he really had to say more, but this was Vivi. She already knew there was more.

"I know I can give you everything you want, but sometimes … not too often but sometimes … I'm gonna need to leave for a while. I won't be gone long and I'll always come back to you, Vivi. You're my woman and I'll always come back to you."

Her brow knotted and she thought for a moment. "I don't think so, Rafe." Her voice was sure and calm. "You can't leave. I can't be without you for a month, or a week, or even a day."

He grinned and leaned in for a sweet kiss. "Already you're talkin' like a wife."

"I'm serious. If you leave, you have to take me with you. You need to teach me how to use a gun and how to ride hard and—"

"Don't be foolish. I ain't never gonna teach you to kill. You ride just fine. And listen to me, woman, even a banker's wife has to face the fact that his work takes him away for a while every now and again."

"A banker's work won't land him in prison, Rafe. Won't put a rope around his neck. You have to take me with you or you can't leave."

A tear glittered in her eye and tugged at his heart so hard it made his chest ache. "Hush now. We got time to work all this out, darlin'." He lowered her to her back and slid his hands beneath the hem of her dress, smoothly tugged her under things off then pushed the skirts to her waist. Quickly opening his britches, he grasped his growing cock, a cock struggling to shrink away from the sudden chill and yet reach for what it needed. He lay over her, nestled against the heat between her thighs and kissed her deeply. "Lots of time, sweetheart. Time to make it all work out."

He couldn't concentrate on what they needed to work out or if he really cared much about it. He could hardly breathe as his hands battled with the tiny buttons of her bodice and finally freed the breasts he craved. Working things out months away had no meaning that moment, only the sensations of his mouth suckling and his flesh deep inside hers. The seeking of heat and satisfaction and completion mattered. Nothing else. He reached for a blanket and buried them beneath it. There, they struggled to free themselves of all clothing and press flesh to flesh then groan with the joyous agony of it.

He feasted on her, intent on offering pleasure where and how he could, but Vivi was determined to be a full participant in the act. Surprising him, she reached and touched and explored, but never with the calculated manner of a whore. She was a woman with the desire to please the man she loved, and suddenly, finally the last piece of the puzzle fell into place for Rafe.

This was what the world knew that he didn't. This was what it felt like to be whole. It wasn't an erotic act being performed on him and it wasn't the surprise of it. It was the loving nature, the yearning, the fullness of it, and when he could hold back no longer, when flashes of hellfire burst behind his eyelids and his entire body knotted then exploded, he knew with his whole heart that she loved him well. That was the only way he would ever think of his Vivi, that she loved him well.

It was a long while before he could breathe evenly or talk. He rolled over her, pinning her beneath him and grinned through what was meant to be a fierce expression.

"So," he said with a grunt. "This is how you plan to keep me close, woman?"

"Yes," she giggled and wriggled but was unable to escape his grasp. The playfulness of their carnal encounters was the fullness of human existence and neither Rafe nor Vivi intended to deny themselves such enjoyment. After all, it was going to be a long winter.

CHAPTER 17

The winds of an endless winter howled outside the thick walls of the cabin and the fire crackled, adding heat to heat and creating speckles of sweat on Rafe's brow. He had long since moved the old bed close to the hearth for their nighttime comfort and that night looked down on Vivi's lovely face beneath him. Her skin glowed golden from the firelight and the glisten of dew created by their exertion. It was long, slow lovemaking, the kind he longed for when he was far from her, freezing, chopping wood, or hunting. It was the real reason he always returned no matter how his restlessness ached inside him. He moved an easy rhythm, deep and retreat, and deep again. The sweetness of her sighs brought contentment and passion together, forming a home in Rafe's soul he'd never known before.

Watching her extraordinary eyes close with the ecstasy of the moment he lowered, licked into her mouth then pressed his lips, driving his tongue to dance with hers as he brought her knees higher to brace for deeper penetration. He hissed with delight, stilled then slid his lips to caress Vivi's tender neck before suckling a starving pull at her nipple.

She moaned, her head rolled and fingers knotted on the rough blankets. This was what he wanted. This he could hold on to for a while, not forever, but a while, enjoying the subtle, teasing trembles against his cock. His Vivi was beautiful. Naked and soft beneath him, giving and receiving at once, the woman he always knew awaited him, always somehow expected, but in truth was always surprised by.

Her soft pants intensified and he rolled them together, lay back and watched her raise above him. His fingers tangled in her dark curls, his thumb found its grip, that pebble hard core awaiting attention. Vivi's head dropped back and her long, midnight black hair tickled and swayed against his thighs. The mere vision of her, glowing by the light of a roaring hearth could have brought him, but Rafe was a man of control, a man determined to make a good thing last as long as he could.

He wanted to see her release, watch it as he had a hundred times. He could never get his fill of the power he had to give her such pleasure. Her breath quickened as her path tightened and he slowed everything, stilled his straining cock, his hands, his own breathing.

A weak cry of disappointment escaped Vivi's lips and he grinned, resumed everything and watched, in tune with the body which seemed a natural extension of his own. Two parts of the human machine meant to work exactly that way, smooth and perfect.

His finger slid easy over her trigger. Their eyes locked and he moved faster. His hips drove up and Vivi pushed hers down. Deep. So deep. So ripe, his Vivi, so ready.

She gasped and he gripped her hip to support her. The tremble around him tightened, intensified and finally she cried out his name just as he felt the beginning of his own offering pulse deep into her. Rolling them over again he thrust deeper, grunted and hissed then shouted as he felt everything clutch tight and explode.

For an eternal moment neither drew breath. Neither moved except from the inside where they shuddered, strained then finally loosened until she dropped over him, his face buried in the soft tangles of her damp hair.

"Fuck, Vivi!" He gasped, slid her to his side and wrapped her into a protective embrace. "Fuck! Darlin', I swear to God I could love you like that forever."

He watched her blushing face in the soft firelight. She turned away with embarrassed modesty but his thumb guided her chin to face him fully.

"No, Vivi. This ain't nothin' to be ashamed of. I love you. Love you when you're just like that, taking me into your heart and your body. It's beautiful. Everything I need. Now," he cuddled her close, kissed her hair and rubbed a soft circle on her back with his hand. "Sleep, Vivi. I think maybe it's time we sleep."

Like the whisper of summer leaves on a warm breeze, he watched her slowly drift into slumber. His eyes took in every curve and valley of her, every reddening mark his desperate hands had made, every gentle wave of her long, wild hair. He pulled the blankets over them and cradled her, kissed her brow tenderly and tried to also sleep, but it wasn't about to come for him. There was too much on Rafe's mind.

Numbers always plagued him, played and tortured, perfect, without flaw, finite, unchangeable. What used to be the amount of cash to be stolen, the number of able members in his crew, or how many served on a posse searching for him, had now changed. The winter was brutal, locking him and Vivi tight to the cabin, but he was going mad with restlessness. He paced his simple duties, chopping only enough wood for a few days and no more, assuring he'd need to go out to do it again. He hunted the same way, providing only enough that would hold them until his need for action and the feel of the rifle or pistol in his hand became too much to ignore. He'd gotten himself into a few tight scrapes along the way. Hunting, or making sure they had enough wood for months, would be far smarter and he knew it, but if he didn't get out of the cabin he feared his mind and needs would destroy everything he had.

Vivi seemed content. It was not an easy life for her. As hard as he worked to keep the cabin warm and stocked with fresh meat, she worked far harder. She kept the place clean and neat, she cooked and hauled water from the stream until it froze solid and he taught her to instead bring in snow to melt in the big pot for cooking or bathing. She cared for the chickens, now snug in a cage at the far corner of the cabin. Rafe wasn't happy with it, but he knew she'd find it too hard to just let the damn birds freeze to death outside, so he allowed it. She kept the cage clean and it didn't even smell so bad. Vivi washed clothes and helped bring in wood, she knew how to restart the hearth fire if it went out while he was away, and she understood the dangers of straying too far from the door.

She understood a lot of things but not everything, and this baffled and sometimes amused him. It was like she never had a mama to teach her, like everything she did, she was learning for the first time. There was joy and concern in that. There was so much Vivi didn't seem aware of, but it wasn't the time to think about that. That night, it was numbers that taunted him. In truth, Rafe Bennett realized that it was all the same. The numbers would all shuffle out, and even if he didn't want to think about some of them, they were still there, determining the sum of everything.

Numbers.

He carefully left the bed, tucked a wool blanket tight around Vivi and added wood to the waning fire. Tugging on all his clothes and Pennywalker's old blanket coat, Rafe went outside to gather more quartered logs to stack near the hearth. He didn't want Vivi waking to find none available and having to do it while he snored, so he stacked his arms high.

He looked at the pile. There was enough there for another few days and his belly rolled. He needed out, needed to move. Tomorrow he'd cut as much as he could, maybe even cut more the next day and the next. He'd cut and quarter the pine logs until the stack reached the overhang roof. That should be enough.

Enough. His heart dropped, he set down the logs and rubbed his eyes. Enough. Raising his face to the star filled heavens he groaned. Numbers again. He had to face the numbers.

In his saddle bags he had money, but not nearly enough. Come spring thaw he could get them as far as the next town but not much further. He had no intentions of riding hard with Vivi all the way to St. Louis. Too far. Too hard for her. He wanted to travel like a fine gentleman, dress his woman beautifully and ride in the luxury of a private railroad car. She deserved that much. There wasn't enough money for that. Oh, there were ways to get it, but not with her at his side. Not ever with Vivi at his side. It wasn't like he'd be willing to work to earn it, and besides, he still had all that money buried down at the Mexico border.

With that cash, the numbers would look better. He'd have his gambling stake, he'd have his fancy hotel room, and there'd be no question that his woman was worthy of respect. His eyes turned to the closed cabin door. Getting that money meant leaving, more numbers to think about, and a few he could no longer ignore.

He sat on the woodpile, his eyes scanning the darkness. He was so restless. Last time he needed out he went too far and had a chance meeting with Pennywalker's griz. The mammoth bear didn't get much, but took a grand swipe at his upper arm and the wound was still healing.

120

Rafe, usually good at paying attention, wasn't good at paying attention when everything was as silent as it could get up there in the mountains. His fertile mind wandered. Got distracted. That's how she crept up on him, that's how he almost became that mama bear's dinner.

She was slow and sluggish, probably awakened from her hibernation by his shotgun blast that missed the elk by less than an inch. No matter, he was lucky that day. He'd killed her with one clean shot but bloodied and shaken, he just climbed onto his horse and left. He was a mile along the frozen stream before he realized the warmth her hide might provide or how much use her meat would be.

He shifted in the saddle and looked back. It was a good kill and they could use it, but when he reached the place, the bloody carcass had already been claimed, dragged along the pristine snow and leaving a bloody trail leading west. Rafe's curiosity peaked and he followed.

Again, numbers. He crouched silently, hidden in the thicket and watched. Indians. A small village but the odds weren't looking so good. He counted ten strapping warriors, six old men and at least thirty women and children. They could keep the damn bear carcass, he wouldn't bother them and had no intention of letting them bother him. But the click of a cocked rifle stiffened his back. Rafe slowly stood then walked toward the village behind a shoving hand and guttural grunts.

Inside a warm teepee he sat and watched all those around him. No one spoke, but how would he know what they were saying if they did? His mind was on Vivi. He had to get back to Vivi. Finally a young brutish man arrived, snorted at him and sat.

"You are the man in the old Pennywalker's cabin."

Rafe blinked at the perfect English, and he wondered if all tribes had such Indians, ready and able to not only communicate so well, but manipulate the English language to their advantage. Either way, the conversation was necessary under the circumstances. He just wasn't willing to look less educated or afraid. Rafe squared his shoulders. "Yeah. You took my bear."

The man grinned. "The bear was a gift from the Great Mystery. We took nothing that was not given to us."

Rafe shrugged. Maybe that would be all there was to it. "Fine." He attempted to stand and push out of the hide door but the man spoke again.

"The woman with you?"

His heart clenched and he said nothing, watched an old woman speak with authority then shift to sit at his side.

"The elder says that your woman is … um … um …" his finger pointed up and moved in a circular motion. "She is … from Spirit."

Rafe turned sharply as the old woman tugged off the shredded, blood soaked sleeve of the blanket coat and proceeded to remove his velvet jacket and shirt. His long john buttons were undone and finally the wounded arm fully exposed. During all this manipulating, she talked and the young man translated.

"The elder speaks of the power of your woman's spirit and the blessing she is to you. But …"

Rafe gasped as fingers deftly cleaned the sliced flesh then wrapped it tight in a pale hide. "But what?" he asked, ignoring the pain and nodding thanks to the elder.

"But, she says that your woman will not be safe when you are gone. She has committed that we will watch over this woman when you leave."

Rafe restrained his shock. "I ain't leavin, ain't goin' nowhere. I'll take care of my own woman."

The grey old crone grinned, patted his shoulder and turned to the young warrior.

"We will watch over her while you are gone, a gift for a gift." he said and pointed for the elder to return Rafe's clothing. "Now, you leave us."

Rafe quickly pulled on his shirt and coats, stood and looked down at the Indians around the fire. He tipped his hat politely to the old woman. "Thank ya, ma'am." Then he gave a curt nod to the men and left unharmed. Numbers. It could've all gone bad, but it didn't. How did they know what was on his mind?

Remembering that afternoon almost a week ago, Rafe stood with an old man grunt Pennywalker would've been proud of. He gathered his wood and went inside. Silent as a mouse he stacked the quartered logs near the hearth and rubbed his freezing hands together. The chickens rustled in their cage and he turned a glare. That damn scrawny rooster was no doubt ready to make his daily ruckus and the sun was nowhere near rising. If Rafe had his way, he'd take the mean, ugly bird outside and wring its neck. It had been a long time since he and Vivi ate chicken, but they needed the feathered bastard. He'd guarantee more chickens to sell or trade come spring, before the long journey to St Louis.

Finally warm, stripped to his skin and under the blankets next to Vivi, he shivered but not from the chill, from the numbers. He knew everything he had to do. Cut enough wood for at least a month. Hunt and butcher enough fresh meat to store in the shed. It would freeze solid, but Vivi could bring it in and cook it well enough. He'd need to get himself ready too, the border was a long way off and the first leg of his travel would be difficult in the deep snow and ever present storms.

While he was south, he'd get his cash, pick up supplies and hightail it back as quickly as possible. His gut told him those Indians were good for their word. Something about Vivi always seemed to reach the Indians. It was strange and curious and he wasn't about to question luck like that, but getting back soon had a lot to do with another number he'd been trying hard not to think about.

His hands slithered around her and she sighed in her sleep. He cupped his body against her back and slowly, easily, slid into her along the moisture of their earlier lovemaking. Reaching his full depth, Vivi moaned delight and bent herself for more. Rafe closed his eyes. As he enjoyed the thrill of moving in the safest, warmest place he knew, the number he'd been avoiding flashed clear in his heart, charging it and softening it with love and pride and joy. The number? Three.

By Rafe's count, Vivi had missed her monthly blood three times. If he was gonna get their lives ready for a good future, he had to do it now while Vivi was able to handle some time alone at the cabin, yet still blissfully unaware of her condition. He grinned and thrust deep, delicious drives that promised to last a while, not forever, but a while.

CHAPTER 18

Vivi stood at the cook stove and stirred a stew. Fresh meat was always nice but that particular icy cold sunny day, they had more than enough. This was one of the good times, one of the moments she felt sure and secure, fully human and pleased with her life. She loved Rafe with every breath she took. She smiled and hummed a sweet melody then turned to reach into the bag of salt for seasoning.

"He's leaving you." The voice was ugly, like it had come from the putrid waste of her own bowels, and her fingers froze in the salt sack. She knew the voice. It wasn't hideous, it was actually beautiful and she knew who was speaking. Stealing herself, she continued what she was doing, ignoring the voice.

"He's leaving you up here all alone, girly. Now what are you going to do?" A hiss of laughter followed and her eyes involuntarily turned. Lucifer stood less than five feet away, his energy radiating and vibrating through the entire cabin. His eyes blazed, his teeth were white as the fresh snow outside the heavy door, and his hair was long, black as night and flowing to his chest. Lucifer strolled around the cabin, touching things, nodding. Then he lifted the long rifle Pennywalker left behind. He fingered the trigger, held it and eyed down the length of the barrel, aiming directly at her heart.

As Vivi watched, refusing to look into his face, she noticed his chest change, reform. It slowly appeared covered with Rafe's shirt, vest, and the lapels of his velvet jacket. She gasped, swallowed as her eyes rose. It was Rafe's face, his grin, his soft chestnut waves flashed golden in the hearth firelight. But something was wrong. Very wrong.

Outside she could hear the slamming of axe against wood. Rafe was not standing before her and she knew it. She cleared her throat and shrugged. "Nice parlor trick," she said and returned her attention to the stew, to the bubbles of flavorful meat, root vegetable and thick juices.

Lucifer set the rifle down, it thudded on the wooden table and she heard the creak of the chair as he lowered his weight onto it. "All alone. Just like him to do it too, leave a helpless woman up here. What are you gonna do now?"

Even his voice had become Rafe's and a shiver ran the length of her spine. "He's not leaving me."

"Yes … he is."

Another shiver shook her to the bone. Words Rafe would say in a voice she knew as well as her own.

"What're ya gonna do now?"

In a flash she turned, gripped the rifle and aimed. Lucifer laughed and vanished as the explosion reverberated in the quiet cabin and strangely, beheaded the old rooster. Before she could breathe again, Rafe charged in the door.

He stood, his breath raspy with exertion and fear. "Vivi?" he said it softly, watching her hold the heavy rifle and stare at an empty chair. His hand slowly came around her, grasped the rifle and set it in the corner. He closed the door against the cold and walked around her, stood at the chair and gripped the back of it tight. "Vivi." He whispered. "What're ya tyin' to do?"

She blinked, raised her eyes and saw his face, his true face, scruffy with a bristled beard and ruddy red from the cold. "Um."

He turned and surveyed the cabin. The hens were wild, squawking and bustling and jumping in the coop around the rooster's mutilated body. He grinned and chuckled. "That ain't how ya kill a chicken, darlin'." But as he turned and took in her paleness and the tremble in her hands, his heart clenched painfully. In two long strides she was in his embrace. Holding her close he kissed the top of her head and sighed. "Vivi, you ain't getting crazy on me, are ya?"

"No." She wriggled, freeing herself and moving to the old cook stove. "Of course not. Um … why have you been out there so long?" He had left their bed at the crack of dawn and hadn't come in for more than a cup of hot coffee since.

Ignoring her question he poured himself coffee. "What were you doing with that rifle?"

She shrugged. "Are you at least going to eat dinner with me? The stew's ready."

"Sure, sure." He dragged off the damp blanket coat and ran a hand through his hair, watching her every move as she served him savory smelling stew and a chunk of fresh bread.

"Waiting for an answer, Vivi."

"So am I. Why are you out there so much? I hate being alone in here, Rafe. You know that."

"Well, don't be getting no cabin fever on me. Can't afford those luxuries yet. When you're a fancy lady in St. Louis you can do that all ya want. Not now. A rifle? Why would you shoot off a rifle in here?"

She huffed and went outside for snow to melt so she could wash the dishes. He watched her put the pot on the cook stove. "Answer me, Vivi."

"I ... something scared me. That's all."

His brow curled. "Ain't nothing in here to scare you but the tit mice living under the coop. Well, maybe that rooster but he's no more. Am I thinking we'll have fried chicken tomorrow?"

She finally smiled and joined him at the table. "There's some fatback, more than enough flour after I sift out the bugs. Tomorrow, fried chicken." At least it promised he'd still be there tomorrow. Happy news, but she felt suddenly exhausted and her shoulders drooped. Fighting Lucifer always drained her.

"You worked hard today, darlin'. Maybe you should get some sleep." Rafe stood and reached for the blanket coat, warm near the hearth.

"Are you leaving me?"

"What?" He'd swung a turn. "'Course I ain't leaving. Got more wood to chop." And he stomped out the door.

Too nervous to rest, Vivi did everything she could to busy her mind as well as her hands. She tugged the dead rooster from the coop, blanched and plucked the skinny thing and wondered if it was too stringy to eat. She took it outside and hung it by the feet, watching Rafe swing the axe again and again. He never even noticed her there, and Vivi wondered.

Cabin fever. Maybe that was it. After all, why would Lucifer waste his time with her? She grinned and chuckled. Foolishness. Maybe she would try harder to convince Rafe to take her along on his next hunting trip, but when would that be? There were two deer and a caribou carcass hanging in the shed. He was chopping enough wood for a whole town. Maybe he was sick of the cold outside and doing all that work so he could be warm and comfortable with her inside the cabin. Images of loving him, laughing and talking, touching, cooking and cleaning around him made her smile, but only briefly. She turned to the empty chair and swallowed the reality. It was late and the light from Rafe's big fire outside was waning, shooting fewer and fewer flashes through the cracks in the closed window shutters. And still, the axe chopped and cracked. She sadly took blankets from the bed and wrapped them around her.

There beneath the sparkling stars, Vivi stood and watched him. In the cold, he had stripped his shirt and she could see the ripples of his back muscles roll and clench beneath sweat-soaked long johns. The waning fire shed little warmth but Rafe set down the heavy axe and ran an arm across his sweating brow, than noticed her, stepped close and hugged her.

"How long you been out in this cold?"

"I'm fine. Rafe, when are you leaving?"

His eyes went blank and he reached for his coat, draped it over her shoulders. "You go inside, this night cold ain't good for you."

"It's not good for you either." Her eyes scanned the mountain of chopped wood. "When are you leaving?"

He cleared his throat, rolled his neck, and sighed. "Soon. Go inside, woman."

"How soon?"

* * *

He finally gathered his shirt and took her arm. Inside, he stood a long time at the hearth, rubbing his hands and thinking. Like usual, Vivi had baffled him. She was astute and unaware at once. He finally sat on the bed and looked up into her beautiful golden eyes.

"Darlin', I gotta go get some money." His hand shot up when her face blanched white. "No, I ain't gotta rob nothin'. I have a lot of money buried at the Mexican border, just gonna take a little trip down, get it, and come right back."

"Why do we need it? Why now? Rafe, it's not like we can spend it here." She paced in front of him and he snatched her hand, pulling her to sit at his side.

"It ain't for here. It's what we'll need in St. Louis. I need stake money to gamble, darlin'."

"Then, take me with you to get it."

"I can't."

"Why not? We'll ride together the same way we came."

"We didn't come here in the deep snows, Vivi. It's too dangerous for you. I'm goin' alone."

She fell silent, still. "Are you coming back?"

"'Course I'm comin' back. Jesus, Vivi. I ain't leavin' you here forever." But again his eyes refused to focus on hers.

She stood and paced. "There's no reason I can't go with you. Don't leave me here alone, Rafe. Please. Take me."

"You ain't coming. Like I said, too dangerous." Again he took her wrist and pulled her to stand between his opened knees. His eyes were compassionate, loving, telling. "You can't come. I'm taking both horses with me, but … tomorrow I'll be bringing you a horse of your own, darlin'."

"A horse? Is there a cabin nearby? A town?" The mere idea of other people thrilled and terrified her.

"Well," he scratched his bristly chin. "No cabin, not a town. Not even white folk. Indians. A village, six miles west of here. There's a clear path to it. A man there, name's Brown Bull, he talks real good English. He's gonna watch out for you while I'm gone. Probably won't bother you, just check on what you need, bring game, wood."

"How long?" Vivi felt her knees weaken and she knelt, laid her head on his knee.

His hand stroked her hair tenderly "I figure a month, maybe less."

"Take me. I can't be without you. Please take me."

His throat tightened but he said it anyway, a croaking sound crawling to his lips. "Can't. Too hard for you ... and not good for the baby."

Her face rose and Rafe could see her mind twisting and tangling, counting. "Oh, God."

"So," he sighed. "A month. But if I something happens and I ain't back by the thaw, Brown Bull's gonna take you down to the nearest town. I'm leaving you the money we have. You use it to get a good city doctor to take care of you and your baby."

"My baby? You mean, our baby, right? Rafe, now you can't leave me like this. Let's just wait until spring and go together, we can—"

"Think, Vivi!" he nearly shouted. "Come spring you're gonna be heavy with child. It's too damn hard a ride all the way to the border then up to St. Louis. This is best. If I go now; you're okay, you can manage fine. When I'm back and the snows are over, we'll take it slow down the mountain, ride in a fancy private railroad car all the way to St. Louis." His eyes twinkled. "Get us a marriage certificate. If I play well, we get us a nice house and raise our kids."

But Vivi's mind was on the other possibilities. "What if something happens to you?"

"It might. That's why I told that Brown Bull fellow to get you down if I ain't back. Two months is too long, Vivi. It will mean either I been caught, or worse."

She became silent, her face beautiful and glistening, falling tears catching the glow from the waning fire.

"Brown Bull's gonna bring an old woman to stay with you if you start getting ... too big ... to carry water or wood. You won't be alone, darlin'. And I will come back. Be back long before your time comes, I swear."

"When will that be?"

Rafe kissed her lips softly. "By my count, July, maybe June. I get back in late February and the storms hold, we can get down first thaw, real careful like."

"But you said the thaw might not come until June!" she gasped.

"Might not, but listen to me. If for some reason you're still alone or we can't get down, that Indian woman will help. Givin' birth is natural, darlin'. Natural as death. Ask the poor rooster hangin' outside," Rafe grinned. "And by the way, shotgun Viv ... don't be looking for baby chickens anytime soon. Those hens need their rooster. Maybe I'll get a rooster on my way back for us." She didn't smile. "Or I can bring up a nice new dress for you?" Still her eyes locked tight and fearful on his. "Or—"

"You, just you come back to me. I need you Rafe Bennett. You are the only reason I breathe."

He kissed her and grinned. "Guess I don't need to be bringing back no romantic story novels for you. You got all that stuff already in your head."

She snuggled close to his chest. "Well, maybe bring back a rooster."

* * *

She stood at the opened door long after he'd disappeared in the distance. Cold wind snapped at her skirts and ice shards burned the skin on her face and hands. She'd begged him not to leave that morning as the coming storm looked ominous even to her untrained eye. Rafe insisted he should move ahead of it, that if he waited he might not get down at all. Bitterly, painfully alone, Vivi turned a gaze into the cabin. Its warmth and comfort were gone, left, riding into the unknown. Even a man like Rafe never risked this kind of weather, but he'd convinced her that it was all for the best. Her eyes probed every corner of the cabin, looking for Lucifer, but he wasn't there. No one was there and even the hearth fired cracked without joy.

One month. Thirty days. She would tick them off and pray as hard as she could. Her hand dropped to her flat belly. When Rafe returned would it still be flat? Would she feel the child moving inside of her? One month … one month … one month.

CHAPTER 19

The trail down was treacherous under good conditions, but as the pass covered with thick, heavy snow, Rafe felt the need to move quicker. A slide could close the pass and hold him tight with his only option to head back. He glanced behind. Back to the warm cabin and Vivi.

What were the chances he could get her through the winter up there? Help bring his own child into the world? He knew a lot about himself, and he knew he couldn't do it. Couldn't face it. Couldn't watch her suffer without the help of at least a midwife. Even the idea of that old Arapaho woman didn't comfort him. No. He had to move ahead. Get down past the storm's danger. Do what he had to do and get back. Climbing up would be easier than going down. He knew that for a fact; had more than once successfully done so, leaving a frustrated posse behind. He had to keep moving. With the money, he could get Vivi safely down the western trail in a lucky early spring thaw. Most of that side of the mountains should be sheltered from the worst of the weather. With a lot of good fortune he could get her to a town before the baby came, get her down to doctors and the kind of care she would need. The kind she deserved. His woman would have the best.

The wind blasted and the horses stumbled, one tumbled down a grade and was nearly buried in the soft snow but soon struggled back to its feet, unharmed and listening for Rafe's whistle in the blizzard. He moved like a machine, without concern, focus intense until the storm lightened and he could sense the end.

Rafe camped in a protected hollow, expecting more weather, but it did not come. He shivered in the bitter cold, his face burned red from the chill and blasting wind. He was wrapped in everything he owned, pieces of old wool blankets torn and rolled around his hands to protect against frostbite. Dawn came dreary and heavy but the further he trekked, the less precarious the trail became.

Three days passed and he found himself removing the blanket coat. He rolled it and tied it to the saddle, re-mounted and moved ahead. It was difficult, slow progress, but finally on the sixth day he recognized the landscape. He'd crossed into the New Mexico Territory but the weather was still blustery, still steeped in a harsh winter. Another few days and he'd be feeling the heat, moving closer to the Mexico border and his stash.

Rafe took a wide circle around populated towns and moved south. He removed the rags on his hands, but not just because they were too warm; because needed to be able to get a good grip on his pistol should the need arise.

* * *

Days passed and Vivi had finally stopped crying. She stopped worrying that Lucifer would appear and she stopped wringing her hands. It was as it was meant to be and she wondered how it would all end, if Rafe would manage to return before the baby came. She decided that she would not leave the cabin, no matter what, she would stay strong and wait for him. She didn't tell him these things, seeing the concern in his eyes and determination on his face. Rafe was positive he was doing the best for them all.

"The best for us all," she sighed and stood at the cook stove, melting snow for tea. Her palm settled tenderly on her flat belly and Vivi marveled that a child was growing there. Her body had become demanding but when she was hungry, it rejected the meal, coming in gurgles and chunks and sometimes without warning. Most times she managed to get past the cabin door, but more often than not she was on her knees, cleaning the foul mess. When she wanted warmth and bundled beneath blankets next to a roaring fire, she became unbelievably hot. She'd leave with a sudden need to stand in the blowing snow for a few moments just to catch her breath again. She could drink water, she could drink tea, but she could not drink coffee as it ached and burned in her stomach, and soon the tea was almost gone. Vivi was reduced to sipping warmed, herbed broth, grateful that Pennywalker had mixed the dried aromatic summer herbs and stored them in an old tin.

The shed held enough meat for seven families, but she could only hold down soft, boiled chicken or a pale soup made from the remaining few root vegetables. Before the third week ended, the chickens were all eaten.

As the fourth week began Vivi felt a thrill. Believing that Rafe would return soon, she felt a surge of energy, hauled in wood and cleaned the cabin. She baked bread with the last of the flour and considered making a more substantial deer stew for her evening meal, something that would also warm and nourish Rafe when he arrived. She carried the skinning knife out to the shed and battled with the frozen butchered pieces of meat, she wanted only a little but finally admitted defeat and took a large chunk to roast in the cook stove's oven. She set the frozen meat in the heated box and sighed, wondering how long it would take to cook.

* * *

Three nights after he circled the dangerous Apache pass, Rafe camped in the open. He made coffee and cocked his pistol, slowly raising it to aim into the darkness just beyond the light of his fire.

"I know you're there," he said but no one responded. "Too late, ya know. You're there and you're probably cold, wanting some warmth. Come on closer." Rafe felt a chill of terror drift across his soul as a dark shadow loomed just far enough from the fire, he couldn't make out a face. It was darker than usual, no moon, the stars faded in the cloudy winter night. "Who are you?"

"Why go back, Rafe Bennett?"

"What?" Rafe shivered, the voice was unnaturally quiet yet somehow booming in his ears.

"You heard me. Why go back? You can't live like that."

"Who are you?" Rafe shouted, stood and squinted into the inky darkness.

"You know who I am. I've been with you all your life, longer than that woman you've got hidden in the Rockies."

Panic soared through him and Rafe squeezed the trigger. The blast lit into the blackness revealing nothing but a smoky, shadowy form. Laughter rang from all around and Rafe spun on his heel. Was he going mad? The laughter drifted into the distance and without warning, the night became normal. He walked around the fire, no one was there, no one could have been anywhere in the clearing where he had camped.

Returning to the fire, he contemplated his mysterious visitor's words. Why go back? Could he live like that? Saddled with a woman and child? Why go back? Hell, that was easy, because of his woman and child. He hunkered close to the fire. No need to lie down, there'd be no sleeping that night.

At sunrise he left to deal with the rattlers and collect the rest of his stash. It was time to get back to Vivi.

* * *

Another week passed. Vivi found a bag of dried corn at her door, saw that her horse was out in the corral. It wasn't the first time. If the Indian, Brown Bull, wanted to hurt her he would've done it by now. She was sad and afraid for Rafe. Another storm had rolled through making it difficult for her to get to the outhouse he'd built for her but she held her skirts high and trudged her way through.

In the smelly darkness, she relieved herself and felt a strange wetness on her pantaloons. Tugging them off, she wondered if she'd waited too long and wet herself. She'd need to wash them now. But as she left, the light bouncing from a mellow sun had shown brilliant on the white fabric. Looking down she found blood. Fingering the small mark, panic pressed in her chest. "The baby! Oh God, my baby!" She gasped a whimper.

As though she had cried out for help, a bent old Indian woman appeared at her side, urging her inside and onto the bed. Vivi was terrified. "My baby! Oh God!" But the old woman was calm, snapping Arapaho instructions to the large man at the door. He stoked the fire, brought in more wood and stood as far away as he could, against the log walls, silent.

The woman reached beneath the blankets and pressed her fingers around Vivi's small mound of a belly, then slid gnarled fingers into her path and smiled kindly. After sipping a warm, foul smelling herbed fluid, Vivi finally relaxed into a quiet sleep devoid of dreams, free from her fear and worry for Rafe.

Three days later the trickling bleeding completely stopped and her appetite returned. The old woman was kind and gentle but insistent that Vivi not stand or move about, even demanding that the warrior carry her outside when she needed the outhouse. Vivi, unable to communicate in the guttural language, simply talked and talked. She talked to God, and Rafe, and Madam Miriam, talked to herself and even though she had again begun to see Lucifer skulking about the cabin, she did not talk to him. The old Medicine woman became agitated when the Devil was there, and at least once opened the door and shouted until the beautiful angel of darkness left.

This was her confinement and Vivi became lost in it, time slid past with little acknowledgment of days or nights or weeks. When she fully came to herself on a lovely dawn, her hand slid to a belly, no longer flat. If Rafe was correct, she would be entering her seventh month of confinement. And if he was correct he should have returned long before. Vivi began to worry that the Indians would try to take her down to a town, but she need not have been concerned. No one, not even an Indian, could get down the passes and even if Rafe was alive, he would never be able to get up to her either. The spring storms were the worst in years.

* * *

For more than the passing of three moons, Brown Bull had come to assist his grandmother, and to watch over this woman with hair as black as night and eyes the color of summer sunshine. He listened to her talk, aimless circles of nonsense, mentioning the names of Rafe and Lucifer and Miriam again and again.

And he struggled with the growing desires in his flesh.

He first saw this white woman when she arrived with her man. Brown Bull had been educated in the east, had more than once tasted the flesh of women so fair and soft it made him groan to remember. But there was something more to this woman, Vivi, something bigger than her body and softer than a gaze from her eyes. Brown Bull had known at the first sight of her, that he would have her. He would kill her man to have her. Even leave his own people to have her.

The old grandmother had many things to say of such ideas and Brown Bull had done what was not natural for the warrior in him. He held himself at great restraint.

When the old woman left for the village to gather medicinal herbs, Brown Bull stood outside the cabin door and wondered what a woman like this Vivi could do to a man. If she knew how to please, what he needed, and he closed his eyes with the imaginings.

"Hello?" Vivi called, sitting up on the edge of the bed. "Hello?"

"I am here," Brown Bull called through the door.

"Brown Bull? Come in, please."

He blinked, squared his bulk and entered, moving directly to ladle a tin cup of water for her as it was most often all she needed. She accepted it from his hand and smiled, disarming him, paralyzing him. Was that power he knew she possessed a wicked magic?

"Thank you." She sipped daintily. "You speak English, right?"

She took his breath away. Her body had begun to show the obvious signs of her condition, it seemed to soften and round the edges of her, make her something he wished to smooth his hands along like a fine, cherished horse ready to foal. He finally shook himself to the moment and stepped back, intending to leave the cabin.

"Please don't go. Please." A tear glittered in her beautiful eye. "Just … talk to me. Brown Bull I'm going crazy, I need to talk to someone who can hold a conversation with me. Please, sit."

He backed to the table, slid around it and lowered to the farthest chair then nodded. "We may talk." Her grateful smile made his heart tremble.

"How did you learn to speak such beautiful English?" she asked softly.

"I was taken by missionary ladies, I was a small boy. I lived in Boston, Massachusetts until I was able to run away and return to my people."

"Wow, that's more than I've heard you say in months," she grinned, a twinkle in her eyes. "Was it hard for you?"

"Being taken was hard, I was not yet a warrior, had only seen seven summers. Living with the Christians was harder. Leaving them," he felt himself grin at the memory, "was easy."

His comment drew a silly giggle from her. "I suppose those are two very different lives."

"No, there is only one life, the life with the people, my people. Arapaho."

"Then it is very good that you came back, Brown Bull. I imagine that your people need you as much as you need them."

He nodded thoughtfully and the woman sighed.

"Where do you think he is?"

Brown Bull did not respond. He did not know where her man was, or why he had not returned yet. He hoped that Rafe Bennett would never return.

"Is he coming back?"

Brown Bull stood and prepared to leave.

"Wait! Please. Tell me if you know. Is Rafe … dead?" Pain rippled across her eyes and her lip trembled.

"He is not dead."

"Are you sure?"

"No."

"Then, how can you say it?"

"The grandmother says he lives, and I will believe he lives." Brown Bull stomped out, angrier than he'd ever been without an enemy to release such fury upon.

"Then, where is he?" she called behind him but he would not answer her.

* * *

The sun heated the next morning and sweat prickled his temples as Rafe waited patiently. Rattlers lazily slithered from the hole, seeking warmth on the hard, sun bleached earth. Thoughts pummeled his mind.

"Why go back?" Hissed the unseen guest from a few nights earlier and without doubt, Rafe knew it to be the voice of Lucifer himself.

"Too dangerous. Gotta get back to Vivi."

Lucifer hissed louder, leaned closer to Rafe's ear. "Forget the woman."

"I got Vivi and I got a baby coming. I'm takin' my money from this hole and going back to that cabin."

"That cabin? A woman? Is that a life for the likes of you? Pampering some prissy spoiled little girl, letting her take your jewels and crush them in her hands just because she opened her legs for you? Use your head, Bennett!"

Rafe blinked, held his breath.

Lucifer paced a thump around him, invisible, yet vibrating the very ground and stirring the snakes. "Women are easy to get. Babies? You already have a few. You don't care about them, no need to care about this one. Besides, she's all alone up there with those savages. She's already been raped or murdered, probably carved for the tribe's feast. She's dead. Gone. Nothing to you. Live the life you're meant to live. There is still money to be had, just for the taking. It's everywhere, Bennett."

Rafe was immobile, unable to move a muscle or draw breath deeply into his lungs.

"The thrill of a take ... or life as an asshole hogtied to a whore's skirts. Use your head, Bennett. Use your head." Lucifer hissed and the rattlers all raised their heads to acknowledge his presence.

CHAPTER 20

Something deep in his soul spoke inside Rafe's heart. It came from a place he never knew was there and it shouted, loud and determined. "Don't think, Rafe!" it cried. "Don't think!"

Don't think? This was not something he thought he could do, but whoever said it, it seemed like good advice. To think would mean to ponder the possibilities of Vivi dead, bloodied, raped. His child, murdered. It would mean the fire of revenge that would cost the lives of every Arapaho in that village.

"Don't think!" the voice came louder, thundering over Lucifer's voice, hot and moist at his left ear like someone was really standing behind him.

"There's ten times more money than you ever had before, all for the taking!"

"Don't think."

"Yours to take! Easy as hell!"

"Don't think."

"You deserve what you want, and you want that money!"

"Don't think."

And finally Rafe didn't think. He let his muscles move against the terror of such a strange impetus. He knelt beside the gaping hole and stuffed bundle after bundle of cash tight into the saddlebag. When he stood and stepped back, he tripped, stumbled hard onto his ass with a grunt and a thud, shaken, watching the writhing snakes all around. Without thinking he scrambled to his feet. He swung a hand, gathered the saddlebag and turned for his horse, walking with long, purposeful strides as rattlers hissed and screamed behind him.

He buckled and secured the saddlebag, mounted and rode hard. Rafe Bennett did something he'd never done before; he didn't think an idea through. Instead he moved with his heart and now he was riding to Vivi. Riding with the money safe in his possession to take care of his woman and child. For the first time in his life, he wondered whose ideas he had been thinking all his life. His, or the Devil's?

Inside the saddlebag, a rattler lay silent, coiled tight and comfortable near the bundled hardtack, deep beneath wads of stolen cash.

* * *

Miriam sat beside Paul at the magnificent marble conference table. It wasn't a full disciplinary council, but the matter at hand was dire.

Young Traffic Angel, Jonathan, stood before them, his eyes steady ahead and his hands clasped tight behind his back. The youthful angel was visibly terrified but standing his ground. He had stated his case, explained his reasoning, but clearly understood the weight of his infraction. There are laws in heaven as well as on earth and he'd admitted that he knew he'd crossed the line, even as he chose to do so.

"Jon, Jon, Jon," Paul groaned, rubbing his eyes for effect. "You must understand what this all means."

"I do understand, sir. But to—"

"To interfere without a clear directive in such simple situations is fully unacceptable!" Miriam said sharply. "What possessed you to do such a thing? The Charge was not your responsibility. The Charge was not in severe danger. The Charge was not your concern! There was no justifiable reason for such action and you know it." She shuffled in her chair and huffed. "It's extremely unclear to me why you would jeopardize your position like this."

Jon cleared his throat, ran a trembling hand over his mussed hair then squared his shoulders. He's been abruptly pulled from his work, nearly slammed into the conference room, swept away from his earthbound activity without the least warning and still not finished with what he was trying to accomplish. He licked his lips and began. "I saw something, Madam Miriam. Isn't it possible that I saw something the department didn't?"

"Highly unlikely," Miriam hissed but Paul's sandaled foot sharply bumped hers beneath the polished table.

"Just what is it you think you saw, Jon?" The Master Guardian asked evenly, his eyes focused on the folder before him, his hand fingering the documents therein.

"I felt more than saw," Jon swallowed hard. "I sensed eminent evil interference ... sensed it so strongly I moved with full intention of deterring Lucifer's objective."

"Lucifer?" Finally Paul's eyes rose to meet the young angel's. "You ... sensed ... Lucifer?"

"I know, sir. I swear I know. It's supposed to be impossible, but I know I felt his presence."

"It is impossible," Miriam spat. "In your angelic state, passing through various earthbound and spiritual planes, you could not have sensed, or felt, or even seen Lucifer, young man. Impossible. You were not even meant to be there! You were far from your assigned position and a thousand miles from your own direct Charge!"

"I know ... I know." The handsome angel's face reddened. "This is so hard to explain, see I—"

"You were not doing your job!" It seemed Madam Miriam had reached her limit and her irritation was legend among the troops. Her temper flared and she pushed her chair back. To stand, to pace, to shout, but Paul's hand stopped the chair then gently pressed her shoulder, holding her to her seat.

"Traffic Angel, Jonathan," Paul said calmly. "You are on probation until you are notified otherwise."

"But—"

"Your Charge will be assigned another guardian and you are to remain in your quarters until summoned by me."

"But, sir—"

"You are dismissed," Paul shouted and watched the young guardian leave. He waited silently. Counted to ten. Still Miriam said nothing, but patience would be most prudent, for he had not been forthcoming with

143

his reasons for intercepting what should have cost young Jonathan his rank. It would not do for Jon to be demoted. He was soon to be promoted in a big way. Now, how to explain it all to Miriam?

Finally she spoke. "I will resign this position, effective immediately," she said.

"Foolishness," he responded.

"Well warranted, I would think, as you have fully usurped my authority," Miriam spat.

"What do I want with your authority? Think, Miriam," he whispered. "Think."

She drew in a deep breath and shook her head. "Think? Just as Jonathan told Mr. Bennett 'Don't think'? What's at play here, Paul?"

"Much, my dear one. Much." He leaned over and gently kissed her brow. Paul had so few moments alone with Miriam, his life had taken on a complexity larger than he had ever imagined since becoming Master Guardian. It would take monumental efforts on both his and Miriam's parts to retain their secret, all-encompassing love.

"I am worried for Vivi," Miriam finally said in a whisper, her anger dissipated within his affection.

"Yes. And I am worried for Bennett. Miriam, if we are not very, very careful here, we could fail this assignment."

Her face rose to eye him suspiciously. "Tell me everything."

* * *

Twice, Rafe raced for safety as posses chasing other outlaws came dangerously close. He hid for days that felt like weeks and counted off time on his fingers. Two times, he found himself in Mexico, searching for a safe way north and circling out of his way for miles. When he finally started to make some headway north, the travel slowly returned to the winter Rafe had left behind. A storm stifled his movement through the night and half the day. Now, light snow swirled and danced around him in the twilight as he viewed the vast distance between him and the foothills of the mountains holding Vivi. He did his damn best not to think of what might have happened to her. The word 'faith' rolled through his head. Faith. Did he know what that was? He could quote a hundred Bible passages containing the word, but did it have meaning for him?

He needed to have faith in those savages, trust that the Arapaho and Brown Bull's word was good. He needed to believe he could get back up those mountains through an extreme winter that looked as though it might never end. When he came down he was positive he could return, but as days and weeks passed, he had his doubts. His mind spun. Numbers. Months. There wasn't much time for Vivi. A few months, no more. Soon it might be more dangerous to try to bring her to civilization than it would be to attempt helping to birth their child in the cabin. Damn.

For five brutal days he ate little from the pouch hanging on his saddle horn, slept less. He was weakening, almost starving as he followed a tight trail through the canyon. As the earth opened before him he noticed a line of smoke drifting up into the winter night sky. A ranch was tucked neatly in a small hollow. Rafe sat still as death and waited for sunrise. Four men, one smaller, probably a boy, left the house. No doubt off to gather cattle as the storm would have surely spooked the beefs off into the hills for shelter.

His mind spun with hunger and his belly growled. Wasn't there one more wrapped bundle of hardtack somewhere in his saddlebag? Either way, the rising tower of smoke from that ranch house chimney was calling to him. He'd go down there, pay whoever was inside for hot food and be on his way. He could hold off just a little longer.

But as he rode, dizziness washed over him. He heeled the animal and lowered to its neck. All he had to do was reach that house. Then he could eat, get some rest, probably in the barn and be long gone before the men returned.

Finally he slowed at the corral. He lowered to the ground on shaking knees then stood and shook his head hard. How long had he been riding? How long was he gone? He unbuckled the saddlebag. Looking toward the shabby door he reached inside for the cash he'd use to pay for hot food and supplies. He intended to pay far more than it would be worth. The ranch looked poor.

Rafe felt the slither of snakeskin against his hand. His eyes widened. The strike was sudden, painful, sharp, burning. He roughly dragged his hand out, the serpent still attached as he shook to free himself. Its rattling tail slapped twice against his thigh. When it released, he gasped and gripped the wound tight. Already his hand was growing numb, his lungs fought for air. Dragging one foot in front of the other, he reached the door and kicked hard with the toe of his boot. When it opened he steadied himself.

The woman was substantial. Her wide face glowed red, her pale hair was a wiry knot at the top of her head and in her hand she held a cocked rifle.

He slumped against the doorjamb. "Rattler," was all he said before he slumped then dropped in a heap at her feet.

* * *

Brown Bull carried wood, hauled fresh snow for his grandmother to melt and use for cooking, and he did his best to avoid looking at the amazing, beautiful white woman. As he left for the village, he heard the old woman call to him. He did not wish to hear what she was about to say, but he could not be disrespectful to an elder. He turned his horse and waited for her to reach him.

"Send a party to find this woman's man."

Brown Bull snorted then grinned. "I can not, grandmother. I can not risk warriors to the storms for him. We must protect the people. If he is returning, let him return at his own risk."

She glared up, and he glared down. "You are lost to the demand of your ego, my grandson. This woman will never be yours. She belongs to him. Send a party to bring him." She turned and walked toward the cabin. It was difficult, living as the white people lived, sealed by walls and disconnected from the earth. Brown Bull knew the old grandmother wished for it all to end so that she could return to her village and her people, but the white woman was frail and required her help. The old grandmother and Brown Bull had told the man they would protect his woman. There was nothing to be done for it. "Send a party!" she called over her shoulder.

"I will not send a party, old woman."

She turned sharply.

"But," he grinned and leaned forward on his horse. "If he does not return by the next full moon, I will go alone to find this man. I will find

146

him and I will return him to this cabin. And before the spring thaw … I will kill him and take his woman for my own."

* * *

Once again Traffic Angel Jonathan stood at the conference table, but this time only Master Guardian Paul was present, watching him closely as though he might see something he was trying to hide. He shuffled his feet. "You called for me, sir?"

"Traffic Guardian Jon, what you did—"

"I know, I know and I am sorry. I swear I will not do such a thing again."

Paul rubbed his eyes. "What you did was extraordinary. Jon, I have only seen two angels at your level in my entire career display such an ability. A valuable, extremely important ability. Thus said, I'm promoting you."

"What? I'm not losing my position?"

"You will work directly under me."

Jon lowered into a chair. "Under you? But sir, Elite Guardians require screening and long term training and …"

Paul cleared his throat. "Not as an Elite Guardian, Jon. Not yet. Before I can even consider placing you in the pool for the Elite Guardian screening, I need you on a special assignment. You'll be serving as a Class Two Elite Guardian assigned to watch over Mr. Rafael Bennett."

Class Two was more than a simple promotion. Class Two was a huge career leap and a category designed for special cases. Jon blinked. Was he happy, or should he be afraid? "What will I be doing?" He tried not to sound excited but the pressure was already mounting, thumping in his chest. He could do this. He always knew he could do this. "I've been sort of, well, secretly watching Bennett since you put me on probation."

"I know. I gave you access," Paul confessed with a grin. "Jon, you will be given a few new powers, but there's no time to prefect your abilities with them. Bennett will be able to hear you, just like he did at the snake pit. But now he'll clearly recognize that he's talking to

147

someone else. At times, he will also see you. He's had this experience before."

"With Vivi," Jon sighed, assuring Paul that he'd already done his homework. Bored and alone in his quarters for days, he was just curious. Now the information was going to be vital.

"Yes, with Vibrant Light. Bennett will hear you and he may become agitated by it, so be careful. You need him to trust you and listen to you. Lucifer's going to be able to see and hear you too so again, be careful."

"So what do I do? Just stay close to Bennett?"

Paul turned a glance to the monitor on the polished marble conference table. "No, he's in good hands for now. Lucifer has no control while Bennett is incapacitated. What do you think you should do?"

"Deter those men from coming back to the ranch house. Weather?"

Paul smiled. "We'll manipulate that for you from here."

"And, Vivi?"

"Not your concern, Jonathan. Don't lose your focus."

"Yes sir."

"Now, go to work."

Jon smiled, even though he was scared to death.

CHAPTER 21

Gordon Heller bristled and swore at his three sons, yelling instructions as they moved, seeking every cow that had run. He was a man displeased with his life, hateful to his good wife and family, and bitter over his questionable finances. It was not supposed to be this way for Gordon, the son of a wealthy oil man back east. He'd originally come to the New Mexico territory with Kathleen because she had given him two strapping sons and all the help he'd need to be successful in his own right. In the beginning, he did well. The boys were young but strong. His wife grew fat and robust. Everything seemed good, but he still was not happy.

He and Kathleen were still young and could have found a certain satisfaction in the life he'd brought her to, but it wasn't enough for him. He gambled badly, drank far too much and took whores as often as he could manage to get away from the ranch. Nothing wrong with that in his mind. Kathleen was his wife and would do as he commanded, stay at the house, raise their sons, and open her legs when he felt the desire.

Poor Kathleen had little pleasure with the life her husband created for her. After years of struggle, she refused to manage all of the work entailed, recruiting her sons to assist which enraged Gordon. He used his fists to bring her to submission and protect his sons from women's work, even though he could see that they loved their mother dearly and didn't mid helping her.

As the years passed, his brutal anger found its way to Kathleen more and more often, sometimes leaving her bloodied and broken, but he refused her a doctor, explaining that she was his to do with as he wanted. And he did. At nearly thirty-four, Kathleen found herself pregnant with their third son. Gordon was beyond angry and determined to murder the child but God above saw fit to let the unborn infant survive his violence.

Money became tighter and tighter, but his expensive habits at the saloon and the whorehouse did not curtail. His ego dictated that he never seek help from his father, and when the old bastard died he left nothing to his rancher son.

Leading the last of the cattle to the corral, he knew he wanted to eliminate everything he hated … the cows, Kathleen, and especially Peter, his belligerent eldest son.

Peter never hid he fact that he despised the ranch and could no longer watch his father hurt his mother. He married early, just past sixteen, and watched his young wife die in childbirth. Not uncommon, and after Peter buried his child bride, Gordon demanded the boy return to the ranch, but it was only at a bruised Kathleen's plea that Peter finally came home to help.

Gordon sat astride his horse, gazed back at the hated ranch and cursed furiously. Peter feared that the old bastard's anger would be taken out on his youngest brother, or worse, his mother. A voice whispered in his head. Peter, now nearly twenty, had never suggested that his father go into town, find a good card game or take a whore, but the thoughts were persistent.

"Pa," he rode up close. "What say me and you and Mitch take a little ride into town?"

The man's sour face brightened and he hissed a laugh. "Feelin' an itch, boy?"

Peter's heart thumped, Gordon could go either way with this, but he returned the grin. "Hell yeah, Pa. Keep thinkin' 'bout that rosy skinned Maybell." To emphasize, he pressed the heel of his hand hard against his crotch. "Feelin' like some whisky too. Mitch might have some fun. We been working hard, Pa."

Gordon grunted an ugly laugh. "Time for Mitch to get his cock inside a nice warm whore's pussy. Send Billy back to the house and let's hightail it outta here."

*　*　*

Class Two Guardian, Jonathan smiled as the riders rode off. He'd just watched poor Kathleen struggle to drag Bennett's unconscious weight inside the house and up onto a bed. She'd quickly taken a skinning knife and sliced his hand over the snake bite then sucked the poison, spitting and doing it again and again until she tasted nothing but healthy, tinny blood in her mouth.

"Now," she whispered kindly, tugging his jacket and boots from him and covering him with blankets. "It's time to pray hard you survive that evil serpent." She sat at his side and soothed his brow with a cool damp cloth.

When ten year old Billy came inside, announcing that the others had gone to town, Jonathan knew it was critical for him to follow. Gordon Heller had to be held far from the house, or Rafe Bennett would be taking his last breath at the business end of the family rifle.

*　*　*

Rafe's head rolled from side to side. His body burned with fever and his mind slid from memories of Vivi, to the snake gnawing on his hand, to the look on that Arapaho's face when he'd promised to watch over his woman. He mumbled and groaned as agony seared him from his soul to his flesh. Shaking with cold and heat he growled to God and man for relief and protection for Vivi and his child.

Pain knotted his muscles into aching spasms, at times the agony so severe he would cry out. Always there came a tender touch, a soft voice, the coolness of a hand. When his fever reached for the heavens, his heart, soul and mind melded into one and Rafe had only two thoughts left to him. Vivi and his child. As his voice crawled and rumbled from a tight throat, he imagined death licking at the edges of his reality and he spoke.

"Jesus saith unto him … I am the way, the truth and the life: no man cometh unto the Father, but by me … And … God spake all these words, saying, I am the Lord thy God, which have brought thee out of the land of Egypt, out of the house of bondage … Thou shalt not take the goddamn name of the Lord thy God in vain ….. arrrrhhhhhhh! … for the Lord will not hold him guiltless that taketh his name in vain … Blessed are they which do hunger and thirst after righteousness: for they shall be filled …Ye are the salt of the earth: but if the salt have lost his savour … wherewith shall it be salted? … It is thenceforth good for nothing, but to be cast out, and to be trodden under foot of men … Ye have heard that it hath been said … An eye for an eye, and a tooth for a tooth: But I say unto you … That ye resist not evil: but whosoever shall smite thee on thy right cheek, turn to him the other also …The Lord is my shepherd; I shall not want …. Ahhhhh fuck … ahhhh … He maketh me to lie down in green pastures: he leadeth me beside the still waters … He restoreth my soul: he leadeth me in the paths of righteousness for his name's sake. Yea, though I walk through the valley of the shadow of death, I will fear no evil: for thou are with me; thy rod and thy staff they comfort me … Thou preparest a table before me in the presence of mine enemies: thou anointest my head with oil; my cup runneth over … Surely goodness and mercy shall follow me all the days of my life: and I will dwell in the house of the Lord forever … Twenty-third motherfucking Psalm … Ahhhhh God help me! … Help Vivi … Ahhhhhhh."

And his fever broke, dropping him into a deep, replenishing sleep soaked with sweat and the comfort of painless peace.

* * *

It was interesting, actually entertaining. Jonathan manipulated person after person, tempting Gordon Heller and his sons into the beds of whores and the den of gambling dandies who threatened to take everything Heller owned, but Jon was watchful, aware that when the time was ripe to let the man return home, he wouldn't be penniless and angry.

So easy was Heller to lure and tease, Jon became comfortable, too sure of himself. His attention was drawn to the events surrounding the younger Heller son and the loss of his virginity, but as he watched the tender scene, a scream and crash came from the room next door. Gordon

Heller, thick with drink and the massive weight of his ego, had begun to mercilessly beat the whore who had simply asked how his sweet wife was feeling. He battered her senseless then charged down to the saloon, his britches still gaping wide to demand repayment for the uncollected service. One thing led to another and the man brutalized several patrons and did substantial damage to the place before he was subdued by several men he'd attempted to cheat at the card tables. They took him to the sheriff.

* * *

Three days had passed and Rafe was beginning to feel alive again. Slowly his eyes opened to the sight of a scruffy yellow-haired boy who simply stared down at him with fascination.

"You a preacher, mister?"

Rafe turned his head slightly, squinted his eyes. "I ain't no preacher." He scanned the room until he saw his loaded saddlebag sitting in the corner. Slowly he groaned and grunted until he was nearly upright, his feet touching the floor and his body trembling and weak.

"Outta here, you," the woman said and the boy scampered away. She pressed Rafe's shoulders back to the lumpy mattress and smiled kindly. "You look better, mister. Here, take some of this. Just some broth. Got nothing else."

He sipped. His throat, at first recoiled against the nourishment, finally relaxed to let it flow warm and soothing to his empty belly. "Thank you, ma'am." He continued to drink slowly, suddenly hungrier than he could ever remember and he gazed up at the woman.

She was soft and round, a subtle rosy tone to her cheeks and lips. Her hair, tight in a knot at the top of her head was streaked with silver but in the light drifting through the window he could clearly see it was mostly a pale yellow like the boy's. Her eyes were plain and brown and filled with compassion. When she talked she was gentle and slightly animated, and when she smiled, an endearing dimple presented and Rafe knew that this poor, overworked woman was once a beauty. She moved her mass with the gracefulness of a young girl and her voice was soft and kind.

After he finished the broth, she brought more. "Good to see you got your appetite back. Name's Kathleen Heller. Who might you be?"

"Rafe," he said, avoiding her eyes. "You been real kind to me, Mrs. Heller and—"

The sound of a madly galloping horse caught his attention and together they turned to the window. Kathleen visibly relaxed the sudden tension that had brought her shoulders almost to her ears.

"Just my son." As she stood to leave the bedroom, the strapping young man burst inside, his eyes wild, his face red from the cold and his breath raspy.

"Peter, what's happened?" Her voice was small and fearful and Rafe struggled to rise on the pillows and watched to see what would happen next.

Peter shot a disinterested glare at him then focused on his mother. "It's Pa. Sheriff's got him. He beat the living shit outta some whore then broke the saloon to hell. They ain't letting him out until he pays for it all! And if that woman dies … they're gonna hang him for murder!"

The expression on Peter's face confused Rafe and he knew something sure as hell wasn't right. He expected the young man to be distressed, but there was a pleased glint in his eye, controlled, but there, and Rafe knew that look.

Kathleen slowly lowered like a mound of melting butter onto the chair next to the bed. "Oh Lord," she sighed.

Now that was true fear, another look Rafe knew too well.

"Who the hell is this?" Peters chin jerked in Rafe's direction and as much as he wanted to respond, his weakened body would not move and no words would form.

"His name's Rafe … rattlesnake … just before you all went to town. Are ya sure they're not letting your father outta jail?" The grin Peter was hiding grew and Kathleen gasped. "Don't be unchristian, Peter! What are we gonna do?"

Finally Rafe's throat felt cooperative. He cleared it quietly and eyed Peter, who's prideful grin was now gone. "What's your daddy owe to get outta jail, son?"

Both Kathleen and Peter glared and no answer came. Rafe knew something needed to be done, he just didn't know why or what. He shuffled higher on the pillow with a groan. "Lemme talk to your mama a minute. You go out there and warm yourself by the fire." He'd said it gently, assuring the young man that nothin' bad was gonna happen and finally Peter left, closing the door quietly behind him.

"Kathleen, tell me about your husband."

After several moments and a bout of quiet sobs, she finally spoke. As she told the story of her pitiful life, suddenly free to release all the demons Gordon had planted inside her, she often stopped to gasp or whimper. Rafe's heart wrenched.

"He beats you, Kathleen?" She didn't say it, but he'd seen women hurt like that, knew they always thought it was their fault, and he knew she wouldn't admit it until he said the words.

She nodded. To Rafe's amazement, she slowly stood. She rolled up the sleeve of her shabby blouse displaying scars that ragged and mangled her flesh. She raised her skirt as far as her knees revealing more, then tearfully opened the top buttons at her neck to expose fresh purple bruises.

Rafe was enraged but showed none of it. "Peter," he called and the young man returned to see Kathleen re-closing her blouse. "What's your daddy owe to get outta jail?"

Kathleen again lowered to the chair, broken and silent.

"Ah … three hundred dollars."

Rafe's brow rose. "Three hundred?"

"The saloon's real busted up. He couldn't pay his losses at the card table and that poor woman … Sheriff says Pa's gotta pay for the doctor."

"Three hundred dollars. Gimme that saddle bag over there, son."

Peter reluctantly did as he was asked, taking a long side glance at his sobbing mother.

Rafe sat up more, grunted and unbuckled the bag. He pulled out his pistol, obviously tucked in there by Kathleen when she dragged him inside, and set it aside. Taking out several bundles of cash, he handed them to Peter.

"You take this into town and get your daddy outta that jail. Take the young'un with you and don't come back right away. There's 'nough there for you to take a hotel room, stay there with your brothers a day or two, you hear me?"

Peter nodded but his eyes were glued to the pistol's shining barrel. "You're … you're Rafe Bennett, ain't you?"

155

"I am. Now, you know what I'm gonna do, so you take your little brother and you stay away." His eyes trailed to Kathleen. "Take your mama too."

"No," she said quietly. "I'll take this sin on my soul with you, Mr. Bennett. Go Peter. Do what he says."

* * *

Jonathan paced, his undetectable, ethereal form drifting from one end of the sheriff's office to the other, and he waited. Something was about to force everything to a head, he could feel it. He wasn't surprised when the doctor shuffled in, closing the cold out as he slammed the door and stomped his feet.

"How's poor Clarisse doin'?" Sheriff Brooks grunted. Jon carefully watched the deputy, a strong, broad shouldered man named Carl Christian, tense.

"No good, Sheriff. She ain't gonna last the night. You got no idea what he did to that poor woman."

The Sheriff nodded and as the doctor turned to leave, Peter Heller pushed inside. He carefully counted out three hundred dollars, tucked the rest into his pocket and slid it across the desk. "That enough?"

Reluctantly Sheriff Brooks took the cash and recounted it. "Let him out, Christian."

"Where'd she get that kinda fuckin' money?" Gordon Heller shouted as he came from the back of the jailhouse. "She's been hiding money on me! I'll kill her!" He charged past his son and outside, mounting Peter's horse and riding hard.

"I'm followin' him," Christian grunted and popped on his hat.

"What for?" the Sheriff asked and all three men glared at him. The doctor grunted disgust and Peter scowled.

Deputy Christian hissed. "If I don't, we're gonna have two fuckin' women to bury come mornin'." He mounted and raced after Heller.

* * *

156

Rafe struggled to stand and Kathleen gasped. "You're too weak! You can't do nothing, you can't fight him, he'll kill you!"

He ignored her. "Move this chair to the window and help me to it." Grunting and breathing deep against a wave of dizziness, he was finally seated at the window. He fought to pull up the sash and she helped. The cold air rushed in and sharpened his senses. Together they waited in the rapidly chilling room until Rafe spotted the cloud of dusty dry snow growing over the ridge.

"Kathleen. Gimme that rifle and my pistol." The weapons in hand, he focused all his attention on the coming menace. "Now, Kathleen, I want you to go out and make some coffee. I'd like some coffee, darlin'."

"I'll stay with you."

"Make coffee, Kathleen. Now." She left, turning a sad but painfully grateful glance.

The rifle felt good across his knees, well balanced, loaded and cocked. Pistol, settled in his ready hand, he carefully aimed as Gordon Heller charged closer and closer to the ranch house.

Rafe rubbed his eyes. His vision had suddenly blurred. He squinted, braced his elbow against the window sill and slowly squeezed the trigger.

Heller plunged from his horse and to the ground like a rock.

With a rumbling groan, Rafe's head dropped back. A sudden wave of exhaustion ripped through his body and he drew several deep breaths, his mind soaring. He'd still need to get out to Heller, take him someplace and bury the asshole. But when he glanced toward the window, what he witnessed made his body twitch and stiffen.

A man riding hard, leapt to the ground at Heller's dead body, as Kathleen ran toward him. In the mellowing light Rafe saw it, the glint of metal on the man's chest. A goddamn sheriff, or at least a deputy. His eyes shot to the horizon. He held his breath and waited several long moments. No one else was coming.

He tried to stand, thought about making a run for it, again he glared out the window. Kathleen and the man were talking. Were they embracing? Rafe's knees trembled then buckled and he fell to the floor with a thud. Gathering the pistol and rifle, he managed to crawl to the bed and hoist himself onto it. Tucking the weapons close to his body, he dragged the blankets over him. An agonizing tremble shook his flesh and sweat gathered at his temples. Another long breath, then another until his heart calmed and he fell into a bottomless sleep almost instantly.

CHAPTER 22

"Jesus! Kathleen!" Christian exclaimed then quickly took her into his arms. "Don't look."

But she did. The bullet had put a perfect whole between her brutal husband's eyes. She gasped, trembled then buried her face into Christian's shoulder.

"I know for a fact, your boys are in town or I'd suspect Peter. Who did this?"

Kathleen stepped back, squared her shoulders and sighed. "I did."

"No, you didn't." His eyes moved to the house, to the window where whoever killed Heller had the perfect shot. "You can't shoot like that, woman. Who's in there?"

"No one, Carl. I shot him, and I'll confess to it. I'll be pleased to hang for it too."

His heart thumped. Carl Christian had loved Kathleen since the moment he laid eyes on her. He'd watched her from afar and knew what her life was like. No man he knew deserved to die more than Gordon Heller, but he wasn't letting her hang for this. Watching her, he recognized that subtle, calm composure that came over her expression, a sweetness he hadn't seen there since Heller started beating her. In that moment she looked young and beautiful again, endearing and tender, more desirable than he ever remembered. He could see it there in her eyes, she was actually satisfied the man was dead. Hell, so was he, but the idea of Kathleen facing a noose for it? No.

"You ain't gonna hang for this. Now, you tell me who's in that house, Kathleen."

"No one, just a man real sick from a rattler bite. He can hardly move." Her eyes begged and Carl became even more concerned.

"Where's he from?"

"I don't know, Carl. He's been unconscious for days."

He paced a circle, looked around and shook with agitation. He didn't want to leave her there with a killer, but he had no choice. None at all. "Go back to the house, but stay away from that man, you hear me?"

"What are you gonna do?"

A groan escaped his chest, released with a billow of steam in the icy air. "I'm gonna take this body and put it where no one's ever gonna find it. Anyone asks, Gordon never came home, you understand?"

She blinked and Carl gripped her shoulders hard.

"Kathleen. I know you're a good Christian woman. I know you don't wanna do anything that could be a sin, but you gotta do this. Anyone asks, anyone ever asks, you never saw your husband again, he never came home. If I do this right, no one will ever suspect anything except that the bastard ran."

She slowly shook her head, tears streaming down her face. "It ain't right, Carl."

"What's right?" He threw up his hands. "That he beats you bloody? Beats your boys? That he beat that whore? Listen to me, Kathleen. Clarisse is gonna die, she may already be dead. Gordon was gonna hang anyway. You're determined to protect the man who pulled the trigger and I'm determined to protect you from looking like you had any part in it. Let me do it my way. Now, you didn't see Gordon, he never came home. Is that clear?"

Finally she nodded agreement and pulled her flimsy shawl tighter around her as she shivered in the cold.

"And you stay away from that man. You don't talk to him." He heaved the dead body over the horse. "You don't go near him." He climbed into his own saddle. "I'll come back when I'm done and take you in to town. Do as I say." He looked down into her eyes. An ache of need pressed in his belly and he leaned down, settled his mouth on her

160

soft, trembling lips for a kiss he'd wanted for years. "Do as I say," he repeated softly and rode off, knowing that he was about to do the first wrong thing he ever did in his whole life.

* * *

With the sound of galloping hoofs riding away, Jonathan actually ran his arm across his brow and watched Kathleen return to the house.

This assignment wasn't nearly as easy as he expected. In fact, the challenges were extraordinary. His own body ached, sensing the misery Rafe felt, but he already knew Kathleen's good heart. She was not about to let his Charge suffer without her caring hands to comfort him through it.

Jon glanced behind. To the left and the right. His brow curled and a hiss escaped his clenched teeth. Where had Lucifer gone? The absence of that malevolence made him feel lighter and far more nervous at once and the angel turned his eyes to heaven. "Can you please make sure Vivi is okay?"

* * *

Vivi was crying again. It seemed all she did lately, trapped in the dark cabin and nary a breath of fresh air to be found unless someone entered or left through the heavy door. Unable to communicate with anyone but Brown Bull, she often sought conversation with him. He was a gruff man, probably ten years Rafe's senior, but there were bright moments when she enjoyed his strange humor and the sound of his guttural accent.

She pondered the loss of her many powers when she'd fallen to earth, her ability to understand the thoughts of human, the languages, and cultures. She'd become steeped in the simple struggles of her existence with Rafe, the easy pleasures of their bodies, and wonderful explorations of ideas. Alone in the dark cabin, Vivi came to realize that she was now somehow even more human than ever.

Trying hard not to count the passing days and weeks, she battled fear and depression, the cumbersome growth of her belly, and miseries of her body. The old Arapaho woman was gentle, even kind, but obviously displeased with having to remain closed with Vivi inside the cabin. Often she'd leave for a several days, but she never left her patient fully alone, and never fully alone with Brown Bull. This was among the few things that made Vivi smile. What did the old woman think she was going to do? Steal the Chief's son away? Drag him off to live a white man's life? Brown Bull had already seen that way of life and made his choice. The old woman had nothing to worry about.

Outside she heard the thump, thumping of an axe. Sadness gripped her as she quickly eliminated the possibility that Rafe had miraculously returned.

* * *

Brown Bull split a log with power and precision and looked around. The old grandmother had left earlier and it was the first time he was completely alone with Vivi. He wished comfort and warmth for her. Even though it was woman's work to gather wood, he found a strange pleasure in doing what Bennett used to do for her, showing her he'd sacrifice for her, work for her. Perhaps soon after the child was born he'd love her even better than the white man could. He'd have a good conversation with Vivi that very day, maybe even touch her, but as he lifted and swung the axe, Brown Bull was rudely reminded that the old grandmother was wise. Coming around the bend to care for Vivi walked not only his first wife, but also his second, and Brown Bull shook his head with a touch of frustration. He curtly handed the ax to Small Feather, his first wife, and then pointed to the shed so that his second wife, Long Willow, would understand that it was her job to butcher the elk he'd brought down.

Brown Bull could have had any beautiful woman of the village. He was strong and powerful and many a pretty girl had cast a gaze his way but as a young warrior, he instead chose Small Feather as his first wife. She was the widow of a man he'd played with as a child and fought beside as a warrior. A man who's raging ego cost him his life in battle.

162

Small Feather was not small at all. She was a large, broad, bad-tempered woman with a stern and often cruel attitude. She was cold among the people and cold beneath his hides and Brown Bull was not happy with her.

Four years after taking Small Feather as wife, her younger sister, Long Willow came of age and he immediately took her as second wife. It was a custom to take sisters, as they had grown together and understood each other. This was done to not only help lighten his first wife's workload, but to bring harmony to his lodge. Long Willow was nothing like her sister. Although she too was thick around the middle, Long Willow was soft and warm, sweet and loving. Unfortunately she was relentlessly bullied by Small Feather and often he would leave the warmth of his lodge to find peace elsewhere, preferably among the men in the council lodge. Sympathetic eyes watched when he would enter, but he ignored them, stating that all men must escape their wives just as they must escape the enemy.

Brown Bull adored Long Willow and found himself taking her beneath his warm hides far more often that her brusque, older sister, usually to comfort the girl's tears and soothe away the sadness in her heart. Had he waited and only taken Long Willow, would he still intend to take Vivi? And how would Vivi handle the mean-spirited first wife she would need to deal with? All his curiosities would play themselves out in time. For now, having put his wives to their tasks, Brown Bull proudly strolled toward the cabin.

"Oh please don't close the door," Vivi called softly from the cavernous depths. "It's so dark and stuffy in here. I just want to feel the cold air."

Brown Bull grinned and nodded, permitting the door to remain opened several inches. "Have you any needs?" he asked.

Vivi grinned. "Just fresh air and some conversation."

Even across the cabin, he could see the concern in her eyes, how her hands locked in her lap. What would it take to make her forget Bennett? "Vivi, Grandmother says you must not be so worried. You know I have vowed to go down and find your man as soon as the trail is passable." He stepped closer and dragged a chair near the bed.

The beautiful woman sighed and it made his heart ache. She slowly swung her bare feet to the floor and sat up, looking directly into his eyes and stealing his breath from him. "Something terrible has happened. Will you be able to reach him soon enough to bring him back safely?"

"Only the Great Mystery knows such things. You will become chilled, lie under the blankets, Vivi."

Instead, she stood and slowly paced across the floor. Her hand braced at the small of her back and the bright light flowing through the door cast a sharp glow through the thin fabric of her sleeping clothes. Her body was luscious, rounded with child, inviting, and Brown Bull grit his teeth to restrain from taking her into his embrace. The woman must know his intentions, but if he did not speak them now, he would go mad from it all.

Taking her hand, he led her back to the mattress then closed the door against the cold that had prickled her flesh and made her cheeks a brilliant red. He stoked the fire and returned to his chair. "Vivi, if it is too late, I will take you into my lodge. You and the child will become mine."

Her eyes widened and she swallowed. "Too late? No, Brown Bull. No. He must return." She stood and scurried across the cabin, pulled opened the heavy door and walked on bare feet out onto the packed snow. "Rafe, oh God!" She sobbed and sat weakly on a pile of chopped wood. The two Indian women gawked curiously at her.

Brown Bull stood at the opened door. "You must know you will always be safe and protected in my lodge. You will be cared for, Vivi. You and your child." There was great comfort in knowing his wives could not understand his words. But with the gentleness of his voice, the relaxed lean of his body against the doorway, he caught the glance that passed between them. Small Feather bestowed and evil glare on the crying white woman, and Long Willow's eyes glowed with sadness. "You will always be protected," he said forcefully, intending to stomp away but stood, frozen before the shuddering, tearful Vivi.

"No, Brown Bull. You don't understand. I do not want to live without Rafe. I will not live. I can not be without him."

Hearing those painful words and observing the frail qualities in the woman he wanted, his breath stopped, locked tight in his lungs. There was only one soft place inside Brown Bull, the place of compassion he held for those he loved. It was time for him to again stand as the warrior. To sacrifice.

164

Taking Vivi against her wishes, whether Bennett lived or died, would destroy the life he loved within her. It would damage the heart of his sweet Long Willow. It would displease his grandmother, and as much as he did not wish to admit, it would give Small Feather yet another reason to torment him by making Vivi her new target. Taking Vivi was not good for his people, for his lodge, or for his own heart. The ache he'd carried since first seeing her intensified. Some things were wrong, and those things brought discontent and trouble among his people. No other white woman lived in his village. He could not ask so much of them all, only to satisfy his carnal desires. If he didn't feel so deeply for Vivi, he could simply take her as a prize then leave her behind or dead. The grandmother's promise to Bennett and his own heart denied him that action. Watching the woman's deep devotion and love for her man hit him like a bullet to the heart. Brown Bull had painfully come to see the truth.

He moved to her and lifted her in his arms, calling to Long Willow to follow him. Inside they made the crying woman warm and comfortable, and as the sun lowered behind the mountains, Brown Bull knew it was time to find Rafe Bennett, no matter the difficulties.

* * *

Rafe's body was in full rebellion. Pain and weakness rippled from his gut to his fingertips as the remaining poison took its last run at his life. He shuddered with agony, stinging misery gripped his belly and his head, and again he drifted in and out of consciousness. Jonathan hovered, paced and watched for hours as Kathleen nursed her patient, washed his sweaty flesh and prayed constantly in a soft, sad voice.

Deep into the night, Carl Christian charged into the cabin, concern and anger evident on his face. Finding Kathleen with the killer, he shook his head then slowly accepted. It was impossible to stop her from caring for the man. It would be like trying to keep the drink away from Gordon Heller.

He sat watch at the open bedroom door but it wasn't until the morning had fully bloomed that his brow curled. Pale light drifted across the sick man's sleeping face and Carl's heart shook.

"Hellfire!" he whispered. He'd seen that man before. That man was the outlaw, Rafe Bennett.

CHAPTER 23

Class Two Guardian Jonathan was correct. Lucifer was nowhere to be felt. Lucifer had withdrawn his earthbound presence. Oh, his minions were well at work, teasing and messing with the angels of the Traffic Department and playing their best hands against the Charges of the Elite Guardians. It continued, but Lucifer had removed himself from that arena, temporarily.

The entire Elite Guardian staff was on edge. Every one of them had received the bold notice, scrolling across their screens at the same moment and stating that Lucifer demanded a face to face meeting with the new Master Guardian, Paul.

Miriam sat curled on the big chair in Paul's massive new office and fought fearful tears. When he walked in, several folders in his hand and a substantial scowl on his face, his expression softened and he sighed. "Not you too?" he said and leaned back against the closed door. She looked like a terrified little girl.

Paul had just left a meeting with the Man upstairs. He was sternly reminded of the importance of preserving Rafael Bennett from Lucifer, and notified of the vast changes about to occur in the heavens. With the new century plowing ahead, humanity was poised to radically change the way protective heavenly departments will watch over the earth. This led back to Bennett and heaven's commitment to preserving him for better things. Bennet had lived eleven times already, and was currently working through his twelfth. Heaven wasn't about to lose him after working so long and so hard. Now, with Lucifer's demands, the only thing to do was feel out the enemy.

"What will you do?" Miriam asked, leaving his chair and sitting on one of the far less comfortable guest chairs.

He thumped into his seat and rolled his neck.

"You can't meet with him."

"Sure I can. Just … not here." Paul stated. Lucifer had pulled some serious weight, dropping fear into the hearts of everyone with his public demand, but Lucifer could demand nothing in heaven. The Devil also knew that Paul had no pull to get him into the celestial domains, even temporarily. There was no way in eternity Lucifer will walk those halls again. If he wanted to meet, he knew well it would require that Paul leave heaven. It would require a neutral ground. Whether Paul met with him or not was never a question. Both angels knew they would face each other. It was inevitable.

"No. Nowhere!" Miriam gasped. "You can't even consider such a thing!" Her voice trembled and a tear slid down her cheek.

"It's my job, my dear." Paul stood his ground. He was the Master Guardian, and Lucifer's demand pertained to an important Charge. Any threat to Rafael Bennett demanded his personal attention. He drew in a deep breath, pursed his lips and exhaled. "I have placed everything in motion to follow through. The meeting is necessary, it is expected, and I will speak with him."

"Why?"

Paul's head tilted, a wave of yellow hair drooped over one eye and he grinned sadly. "Miriam, you know Luc and I have history. You know it had much to do with His decision to place me as head of this department. You know I must go."

"What does Lucifer want?" she sniffled.

"What do you think he wants? He might suspect something is in the works. It's my job to convince him otherwise."

"And." she stood and crawled like a child onto his lap. "Is there something in the works?"

His hand soothed circles on her back and his face leaned down against her soft hair. "Nothing for you to be concerned with."

Another storm howled through the mountains. It had been many moons since Bennett left his woman and not once had the spirits seen fit to lighten the weather and allow Brown Bull to leave for his search. His mind rolled with concerns. Although Vivi still had time, should he not leave soon, Rafe would never be returned to her side before his child was born.

The grandmother was also concerned. She did not wish to be trapped at the cabin and forced to assist with the birth in the foreign log prison. She had begun to talk of taking Vivi to the village to assure a birthing the old woman could support. Brown Bull was against this, fearful that Vivi would not understand. That she might try to run and possibly die in the harsh weather.

"Then you must explain this to her." The grandmother grunted as she mounted her horse to take another leave from the cabin's gloomy captivity.

"I have tried. She demands that she wait for her man."

"Then," the old woman leveled a glare on the chief's son. "You must go and get him."

Snow pelted them, relentless shards of ice that burned and hissed as it touched their exposed face and hands. He did not wish to die searching a man he hoped was already dead, but the grandmother already knew this. Her eyes trailed to a rise behind the cabin and she snorted before riding off.

The rise. A place of prayer. It was the only reason his people had remained peaceful with old Pennywalker. Young men and seasoned warriors alike went to that place for focus and guidance, but what guidance could Brown Bull find there? It was not that he suspected spirit had no plan for him, nor that he feared the cold or even the trek to the lowlands through the treacherous passes. No, the answers were already clear but with one nod from the old woman, he had no choice but to honor her wish.

When a medicine woman commands that a warrior seek the guidance of spirit, she already knows what is in his heart. His father will soon know of her directive, or perhaps they had already discussed it. Brown Bull may be a chief's son, he may be a very wealthy and powerful man among his people, a man of great honor having done many great deeds, but at that moment he was a lost man seeking guidance and would follow through.

He spoke briefly to Long Willow, pleased to see that his sweet second wife, along with Calling Crowe, a strong, kind elder woman of the tribe, would remain with Vivi.

"I am leaving for the hill. Grandmother will send a warrior to protect you all. When I return, I will be leaving to find this woman's man."

"Husband?" Long Willow spoke softly, as Vivi slept fitfully across the cabin. "What if he is already dead?"

He stroked a large hand down her silky black hair. "I am to find him and return him, alive or dead. Care for this woman."

* * *

Rafe was dreaming. His mind finally slowed to a rhythm, a natural throb of heartbeat and health. His body relaxed beneath the sweaty sheets and a part of him was aware he was in Kathleen Heller's care. Ah, but a part of him was elsewhere.

He was in a fine ballroom he once saw in St. Louis, a place that glittered with gold, fancy paintings along the walls, and high arched ceilings. There were people all around dressed in their best, men dapper and straight, their clothing crisp and sharp, their movements and attitudes that of old money. There were beautiful women, their lovely gowns glowing and their ears and necks sparkling with jewels that flashed in the soft lamplights. And the music. The music. It pulsed with his heartbeat.

He gazed down at Vivi in his arms as he moved and danced, swayed with her body close. Her belly was large, pressed against his hips and he felt the soft roll of the infant, a tender calling to his flesh from the child within her. Vivi's eyes were amazing as always, the depth and golden hue teased and excited him. They were joyful and she laughed her soft laugh as they moved like smooth liquid on the ballroom floor.

The waltz altered. The beat stuttered, it stopped and began again, the melody dissolved into dissonance and a terror tore through his heart.

As beautiful as the vision of Vivi was, even amidst the discord of the evil energy around him, Rafe knew he had to wake. He had to think. He had to get back.

How long had he been gone? Numbers played in his brain, the background hissed with the confusion of Bible quotes and the sound of guns blazing and the thudding of racing hoofs. Numbers. It took him nearly three weeks to reach his stash, another five weeks to reach the Heller Ranch. He was at least another three or more weeks from reaching the cabin in the intense winter weather, and that only if the trails and passes were open. How long had he been in Kathleen's care? How long before he could leave? Vivi was nearing her time, he could feel it in the dream. His voice resonated, a raw crawling groan from his throat.

"The Lord is my shepherd … Surely goodness and mercy shall follow me all the days of my life: and I will dwell in the house of the Lord forever …"

"Psalm twenty-three," said a man's voice.

Rafe's eyes snapped opened. He blinked and begged focus, turned. It was not Kathleen's son. Kathleen was nowhere in the room. It was dark and one candle glowed at his bedside. "Who are you?"

"Name's Carl Christian. Guess I'll be famous. I'm the man gonna bring Rafe Bennett to justice."

Terror slithered through Rafe but even against his weakness, he was able to hide it. Making a slow movement beneath the sheets, he spoke calmly. "Then take this," he said and tugged pistol from its hiding place at his side. He reached it to the man. "Kill me now, 'cause you try and stop me from leavin' this place, I will kill you, Carl Christian."

The man never moved. "You can hardly lift that goddamn gun. 'Sides, Kathleen'll have my head if I kill you. I'll leave that for the hangman."

Rafe shuffled on the pillows, groaned and crawled until he could lean back against the rusted old brass headboard, his pistol still in his hand. The man underestimated him. He might be weak, but he felt stronger than when he took Gordon Heller down. He could easily end Christian's life in the blink of an eye. But why hadn't the man taken him in yet? What hold did Kathleen have on Christian? What prevented him from throwing Rafe over a saddle and hauling him off to jail?

The candlelight fluttered and flashed off the badge and Rafe felt a grin rise at the corner of his mouth. That's why. A good gambler always knew when he was holding the winning card, and Rafe knew what he had on Christian. It was a bluff, it was a hunch, but it was solid enough.

"As I see it, no one knows I'm here yet … and … no one knows you're the one buried Heller's body. Now, Carl Christian." Rafe reached for the tin cup of water at the bedside and sipped. "Looks like you and me, we both got us a few secrets."

Christian stiffened in his chair, his eyes narrowed and he didn't speak.

"Heller had to die. It was him or Kathleen and we both know it. You got feelings for that woman and frankly," Rafe's eyes twinkled knowingly, "don't you think she's suffered enough?"

The man remained silent, he glanced back and Rafe could see Kathleen's movements in the kitchen. With a smooth quiet sigh, Christian reached and pulled the door closed.

"Don't think for a minute I won't kill you," Rafe grinned maniacally.

"Oh, you got no problem killin'. But you ain't gonna kill me."

"I ain't?" A brow rose and he fingered the trigger.

"No. You ain't gonna kill me 'cause you already know I'm lettin' you go."

Rafe didn't know such a thing, but his expression never changed. Instead he nodded congenially. "Nice of ya."

Christian stood and slowly paced at the foot of the bed, his eyes constantly on Rafe and his pistol securely deep in his holster. "I been watching you for more than a week, Bennett. Watchin' and listenin' to you talking with fever. You got someplace to be, don'tcha? You ain't gonna do nothin' to keep you from getting to your woman. And you're figurin' you got a better chance escaping if I try to take you in alone." His pace stopped and his glare intensified. "Here's the deal. You got three days and no more. I'm takin' Kathleen into town. Sheriff thinks I been trackin' Gordon Heller. There will be a posse out for him within hours."

"The woman died?" Rafe almost choked, thinking of the poor dead whore, of the brutality Kathleen had miraculously survived.

"She did. In three days, that posse's gonna suspect maybe Heller came back here. So, you got three days to get outta here." He pushed

172

the door open with one finger, Kathleen stood close, her eyes fearful and on Rafe. "Out there," Christian continued, "across the house is your saddlebag. All your cash is in it. When you're strong enough to get to it, you're strong enough to leave. I never wanna see your face again, you hear?"

"You ain't ever gonna see me again, Christian. Take some of that money for Kathleen."

"She don't need your stolen cash. She already accepted enough of your help."

Kathleen pushed into the bedroom and Christian gripped her elbow tenderly. "One minute, Carl. Just gimme a minute." He nodded but stood firm at the foot of the bed as she lowered herself to sit at Rafe's side.

"Mr. Bennett, I wanna thank you," she whispered, ran a hand over his cool brow and smiled sadly. "There's food for ya, everything you need. You get strong before you leave."

"I'll be gone today," he said softly, holding her plump hand in his.

"No, wait 'til you're strong enough. I'll keep you in my prayers. You and Vivi."

Rafe blinked, his heart stuttered and his eyes burned. He nodded, wordless as she lowered to embrace him. Finally he spoke into her ear. "You live a good life, Kathleen."

"S'go." Christian said and she stood, straightened her skirts and left the room. "Three days."

"Christian," Rafe called and the man turned. "You be good to her." "Three days."

* * *

Messages shot back and forth, Lucifer beginning his negotiations for a perfect meeting location in the most appropriate place, earth. Of course, Paul's reaction was to laugh. "Be reasonable, Luc," he typed. "We both know that only neutral ground will suffice."

"Ah, then I will assume that hell is out of the question," came the glib response.

"I've no interest in seeing the inside or your office, my friend."

"Oh, but I was looking forward to seeing the inside of yours. Such a promotion, my dear Paul. You must be bursting with pride."

Paul ignored the comment. "Will you consider the Platine Galaxy?"

"I was not aware that you had such an interest in ancient ruins, my brother. It would serve as a bit of nostalgia for me. I would enjoy that. Miniara?"

The planet Miniara was once a beautiful place, populated with beautiful humans, peaceful and promising, as were so many of the planets in several galaxies across the vast universe. But Miniara also held a bit of nostalgia for Paul, it was the first planet to fight Lucifer. Oh, it fell and fell hard, many of its inhabitants now working diligently at Satan's business and many simply struggling to pay their dues, but for one shining moment in Miniara's history, even God smiled. What began there has continued for eons and now, earth carried on the fight against Lucifer.

"Miniara. It is settled."

* * *

Brown Bull knew there was little time and he sensed the spirits would be harsh and quick. He sat in the freezing wind at the top of the sacred hill and closed his eyes. His prayers floated to the surface of his exposed chest and poured out to the heavens. Emptying of his ego, of his concerns and confusions, he quickly endured the pounding of power upon his soul. Strong wind slammed his body and knocked him to his back on the frozen, snow covered ground. Mother Earth caressed him, the cold snow warmed and soaked his back as the brilliance of the milky white sky split opened and sunlight sheared through the clouds onto his face.

As suddenly as it began, all was made apparent. The journey would be difficult, a true test of the warrior, but at the end, he was assured he would find Bennett alive and struggling, making his way back. Brown Bull was given a clear vision of exactly where he would find the man, broken and prostrate beneath a curled rock in a deep canyon. He did not question where this canyon was, for he knew the signs would be given as he needed them.

The profound energy of the Great Spirit released him with a jolt and Brown Bull gasped as though he hadn't breathed for a very long time, as though he had just been given life again. He slowly stood and gazed down at the cabin. A warrior was riding to the door on his pony. All was set and right. Brown Bull mounted his horse and headed south.

CHAPTER 24

It took Rafe two days to be able to stand and walk all the way to his saddlebag. He packed the dried meats and hardtack Kathleen had left him, mounted his horse and rode north, looking back once to see a distant coming of the posse Christian had warned him about. He picked up the pace and was soon deep in the low foothills and heading toward Vivi.

Four more days passed. Beside him, Jonathan had changed his approach. He now wore human clothes, a hat, a blanket coat similar to Rafe's, and rode a fine grey steed. He watched the man wobble and groan but often gave a soft clicking sound of his tongue to keep both animals moving ahead. Near sunset, Rafe had lowered his head to the horse's neck, his hands drooping at the reins and his breath heavy.

"Come on, Rafe. Vivi is waiting," Jonathan said quietly and to his surprise, Bennett slowly rose and looked right at him.

"Who the hell are you?"

Jon gulped. This was a new development, one he certainly didn't expect. He had only chosen human trappings to better understand the difficulties his Charge faced and hopefully assist where needed. Jon mistakenly expected that he would have control over whether Rafe would be able to see him or not. Apparently, that was not so. Ah well, best to just roll with it. He reached over and took the reins from Rafe's weak grip. "Name's Jon, and I'm just a friend. We've got a long way to go, Bennett. Can you keep moving?"

Rafe nodded, tugged the reins free and cleared his throat. "Yeah, I can keep moving."

Jon urged Bennett and his tired horse deeper into the mountains, slowly led them through a pass, and up higher. At the vista they could see the glory of the Rockies, looming powerful and half veiled by fierce spring snow storms, their ragged, rocky peaks boldly spearing the sky far above the milky robe. They rode into the night, and suddenly, Bennett dropped with a grunt to the ground. Jon helped him to a wall of rock sheltering him from the weather and built a fire. He dug into Rafe's saddlebag, retrieving the last of the provisions, pitiful little, no wonder the man was weakening at an alarming rate.

He glanced around them. A long way to go was a gross understatement. It could be weeks of travel hindered by whatever the weather saw fit to throw their way. At least most posses avoided following in such treacherous terrain. Most of the native peoples were huddled close to their fires during a storm, but unfortunately, most of the game was also hunkered deep and safe against it too.

It was like a whisper, a tease, and Jon turned. There, at a nearby stream, the last unfrozen and free flowing water they were likely to see from there on, stood a deer. She was lit by the mottled full moon peeking through the clouds and bouncing off the pure white snow. Delicately leaning toward the water, Jon knew she was a gift to the human in his care. He reached carefully and drew Rafe's rifle from the saddle holster.

"What do you think you're doing?" groaned Rafe and Jon shushed him quietly. He stepped cautiously around the horse and aimed, shot, and said a silent prayer as the deer fell gracefully to the ground. Jon turned a grin to Bennett. "We eat meat tonight."

* * *

Paul soared then landed on the third planet from the second sun of the Platine Galaxy. His feet settled in the once lovely city of Miniara, the main town square that once bustled with life and vitality so very long ago. His wings folded elegantly at his back and he sighed. Such a feeling, flight. Something Paul hadn't done in many, many centuries.

As promised, Lucifer sat at the fountain. The pool sprinkled water and sang musically, a touch the dark angel probably thought to be both soothing and playful, something to lighten the mood and please his long time friend. Lucifer was not a devil, he was never evil and his motives were far more noble than any human could imagine. Yes, he vied for the souls of men and women alike, rich and poor, people of high standards and people of low morals, but his reasons were his own. It was and always had been his deepest desire to protect God from the monster He had created by giving humankind free will.

Paul remembered the explosion as though it was only yesterday. Lucifer standing before the Grand Committee and begging the omnipotent Creator to back off, deny humans the opportunity to hurt Him. When God refused, pointing out that man must earn heaven by making the right choices during his life, Lucifer went mad with the decision.

"I will prove it to you, my Father! I will show you how weak and unworthy these beings truly are! Let me show you how evil they can be! I can prove it! If I show you, will you then deny them this right of free will?"

"I will not," God spoke and thus the war began, a war that has from its inception actually been the necessary balance of all things. Lucifer was banished from the heavens and his enormous ego alone still told him he would win, would prove his point and protect the Father from these creatures that did not, and never would, deserve His love. This fundamental difference in philosophy alone should have destroyed the friendship between Paul and Lucifer, but it had not. They loved and hated each other, respected and thwarted each other, were worthy adversaries and respectful comrades.

They seldom spoke, and thus the reason heaven was so shaken by the demanded meeting. Lucifer had always kept Paul in his prayers and Paul always kept Lucifer in his. God alone heard it all.

Paul walked toward the stone fountain and Lucifer stood, smiled and reached out a hand. He took Paul's tight in his own and pulled him into a hardy embrace. "How was your flight?"

Paul grinned and shook his head.

"Must be nice to get out of the office, my friend."

179

"How are you, Luc?"

"As well as can be expected. You look tired, older. All that sitting behind a desk must be aging you, brother."

"Thanks so much." They settled at the edge of the fountain. "What is it you want, Luc?"

"Rafael Bennett."

"Denied."

"Ah, but you know that eventually I will have him. Brother, this is his twelfth life and I have come this close eleven times."

"You have failed eleven times. You will never have him. I will make sure of that."

"Not you, Paul. He was easy pickings this time around, until you sent Vivi. Now that was an interesting battle but again, I won."

"You did not win, Luc," Paul turned a knowing grin. "She fell in love. It happens, you know that. Not the first time, won't be the last. She was green, perhaps another would have held on longer, but a human praying and hoping for Bennett is nearly as good as an angel."

Lucifer grunted. "And now, another green one, a newly assigned Class Two Guardian. Jonathan. He's not even sure of his powers, are you aware of that?"

Paul ignored the comment, running his fingers through the warm, swirling water in the fountain.

"Ah well, I shouldn't tease you." Lucifer sighed. "Lord knows I have issues finding good help too." They were silent for several moments. "I will have him. I've earned him. Whatever you throw in my path, I will prevail and you know it."

"I know no such thing. Tell me, Luc. Why Bennett?"

"Because you won't back off. Because you refuse me. Because you want him so badly."

"Not me, my friend. Not me. I follow orders, make no judgments and do my job. Nothing more."

And the two angels looked off into the distance, at the destroyed terrain of a once magnificent planet, ruined to annihilation by the taunting of Lucifer and at the hands of beings who knew nothing of what they were doing.

* * *

Brown Bull pressed ahead against snow and sleet and freezing cold, heated by his quest to find the man he was to bring safely into Vivi's arms. He suffered, and he prayed, each night calling out to the spirits with sacred words and songs. Three days, six, a week then two. He moved ahead, led by nothing but the belief that he would be taken to the exact place where Rafe Bennett would need him most. At one point he was guided to turn back, circle around and move to a place far closer to the cabin. On the third day of the third week, his pace slowed and he stopped, climbed to a protected area on a ridge above the canyon he recognized from his vision, and he waited.

* * *

Rafe grew strong and the travel continued. He spoke little to his companion who oddly reminded him of a young Frank Pennywalker. He watched over the man as the man watched over him. As they moved into a deep canyon, their horses picked carefully along the ridge then moved single file on a flat, narrow path, a treacherous ravine to the right, a sheer wall of rock to the left. The path widened as the day waned and Rafe cleared his throat.

"We'll camp 'til daybreak. This path is too dangerous to travel at night." He turned back and looked at Jon. "Ya hear me?"

"Yeah, I heard you. Listen Rafe, I'm gonna be leaving you soon."

"What?" Rafe chuckled, watching his breath steam in billows from his grinning mouth. "You going all the way back to the lowlands alone? That's stupid. We're a day, maybe two from the cabin. Stay with us, keep warm 'til the weather breaks before you go back down."

"Nope, I'll be leaving tonight. You'll be fine, you won't be alone."

"Oh, I'll be fine." Rafe grunted. "It's you I was thinkin' about, you fool. Don't be an idiot."

Silence.

"Ya hear me, Jon?"

Silence. Rafe turned, his saddle creaked and he twisted his back. Jon was nowhere in sight, not behind on the long narrow path. He'd have heard if the man and horse had fallen. There was no explanation, he'd simply disappeared, and this wasn't the first time Rafe Bennett had had this kind of peculiar experience.

"Fuck," he hissed and plowed ahead. As the canyon widened, he spurred his horse with frustration. Had he gone mad? No matter, Vivi needed him and whatever his crazed mind invented to help him to reach her, he'd accept. Without Jon to worry about, he decided to ride as far as he could. He was familiar with that particular canyon. There were several miles before it again narrowed, so he could cover some distance before stopping for the night.

"S'go," he whispered to the horse and the animal moved to a trot. Another poke of his heels at the horse's sides and it was a near gallop. Then, abruptly the animal jerked, twisted in a soft patch of snow and threw Rafe into a shallow gully with a squeal and shuffle. The horse dropped to his side and struggled then managed to regain his footing. Rafe yelped, shook his head and attempted to stand.

"Dammit!" he shouted, dragged himself toward a curled rock and struggled to remove his boot. His ankle was swelling quickly. "Dammit!" The horse stepped close, nuzzled against Rafe's shoulder and whinnied. "Not your fault. Mine. Hush now." He smoothed fingers between the animal's ears and finally the horse stepped back. Rafe packed snow around his painful ankle and groaned. "Dammit," he said one more time.

"I did not expect you to be so foolish, Rafe Bennett."

The voice came from the darkness, and in a flash, Rafe gripped and aimed his pistol. "Show yourself."

Brown Bull raised his hands and stepped closer, chuckling. "It is I."

Rafe dropped the pistol, shook his head and shifted his position. He rubbed his eyes and rolled his neck. "Vivi, okay?"

Brown Bull stepped forward to take a look at the injured ankle. He scowled and leaned back on his heels. "She is near her time. Can you ride or must we wait until morning?"

"I can ride. Just help me onto my damn horse."

* * *

With the first ripple of a contraction Miriam felt Vivi's fear and pain and made a decision. Paul was still gone, still meeting with Lucifer and every resident in the heavens held great concern for him. She was helpless to assist the one she loved, so she chose to go where she could be of some good. Permission was granted the moment the idea drifted into her mind and she took leave of her post.

In the blink of an eye, she stood inside the cabin and watched the old Arapaho woman shake her head. It would be a long, difficult labor and she too had made a decision. She wrapped the writhing woman in a mountain of blankets and created a device from long wood poles to drag Vivi away.

"No! No!" Vivi cried and slapped away the hands attempting to take her from the bed. Miriam stepped forward.

"Let it be as it must, Vibrant Light," she whispered and Vivi gasped, looked into Miriam's face.

"I'm so afraid! Where is Rafe?"

Miriam smiled. "He is almost here, but these women must take you to their village. This will be difficult for you, but I will remain at your side through it all. Do not be afraid, little one. Do not be afraid."

The old woman grunted and also looked directly into Miriam's face.

"I am here to pray and assist, old grandmother," Miriam said respectfully.

The ancient medicine woman nodded and helped Vivi onto the travois.

CHAPTER 25

The old grandmother looked back as the ugly log cabin dissolved behind the winter worn spindly trees and drifting snow. As the panting white woman cried out in pain on the travois they slowly made their way along the trail to the village. Walking beside Vivi was the ethereal form of Miriam and the grandmother wondered, at what time had she ever been told that so many of the spirit would come to her? Had she missed a sign? Misinterpreted guidance? Was the presence of these strong spirits, one laboring as woman and one floating as spirit, a bad omen? A good prediction? Did it have nothing at all to do with her or her people? It would not be the first time she had been called to assist where she could not understand. Not the first time at all.

In her youth, the old grandmother was known as Moon Seeker. She was Comanche and she was born a twin, a serious crime that nearly cost her life even as she slid from her mother's womb; it was believed that the second twin was cursed. Moon Seeker was a quiet, plain child but her sister, Fawn, was beloved and beautiful. In their fifteenth summer, it was clear that just as spirit saw fit to bestow much beauty upon Fawn, spirit also saw fit to fill Moon Seeker with great power. Already she had become known for her skills and ability to heal wounds, find game and warn of enemy attack through prayer and visions alone.

Jealousy within the band grew. The established Holy Man declared he would provide no guidance for controlling Moon Seeker's abilities

185

and he warned of terrible disasters ahead. He found himself confused and impotent when Moon Seeker was present. It became heartbreakingly obvious to their father that the only way Fawn would become wife to a warrior of quality, was if her sister was to die.

Fawn was given more than beauty; she was given a deep compassion of heart and a strong intellect that would prove intriguing to her future young husband. Before her admirer dared collect horses to buy her from their father, Fawn proposed a small hunting trip alone with her sister. The women of the band often hunted together, it was excellent practice with bow and arrow and took care of them all when the warriors were off in battle. Nothing was thought of the short trip and the girls happily rode into the hills.

"Moon Seeker, I will not let them kill you," Fawn said softly as they settled to watch for game.

"Is it your plan to kill me yourself then?" One brow rose and Moon Seeker bumped her twin's shoulder playfully. "Worry not, I already understand your plan."

Tears slid down Fawn's lovely face. "Where will you go?"

"North."

"Will you be safe?"

Moon Seeker smiled. "I will be safe and loved and I will live long. You … will have many fat children and a fat husband who will be honored for his strength and bravery."

"No … I will wed Strong Arrow. He is thin as a reed!"

"Not for long," Moon Seeker stood and embraced her twin. "I will miss you."

It took several moons to arrive with the Arapaho. Sign language alone saved Moon Seeker. The warriors of many peoples had already become leery of strangers. They were as highly skilled with rifle and pistol as with blade and arrow. She was taken in and indeed safe. Respected. Honored. Loved by a chief, mother to a chief, and grandmother to a man soon to be chief, her life had been lived as she envisioned. But she worried for her grandson, for there were many difficulties in the trails ahead for Brown Bull.

She looked back at the laboring white woman. The grandmother chewed her lip with toothless gums and worried that the travois would cause damage to the infant. She worried that they could not travel quickly enough. She worried that Vivi was not warm enough. She wondered at the calming spirit woman with them. And as they trekked the slippery miles to the village, she wondered what would come of the birthing event ahead.

The lovely white woman might die, for spirit had a way of choosing a mother for a child, or a child for a mother, but death would not come easily on her watch. She understood little of the strange white people, but she did know that it was her responsibility to use all her skills to protect Vivi and bring her child safely into her arms. With the blessings of Great Mystery, Brown Bull would return with Bennett and all would settle as it should be.

The village women assisted Vivi as the old grandmother entered the birthing lodge to see that all was in order. She birthed her Arapaho village women in the way of the Comanche. She nodded approval as she walked around the center post, a sturdy, smoothed tree trunk buried deep in the earth and standing straight and tall. At the foot of the post, a shallow ditch lined with soft skins to receive the new infant. At the side, another mound of soft skins for the laboring woman to rest upon until her time arrived. There was a small fire and the mellow smoke of burning sage and cedar. The smoke hole above pulled the holy scents to the heavens. Herb tea prepared was and ready. All was in place and the old woman was pleased.

* * *

Vivi shuddered with fear. Her eyes circled then rose to the small smoke hole where a shred of brilliant light dripped into the dimness. Panic gripped her but Miriam's voice soothed her. "You will be fine, sweet Vivi. Do as you are told and you will be fine."

"Rafe," she cried out as she lowered to the nest of skins and rolled to her side in agony.

"Hush, Vivi. He will be here soon. This is all you must focus on now." Miriam settled beside Vivi and sighed softly. "If you listen carefully, you will understand the old woman's instructions. Listen very, very carefully."

And for several torturous hours Vivi tried to understand. It was not until her pains had grown beyond reason and her mind could no longer comprehend what her body was attempting to accomplish that she truly understood the old woman's words. It was an astounding moment and she smiled wide, her face covered with sweat, hair soaked and permeated with the scent of the burning herbs.

"You understand?" The old woman gave a toothless grin and a childish wink.

"I do. Tell me what to do Grandmother. Tell me. This can not continue, for I fear I will die."

"No, you will not die. You will give life and it is right and good … as it should be. Are you ready?"

A rippling pain wracked her and she cried out, but the moment she could breathe again, she looked into the grandmother's eyes and nodded. "I am ready," she gasped and was helped to her feet.

Vivi stood, wearing her sweat soaked, tattered night shirt. Her feet straddled the skin-lined indention and her shaking hands gripped the wooden pole tightly. Her face leaned in, pressed against her fingers and she sniffled, gasped and prepared for the onslaught of yet another contraction. She screamed again, loud and desperate and wrapped her arms around the pole, her brow pressed hard against the wood, her heart determined to hold herself to the task of giving life to her child.

Visions swept and flurried like a whirling snowstorm behind her tightly closed eyes, images of heaven, the faces of Paul and Lucifer, of Rafe and Miriam, of the old woman and the others assisting, mixed and melted together. Another contraction and then another came immediately on its heels. Vivi shrieked; pressed down as the old Grandmother sang softly, Arapaho words of courage and strength.

"Soon, Vivi," shouted Miriam.

"Soon," bellowed the old woman and she nodded her head quickly. The younger women assisting held Vivi's hips firmly as the old woman reached between her shaking thighs. Vivi cried out again, trembled but refused to collapse and suddenly she felt it, the tear of soft flesh and the slither of tiny new life. With another push, the placenta and baby were gently, tenderly laid in the shallow cradle of soft hides. Vivi was shuffled to her own nest and watched desperately as the Grandmother worked over the child.

Holding her breath and praying, Vivi could feel Miriam's hand squeeze hers. She sobbed. "Tell me it lives!"

The old women bent low over the hides and slit the umbilical cord to free the wriggling infant who suddenly, as though on cue, wailed out its presence.

"It is a daughter," the old woman handed the bundled child into Vivi's outstretched arms. "A girl."

Vivi had lost her ability to understand Arapaho as quickly as she had gained it. All her attention was on the tiny creature in her arms. A wriggling, wailing girl child with wild, soaked dark curls.

* * *

Rafe rode hard, Brown Bull at his side. They galloped the open spaces and charged through the trees, along the frozen stream and up the final rise. Heedless of mountain lion or grizzly, of freezing wind or icy obstacles, the men plowed ahead, hardly slowing even for the deep darkness of a moonless night.

The next morning blazed clear with brilliant blue skies. Rafe stopped, hobbled on his swollen ankle to the small pond and pounded the heel of his fist against the crackling ice. Water trickled up through the cracks and he moved for his thirsty horse to reach the life giving liquid. His eyes squinted against the bright day and he shivered. The long winter would end, spring was coming sure as salvation, it was coming. He would take Vivi and his child to the flatlands and begin their lives. There was plenty of money to stake the card games in St. Louis and take care of his family until he decided what to do next.

When the animal moved aside, Rafe reached for Brown Bull's horse then urged the Arapaho to drink before lowering to a knee and gulping the icy water himself.

What to do next? He could hardly think about the next day, or the next week. He refused to think the worst, but what if he is too late? What if Vivi didn't survive the birth? What if … what if … what if …

"Six, seven hours," he said and ran a sleeve across his wet chin. "We'll be there before dark." His eyes took in the robust Arapaho, his swagger and surety and as sudden as though a bullet had struck, he was saw something far different from the helpful man riding at his side.

Voices spoke and overlapped in Rafe's brain. Taunted, teased, agitated him.

"He's a liar. He's already killed Vivi. He's raped her and murdered her and your child," rumbled the ugly words, bouncing inside his mind, confusing him, terrifying him, pressing anger like heated blood through him.

Rafe drew in a deep breath and released it in a cloud of steam. Cooled of the ugly thoughts he shook his head to clear it. "S'go." They mounted and rode on.

The voices and thoughts continued and Rafe fought them, focused on reaching Vivi, seeing her healthy and safe and waiting for him. Several times he gasped, pushed back his hair, his brow furrowed with the confusion inside his head.

The path narrowed but he pressed his horse, Brown Bull tight behind as he broke into the clearing and spurred to a gallop. Panic soared through his soul. There was no smoke at the chimney, the heavy door was opened wide, yawning, exposing dark emptiness.

He leapt to the ground, limped as fast as his damaged ankle would allow and stood at the bed, the bedclothes rumpled, cold to the touch. The hearth had been silent for some time as well.

* * *

"Where is she?" An evil growl crawled from Bennett's throat. He slowly turned to face Brown Bull who said nothing, braced himself, readied for the attack as no answer would suffice at that moment.

Brown Bull had sensed the overwhelming evil energy weaving tighter and tighter around Bennett for miles and he already knew what he must do. Inside his head, he too had heard a voice, a different, guiding and insistent voice.

"Protect Bennett against himself and his tormentor, Brown Bull," it said, calm but insistent.

When Rafe drew his pistol, he was crazed. "Where is she?" He shouted and moved closer until the barrel pressed against Brown Bull's chest. "Where ... is ... she?"

Brown Bull slowly raised his hand, gripped the pistol barrel then suddenly dropped to the ground and swept a powerful leg, knocking Bennett on his ass. The pistol fell and slid across the rough wooden floor. Brown Bull was immediately on his feet staring down with a scowl. His heel jammed hard into the man's gut and Bennett rolled but not far.

"I will kill you for this, you asshole! Where is Vivi? Answer me! Where is—"

Brown Bull aimed, slammed a foot down and Bennett was cut off in a gush of blood from his broken nose. Unconsciousness immediately followed and Brown Bull rubbed his aching heel.

"You have one very hard head," he said with a growl, wiped sweat from his face then heaved the man over his shoulder. With an unceremonious toss, Bennett was over the saddle of his horse and Brown Bull led the animal to the village.

The chief's son responded to none of the shouting welcomes as he rode toward the birthing lodge. There he simply dumped Bennett with a thud to the frozen ground. He freed the man's horse of the saddle and slapped the animal's rump to join the others at the river. Brown Bull glanced back only once before heading to his own wives and warm fire.

* * *

And Lucifer scowled but accepted his loss in this round for Rafe Bennett's soul.

* * *

The gritty, bitter bite of icy hard-packed snow burned against his swollen eye, then the sensation of lifting, lifting, lifting from dark unconsciousness, and the soft, muffled sound of a tiny cry. An infant.

Rafe's eyes fluttered opened and he shuffled to sit up, rubbing the ache at his nose as he looked around. Behind him, the Arapaho village, people moving about and completely ignoring him. In front of him, a

191

conical hide lodge, warmth flowing from the slight opening at the door flap and the soft shushing sound of a woman's voice drifted to him.

"Vivi?" He gasped and scrambled to his knees, pushed aside the soft flap and peered into the dimness. There, lying on a mountain of soft hides, the tiny infant at her breast and tears in her eyes, his Vivi. Rafe crept his way quietly to her side.

Her free arm reached out to him and he pressed his face against her shoulder, drawing in the comfort of his woman and child. He maneuvered to lay close, warm against her, words lost both inside his heart and head. Vivi sobbed softly as his large, cold, and dirty hand hovered over the small fuzzy head of his child.

"A girl," she whispered and Rafe released a pleased sigh, chuckled softly and raised his face to kiss Vivi's quivering lips.

"I'm sorry, darlin'. I tried to get here in time. I tried."

"Are you okay?" she whispered and carefully moved the infant from one breast to the other. Rafe cuddled closer, his hand resting along her arm, cradling his precious family to his heart.

"Fine. Just fine."

Two days later, Rafe stoked the fire in the cabin's hearth. On the bed, Vivi slept peacefully and outside, winter's last blast covered the mountains with a blanket of purity under a glowing full moon. He sat in the warmth and held his daughter on his knees, marveling at the softness and smallness of her.

They had chosen to call her Louise. "Lovely little Louise," he whispered. "What will we do next? Where will we go?" In his mind he saw a golden road, a comfortable life for them all, but it would take more money than he had stuffed in his saddle bags and buried under the cabin floor. Much more. Getting it would not be as fast or easy as he was used to, and the vision of a grand house and safe haven for Vivi and Louise demanded that he get that money in a better way. He couldn't risk the folly of his past. Even as a plan formed, he grinned at the tiny squirming babe in his big hands and sighed. "What will we do next?"

CHAPTER 26

By spring's first thaw, Vivi and the child were strong enough to travel so he took them to a fine hotel suite in St Louis. He bought himself a fancy satin vest and a new velvet jacket, purchased expensive snakeskin boots and had himself a visit with the barber. Then he polished up his pearl-handled pistol and announced that he'd be gone for a few hours.

Vivi's eyes widened but he soothed her with a tender pat on the shoulder. "Just headin' out to see what I can see, darlin'. I'll be back before you know it. And remember, our name is Forester. I'm Rafe Forester and you're Vivi Forester."

He strolled past the bank he always wanted to rob, tipped his hat to an acquaintance then stepped aside as a few fine ladies walked past. Spying the newest gambling house, he pushed his jacket behind his pearl pistol handle, entered with a comfortable swagger, and walked to the bar. Along the way he saw them all, pointing or talking quietly, some grinning wide, some leaning back in dismay and Rafe couldn't help but smile.

Even during the height of his outlaw activities, no one in St. Louis ever recognized Rafe Bennett as the outlaw he was. All the big money men recognized was his pistol handle and the fact that when Rafael Forester came to town, good card games were sure to follow. Horace Hook was there, surrounded by other players smelling of wealth and gambling fever. St. Louis gambling fever looked different than it did on desperate men playing in poor towns. These men moved smooth as silk, the only giveaway, that starving glint in their eyes. There were lots of ways to become wealthy in the growing country, and men with money often fell prey to the idea that poker was the best and easiest. Those men seldom lasted long.

Collier Pierce nodded a perfectly trimmed bearded chin his way and Rafe returned the salute. Phillip Logan too was at the tables, concentrating with his carefully perfected bluff, but still able to flash a grin. These men paved the road to what Rafe wanted, but as usual, this would take timing and calculation. He figured to stick around for four or five months. Usually he'd come and go quicker, but he had Vivi to think about, so what he intended to gain required careful planning.

Sipping whisky from a heavy crystal tumbler, he stepped close to Hook who instinctively tucked his hand tight to his chest. He turned and smiled. "Rafael Forester. Care to join us for a few hands?"

"Good to see you, and good to see you're still wearing that diamond tie pin," Rafe teased with a chuckle. "No, thanks, gentlemen. Just got in to town."

"He's not finished checking out all the games yet," grunted Pierce good-naturedly. "Forester only gambles where the biggest money plays."

Rafe grinned. "I try to keep the gambling to a minimum."

"How about tomorrow night?" Hook asked, checking his cards as though something might have changed in the past few moments. "We're planning a big one. Logan's leaving for San Francisco and we're hoping to regain our losses."

Logan was a man Rafe vowed never to play against. The man was a master at cheating, so good that no one else could tell. Easily as good as Rafe. A hand of poker with Philip Logan was likely to take Rafe too close to killing the man where he sat. "Maybe," he said then raised his glass. "Win well, gentlemen." He left, having gathered all the information he needed.

Since the last time he was in town, they had all moved their play to the new, opulent gambling house owned by none of the players and deemed to be fair, neutral territory. They were, as usual, salivating for a little gaming with him and would most likely spread the word in hopes of setting up a high stakes match. Such games lasted days where the wealthiest would participate or observe. Rafe knew how to play those men. He'd cautiously win and lose, all in a calculated effort to make them comfortable, and then he'd drive ahead for the big take. After that, he'd leave town amongst congratulations and congenial grumbles about getting even next time. No one knew where he came from, and no one ever knew where he went. They never noticed how much he won because he won so subtly. They never realized how much they'd lost because of the intrigue of the game. For Rafe, it was all part of a plan he intended to pull off one last time. It had to be big, because what he wanted next required big money, more than he'd ever had at once in his life.

It was early and he'd be back at the hotel in time for supper with Vivi. All was well with his world, but something didn't feel right. It wasn't that bad feeling he got when danger was close, and it wasn't that burn that told him something was going to go wrong. It was something else.

The following rainy morning, lying warm and tight against his woman the feeling grew and loomed then blazed clear. If he wanted the golden life he envisioned, he had something important to do first. Rafe woke his little family and quickly took them to an outlying town to locate a minister.

"Why?" Vivi asked. Rain tapped on the roof of the hired carriage and she bundled the baby tighter in a blanket. "Why today? Why at all? I'm so afraid someone will recognize you."

Rafe rubbed his nose and the crooked bump on it from the Arapaho's moccasin. He figured it made him look different enough, and she'd said it made him more handsome. "Can't live the way I want us to life by hiding, Vivi. And you can't be lying all the time, pretending anymore. If we say we're saying we're man and wife, we're gonna be man and wife."

"But—"

"I ain't done much right in my life, darlin'. Let me do right by you and my little girl."

The hairless minister's head shined in the dull daylight. He was reluctant, eyeing the well-dressed man, his poorly dressed woman and the squirming tiny babe. "You steal this woman from another man, mister?"

"No, sir. I've loved this woman my whole life and it's time to make her my wife."

"Well past time, as I see it," he said with a growl, blocking their entry to the small church. He scowled at the baby and little Louise howled in response.

A small, thin woman with hair as white as mountain snow joined him at the door. She eyed Vivi and the infant sympathetically then smiled kindly up at Rafe. "Marry them, Howard. They came before God to live a good Christian life."

Rafe immediately liked the minister's wife. She'd compassionately looked at them without judgment, but he did regret forgetting to buy Vivi a new dress and vowed to never let his woman face such scrutiny again.

"I ain't marrying them, Blanche! He's a gambler. I've seen him in St. Louis. He's a sinner, I know it. She's probably a whore—"

"I am not!" Vivi bristled and Rafe grinned. His Vivi was a spitfire.

"Marry them, Howard," Blanche hissed and stamped her foot. The old man finally stepped aside to let them enter.

The minister sneered as though his church sanctuary had been soiled, but he opened the book and solemnly read, emphasizing the parts about faithfulness in sickness and health until death.

Rafe and his love stood at the altar before God and man and spoke vows with such depth and intensity it brought tears to his eyes. He may have forgotten to dress his bride properly, but he didn't forget to buy a ring for her, a plain gold band that fit her finger perfectly.

"You're man and wife. Leave."

"Now, baptize my daughter," Rafe grunted to the minister who'd already turned to leave.

The man swung around with a scowl, prepared to argue but light drifting through a stained glass window glinted off Rafe's strategically exposed pearl pistol handle.

"Blanche, go get some water."

* * *

Months had passed. Rafe explained that it would take time to gain the financing he wanted though gambling, but it seemed endless to Vivi. Knowing her time in the St. Louis hotel was temporary, she longed for the stability of the future he promised. Behind her on the big bed, Rafe snuffled his rhythmic snore and it was comforting. Beside her, little Louise gurgled playfully in the cradle she would soon outgrow.

Vivi pulled a brush through her long dark hair and looked into the mirror. She fussed with the white lace at her boned, high collar, and wondered about all the beautiful clothes Rafe had purchased for her. How many clothes did a woman need? There were several long flowing skirts, many pristine blouses, under things galore, special dresses adorned with fancy glowing details and soft cotton dresses. She marveled, and gazing at her reflection, remembered. Long ago she'd researched the women's clothing of the time and secretly wondered what it would be like to dress in such a way. It was a far cry from the soft tunics and sandals of heaven, nothing like the life she knew before falling. Her corset pinched and feet felt smashed in her tight high-heeled shoes, but as in her imagination, it was a glorious feeling to be a human woman. Of course there were massive difficulties, especially learning the joys and miseries of motherhood.

Rafe had purchased a lovely baby carriage so that she could take Louise out for daily strolls along the beautiful streets, but the summer had grown unbearably hot, so she preferred to stay in the suite and play with the baby while sipping iced tea.

She pinned her hair high, delighted to have finally mastered a simple style, then she smoothed a hand over her cheeks. She had recovered well after the birth but honestly wondered why she hadn't become pregnant again. She had not discouraged Rafe and often felt a prickling desire to give him another child, hopefully a son. With a sigh her eyes rose to the ceiling. God decided such things and she would be patient.

There was a shuffling sound outside the door and Vivi brightened with delight. She gathered Louise to her shoulder and left the bedroom to visit with her only friend in St. Louis, the sweet young maid who cleaned their suite. Melody Chase was no more than sixteen, but a hard worker who carefully planned her duties so that she would come to clean the Forester's rooms last every day. That gave her time to fuss over the baby and chat pleasantly with Vivi. It amazed her how important the young maid had become to her. She was tender with Louise and always smiling and those qualities brought an element of joy into Vivi's lonely days.

Rafe often left as early a noon for the gambling hall and never returned until almost dawn. From the soft feather pillow, she would watch him quietly tuck his winnings deep into a polished brass studded trunk, and carefully jot numbers into a small leather bound book before joining her in the warm bed. He would love her passionately, smelling mildly of fine whisky and cigars then fall into a deep restful sleep.

Vivi found it hard to relax afterward, wondering when he would talk with her about how much more he wanted to win, when they might leave St. Louis, and most importantly, if he was cheating at the tables. This often burned in her heart. She was no fool. Vivi understood what Rafe was and knew he was most likely not playing fairly. It terrified her that he might continue in the ways that threatened his salvation, but could not bring herself to ask about it. Being human, his lover and wife, had taken her far from her original responsibilities for his soul, but still, she worried.

With Melody, those worries fell to the back of her mind. She put on a cheerful face and carefully closed the door between the bedroom and parlor, assuring that they wouldn't disturb Rafe's rest.

"How are you this beautiful day, Melody?"

The girl smiled and reached for the baby. "I'm well! And how is lovely little Louise? Did she sleep?"

The baby had begun teething a few weeks earlier and Rafe, exhausted from lack of sleep, had grown terribly concerned. Against his insistence that a doctor be called to the baby's side, Melody calmly convinced him that she knew a better way.

"It's only her milk teeth commin' in, Mister Forester. The doctor will give her that awful snake oil medicine and I've seen many a babe die from that poison. Let me show you how to help little Louise, please," she begged and Vivi was grateful when he finally agreed.

The solution was a simple rubbing of whisky on the baby's gums. Quite possibly little Louise was just too drunk to realize she was in pain, but either way, she always calmed and slept better, and that permitted Vivi and Rafe the same benefits.

With a smiling Louise on her hip, Melody bustled around the suite, dusting and chattering about the hot summer, the hope for some rain, or what the cooks had prepared for dinner in the hotel dining room.

Rafe rose, ate breakfast and played with the baby so that the maid could tend to the bedroom. "She's a big help to you, isn't she?" he asked without looking at Vivi, all his attention on Louise.

"Melody's a dear. I will miss her when we move on." She sighed sadly.

Rafe nuzzle the baby's neck, making Louise giggle and hug him tightly around his neck. He turned to Vivi with a broad smile. "Darlin', maybe you won't have a reason to miss Melody."

Again, Vivi bit her tongue, afraid to ask. Did he intend to stay in St. Louis? Would she raise Louise alone in a hotel room while he gambled every day? She remained silent, spreading jam on her bread and wondering how to convince him otherwise. The hotel was beautiful, but she wanted a home of their own.

When the rooms were sparkling clean, Rafe stood, put on his jacket, tugged at his shiny vest and winked at Vivi. "Miss Melody?" he called before she left the suite.

"Yes, Mr. Forester?"

"May I accompany you to your home today?" He watched the shy, concerned expression grow on her face and smiled. "I've hired a carriage for the day and it's no trouble. After everything you've done for Vivi, it's the least I can do."

"All right, thank you."

"Meet me in the lobby in ten minutes?"

She blushed. "I'm not allowed to be in the lobby, sir. Not unless I'm cleaning it."

"Well, then meet me outside the front door. Surely you can stand there?"

Her blush deepened. "Yes, I can."

"Ten minutes, Melody."

Vivi waited until the girl had left then turned a squint at Rafe. "What are you planning?"

"You know me too well, darlin'." He smiled. "We'll see. I want you to do something for me today."

"What?"

199

"Begin to pack our things. We may be leaving as soon as tomorrow. Friday, at the latest."

"Really?" She was breathless with excitement and wrapped her arms around his neck. "Really?"

"Possibly tomorrow, but most likely Friday. Best to be ready."

"How? What's changed?" Already she'd begun to look around the room, mentally collecting their personal belongings and estimating how to fit it all in their new trunks.

"Don't worry you're little head. I gotta go now. I have a date with the maid." He kissed her lips softly and walked out, leaving Vivi so thrilled about the move, she'd completely forgotten her concerns.

CHAPTER 27

That night at the tables Rafe felt confident. He'd been watching them all carefully for months, sharpened his ability to count cards, and was sure that he could move from fair play to a little cheating without effort or detection. He was so good at it that it had been difficult not to slip a card in or out of his hand since he came to town, but he'd been winning fair and square. He knew Vivi was ready to move on, and so was he, so he'd played with skill and careful strategy until late that night when he was sure he had the winning hand. He didn't. When Pierce laid out his royal flush, Rafe blinked in shock. He was positive he'd counted that queen of hearts earlier, but he could be wrong. He could be still tired from the long sleepless nights when the baby wailed in pain. He'd intended to win fairly, but instead lost nearly five thousand dollars.

He grinned congenially and congratulated Pierce, sure that somehow the man had either managed a miracle, or created one on his own. He'd never noticed Pierce cheating before, but if a man was going to learn how to do it well, the St. Louis tables were the place to do so. Rafe chuckled and gulped his whisky. "So, gentlemen. Shall we go again tomorrow? Maybe raise the stakes to make it a little more interesting?"

They all nodded and groaned from the table. Every one of them had a wife at home, waiting, just like Vivi.

He sat beside their bed until the dawn and reviewed all the numbers in his little ledger. There was no other way to do this, he had to have a huge take and he had to make his move cautiously then get out of town.

"How much did you lose?" Vivi said softly but he startled at the sound of her voice.

He shrugged and groaned, rubbed his eyes then shook his head slowly. "Lots. Bad night, darlin'. But I'm gonna fix it all, so don't worry your pretty head. We're still leaving town tomorrow."

A tap on the door and he grunted to his feet while Vivi tied her dressing gown. "Who could that be?" she asked, following Rafe to the door.

"Welcome, Miss Melody." His voice was tired but he smiled, stepped aside and elegantly waved the girl into the suite. "Why don't you go on in and take care of Louise, she's waking a bit fuzzy."

The girl smiled happily, rushed to hug Vivi then quickly disappeared into the bedroom.

"She never comes until later. I don't understand?" Vivi eyed her husband suspiciously.

"Well, it's simple. I bought you a maid." His grin was smug and proud, but she continued to look at him as though he'd spoken pigeon. "Vivi, I didn't realize how poor Melody and her family are. I offered her a job. Her daddy wasn't keen on losing her when we take her to Denver ... he wasn't keen on losing the money she brings home. So I offered triple her salary and promised to send half of it back to her family every month. Now you won't miss Melody when we leave."

"You bought me a friend?"

"No, woman. I hired domestic help for when we move to Denver. She's good company for you, and good with the baby. I thought you'd be happy."

"But ... but ... I thought you lost last night. I thought we ..."

"I'll get it all back and I'll do it tonight. I told you, we leave tomorrow." Irritation ragged at the edges of his voice. He was pissed that Pierce had bettered him at the tables, that he risked so much money and worse yet, that his fair and square winning streak had come to an abrupt end. He had no choice and like always, he didn't like Vivi voicing her opinion about his plans. She'd do it anyway.

"You're going to cheat," she whispered.

"Woman, you know who I am. I'll do what I gotta do so we can move on. That's the end of it."

"Rafe, please, please don't cheat." She spoke softly forcing him to listen hard. "We need to start doing this the right way. I can't protect you if—"

"Protect me? I don't need your damn protection. I know who I am. Christ, sometimes I gotta say my real name out loud just to remind myself!"

"No! Don't remind yourself. You are Rafael Forester!" Her voice was a controlled hiss.

"I'm fucking Rafe Bennett—" he shouted but her hand clamped tight over his mouth, silencing him as tears slipped down her cheeks.

"Shhh." She glanced to the closed bedroom door, terror in her eyes,

He leaned close and whispered. "Hush, darlin'. She won't tell no one, she needs the money for her family."

"What if she does? The bounty on your head is a lot more than her salary will be. Oh, God, what if she ..." More tears soaked her face, the kind of tears that tore at his heart.

He really had no choice now. His stupid mouth could be the death of him and he needed Vivi to help him get through the day alive. He held her close and whispered. "She won't say nothing, she won't. But keep her in your sight all day, Vivi. Don't leave the hotel for anything and keep that girl close. Don't let her talk to the busboys or maids or anyone, you hear?"

Vivi nodded against his chest, sobbing quietly but standing strong.

"Pack everything, all of it. I'll buy train tickets for tomorrow morning and hire a private car for us ... but if we gotta run, I'll have a carriage ready too. Don't worry, Vivi. It's gonna work out just fine."

She nodded again and he held her tighter.

"Vivi," he said in a hushed voice. "And listen ... listen ... if I don't come back by morning, you take Louise and the money in the trunk and get on a train for anywhere. I'll find you. I swear ... I'll find you wherever you go."

And he left before she could protest or beg him to take them away now, before he could regain his losses.

* * *

She watched Melody like a hawk, but the girl showed no sign of overhearing that her new employer was the outlaw Rafe Bennett. She fussed with the baby, talked excitedly about Denver and helped Vivi pack. When their meals arrived, Melody paid no attention to the hotel workers and focused on her new responsibilities. By evening, Vivi began to feel confident that things just might work out. That night Melody would sleep in the big bed with Vivi and the baby, and Rafe would sleep on the fancy parlor divan when he returned to the suite. That way, he could be vigilant if Melody tried to leave. Of course, Vivi intended to wait until he arrived before laying her own head down. It would all be fine. Fine like he promised.

But only if Rafe came back at all, and Vivi fearfully wondered if cheating gamblers were hung. Seeing Rafe with a noose around his neck again made her tremble and she prayed harder than she ever had, before or after becoming human. Losing Rafe would make her life unbearable.

* * *

He'd gotten as much rest as possible but worried that he might not be sharp enough, so counting cards would not be his best plan. All he wanted was his five thousand dollars back. Rafe wasn't desperate to have more. In fact, for weeks he'd had more than enough to take his family to Denver and start their new life. Getting greedy always burns a man, and Rafe still felt the sting of it.

Hand after hand was dealt. He took four games and lost two, then won the next two, and he started to wonder if his winning streak was back.

Over the months in St. Louis, he'd had several conversations with a construction tycoon who told him that land in the mountains around Denver was rich with some of the best lumber a man could buy, so Rafe intended to own a lumber business. A few weeks earlier, he'd chatted with a banker at the hotel saloon who told him about a gold mine near Denver for sale. Of course, no one would part with a producing gold mine, and this particular mine had only shown small rewards. The owner needed to sell the mine and go back east to rebuild his life.

"Why would I buy a gold mine that's worth nothing?" Rafe asked, a glint in his eye and sure there was a joke coming next.

But the banker simply shrugged. "Truth? You probably shouldn't. But this guy … I don't know why … but I'm sure he just didn't dig far enough … gave up too quickly."

"You handling the sale of this particular gold mine?" Naturally Rafe was suspicious.

"No, no. I know the man though. He came to me for a loan to keep the mine going and I intended to give it to him. Poor man, he just lost his hope, I suppose."

Rafe's imagination soared with the possibilities of making money hand over fist in lumber, and maybe striking it big with a gold mine of his own too. There was gold near Denver, he figured he had as good a chance to find it as any man. The lumber would take care of his family, a mine would help him feel the thrill of the challenge.

The next few hands were lost, but he hadn't bet much. His mind buzzed with numbers. How much of his losses had he regained? How many cards had he seen that game? And was Pierce counting cards too? If so, a little slight of hand wouldn't be enough. He'd be caught. He folded a good hand and waited for the next deal.

Images of Vivi living like a fine wealthy man's wife in a big house on a hill played behind his counting. Thoughts of Louise growing into a beautiful young woman teased at his pride. And suddenly, strangely, something happened.

When Rafe stopped counting, he started winning. Hand after hand. The only way this ever happened before was when he was cheating like an expert, but Rafe had yet to pull one manipulation. His five thousand was back in his hands, and he kept winning. Five out of every six hands went to him and he knew he should stop while he was ahead, but the others wanted the chance to get some back for their own pockets. Again and again, he won and the cash piled high. Gambling fever had taken over every one of the men at the table, except Rafe. For the first time in his life, he was actually having fun.

Men and showgirls, bankers and people off the street came in, crowded around the table and shouted or cheered each time he reached for the pot. Outside the window it was darker than dark, the way it is right before dawn. He thought to stretch and yawn and voice his concerns about going back to an angry wife, but they all knew he was leaving town in the morning and weren't about to let him leave so easily. He feared Vivi might take the baby and run like he told her to if he played much longer, so Rafe made a different plan than he ever did in his life. He planned to lose.

He's won twelve thousand dollars overall, so with calculated strategy, he managed to lose twenty five hundred in the next four hands. The spectacle was over, the crowd dispersed, and the others finally grumbled about getting to a warm bed and bristly wife before the sun rose.

He walked back to the hotel, completely baffled by how the evening unfolded. His only real concern was Melody. Would she tell someone his real name? Ever? Should he dispose of her before it was too late? Or, maybe he should just take a chance. After all, his luck was running good.

Vivi was sitting on the velvet divan, nervously wringing her hands when he came through the door. "Oh God! You're here. You're safe!"

"I got it all back and more … and here's the best part, darlin'." He kissed her deeply then whispered. "I never had to cheat."

CHAPTER 28

It had been a very long time since Vivi was in a crowd. She nervously shifted from foot to foot, clinging tight to the baby, standing close to Rafe and avoiding the bustling throng. The train huffed in slowly and she wondered how they'd get on board without being trampled. Odd, people never bothered her before, but her confinement in Pennywalker's cabin and months in the privacy of their hotel suite had obviously taken its toll. She thought to shake off her silly fears, to smile and make small talk with the ladies cooing over little Louise, but it was too much to handle.

Her worries were for nothing. The porter rushed to them, led them down the platform and helped them onto the train at their own beautiful private car. The space was well appointed with elegant furniture, sleeping compartments and a well stocked bar that Rafe immediately took advantage of. As he filled his glass with golden whisky, the porter explained that he was at their service. He would come to take their meal orders and ensure they wanted for nothing. In many ways it was delightful, but in others it felt strangely like living at the hotel, only their suite was moving across the country.

Panoramic views slid past the polished windows and the gentle clacking of the wheels beneath her feet threatened to lull her to sleep. Rafe leaned close, smiled and sipped from his glass. "I'll take the first watch, darlin'," he whispered with a teasing glint in his eyes. "Go on and sleep in the bed. We're fine here."

As tired as she was, she couldn't bring herself to rest. After so many months of waiting, the past two days had been a barrage of excitement, terror, and jangled nerves. Fidgety and restless in spite of her exhaustion, Vivi decided that it was time to move around, interact and be part of the human race again. After all, she was human. She stood from the fancy settee and brushed a hand down the skirt of her dark blue taffeta traveling suit. All eyes, even little Louise's, looked up at her.

"I need to stretch my legs. I'm going down to the dining car to order our lunch."

"The porter will be here soon, Vivi." Rafe folded his newspaper, his head tilted and eyes questioning.

"I know. I just need to move around, that's all." Before they could protest or insist on accompanying her, she slipped out the door and onto the breezy walkway between their private abode and a passenger car. Vivi didn't realize she would need to pass through several cars before reaching her destination and decided to enjoy the trek. She walked along the aisles and smiled at passengers. She went from one car to the next, and yet another, before entering a crowded kind of saloon. Remembering her first experience in a saloon made her step briskly and keep her eyes down, sliding past grinning men quickly before entering yet another passenger car.

Stepping onto the next connecting walkway, the passing world caught her attention and she stilled. Beneath the loud rumbling of wheels and rushing wind there was a silence she craved. In that peaceful bubble, her mind calmed and she found herself taking inventory of her life. The shock she never permitted overtook her and came in waves. She had lost her heavenly world completely with one tender kiss from Rafe. Lost was the surety of heaven, the security of redemption and startlingly, the reality of hell pulsed beneath her very human flesh.

Lucifer's domain was so precariously close to human existence, she wondered how it all worked. God assigned heavenly beings to assist and watch over human souls, but Lucifer was always physically present in their lives, taunting, teasing, threatening. Recruiting.

Pressing a hand to her wild heart, thoughts of her life, of any human's life, and the choices they were forced to make felt like heavy weights on her chest. How could God ask so much of such frail beings?

How could he expect them to choose good over protecting the ones they love? How could she ever choose eternal salvation over sin if Rafe was in danger? The full impact of her fall crushed her soul and Vivi held tight to the railing, afraid she'd collapse from the burden of it all.

Was she ever worthy of her angelic status? Would she ever be worthy of heaven again? She tried with all her might to envision Mr. Paul and Madame Miriam, the faces of her wonderful colleagues above, but with all her efforts she could not see them. They were truly, completely lost to her. A prayer slid from her lips and her eyes drifted closed.

"God … you may remember me. My name was Vibrant Light and I was an angel in your army once. It seems so long ago. So very, very long ago. I was given an assignment to watch over an outlaw … Rafe Bennett … and I really did my best to carry it out … but I … well, I broke a rule … something I used to do a lot, I'm afraid. I guess it was the last rule you were ever going to let me break because now I have done the unthinkable, and fallen. Not only have I fallen from the heavens and become human, but I fear Lucifer himself is right at my shoulder at all times. I can't shake him. He is relentless. Not only to gain Rafe's soul, but mine too.

"I'm so very afraid. I know that I can not live in this difficult and challenging world without Rafe. I know it, but of course that's a selfish thought and not really my prayer.

"This is my prayer, Father, and if You still hear me, I want to ask … no beg … that You protect Rafe. Protect him and love him. He is a good man. Beneath his human weaknesses he is a very, very good man. Protect him and protect our beautiful daughter, Louise. It's all I ask. I know I am doomed for eternal damnation for all my flaws and bad choices, but let me take on the punishment for anything Rafe has done. I take it willingly. Just please, oh please, watch over and take care of him.

Vivi sighed then cleared her throat. "Oh, and just so you know, we are now going by the name of Rafael and Vivi Forester. Yes, it's a lie, but we are doing our best to live right. Thank you. Thank you. Thank you."

As her eye drifted open, the noise returned and the green earth raced past as a sudden jolt rushed through her. Vivi realized that she had done all that a human could do. She protected those she loved, she prayed for them, and she had only one thing left to her. To live. She would do it to the best of her ability, watch carefully, avoid sin as much as possible and never, ever again acknowledge the presence of Lucifer at her side. "You have no power over me," she shouted into the wind, but as she entered the dining car with newly restored vitality and drive, she could swear she heard low, growling laughter on the wind.

* * *

Rafe set aside his newspaper and cleared his throat. "Melody," he said and she suddenly stiffened nervously.

"Yes, sir." Her voice was a child's squeak.

He smiled and leaned forward, propping his elbows on knees, careful to sound and appear as kind as possible. "Melody, Vivi will need your help when we get to Denver. I'm sure you can see that she ... well my wife has lived a very protected life and isn't really prepared for a lot of things." He waited and the maid offered a subtle nod of agreement. "I've commissioned a house for construction. Don't tell her, I want to surprise her." He winked. "She'll need your help in setting up the household ... hire a cook, housekeeper, maid, gardener—"

"I will be your maid." She smiled proudly.

"No, Melody. You have only one responsibility, to take care of Vivi and little Louise. Understood?"

"But sir, you pay me so well, surely I must work harder to earn it."

"You have only one responsibility, to take care of Vivi and little Louise. Understood?" he repeated and she finally nodded again.

"Good. The house won't be finished for a few weeks. I'll show it to her when I feel it's good enough for a woman's eye, and then you'll help her hire the staff. The more ready she is, the smoother the move will be."

Melody lowered her eyes, her fingers twisted and knotted in her lap. "Yes sir ... but ... when all that's finished, when Vivi knows how to run your household and ... and children grow up, Mr. Forester ... well, there will be little for me to do." She looked up with tear glittered eyes. "Surely there is more you want from me. More I can do ... for you. I will do anything ... anything you want."

210

Rafe suddenly felt uncomfortable, the way he felt that day the noose tightened around his neck. He looked to the door, wishing Vivi would return that moment. "Ah, no, nothing. And yes, of course I know Louise will grow up but there will be more children. Don't worry your head, there will always be work for you, and your family will continue to receive money from me." It came out gruffer than he intended but he found comfort in the fact that the young maid had visibly melted. Her shoulders slightly curled in and blessedly she stopped looking at him like a hungry puppy.

"Ah! There you are!" He stood and rushed to Vivi before she even closed the door, swept her into a tight embrace and kissed her hard.

"Well," she gasped and struggled to regain her footing. "The porter will bring our meal soon. I didn't realize you were so hungry," she said with a wide grin.

"Uh … right. I'm going for a drink. Be back in a bit." He had to get away. Yes, he was hungry and a hot meal was on the way, but the burn of whisky and the company of men was what he needed that moment. That, and a plan to stay as far from the maid as possible. He ran a hand down his face and walked past seated passengers. Maybe a few hands of poker would set him right.

The saloon car employed no fancy dancers or bar maids, just a dignified Negro bartender. Men of means sat on silk brocade chairs and around tables, some shuffling cards, others talking quietly, all smoking expensive cigars and sipping imported liquor. Something inside him rattled and shook. He didn't want company or cards, the whisky would calm him, but his mind was locked onto a remembered sensation. He knew this feeling. It was impending trouble. Did Melody hear him shout his real name? Did she intend to use it? Did she want what he thought she wanted from him? Damn, he should have taken care of the problem two days ago, taken her outside of town and put a bullet through her head.

But with that thought another set of fears rushed through his heart like a herd of buffalo. Vivi would have never forgiven him.

One drink sizzled down his throat. Another. Then another, and finally things started to look different. Denver would be his real start. Their lives would be the way he wanted it to be. Maybe he was mistaken about the girl's insinuation. What would a young thing like that want with him? Even if she did know who he really was, it made no sense.

When he rode as Rafe Bennett, girls like Melody were a dime a dozen, but long ago they'd lost their sparkle for him. Now, he had Vivi.

He ordered another drink, sipping it slowly. He'd watch that little maid closely. If she made one more comment or, God forbid, move toward him, she would find herself falling from a speeding train late at night. He'd have no regrets. An accident is an accident. He chuckled quietly and the bartender raised black brows on his very dark face. Rafe shrugged. "Women troubles."

The man returned the shrug and topped off Rafe's glass.

Melody was a pretty girl, would it be so bad? If it ensured she'd keep his secret, would it really be that bad to bed the bitch? Blackmail. She'd hold him to her the rest of his life. The last thing he could ever confess to Vivi was unfaithfulness for any reason. He would lose her, and that could not happen. Glancing out a window he wondered how fast the train was moving, if the girl would die quickly or suffer, where could he toss her so that she'd never be found.

Then he came to his senses. Having a plan was good, but using it only if he needed to was better. He'd wait to see if she'd try to seduce him. A laugh burst from his lips. Seduce him? He wasn't even really sure if that's what she'd attempted in the first place. Maybe she was just thinking of her family. He caught a glimpse of his own reflection in the mirror behind the bar. Was he a man such a pretty young girl would want? Did it matter? He and Vivi had important living to do. He'd waited his whole life for a shot at the life ahead in Denver. No, it didn't matter. He had no way of knowing if the maid overheard the name Rafe Bennett or not. It was like taking a bank. He'd need a plan for every possible situation. He would not risk Vivi, his baby daughter and the life he wanted.

"How fast does this train go?"

The bartender blinked. "They tell me as fast as thirty miles in a single hour, sir."

* * *

Denver was even more populated than St. Louis, lively with rough miners and loggers, Chinese, Irish, Italian, merchants of all kinds, and money men from all over the country. Rafe quickly settled his family into a large hotel suite in the wealthy center of the burgeoning city. He'd privately instructed Vivi to continue to keep a sharp eye on Melody, who had not spoken another word to him since the incident on the train, and thus hadn't found herself dead in a gully along the Northern Pacific Railroad tracks. During the days, he left to explore the city and his options, and he was close to making a few business decisions that would set them up well for a very long time.

Rafe was a calculated man, a man with a plan for everything and nothing escaped his mind, no matter how trivial. One morning he walked into the suite with a flourish and held out a small box to his wife. Vivi was seated at her dressing table, looking over a mountain of new clothing for their growing daughter. She handed a sweet little white lace dress to Melody then eyed the box.

"What's this?"

He smiled and opened it, revealing a diamond and sapphire necklace that cost him more than he intended. Vivi was not a woman desirous of such things, but he had his reasons. Her eyes widened with surprise and he stepped behind to clasp it around her beautiful neck. Her finger grazed the jewel delicately then he kissed her shoulder.

"Oh, Rafe! What is this for?"

"Because I love you, darlin'. Do you like it?" A quick glance confirmed Melody's disappointment before the maid turned her back to dress the baby. Rafe stifled a satisfied grin. That girl needed to know her place.

"It's so beautiful! But it's too much. Where would I wear such a necklace?"

"There's an opera house in town, someday we'll take in the music and I can show off my beautiful wife to all of Denver." He kissed her deeply, his tongue softly playing in her mouth, savoring her flavor. Lowering on one knee near the baby, he placed another box into the child's hand. "This is for lovely little Louise."

"What on earth?" Vivi smiled when he opened the box and held out a sparkling silver spoon. The baby's eyes glittered with excitement and she giggled, awkwardly gripped the spoon then pounded it onto the floor.

"She has no idea what to do with it." Vivi laughed.

"It's for her future, in hopes that she'll never want for anything." Rafe stood and pulled yet another package from under his arm, wrapped in brown paper and tied with ugly twine. "This is for you." He pushed it into Melody's hands and stepped back.

Melody constantly pushed his limits for irritation, never speaking directly to him but always watching him longingly. His intentions were to show just enough kindness to keep the girl quiet and close, but to never give her an impression that she had a damn thing on him. It was a strategy he knew all too well, having used it to his advantage with the men who rode with him. With her eyes down, she fingered the rough twine.

"Open it," he said, nothing near pleasure in his expression, but Vivi smiled happily and watched.

In the package was a simple shawl, the ugliest one he could find in the roughest mercantile in town.

"Thank you, Mr. Forester."

"Yes ... well ... now," he said with a clap of his hands. "Ladies, put on your bonnets, there's something I want to show you."

Melody had grown sullen and a little pale. "Ma'am, I don't feel very well. If you don't mind, I'd like to stay behind."

"No." Rafe snapped. "It's a beautiful day, a little sunshine ain't gonna hurt you none."

Vivi blinked at his brusqueness but said nothing and hurried them along. The day would go as he planned without her input, perhaps for the first time since he laid eyes on her. He loved Vivi with all his heart, but never cared for her mouth where his intentions were concerned. Glad for small blessings, he drove the carriage through the city and up a hill. Many waved or called out to greet him along the way, men he'd been cultivating as future business partners, good poker players and prospective associates. Every moment of his day was part of a grand plan and not one of those moments could be wasted. He smiled or nodded and at least twice stopped the carriage to introduce Vivi to affluent passersby.

Atop the hill, construction and dirt and grunting men moved in whirlwinds around the almost finished structure. He'd been visiting daily, watching every detail and although it still required work before they could take residence, he felt it was time to show his wife. The house had grown skin over its bones of fine Denver lumber. It boasted a large porch that elegantly wrapped around the entire structure, curly wooden millwork adorned the high pointed roof peaks, and men precariously hung from ropes to paint the exterior a lovely shade of blue.

"Welcome home, Vivi." He watched her carefully.

She didn't squeal with excitement or leap into his arms; instead she slowly, thoughtfully walked close to the front door then around the entire house. He held his breath. Did she hate it? Maybe he should've asked her opinion earlier. When she rejoined him a smile rose at the corners of her mouth and he finally sighed with relief. "I've been watching this house being built, and Rafe, I hate to admit it, but I actually hoped it was for us."

"Let's take a look inside." His chest puffed with pride, knowing that if she appreciated the outside, she would love the inside. He toured them from room to room, explaining what each space was for and how they were designed to catch the morning or evening light. Up a grand, curving staircase, he showed them a lovely sitting room, numerous bedrooms and a room just for him. "A place where I can meet with men, talk business," he explained. "Have a desk … some books … the builder calls it a gentleman's study."

"Yes, I see." Vivi smiled and moved into a massive room across the hall. "And this?"

"Our bedroom," he said in a soft whisper.

Melody sniffled softly then carried little Louise into the rooms designated as the nursery and disappeared around a corner.

Rafe turned to Vivi. "I've ordered Melody to—"

"Ordered her?" Vivi's brow rose in distaste and he cleared his throat.

"I've asked her to help you set up housekeeping. We can move here as soon as next week if you'd like, unless there's something else you'd like to see added."

She smiled and his aching heart relaxed. "It's perfect, so much more than I ever dreamed."

She stepped to a window and wrapping his arms around her, he propped his chin on her head and took in the view of Denver below.

"Rafe?"

"There will be gardens down there, a greenhouse, pond."

"Rafe?"

"Perfect for ladies garden parties I suppose. You're going to be a big part of Denver society, darlin'. You'll entertain and—"

"Rafe, are you angry with Melody?"

Of course she'd ask, and of course, he'd have to answer. "Don't trust her."

"She's been so good to me and the baby ... but maybe ... maybe we should send her home to St. Louis."

"Trust her even less three hundred miles away. It's fine, darlin'." She leaned back against his chest and he enjoyed the warmth of her, but Rafe found it unsettling that her every frown or smile moved him so deeply. A woman shouldn't have that kind of power over a man, but he couldn't change it.

Outside, a burly man bustled about, pointing to the men and shouting orders. Rafe helped the ladies into the carriage then walked over to him.

"Mr. Collier?"

The man turned. He had several inches on Rafe, far broader shoulders and an ugly dark scar across his cheekbone but when he smiled and reached out his hand, he looked like a happy child. "Mr. Forester. Does everything meet with your approval?"

"My wife says so, so yes, it does. Was this house built with your lumber?"

The man shuffled from foot to foot. "The best Denver lumber, I guarantee."

Rafe nodded and looked at the house. "Mr. Collier, I wonder if I can take a look at your operation."

"What? The logging? The mill?" Obviously no one had ever asked such a thing before.

"Yes, the logging and the mill."

"Uh ... sure. I'm not heading back there for a few hours yet though."

"That's fine. I'll take my family back to the hotel and meet you're here at, say one?"

Collier scratched his head. "Yeah, one o'clock."

* * *

The baby cried, overtired from the abrupt change in her napping routine. The moment they entered the suite, Rafe, again with an angry edge to his voice, ordered Melody to take Louise to the nursery and quiet the child.

Vivi's chest ached and tears threatened. Something was wrong. She knew his patterns and mannerisms so well that the change in his personality shook her to the bone. The baby's sobs continued behind the closed door, but ignoring her motherly instincts to comfort her child, Vivi instead focused on comforting Rafe.

She led him to their bedroom and quietly closed the door. "Please tell me why you're so angry."

"I ain't angry, woman. I got things on my mind, things to do. I'm leaving for the rest of the day, might not be back 'til after dark. Watch that girl, ya hear."

Even the way Rafe spoke had changed. He had returned to using words he used as an outlaw and she trembled with anger and fear for him. "No," she said sternly and stood her ground as he turned a vicious glare on her.

"No?" He moved to push past but she spoke softly, in a way she knew would reach him.

"No, Rafe. You can't leave until I understand what's going on."

When he finally looked into her eyes she could see the irritation and growing rage there. "Why are you so angry?"

"I gotta go."

"No."

He stood still as death. He could have easily pushed her aside and walked out, but their eyes locked and together they were inside a powerful world all their own. In that brief moment, she felt the connection she had with his heart and soul before falling from heaven but it passed quickly, a cruel reminder that as a human woman, she could only help him one way. "Are you doing something illegal?"

"I am not."

"Are you in some kind of trouble?"

"No."

"Has someone recognized you?"

He shifted an irritated glare toward the closed door. "Don't let that girl out of your sight."

"Rafe." Vivi reached out and wrapped her arms around him, kissed his neck and held him tight but he did not return the embrace. "We can't live like that. If we can't trust her we have to do something ... send her away ... keep her quiet somehow."

"You know the only way to keep her mouth shut."

Vivi drew in a sharp breath and stepped away. "Don't. Please, don't. Listen." She paced, her mind racing. Somehow she had to take this responsibility from his shoulders. She couldn't bear the thought of another murder staining his soul. "Okay, okay, listen, Rafe. Don't worry about Melody. I can watch over her, keep her close. I can be sure she knows how good she has it here with us. I can remind her how much her family needs the money. Let me take care of it, please."

A sad smile pulled at Rafe's lips. "Like you said, darlin'. We can't live like that. Besides, it's more than money she wants, I think."

"What? She doesn't seem like a girl to be so manipulative."

"Vivi." He gave a snort. "How can you be a woman and not know a damn thing about women?"

"It doesn't matter, I have good senses. I can handle this, so please don't worry about her anymore. Let me do this for you."

"You can try." He reached for his hat. "Right now, I gotta go meet with Collier."

"The builder?"

"And the biggest lumber man in Denver."

She smiled, knowing Rafe wished to also own a lumber business, and pleased beyond words that his focus remained on things that wouldn't get him discovered or killed. "I see. Do have a good meeting and don't worry about anything. Trust me, I will take care of this."

He finally touched her, running a tender finger along her cheek that sent a thrill through her veins. "You, beautiful Vivi, will do anything to protect me, but darlin', I can protect myself. Just watch her. This might all be for nothing. She might not tell anyone, she might not even know what we think she knows. Look." He brushed a soft kiss against her lips. "I'll be nicer to her. You keep her busy and close. It'll all work out fine."

He left without another word and Vivi sat on the edge of the bed, knowing full well that things could easily go sour. Poor Melody could be dead sooner than later, crushing the last hope for Rafe's redemption unless she could somehow force the girl's loyalty.

"Friendship," Vivi whispered and blinked. No one betrays a real friend. Ever since she met Melody Chase at the St. Louis Hotel, she had treated her the way all hotel guests treat the maid. A little kindness, some light conversation and an occasional small tip as thanks for services above her regular duties. It had always been Melody who brought joy and laughter to Vivi, not the other way around. Vivi vowed from that moment on to never treat Melody as a maid, but instead as a loved younger sister. She'd talk with her more, learn more about her and spend personal time with her instead of just expecting services to be rendered. They would go to the shops together and Vivi would be sure to purchase something for Melody too. She would become Melody's friend, and in turn gain the girl's devotion.

It was the best way she could think of to save Melody's life and Rafe's soul.

CHAPTER 29

Morgan Collier drove Rafe into the foothills, chattering all the way and often apologizing for the roughness of the buckboard ride. "No point in driving a fancy carriage up here … just get all messed up."

"I'm no stranger to a rough ride, Mr. Collier." Rafe smiled, enjoying the sunny day and the surroundings. The mountains boasted rich, valuable Colorado lumber as far as the eye could see. They drove along a wide river covered with downed logs, moving lazily toward a confluence where men reaching with long poles guided the lumber toward the mill situated a mile further down the bank.

"River's the only way to deal with moving the logs," Collier said, sounding like the teacher Rafe hoped he'd be. "I originally built the mill near the harvest, but getting the lumber down turned out to be one hell of a feat, so five years ago I dismantled the whole damn mill and moved it down here."

Rafe nodded, his brow curled and his mind processed everything Collier said. They drove past the mill and higher up. Already he could see thinned areas of the mountains, but none of the patches were completely devoid of trees.

"I only harvest about eighty percent in each area, leaving some to continue to grow, mostly the young trees, not ready or strong enough for quality lumber. Some loggers down them all 'cause it makes it easier to move the logs, but I'm thinking about the future. Works out real good.

See up there?" Collier pointed and Rafe squinted in the speckled shadow and sunlight to focus. The area was obviously harvested some years earlier but now blazed green with strong new growth. "In another five years, I can go back up there and do it again. It's what keeps my business alive, Mr. Forester."

With a seemingly endless supply of lumber as far as the eye could see, Collier had chosen to keep his property productive and Rafe was impressed, but even more impressed with the activity around them. All around, men removed limbs, chopped, and sawed with a rhythm that sounded like music to his ears. Others dragged downed logs to a gathering point. They'd turned and begun the drive back, but still Rafe twisted on the buckboard to watch the activity. "How many acres do you own, Mr. Collier?"

"Call me Morgan." The man halted the horses near the mill then hopped down. "Forty acres, but I buy about ten new acres every year lately. Business is good."

Rafe followed him. They toured through the noisy mill where thirty men efficiently cleaned bark from dried logs and sliced them into perfect planks for construction. He checked his pocket watch; fifteen minutes from start to finish. Astounding.

"It's remarkable," Rafe said with a smile. "Very impressive."

"So, now you gonna tell me why you wanted to see all this?"

"Let's talk somewhere quieter."

They entered the small building emblazoned with a large sign boasting Collier's Denver Lumber, The Best in the World. Rafe accepted a glass of whisky and sat in the cluttered office. "Morgan, I'm going to be up front with you. I want a logging business and I'd like to make you an offer."

The big man choked, snorted, wiped whisky that had sprayed from his mouth then giggled like a girl. "What? An offer for my business?"

"Yes, a generous one. It seems to me you've done this well and all the groundwork is laid for a huge business that can cover hundreds of acres."

"And you think I'd sell all my good work?"

"For a good price, yes I do."

Collier's marred face displayed a number of emotions, one after the other and it was fascinating to watch. Indignity, anger, thoughtfulness then finally something close to pure confusion marked his expressions.

Rafe kept his own face calm and steady. This was a card game, and he needed his best poker face to win the hand. "Fifty thousand," Rafe said and sipped whisky.

Morgan Collier stiffened in his chair and all the color drained from his face. Rafe wasn't sure if he'd insulted the man or impressed him beyond words. Rather than wait for a response, Rafe stood and set the glass on Collier's desk. "It's my final offer."

It wasn't until Rafe reached for the doorknob that the man spoke. "Mr. Forester, my business isn't for sale." Rafe turned to see the face of a man so sincere it almost broke his heart. Rafe was under the lifelong impression that everything was for sale. Maybe not. He returned to his seat and waited.

"It's a good offer, a great offer. You got no sons, Mr. Forester. Maybe you don't understand. See, I got four sons, and three of them already work the mill. This place, this work, those trees, and that mill are for them and maybe even for their grandsons. My business isn't for sale. Thanks, but no thanks."

He'd lost the hand but learned so much from Morgan Collier, he couldn't help but feel grateful. That meant a little more diplomacy than he'd originally planned on. "Morgan, you certainly are a man looking to the future and I respect that. But I'm gonna be real fair with you. I intend to own a logging business, one much bigger than yours."

The man tightened his fists on the desk.

"Now, it isn't my plan or intent to put you out of business, Morgan. I'll buy land across the river and grow to the north, leaving you the land west and south of the river for your growth. We are going to do this fair and square and not do anything to hurt the other."

"Of course. But the river ..."

Rafe's land would be above the confluence of Collier's tributary and unless he built his mill above the tributary, there could be trouble, log jams and arguments. Rafe rubbed his chin and thought a moment. "Listen, we'll work that out. I'll see where my mill will work best and if it does compromise the water flow, we'll arrange a fair time share for log traffic. Sound good to you?"

"Except for one thing. Mr, Forester, that river will be on your property. You can control it and get my business anyway if you want." The man, proud and happy all day, suddenly seemed broken.

"We'll draw up papers, Morgan. It isn't my goal to put you and your great grandsons out of business." He smiled.

The ride back to Denver was quiet, both men deep in thought. Rafe did have good intentions, but intentions, like legal agreements, tend to change and be destroyed with time, desire, and need. He knew there'd be trouble down the road. Rafe would be purchasing a hundred acres to start and be logging at twice the rate Collier was capable of milling. One day, maybe not soon, but eventually, that confluence and all their fair and square planning would come to a river war. He knew it, and would bet his bottom dollar that Morgan Collier knew it too.

But as he mounted his horse at the Denver stables, Rafe did what he did best. He tucked the future trouble with Collier into a small nook deep in the back of his mind and moved forward.

He'd already had a look at the gold mine he wanted, but not a close look. He rode west to the location and hoped for a few moments alone before the owner arrived to meet with him. The last time he was there workers bustled in and out of the mine, but that day it was silent, perhaps deemed already dead. At the yawning mouth of the tunnel, Rafe stood still and frozen. Darkness and chilled air reached out at him like deadly fingers. It felt like a prison cell, something he never really liked. The feel of chains on his wrists, the idea of lost freedom and the desperate need for fresh air pummeled him, but as frightening as it was, there was a rush of anticipation too. Logging would be his business. It would support the life he wanted. But mining? That would be his fun, his risk, and his blood pumped wild under his skin with the excitement of a big strike. He knew he could get the mine for a song. Having saved so much with Colliers refusal to sell, he still knew he'd be spending a huge amount on the tract of land north of the river. Pinching a penny or two wouldn't be bad for a mine that could make him millions.

"Are you Mr. Forester? Rafe Forester?"

Rafe turned with a smile. "And you must be Mr. Billings." He'd heard that the man was young, but Billings looked like a boy, fingering his hat nervously, his eyes wide and sad.

"Yes." He reached out a hand. "Peter Billings. Nice to meet you. Would you like to go inside?"

Rafe thought to refuse, already feeling the dark walls tighten in on him, but he waved a hand and followed. Billings carried a lamp as they walked into the darkness. "We dug two miles that way." He raised the lamp higher and pointed. "Another mile that way, and started to dig over here too. There was a small vein back here, but it played out quickly, making me about three thousand that I used to mine deeper."

"How much are you asking?" Rafe said, knowing full well the man only wanted a thousand dollars for the mine.

Silence mixed with waves of energy that raised the hair on the back of Rafe's neck. For a moment, he could have sworn that he saw a dark, ominous figure standing just beyond the lamplight's reach. Blessedly, Billings turned to lead them outside.

The man hadn't answered but suddenly Rafe wanted that mine more than anything. "I'll give you five thousand dollars."

Billing stopped abruptly and Rafe awkwardly slammed right into his back, gripped the young man's arm and guided him into the sunlight. "Well?"

Billings sat on a boulder and set the lamp down. "Mr. Forester, I need to be honest with you. I think this mine is dead, finished, played out as far as it'll go. That's a lot of money for such a risk."

"I have enough money to take a risk, son."

Billings rubbed is eyes and shook his head slowly. "Listen, I don't feel right taking so much. All I need is a thousand to pay off my debts, pay my men, and get me back east."

"And no one else was willing to give you a thousand?"

"Truthfully? I turned down the last offer, it was a month ago and I thought … I thought … I thought I was close to hitting a big vein. It didn't happen, so now I have no choice."

"Where back east?"

"New York. My family. There's a woman there I want to marry."

"And what will you do?"

Billings grinned and shrugged. "I'm good with numbers, a graduate of the Columbia University of New York City. I was to be a banker but I wanted adventure. Now I'm broke and have no choice but to go back."

Rafe leaned against the mine's rocky wall, crossed his ankles and thought. The kid's family was probably demanding his return. The fiancée was probably losing interest. Billings was definitely in a tight spot, but wouldn't take five times his asking price. It was admirable. Damn, he liked the young man. "All right," he said smoothly. "How about this … I'll give you a thousand dollars for this mine, you send for your girl, marry her here then work for me."

Billings blinked. "Work for you? In the mine?"

Rafe laughed. "No, I need someone good with numbers, a real business accountant. Mining won't be my only venture. What do you think?"

He watched the man rub his chin, weighing all the options. Rafe was betting the kid had little interest in New York, aside from his woman. Perhaps he should sweeten the pot to get himself a Columbia University of New York trained numbers man. "And."

Billings looked up.

"I'll give you a half percent for any gold I find in this mine."

"That could be a half percent of nothing."

"Could be, but I'm guessing you'd rather work for me here in Denver than go back east."

"Done."

And so within a week, Rafe bought a hundred acres of prime lumber land, a gold mine and a loyal accountant. Now it was time to make some money, the coffers were getting low and his life was a far cry from how it used to be.

* * *

Just as morning broke, Vivi slipped out of bed and went to the bathroom. Rafe snuffled a soft snore behind her and she smiled, filled with the joy of having him all to herself during their private hours. In their big bed, she gave herself completely to the intensity of his touch, the exciting rumble of his soft resonant voice, and the power of his passion. Her life was beautiful. The household ran perfectly, well staffed with all the help a woman could possibly need. The friendship she'd cultivated with Melody had become what she'd hoped, and Vivi, believing she had the sister she could love for life, no longer worried over what the girl had overheard or not. Little Louise, now four years old, had grown strong and sturdy with dark ringlets of soft glowing hair and eyes that told of both her parents. They were startling, a rich dark blue with distinct speckles of gold.

His lumber business boomed but the mine had yet to strike big. "That damn vein is doing the two step with me, Vivi," he'd say at least once every week. What might have been disappointing to another man gave Rafe delight in that he truly believed that one day soon, he'd be the wealthiest man in America.

To her, they were already the wealthiest people anywhere, although she would have been just as happy living in Pennywalker's cabin. She understood that everything he'd given her was a blessing, but struggled when seeing those less fortunate around her. Ever vigilant for the salvation of his soul, she actively assisted where possible, nudging Rafe to make cash donations for the Denver hospital and orphanage. She'd even encouraged him to support a few poor families, allowing their children to gain higher education as colleges sprouted up to serve the growing country's needs. One of her most proud moments was the day she managed to convince him to donate a large sum to help finish construction on beautiful St. Elizabeth's Church.

It was Sunday morning and they would all be going mass together, an attendance Rafe grudgingly agreed to every week with a glib "Can't hurt" comment just before entering the big doors.

Yes, her life was indeed full and happy, but standing over the sink, rinsing blood from her nightgown, Vivi felt the crush of yet another month without conception. Tears slid and dripped from her chin and she looked into her own reflection. For four years she had hoped and prayed for another child, for the chance to give Rafe a son, but it wasn't to be. Like clockwork, every full moon her monthly blood came, reminding her of the truth. This was her punishment for falling, but was it really punishment? She'd been spared the terror and pain of a dangerous miscarriage which many women died from. She'd lived well and been healthy. Perhaps this was just the way of it.

"There will be no more children," she whispered to the mirror and finally accepted with an aching heart. "There will be no more children."

Tears wiped away, dressed and primped, she gathered her family and they went to mass. Melody sat deep in the pew and Vivi and Rafe sat with a precocious, fidgety Louise between them. Melody seemed to be praying hard, as usual, her eyes closed tight and hands clasped at her chest. Vivi figured that Rafe wasn't exactly praying, especially after he'd nodded to that nice Mr. Billings who kept the books for his logging company. Knowing Rafe, he was thinking of ways to make the mill more efficient or when he'd get lucky with the mine. They'd made money on the gold dug from those ugly caverns but Rafe believed there was more, just inches away, and he was determined to find it. The mine made him happy and even thought she never feared for his life because he never entered the dusty, dangerous place, she still worried for his obsession over it.

After the long service they streamed past the priest and shook his hand. It was a far cry from the first time she and Rafe went to a church to be married. Father Montgomery was always thrilled to see and chat with them, always grateful for the fact that his church was finished.

There will be no more children. There will be no more children. So what will I do now? How shall I live my life with this sadness? Vivi's mind ached with her thoughts.

"Pay attention," came an ethereal voice whispering in her ear. "Vivi, pay attention!"

She blinked and looked around and as Rafe drove the carriage home, she could swear she heard *Pay Attention* in the whinny of the horses. Later, she heard it in little Louise's laughter, and at night in Rafe's soft snores. She heard *Pay Attention* in the bird song and the wind through the leaves in her garden. So Vivi paid attention. She paid attention inside her house, looking through every room and wondering what she was to find. She paid attention to her prayers and her conversations. She paid attention in the kitchen, while helping the cook peel potatoes.

Pay Attention. This time it came in the bubbling sound of boiling water on the cook stove. "What time will dinner be served?" Vivi casually asked.

"Oh, ma'am, not for hours yet," cook answered with her thick Irish brogue.

Vivi quickly removed her apron and left for the stables. There she found Rafe preening and grooming his horse, a pastime he often enjoyed when he was home and without demands at his office in town.

"Let's go for a walk," Vivi said softly and he turned a tender smile, leaned in and kissed her lips.

She held her breath. She seldom knew Rafe to stop any task before he was satisfied it was perfectly executed, but that fine afternoon he shrugged and set down the brush. "All right darlin'. Just let me wash up a bit."

She located Melody and Louise playing in the garden and announced they were off for a walk into town. Melody seemed cool to the idea until Louise asked, "Daddy, too?"

"Yes, daddy, too."

At that, the maid rushed for her hat and was ready at the door.

They strolled down the hill and into several stores, talked of the lovely summer weather and winter's wrath, never far from Denver and always brutal. All the while Vivi heard, *Pay Attention* again and again, as though someone walked at her shoulder, whispered right into her ear. Weeks had passed since the message first came to her and she'd paid as much attention as she could. That lovely afternoon, just after chatting with Mr. Billings' pretty young wife, Vivi witnessed what she was guided to see, and her miracle appeared. It didn't seem like a miracle at the moment, but it took less than the blink of an eye to understand.

Rafe with little Louise in his arms, pointed out things for her to see, made her giggle, and received warm hugs around his neck. Vivi watched his eyes close in ecstasy and wondered if she should stop feeling so sorry for herself that there would be no more children. Perhaps she was to pay attention to the life she had, and know that it was enough.

"Damn you little Injun bastard!"

The bellow startled her and what she saw next froze her feet to the spot. A gruff man repeatedly punched and slapped at a struggling child until it finally went limp. With that, he lifted it by the collar and tossed it from the buckboard. A small boy, no more than six or seven, lay unconscious at her feet.

The man spat and reached for the reins, but before he could drive away, Rafe had pushed Louise into Melody's arms. In two long strides he reached up and dragged him from the wagon. "What the hell are you doing?" Rafe shouted.

The man straightened his shoulders, puffed out his chest and pushed his nose dangerously close to Rafe's. "None of your damn business. Fucking kid's worthless." He turned to climb up, only to be jerked away again.

"You can't leave that boy here." Rafe growled, his eyes afire and a tight grip on the man's arm.

"He's useless! You want him, he's yours."

Vivi was paralyzed by the cruelty, but when Melody reached with the tip of her boot and roughly pushed at the little boy, she found the power to move. "Don't!" She dropped to her knees, hands hovering over the broken child. "Who is this boy?"

"Don't know," yelped the man, still held firm in Rafe's grip. "Got him and two women some months ago. Somewhere in Arizona. Those women were useless too, thought they could help with my motherless kids, but hell no. They both died."

"Arizona? Rafe?" She looked from the boy's angelic face to her husband. "Apache."

Rafe blinked and freed the man. "You can't just leave him here."

"He ain't my kid. Take him to an orphanage ... leave him there to die. I don't give a good goddamn!" He huffed his way back onto the wagon.

"What kind of man are you?" Vivi screeched.

"A man looking for work. Anyone know where I can find Forester?" He shouted to the gathered crowd.

Many chuckled and finally one pointed. "You found him, and I ain't thinking he's gonna hire you."

With a scowl he shouted louder. "Then where's Collier's place?" No one answered and the man drove off trailing a litany of obscenities.

Rafe knelt at the unconscious child's side and gently pushed his thick black hair back, revealing growing bruises and blood. Looking up, he called out. "Butler."

"Yes, Mr. Forester?" A dapper round young man with red cheeks and a shock of orange hair stepped forward while the others drifted away. It seemed the excitement was over and they had more pressing things to do.

"Get the doctor and send him up to my house."

The young man ran off and Rafe carefully lifted the boy into his arms and hurried up the hill. Vivi and Melody with little Louise in tow scrambled to keep up.

Vivi's mind sparked with wonder. She did as she was told and paid attention, and what she knew shook her to her soul. She recognized the child. It had been five years since last she saw him, a broken toddler heaped in a ditch with so many dead Apache elders, women and children, but his features were unmistakable. If he survived the brutal beating, Rafe would have saved the boy's life a second time.

At the house and out of breath, Vivi quickly sent Louise off to the nursery. She and Melody stayed close to the bed while Doctor Smythe worked over the child, but Rafe stood in the far corner, his expression a combination of concern and curiosity. Removing filthy, tattered clothing revealed damage over most of the child's body, many at various stages of healing. Finally the doctor turned with a sigh.

"Well," he announced. "This boy is still unconscious and that's not a good sign."

Rafe stepped closer and Vivi clasped her hands tight at her chest, her heart wild with fear as prayers repeated endlessly inside her mind.

"He's got at least two broken ribs. The cuts and bruises will heal well enough, but that wound on his leg could be a problem. The dressing must be changed tonight and again in the morning."

Vivi nodded and blinked back a tear but the old doctor smiled kindly and patted her shoulder. "I'll come by to check on him tomorrow. If he hasn't opened his eyes, we'll take him to the hospital and see what we can do. He could have a serious injury to the head and ... well ..." He shrugged sadly.

"Thank you," Rafe said and the man left.

"What are we gonna do with him, Vivi?" Rafe sat on a chair near the bed, his eyes exploring every corner of the boy's face. "If he survives, we can take him to the orphanage."

"Orphanage? No, Rafe. No ... we ... we have to adopt him."

"Vivi, darlin', isn't that a little much? I know he's alone, but he's ... he's—"

"Apache, Rafe. We have to adopt this boy."

He stood and tenderly gripped her shoulders, looking deep into her eyes. The room was heavy with the scent of soap and blood, and growing darkness outside the window threatened a coming storm. "Vivi, listen sweetheart, doing something like that is—"

"What?" She squared her shoulders, her jaw tight and determined. "Is there something wrong with adopting a child who needs a home?"

"Vivi, we can keep him here, take care of him ... but adoption?"

"We need to adopt this boy, Rafe." Her words rode over her tongue like gravel, insistent, demanding.

Melody, quiet since the incident in town, suddenly came to life. "Vivi, it's not right."

"How can you say that?"

"Ma'am, I truly understand how much you want another child, but if Mr. Forester adopts this Indian boy ... if he gives him his name ...

it's going to give people the wrong idea!" The maid actually stamped her foot and looked to Rafe for confirmation.

"And what, pray tell, is the wrong idea?" Vivi's fists knotted.

Melody rolled her eyes then huffed. "Vivi, for goodness sake! A man of Mr. Forester's standing only adopts such a child if he's … well … fathered it! Everyone will think that dirty little Indian," she pointed viciously, "is Rafe's bastard son. He can't adopt that boy."

"Woman! Get out of my sight!" Rafe hissed and just as the color drained from her face, Melody turned and ran from the room. "That girl is out of hand, Vivi."

"Forget about her. Rafe, listen to me. We have to adopt this child. We have to!"

He gripped her shoulders and kissed the top of her head. "I know darlin', I know you want another child, but this is foolish."

"Is it?" She stepped back. "Is it? Look at him. Rafe, you know who this boy is."

He sighed and turned to do as she asked.

"This boy was in your care once before. He's the reason you got safely through the pass so long ago. This is the boy."

Rafe blinked. "What? How could you know about that?"

Her heart jerked and she swallowed hard before responding. "You talk in your sleep," Vivi lied.

"No, I don't."

With a shrug and wave of a hand she dismissed him and sat at the boy's side.

"You were there. How could you know about that if you weren't there?" Rafe's voice was a tortured whisper.

Finally she faced him, compassion in her heart and concern for what she'd said. Lying was not natural to her and she feared she'd do it so badly, everything would change. She had to convince him, so she put on her best matter-of-fact wifely expression and tilted her head for emphasis. "I couldn't have been there, Rafe. You told me in your sleep, and I truly believe that this is that boy."

"It's not possible. Vivi, you're overly upset. Let's leave this poor child to rest. You need some rest."

"No!" She stood and this time it was Vivi's foot that stomped, vibrating the floor beneath them. "Rafe, I've never asked you for anything! Never once. I'm asking you now. I want to adopt this boy, give him your name, raise him as our own son."

He was silent, but his eyes spoke of the curiosities fighting behind them.

"Please Rafe. I'll never ask for anything again. This boy is our responsibility. We must adopt him." The floodgates had opened and her face glistened with tears. Rafe held her close but tight in the comfort of his embrace, Vivi realized that she had in truth asked for a lot since falling from heaven into his arms. She'd asked him to love her as she loved him. She'd pleaded with him to support charities and help build a church. Perhaps this time she asked too much. "Please," she begged between sobs. "Please, Rafe."

"Hush, darlin'. Hush. I'll think about it. But Vivi, as much as that damn Melody irritates me, she's right. Folks will treat us differently. It might mean—"

"I don't care what it means. I don't care if we have to move back to the cabin. It's the right thing to do, Rafe."

"Yeah, maybe it is. Maybe it is. I'll think about it."

* * *

Vivi had calmed, her remaining tears a sign of hopefulness after his hard won agreement to consider adoption. He would think on it and reflect on all the consequences, but something had to be done about Melody. Leaving his wife to nurse the wounded boy, Rafe walked directly into the nursery and poked his head in.

"Melody … in my study. Now." What he intended to say or do wasn't clear yet, only that his distaste for her demanded response.

Blessedly, in the time it took for her to walk down the hall, he had chosen his plan. As expected, she had smoothed her hair and pinched her cheeks. A crisp, fresh apron covered her plain skirt and a smile tugged at the corner of her lips. "Sir? You wanted to see me?"

He leaned back in the big leather chair and looked her over for several long moments, just like he expected she wanted him to. Her eyes lowered modestly, but her smile grew, bringing even more anger to his pumping veins. Remaining silent, he waited patiently, knowing full well that she would start the conversation herself and create the perfect opening for his intent.

"Rafe, I am so sorry about Vivi," Melody began in a calculated tone. "I swear, I've tried very hard to make her understand how to behave and grace the position you've made for her, but sometimes she is, well, I'm so sorry to say, simply not able to understand. I hope I helped by explaining how adopting that heathen isn't done in high society."

Rafe raised his chin, listened carefully and held his tongue. Just a few more moments and he'd have his opportunity. Just a few more moments.

"May I pour you a drink?" She turned, idly undid the tie of her apron and set it aside then poured his favorite whisky into a sparkling glass. Setting it at his fingertips, she casually sat in a chair and continued. "It must be so difficult for you, Rafe, to have a wife so backward and stupid as to ask such a thing. I shudder to imagine what else she tests you with."

He didn't touch the glass, didn't take his eyes from her, but he did struggle to control the rage brewing in his gut. Finally, she realized that she was not in his favor and slowly, as though he'd jump out and attack her, reached for her apron and stood to leave. Her face reddened with embarrassment, she cleared her throat. "Mr. Forester, is there anything else you need?"

He made no response and she turned to leave.

"Melody."

"Yes?" She swung around, but he was careful not to look at her, but instead sift through a stack of correspondence on his desk.

"Don't ever … and I repeat … ever … open your mouth again regarding matters of my wife, my family, or my decisions. Is that clear?" He'd spoken with a controlled serenity meant to deceive her. "Vivi cares for you, and I would hate to sadden her by dismissing you."

She curtsied politely and left. In one gulp the whisky was gone, but it didn't wash away the intense desire to rid himself of Melody Chase, once and for all. Her silly desire for him aside, he knew in his gut that she held the truth over his head, and he believed that without a second thought, she would turn him in to be hanged. He filtered through his mind, reviewing every idea he'd had about the easiest ways to kill the bitch, the best places to dispose of her body and the most effective means to use. There were his bare hands, poison, a well planned accident and of course, just taking her out to the mine one night and putting a bullet through her head. He'd rehearsed all the explanations, all the pretense required for when the maid disappeared without a trace. Only one thing deterred him. Vivi. Could he bear to tell her that lie, knowing she would see the truth in his heart? "You're one lucky, scheming woman, Melody Chase," he said in a whisper, filling and raising a glass before gulping it down. "But luck always runs out."

CHAPTER 30

Vivi had fought hard to keep the wounded boy out of the hospital, fearful he'd be deemed unimportant, ill-treated or worse yet, left unattended to die. On the third night, the young Apache child finally opened his eyes. Strangely, it was Rafe at his side.

He'd chosen to sit with the boy after the household was asleep every night, examining every angle of the child's face in the soft lamplight, speculating, wondering, marveling. The child's features were distinctly Apache, but poor Vivi had no way of knowing how many Indian children had found themselves in the same dire situation. As the white man's world grew and prospered, the red man had been pushed aside, murdered or forced onto reservations to protect America's Manifest Destiny. Only her imagination could have told her it was the same boy he'd rescued years ago. The fact that it was impossible for her to even be aware of the incident escaped his understanding, and thinking on it confused him so deeply he chose to accept that just maybe he did talk in his sleep. If so, what else did she know about him? What else should he be afraid he'd mumble during his fitful dreams? But, was it possible? What would it mean if this was the same boy? Did he owe the child more? After all, the rescued boy's father had already returned the favor, saving Rafe from sure annihilation at a posse's hands.

"She's coming," the young warrior chief had said before riding off. Did he really say that, or had Rafe imagined it? How could the Indian know about Vivi? About the future? Was this why he saved Rafe? To once again preserve his own son's life?

Rafe was a man ready and able to manage a rich man's life, a gambler's life, and an outlaw's life. These questions were beyond him and with a frustrated grunt he crossed his legs and chose to discount it all. It was just a hurt little boy. Vivi's gentle heart wanted this child and he promised her that he'd consider adoption.

The boy moaned softly. Rafe leaned closer and watched the small body struggle its way up into consciousness. When his coal black eyes finally slit open, obvious fear rippled along with pain across the child's face.

"Hush, now, you're okay. You're safe here. Hush." He smoothed the blankets over the boy's shoulders. "You're okay."

The boy abruptly tried to move, sit up, push himself free of the bed but cried out then whimpered and permitted Rafe to again tuck the blankets tight around him.

"Now, it's too early to be moving around like that. You have nothing to be afraid of. You're safe here." He spoke as calmly as he could even though concern for the broken ribs pounded in his heart. The doctor told them that the damaged bones could cause more harm, rip through a lung, or worse yet, puncture the small beating heart. When the boy settled, Rafe sat back and mused at how they watch each other, like circling wolves, unsure, stubborn to survive a fight ahead.

"You speak any English?"

Sweat speckled the boy's brow and his voice came soft but determined. "Yes, sir."

And with those two small words the decision was made. The fact that the Apache child spoke English meant little in the matter. Difficulties and challenges would come, some possibly harder than Rafe imagined, but without rhyme or reason, he knew he would adopt this boy. Visions of raising a son, seeing him grow into a man and having pride for what would come of the decision washed over him like spring rain.

"What's your name, son?"

"Manuel."

"It's a good name."

The boy shifted painfully on the pillow. "My father was a chief. He taught me English. He believed it would ... protect me."

And so it had, Rafe thought with a growing smile. "Where is your father?"

"He has gone to the Spirit World."

Rafe's mind chewed on that, recalling the young chief who saved his life and sad for such a loss. Every band of Apache had a chief. Was it wise to believe that this boy was that particular man's son? And did he and Vivi have the right to take this child and raise him as a white man? Life would be hard for him, never as easy as it should be, but Rafe would stand by him and protect him. He wanted to do so with all his heart, but first he had to be sure of the boy's desires.

"Manuel, would you like me to take you back to your people?"

A tear slipped from the child's eye. "They are all gone."

"I am sorry to hear that. More than you can know." Such a proud people. Such a loss. "I want to ask you something, son."

Those dark eyes focused on Rafe's face thoughtfully, so he carefully formed the words he'd use.

"Manuel, you have nowhere to go. Would you want to stay here? Live in this house with my wife and daughter ... and me?"

"What work will I do?"

Rafe blinked. The boy didn't understand. "No. Not to work. You will live here ... I'll raise you ... as my son."

"What do you want from me?" More tears soaked the pillow.

"I want you to be well and strong, go to school ... grow to be a good man."

The boy remained silent.

"I know I'm a white man and—"

"My father told me that once a white man saved my life."

Rafe held his breath.

"Maybe this is how I can complete the circle. I can be a good son to a white man."

"I see." Rafe said thoughtfully. "And you will stay here, let me adopt you as my own son."

"And I will do my best to grow to be a good man."

"Rest now."

"I am a warrior, sir."

A chuckle escaped Rafe's throat and he did his best to hide it and show no disrespect. This seven year old Apache could be a formidable opponent. "Well, son, that could be a bit of a problem. See, I'm the only warrior in this house. Maybe one day, we'll take turns."

"What is your name?"

"My name's Rafe Forester and you'll be calling me Father."

"Yes, Father. I will pray to the Spirits for you."

"'Round here, my wife prays to God and I pray for a nice juicy vein of gold to whoever listens to such prayers." Rafe grinned and stood. Dawn crept through the window with a pale pink light that made the boy look even weaker and more frail. "You need your rest, Manuel. Go to sleep now."

"Yes … sleep …"

* * *

Difficulties did come, but not as Rafe had warned Vivi. Those in their social circle seemed accepting of their decision to adopt and raise the young Apache orphan. Either the wives of friends and associates knew of her deep desire for another child, or they kindly avoided discussion about it when in their presence. No, the difficulties didn't come as Rafe warned, they came in other ways.

Poor Manuel had been raised wild among a wild people, but he had also endured the constant threat to life and limb. The security she and Rafe offered was unfortunately incomprehensible to him and often Manuel would grow skittish with a jittery manner about him, or sullen and near tears. Vivi did her best to comfort him, but realized quickly that having learned how to comfort her daughter wasn't the best training for soothing the fears of an emotionally damaged little boy.

For the most part, life went on as usual, Rafe's logging business continued to grow and prosper, while the mine teased and played with him. Winter had arrived and Manuel had been going to school every day with the white children of the city. Vivi worried how they might shun or torment him, and worried even more at how the average Apache boy retaliated for such treatment. The next year, Louise would also begin going to school and Vivi believed school days would be very different for Manuel. If there was one thing she could count on, it was the fact that Manuel had taken his little sister under his wing and would do anything to protect her. It was lovely to watch the two play together, how he would move items to assure Louise would never trip and fall, the way he'd help her put on her coat or button her little shoes.

"Look at this," Melody said sharply and Vivi turned from her thoughts to see a tattered bundle in the maid's hands.

"What is it?"

"Disgusting things that have no place in a good Christian home! I found this in Manuel's room. He didn't even have the decency to hide it. It's an abomination!" She unrolled the bundle to display a rabbit skin, a small dead bird, a claw from a bird of prey, what appeared to be a wolf's canine and something Vivi instinctively recognized as a medicine wheel – a small hoop wrapped with four different colors of yarn. She fingered the wheel and sighed.

"He probably stole the yarn from your knitting basket too. I warned you that adopting this savage child was wrong."

"Give me those things."

"Promise me you'll have them destroyed," Melody said, her voice shrill and demanding. "The gardener will burn them."

"No one will destroy these things. I will return them where they belong, Melody."

"Vivi! Surly you must understand. This can't happen. I hear them, everywhere. In town, here in the house, the cook, the housekeeper, they all feel as I do! Adopting this heathen will bring terrible things to you."

"I care little of what people say. Rafe and I don't seek their approval and if the cook or the housekeeper find it so distasteful to work for us, they are certainly free to leave. We can replace them, but you, my dear Melody, I could never replace you. Please find compassion for Manuel. He has lived a very difficult life. These are his things and they remind him of his life before he came to be with us."

"He should forget such things. They look like things of the Devil."

Vivi shuddered. "No. These are things of God, Melody."

"Can you be sure?" Melody eyed the bundle in Vivi's hands and trembled.

"I am very sure. Please don't worry over this." Finally Melody nodded and gave a submissive yet vaguely condescending smile.

Opening the bedroom door, Vivi found Manuel at the window, standing with locked knees, watching the fat snowflakes drift on the air.

He didn't turn, so she spoke. "Manuel, please tell me where these things belong so I can put them back."

He turned red eyes, but his tight lips didn't open and he pointed to the corner of the dresser. She set the bundle down and opened it. Stepping a little closer, he watched her and finally spoke.

"First, the rabbit skin."

With great respect, she laid the soft pelt flat on the wood surface then turned for further instruction.

"The medicine wheel in the center."

Tenderly, she laid it in position.

"The bird goes in the north."

Vivi lifted the tiny feathered carcass, it felt light as air. Then she thought. Which way was north?

"There," Manuel pointed and stepped even closer.

She carefully placed the bird, ran a gentle finger along the feathers then looked to him and waited.

"The wolf's fang in the west." He nodded approval like a wise old man. "That hawk's talon, in the south."

She looked over the arrangement, at the space void of representation. "What belongs there?"

"That is the east ... the future. I don't know what belongs in the future."

Her hand lovingly settled on his frail shoulder and she tugged him close to her hip. "You will. Soon you will understand."

He nodded sadly and she looked down into his eyes. "Manuel, I'm sorry Melody took these things from you. She doesn't understand. I want you to know you have nothing to be afraid of."

He stiffened and stepped away. "I am a warrior."

Vivi sat at the edge of his bed. "You are the warrior son of a warrior chief and have nothing to ever be afraid of." He nodded and sat beside her. "But I want you to understand that your father and I will always watch over you, always protect you and always take care of you."

Another nod then he turned to face her. "Until the time when I am grown, then I will take care of you."

Vivi blinked, wanting to hug him tight to her breast and proclaim her love, but Manuel was not comfortable with such shows of affection and seemed to be unclear as to what the word love meant. She smiled and gripped his small hand. "And we will be proud to have such a son."

They sat in silence, together watching the window where winter had come to Denver with the first gentle snow of the year. Finally, she stood and smoothed her skirt. Time to be mother. "Finish your studies then come down to dinner. It's freezing and wet outside. When your father gets home he'll be cold and grumpy." They shared a knowing grin. "We'll need you to regale us with one of your stories." Often he'd tell his Apache creation stories and legends. The boy was excellent at conveying the richness of his oral tradition with flair and color and her family greatly enjoyed hearing them.

"Maybe I will tell white man stories, but I know only a few. What they call fairy tales." His nose curled. It appeared that fairy tales bored the little warrior.

"Well, when you learn more interesting white man stories we'd love to hear those too, but Manuel, you are Apache, and you have much to teach us. Now, to your studies."

* * *

He'd had an extraordinarily difficult day. It began with an early morning scuffle at the river's confluence. Both Rafe's Colorado Logging Company and Collier's Denver Lumber Company were racing to fill orders before winter gripped the mountains and froze the river solid. Careful negotiation and the joint decision to create a gate designed to seal off Rafe's or Collier's log flow on opposite days calmed the threatening crisis, but again Rafe wondered when such simple solutions would no longer work. Already he owned and harvested from nearly two-hundred acres of rich wooded land, almost triple Collier's acreage. Both businesses were profitable and often he pondered at the likelihood of the two becoming partners. Naturally, Collier waved off even the slightest mention of such a merger. He respected that. Morgan Collier was his own man. The river, however, was another story. That day, it all smoothed out nicely. Perhaps one day soon, it wouldn't.

Rafe worked at his office in town until early afternoon, reviewing lumber orders and discussing profits with young Pete Billings, who again strongly suggested that he sell the mine.

"It costs more than it profits, Mr. Forester. It's not worth the risk."

Rafe shrugged. "Like I said, I have the money to risk."

Billings shook his head and left for the day. It was Rafe's full intention to do the same, surprise Vivi, maybe even lure her into their big bed so he could love her before dinner. The softness of her flesh enticed him, even when he was away from her. He could taste her on his tongue, sense her heat from across town, hear her soft sighs and squeals of excitement beneath the endless business conversations and negotiations. Neither the life of an outlaw, nor the wealth of his current status, held a candle to his insatiable need for her. At times he felt as he did long ago, suffering and struggling to get back to her, afraid he'd never see her again, terrified that she'd die in childbirth. Through his big office window he could see the house, grand and safe and sturdy behind a curtain of drifting snow flakes. It was time to go home to Vivi.

But as he shrugged into his heavy coat, tugged the collar up and mounted his horse, a wild call came from behind. Running toward him was a young man he recognized from the mine.

"What's happened?"

"Trouble at the mine ... two miles in ... Mayfield's hurt bad." The young man gasped for air.

Rafe reached down, gripped his arm and swung him up onto the horse then raced for the mine. He lost more men logging than in that damn mine, but something about a man dying there, in the deep darkness of hell, made Rafe shudder with fear against the icy cold. William Mayfield was the foreman. He worked the men hard but had a good, calculating mind that often redirected the constant blasting and digging to reveal small veins of gold. Losing him would set things back, possibly so far that Rafe would need to seriously consider Billings' suggestion. Mining was about more than desire or the hunger for gold. It required a nose for it. Often he compared Mayfield to a shooter he once road with. That man had an instinct and he knew which way the posse would come, long before there was any sign. Replacing a man like that was nearly impossible.

Everything was in turmoil at the mouth of the mine, men shouting and milling about. A large bonfire lit the clearing, warming men and revealing faces painted in black dust and terror. All eyes turned to Rafe and without thought he charged inside, following the glow of his lantern and hoping Mayfield was still alive. By the time he reached them, they'd

244

freed the man from rubble and large rocks that could have easily crushed him to a pulp.

A loud stream of cursing flowed on Mayfield's voice and Rafe released a sigh of relief. He knelt close to the man.

"You okay?"

"Arm's fucking broke, leg's kinda torn up, but I'm fine. Get these men back to work!" he shouted, looking past Rafe at the men around them. "Clean this mess. Fortify that damned brace over there."

Rafe stood and chuckled. "No more tonight. Take him to town. Doctor Smythe will set that arm. We'll get back to this tomorrow."

He was obeyed without question and Mayfair was laid on a flat board and unceremoniously dragged out, still shouting obscenities.

Alone, Rafe held his lantern high to examine the damage. An entire hard-earned portion of the mine was completely blocked off. He moved closer and pushed a foot against the boulders. Dust filtered from above and he shook his head. The collapse was bad, but blessedly not a disaster. No one died in the mishap. Mayfair was alive. But was it all worth it?

An ominous tingle ran down Rafe's spine and he stilled, listened for shifting around him and ready to run but there was nothing but deadly silence. The hair on the back of his neck rose and just like the first time he entered the mine, he felt the presence of another man. Instead of leaving and against all his better judgment, he moved toward it, holding the lantern high but he saw nothing.

"The biggest vein in all of Colorado is less than a quarter mile east," a voice said.

Rafe moved closer to it with an angry stomp. "Who's there? Show yourself!"

To his amazement a man did appear. At first a shadow, black as night, and then the form became more defined as the lamp light illuminated it.

"Just a quarter mile, Bennett. It's what you want. It's all you want. In fact," the low rumbling voice laughed, "it's all you need. That way." The figure's arm stretched out and an abnormally long finger pointed east.

"Who the hell are you?"

Again the figure laughed and before Rafe's eyes, it dissolved as though it was never there.

"You know me. You've known me your whole life, Rafael Bennett."

The following silence pressed against his heart and he suddenly looked back, fearful that someone might have overheard the name Bennett. He left, carrying the weight of the unexplainable incident in his throbbing chest, following the glow of his lantern and pondering the words spoken.

Outside, the men dispersed, some calling out their thanks for giving them the night off, others nodding a salute or simply watching. He'd never entered the mine before in their presence, and had somehow gained respect for doing so under such dangerous circumstances. He rode off without a word, slowly picking his way back to Denver in the darkness through the falling snow.

At the gate to his own home, Rafe stopped, sat astride the horse and listened to his own beating heart. For the first time he seriously considered riding away, disappearing, once again becoming the outlaw he truly was. The Devil himself was following him, he knew it, and he had to protect his family from such horrific evil.

But just as he was about to click his tongue and tug on the reins, leave it all behind forever, his eye caught movement in an upstairs window. Louise waved and bounced excitedly in the nursery window, her dark curls happily leaping right with her. Beside her, Manuel smiled broadly. Rafe's heart heated, pumped more intensely. Inside that house was Vivi. He needed Vivi, needed her more than air.

The stable man trotted over. "Mr. Forester. Everything okay?"

"Yes, yes. Fine." He climbed down, passed the reins over and entered the front door.

"Oh my!" Vivi teased. "You're covered with snow! You've missed dinner. I'll have cook set a plate for you. Look at you! You look like Pennywalker, all snow white haired and ... Rafe? Are you all right?"

He took her warm hand in his freezing fingers and led her upstairs. Desperation ached in every muscle of his body as he closed their bedroom door and reached for her. He kissed her hard, not realizing that he'd cut her lip against his teeth until the salty taste of blood met his tongue. Still he couldn't stop. His need had grown beyond reason and he tore at her clothes. Vivi said nothing, didn't fight him or demand explanation, simply moved with him, allowing him whatever he required. Flesh to flesh, pressing her deep into the mattress, Rafe feared his entire body would explode. Tears ran down his face along with beads of sweat that slipped and slithered their bodies smoothly against each other. When he finally reached his climax, all of his life flashed behind his tightly closed eyes. Visions of the dead men he'd stepped over, holding his squirming tiny daughter in his arms, sitting behind bars, the smell of carnage, the scent of his woman and the dust floating endlessly inside the collapsed mine shaft.

Dragging himself from Vivi, he dropped what felt like a hundred miles from her heat and laid an arm across his eyes. She snuggled close and covered them with blankets.

"Tell me what's happened. Please Rafe, tell me," she whispered.

He answered quietly, his voice a monotone, void of the emotion twisting his heart. "Trouble at the mine. Mayfair's hurt."

"Oh no! Will he be—"

"He's fine." Finally he pulled his arm away and looked into her face, the face he loved so close to his, her cool fingers soothing his brow. "Vivi, the Devil's following me."

Vivi stiffened, waited silently for him to explain.

"I saw him in the mine. He spoke. Told me the gold was a quarter mile east of where we're digging. He called me … Bennett." He whispered the last word and squeezed his eyes tight. "The Devil, he's following me. Said he always has been."

He pulled her close to his chest and held on for his life.

"You went inside the mine?" Her voice came quiet and soft.

"Yeah, it's a fucking mess. A whole shaft is blocked in the collapse."

"Inside that mine? Rafe, you know how that place terrifies you. You didn't see anything. It was your mind playing tricks, that's all. God is with us, not the Devil. Lucifer will never have you, Rafe. Never."

She'd told him that once before, but it was before he ever had her as his own, as the woman in his arms. She'd told him many things during his life, given him so much guidance since he was a boy, most he'd refused to follow. He could no longer ignore the truth. How it was possible would forever elude him, but that wasn't important. It was time to recall all she'd always been to him, done for him, and taught him, and accept it. He kissed her tenderly, running his tongue along her torn lip. "Are you sure, Vivi?"

She returned the kiss and looked deep into his eyes, her hand on his face, her heart thudding against his. "Lucifer will never have you."

* * *

It shook Vivi to her core, knowing full well that Rafe was correct and Lucifer was always at his side. Her daily focus had shifted, drifting from the contentment of human life and into a world of fearful prayer, endlessly beseeching the heavens for assistance. Every day for months she left to spend her afternoons in the cavernous, empty church, on her knees and fingering rosary beads until her back ached. Often she stood alone in Manuel's room, whispering prayers to his unfinished little Apache altar, knowing that every way to God was a good path and she'd leave none unused. She prayed while making love with Rafe, prayed as she drifted off to sleep and prayed every waking moment.

Everything she'd learned from the priest and her well-worn Bible held none of the truths she knew of a heavenly, loving and helpful God. Man's God was filled with anger and fire and brimstone. Man's God demanded sacrifice and groveling. What she recalled was a joyful God, willing to laugh with man, assist him with angelic guidance, and respond with compassion when he fell prey to Lucifer's tests. That reality was far from her now. She was human and had begun to think and respond and feel fear as a human.

Her biggest trepidation was that she'd grown to love Rafe more than God, but that would be her sin, not Rafe's, so she permitted herself to be deeply embedded in her husband's heart while shooting prayers like arrows for his protection from eternal damnation. Could she be damned for loving a man so much? Loving this man? It was a foolish question to ponder as there could be no solution. To stop loving Rafe was to stop breathing.

She'd also begun to seek Lucifer, look for him in every corner of her house, the city, even the church. If he was there, he would not reveal himself to her. It was Rafe he wanted, she knew the Devil was following Rafe and always had been. That specific memory of her former existence never left.

Her days and nights had become a litany of imploring petitions, hopes, and terror, and as a result, Rafe had become deeply concerned for her. "You're pale. You're weak. I'm afraid something's wrong." He sent for the doctor, but the old man had no diagnosis. She knew he wouldn't. No doctor could uncover or cure a terrified soul.

Winter passed then spring but it wasn't until summer that Vivi slowly awakened from her nightmarish sleep. If Lucifer was tormenting Rafe, he'd stopped because the man she loved had grown happy, his middle widened and his joy radiated. Rafe often spent time with Louise, playing and teasing her into giggles, and he'd always found time to talk with Manuel alone in the study. It warmed her heart to see them together in that room meant for men. She'd stand just out of sight near the open doorway and listen while Rafe helped the boy with his arithmetic or talked about how logs were made into planks for building houses, or why he liked having a gold mine. Young Manuel would listen, awestruck and quiet, his eyes aglow. Her family was strong and whole, and the Devil had no place in it.

It was no longer a constant vigil, but still she often looked for signs of him. Lucifer was crafty, could show himself in any form or event, in the storm that brought down an ancient oak tree, the ever elusive vein of gold, even the fact that she could not conceive. On a beautiful sunny afternoon she realized that nature was not the Devil, and that Lucifer must have moved on to another target, leaving Rafe to the good man's life he now lived. She could not have been more proud of the former outlaw. Thoughts of theft and murder had left Rafe's mind, he now spent his days in honesty and fairness, and his nights in love with her.

A light chuckle drifted from her throat and Vivi looked up at the elegant white clouds. If Lucifer did show up, she'd revel in fighting him with her bare hands. As long as she could battle, he'd never have Rafe's soul. Never. She could keep Lucifer at bay. She'd been doing it since Rafe was a small boy and she'd do it forever if necessary.

She walked pleasantly with Melody through her gardens, enjoying the warm breeze and chatter of birds. At that moment, just as she'd given herself fully to human joy, she heard what she could swear was the massive, shuffling movement of Lucifer's wings. A hot blast of air brushed past her and after a brief second to gain her courage, Vivi turned. All she saw was Melody, bent over to admire the lovely yellow rose bush and relief rushed from her lungs. Fear was a funny thing, it could create nothing but more fear and Vivi was finished with it.

"These are so beautiful!" Melody sang. "We should cut some of them for Mr. Forester's study."

Vivi smiled. "They would brighten the room nicely, but I have another idea. Melody, let's go into town and buy you a new hat."

"Me? Why would I need such a thing?" She continued to finger a rose then finally turned. "I have no need for pretty hats."

Vivi tucked her arm under Melody's. "Every girl needs a pretty hat. Maybe a new dress too, a lovely one to match the hat."

Melody blinked, her expression blank.

"My dear, dear friend. You've grown to be a beautiful woman. It's time for you to think about a husband. There are many handsome young men in Denver looking for wives."

"Vivi, I have no desire to marry or leave here."

"Oh now, you must be thinking about it, a household all your own, the love of a good man, children."

"I haven't thought of such things, Vivi."

"Well you should. Come, let's go show Denver how lovely you are."

CHAPTER 31

It took five more years, but the river war Rafe foresaw came hard and fast. Some months earlier, he'd challenged his logging manager, a man named Stedtler, to bring down more trees faster in order to get them down the river, to the mill and ready for processing. It was the largest order The Colorado Lumber Company had ever received, and he wanted to be sure it was delivered on time. Having accomplished the feat, Rafe paid the man a handsome bonus.

Stedtler grew greedy and continued to push the loggers at the same pace, driving a massive number of logs down the river's flow and creating severe log jams in the process. More than once Rafe was called to the confluence to smooth ruffled feathers and he'd ordered Stedtler to place more men on the river to assure even and safe log movement. Stedtler did so, but pushed even harder with his axmen, expecting another bonus for producing repeated high volume for the boss. It seemed the man never noticed that congratulations or another cash reward wasn't in the cards for him, only reprimands. Stedtler was either stupid or determined to push his employer into doing things his way. Rafe believed both and had already begun to look for another qualified logging manager to replace him. The headaches Stedtler caused were not worth high production, and his relationship with Collier had grown precarious.

Autumn and the bare bones of the trees glistened with endless rainfall as Rafe raced to the confluence. Stedtler had apparently posted armed men at the gate, so when Collier's men came to cut off Rafe's log flow to make way for their own, all hell broke loose. The sound of gunshots reached him and Rafe spurred the horse harder. From his saddle he took in the whole scene. Men ran from Collier's camp waving shotguns in response to the threat Stedtler's men doled out. Rafe gripped his pistol, shot into the air and shouted, "Enough!"

Everyone stilled except Stedtler who took aim directly at one of Collier's unarmed men. Without thought, purely by instinct, Rafe aimed and fired twice, once into Stedtler's arm and the second bullet catching the man's hip. Adrenalin soared through his veins and his fingers itched to do more damage but the awe and amazement on the once battling men's faces changed all that. Rafe shrugged.

"Lucky shot. He, okay?"

Stedtler rolled on the ground and hissed up at Rafe. "I want that bonus!"

"I offered you no damn bonus! Did you place these men at the gate? Armed?"

"We got a big order! I wasn't gonna let it be late because of Collier's penny ante bullshit!"

"Damn you!" Rafe lowered to the ground and stared down at the wounded man. "There's more than enough wood at the mill and you know it! This is the last straw. Get your ass off my land!"

Stedtler rolled to his knees and grunted to his feet, blood running down his arm and leg. "You ain't never gonna find a better logging man! Nowhere! No how!"

"Fine by me. Get outta my sight!" He looked around. "Anyone else hurt?"

Heads shook, Collier's men with scowls and his own looking embarrassed and confused.

"Get this gate moved! Now!"

"Mr. Forester, that's gonna take ten men," one brave young logger said.

"I don't give a good God damn if it takes twenty men! Get this gate moved!"

Collier arrived at a gallop, dismounted and rushed at Rafe, his fists ready and face red as hell.

"Morgan, I'm sorry. I didn't know nothin' about this."

"I've lost hours, you bastard! You're not the only one up here with big orders!"

Rafe stood still, allowing the man all the time he needed to swing at him, but Collier simply glared, seething.

Putting his hands out, Rafe spoke calmly. "I know. I know. And I don't even have a big order. Stedtler acted on his own."

"Hours!" Collier repeated. "I've lost hours!"

"I'm gonna make this up to you."

Collier ordered several of his men to help with the gate. The task was extremely difficult, a simple iron gate pushing against the press of Rafe's logs covering from shore to shore and moving fast with the rain-swollen river flow. Rafe and Collier jumped in and with great effort, grunts and shouts the gate was finally sealed.

"Do I gotta post armed men here, Forester?"

"No, this won't ever happen again. Stedtler's gone."

Collier blinked. "You fired the best logging manager in the territory?"

"Shot him too," Rafe said with a grin. "Listen, I wanna make this up to you. Take whatever logs you need from my harvest."

"No."

"Let me send men to help at your mill."

"No, damn it. Can I count on you to make sure this shit never happens again?"

"Morgan, I swear it. Maybe we should talk?"

"I ain't selling to you and don't want to be partners with you! There's nothing to talk about."

"Morgan …"

Collier waved him off, mounted and left.

The incident ragged at Rafe's nerves. He honestly didn't realize what Stedtler was up to. Perhaps too much contentment had blinded him to the obvious. Either way, he should have sensed trouble and sidetracked the whole thing. He wanted to make some kind of gesture for peace so he followed Collier to the mill and walked right into the man's office.

"We're done talking." Collier thumped into his chair and glared.

"Listen, I can get a deal on a vast piece of property on your side of the mountain. Over a hundred and fifty prime acres."

"You said you'd stay on your own side of the fucking river."

"Not for me, you fool. Let me buy it for you. The owner won't sell to you at the low price he'll sell it to me."

"So Beecher's singling me out? Doesn't want me buying any more land? He's planning to shut me off?" Collier was on his feet but Rafe just chuckled.

"No. I play poker with him, he owes me big. I wanna cash it in and make things right between us."

Back in his chair, Collier rubbed his eyes. "No. Can't deal with expanding right now. No."

"But ..."

"No. Just don't ever let that shit at the river happen again."

It didn't turn out like he wanted, but at least a river war had been avoided. It didn't look like Collier was out for blood over the whole mess either. He should have been pleased, but Rafe felt desperate to make sure the man knew he was sincere.

First he had to find a new logging manager, then he had to fend off Billing's daily onslaught of reasons to close or sell the mine, then, blessedly, he could go home to Vivi. Maybe she'd have an idea. The last thing Rafe needed was an enemy, but beyond that, he liked Morgan Collier and wanted to smooth things over.

But that evening he didn't discuss the situation with Vivi, in fact, he could hardly talk about it to anyone. For weeks he thought and wondered and puzzled over it, even tried to contact Collier in hopes of reopening the conversation. On a cold afternoon, he left his office and rode to the mountain, determined to face Collier and make him understand. Fair was fair and, as new as fairness was to Rafe, he wanted to see it through. The scuffle at the river's gate was bound to happen but Rafe didn't want war, he wanted to find a way to keep them both in business. He wanted to be noble.

"But Bennett, you're not noble."

The voice was right at his side and Rafe startled to see a rider who wasn't there a moment ago. The man wore black from his hat to the tips of his snakeskin boots. His face was in shadow, his body fit and strong, his back, straight as an arrow and his fingers, unnaturally long. He rode a black stallion and sat on a saddle embellished with rattlesnake engravings. Rafe gasped, blinked, hoping the figure would disappear like it did in the mine.

"You can't make me go away. I'm the biggest part of you, Rafe Bennett. Now, let's have a talk about Collier." The man turned in the saddle with a grin.

The face was striking, perfect and terrifying at the same time. Rafe wanted to slap the reins, race away, but not a muscle would move. He was in the Devil's spell and there was nothing he could do about it. All around him the sun dripped down from a clear cold sky. Not a bird chirped or sound of wildlife reached him. The silence was so heavy, he could hardly breathe.

"Now think about this," Lucifer continued, casual as you please, as though they were two riders passing the afternoon with a pleasant chat. "Morgan Collier is an idiot. He certainly doesn't listen to reason, and you've tried, my man. You have certainly tried. So tell me, why are you putting up with this shit? It's not like any of it matters."

Rafe blinked hard, his mind begging the vision to dissipate. Was he mad? No. He'd heard Vivi's voice before he touched her. He saw her the same way back then too, like an image, there but not truly there. With Vivi, it was comfort and light. With this evil, it was darkness and danger.

"Listen to me, Bennett. That river is yours, there's nothing wrong with using it for your own benefit. You believe fair is fair, so be fair to yourself. Cut off his access. Putting Collier out of business is only a natural order of things, survival of the fittest. He can't compete with you, so why are you trying so hard to make this work?" His voice was smooth as silk, moving through Rafe like heated honey. "Stop all this foolishness. You're not a noble man. You're a man to be reckoned with. A brilliant strategist, a man who knows not only how to get what he wants, but how to take it any time he pleases. I made you this way, and son, and I am proud."

Rafe opened his mouth to speak, but no words came. His tongue was locked and his ears listened against his will.

"And the mine, Bennett, you need to pay attention to me. I'll make you the richest man in America. East. Dig east. There's so much gold there you can take it and just walk away from all this bullshit. You've grown soft in this fancy life. It's time to get your take and cut away from all this foolishness."

Rafe's hands trembled. It was the truth, he was not a noble or good man, he was Rafe Bennett, an outlaw. But Vivi? Vivi.

"Forget that stupid woman. You know damn well that women are to be toyed with then tossed aside. You've known this since the first girl you fucked."

Vivi. With the powerful memory of her face, Rafe found the ability to finally react, but not with rebuttal or argument, not with his fists or his pistol which he honestly feared would do no good, instead he moved with his own intentions. He clicked his tongue and led the horse away, not to Collier's mill, not to his plush office in Denver, but home.

"You know I'm right.," Lucifer called then laughed so loud the trees trembled.

Rafe didn't turn, afraid the image was still there, but more than that he feared the Devil was correct. His mind pounded thoughts faster than his heart pounded blood. Could Lucifer be right?

For five days he didn't go into his office, he didn't check on the mine or the mill, and ignored messages sent from his managers and foremen. He sat alone in his study and thought and drank and drank. Each night he dropped onto the bed beside Vivi and fell into a drunken sleep. On the fifth afternoon there was a knock on the door.

"Go away," he shouted but Vivi entered, closing the door quietly behind her.

"I said go away, woman."

"No."

He shot a scowl at her but she sat on the big leather chair Manuel was so fond of. "Rafe, come down and sit in the parlor with us."

"I'm busy."

"You're brooding."

Another scowl but Vivi simply smoothed her skirt and watched him.

"Vivi, just leave me be."

"You have to stop this. Be fair. Morgan Collier might want a little time alone too. He might be angry or just not want any help. He's a proud man."

"What's the point?"

"Simple. When he's ready for open peace between you, he'll come to you. You're trying so hard to make things right, you're forgetting everything else, your businesses, your family."

He shot her a glare that would have made an outlaw piss his pants but she continued.

256

"Just let it go for a while. It will get better."

"How do you know?"

Vivi drew in a long breath and let it out slowly. He watched her face carefully, wondering what thoughts could be running through her pretty little head. What she said next shocked him.

"Lucifer doesn't make your decisions, Rafe. You do. It's how he works, setting ideas and thoughts inside your mind and letting you decide how you will deal with them. He has no real power. And now that you are a good man, he's desperate, trying harder, afraid he's lost your attention. He has no power over you. Trust me."

"How can you know this?"

She shrugged. "I know you saw him again, and I believe you. Please don't let him ruin your life here with us."

"What does it fucking matter? It's too late. What good does any of this do?"

"So you think you can just ride away? Let the Devil lead you straight to hell?" Her voice was a whisper, her eyes sparkled with tears. "Oh yes, I know you've thought about it, but Rafe, look at yourself. You're no longer an outlaw. You can't go back to that life. You're fat and happy and—"

"Vivi."

"It's the truth. You're not suited for that life anymore. It never served you the way this life does."

He grew silent, his mind chewing on her words. He knew his trigger finger was good; he used it to protect Collier's man at the river. Yes, he wasn't the lean, strong young man he once was, but he could toughen up again, or get himself shot to death trying. What was he trying to do? Be noble? Good? How could it make any difference? What God would forgive a scarred soul like him? He'd allowed Vivi to push him toward doing good things, but were those his accomplishments or hers? Did he ever think of not doing what she asked? No, he'd deny her nothing, but he'd never imagine doing those things without her gentle push. Wanting to make things right with Collier was his idea, his obsession, his hope, and it seemed all useless effort.

"Rafe, please don't leave me."

He blinked, suddenly realizing she was still there. "Never, but …"

She sadly stood and walked out.

If there was no hope for his salvation, what was the point of it all? He blinked at the answer, blazing so clear. Vivi. His family. They were the point. If he couldn't get himself into heaven when death finally came, just maybe he could help secure a place for his family. He'd feverishly created a good life for them here and now, but maybe he could help get them into a good place when it was all over. It was time to pay attention to the way he walked his own life so that Louise and Manuel would learn from him. His own parents were not good people and it was time to do what they failed so miserably at. He pushed away his glass of whisky. Walking down to the parlor he heard Vivi talking to the children. Her words were motherly encouragement for their chess play, but he recognized the waver in it, the shaky sound of the voice he loved, fighting off threatening tears.

"Well, who's winning?" he asked, stepping up to the table and laying a gentle hand on his pretty daughter's hair. Louise was now ten and Manuel had grown into a young boy of thirteen, all elbows and knees and ears, but remarkably smart.

"I am, of course," Louise glowed but Rafe winked at Manuel who shrugged, confirming his suspicion that the boy was again letting his sister win. Rafe playfully reached out and slid a pawn ahead for her then sat next to Vivi.

He leaned close. "I'm sorry," he whispered then drew in the scent of her.

She smiled then cleared her throat. "Louise, perhaps you should let Manuel win a few games, dear."

"But when I let him win, the games are over too fast."

Rafe chuckled and rubbed his aching eyes, feeling the miseries in his heart ebb away. Was Collier's family comforting him? Did they want or need anything Rafe could give them? Would the man even accept?

Vivi chattered about the household help, the beautiful white horse he'd purchased for her, and her daily adventures in Denver. "Melody and I were in town this morning and I heard something interesting. Rafe, did you know that Morgan Collier's youngest son is very sick? Mary Bridges told me that something is terribly wrong with his back."

"Scoliosis," Manuel announced and both Rafe and Vivi looked up at the boy who continued to focus his concentration on the chess board.

"What's Scol…" Rafe stumbled over the word he'd never heard before and the boy turned to face his parents.

"Bennie Collier has scoliosis. That means his back is twisted so bad he can hardly walk. Sometimes he comes to school, but mostly he doesn't."

"How do you know this, son?" Rafe was constantly baffled by Manuel's intellect.

"I help Dr. Smythe sometime after school. He lets me carry things and read some of his books."

"He doesn't mind?" Vivi asked.

"No, he told me to come any time. It's interesting, more interesting than schoolwork. He said that scoliosis is really bad and poor Bennie might be totally crippled soon."

"Nothing can be done to help him?" Rafe was locked onto an idea and prepared to wrestle it into submission.

Manuel shrugged, a habit learned all too well from Rafe. "Doctor said there's an operation, but there aren't any doctors in Denver who can do it. Bennie's father would have to take him to New York. Check mate." He grinned at his sister who giggled and reset the board.

"And from the mouth of babes," whispered Vivi.

"Indeed." He'd go into town that very afternoon, have himself a chat with Dr. Smythe, then contact the miracle worker in New York and bring him to Denver to help Collier's son. His only challenge would be convincing Morgan it was pure coincidence that the only surgeon capable of helping the sick boy happened to be in town. He'd work that one out when he had to.

There it was, Rafe's first ever noble choice. Yes, Vivi conveyed the information, yes his adopted Apache son held the facts, but he alone would act on them by his own choice.

* * *

Outside the window, Lucifer seethed.

* * *

259

In the heavens, an emergency high-level meeting was called. The guest of honor, angelic guardian, Jonathan, stood blinking before the committee and idly brushed dirt from his overalls. "Have I done something wrong?"

CHAPTER 32

Seldom had Master Guardian Paul experienced the kind of trepidation he felt sitting at the head of the large marble conference table. This was the first time since his promotion that he held the responsibility of steering the ship for an important soul. No, Rafael Bennett wasn't particularly significant, but his soul was part of a long running battle between heaven and hell. Much had gone into protecting it through lifetime after lifetime. This could easily go on for eternity, but the man had suddenly changed the game drastically and now certain actions were necessary.

At Paul's side sat Madame Miriam, director for the Angel Traffic Division. Six other directors of major Angelic Protection Divisions rounded out the table, all as curious as young Jonathan as to why they were so abruptly called to meet.

Word had come down from above. Paul was warned that there would be rebuttal and arguments, advised to be stern and ordered to see this through. He steeled his nerves and prepared for the battle ahead. Everyone at that table had some hand in bringing the soul within Rafael Bennett this far, and not one of them would be willing to stand by quietly for what was to come.

Jonathan shuffled his feet and looked into each face. "Have I done something wrong?" he asked again. "I've done my best, I swear."

"You've done an exemplary job, Jonathan," Paul said kindly.

"Well, can I get back to it? Lucifer's at Bennett's side almost constantly. Keeping the Devil distracted has been tough, but I think I can keep it up. I know I can. Sometimes it's hard but—"

Miriam smiled, flipped through a stack of papers. "As Master Guardian Paul said, you have done extremely well. Pulling Lucifer from any man is a major challenge, and you've done it six out of seven times just in the past few weeks. Truly sterling work."

"Jonathan," Paul added. "I've called you here to inform you have been removed from Bennett's protection."

"What? If I've done so well why am I being taken off the case? I've been with this man for over ten years. I know him better than any other angel possibly can. It's a critical time. Please let me finish this job." Jonathan had the look of desperation in his eyes.

Paul simply shook his head. "The job is finished, my young friend. You are ordered a time of rest then you are assigned for Elite Guardian training."

As expected, the young angel's face brightened. "Elite Guardian training? Thank you so much … but if I could just stay with Bennett a little longer I know I can—"

"You are dismissed." Paul purposely looked down at his own reports and waited until the door close behind Jonathan. Then, of course, the predicted arguments came in a deluge. Voices rang, some shouted, others bickered among themselves and when the clamor became too much to bear, Paul simply raised his hands and spoke with authority. "Quiet!"

A welcome silence lasted but a brief moment. Lucas, Director of Life Count, spoke up first. "You must be mistaken, Paul."

"Must I?"

"Yes. This soul has been in our critical care for twelve lives. Surely there's a mistake. This has been a major effort and—"

"The decision has been made, Lucas."

Jophiel shook his mass of white hair and rubbed his eyes. "Paul, my brother, you are new at this position of Master Guardian. Our Father speaks often in riddles meant to make us think and solve the problems of humanity more precisely and strategically. Perhaps you've overreacted to the directive?"

"I have not."

"But the soul … this soul!" Gabriel himself stood and paced. "The soul is a muscle and the soul inside Rafael Bennett is a sinning muscle that remembers most how to sin. Yes, I do understand that he's made an excellent choice and I certainly see the significance of him making such a choice for goodness and kindness, a choice that doesn't require him to sin in order to accomplish the deed, but surely you realize he hasn't yet acted on that choice."

"And he may not," added Lucas with a knowing nod.

"He may," Paul said with a sigh.

"Twelve lives. Twelve sinful, murderous, heinous lives. What can make us trust that this damaged and blackened soul can ever find its way?" Haamiah pushed his golden hair back with a crackle of sparks and looked to his colleagues for agreement but it was Amitiel, and not Paul, who spoke truth with a timely rebuttal.

"My dear Haamiah, what was the reason for all our protection and guidance if not for this day? We should rejoice, not grumble and worry."

A murmur began then grew into shouts and finally Paul stood. "Is it for us to question?" All became silent. He gathered his papers and tapped them onto the marble table top. "I alone will monitor this situation and keep you all abreast of Bennett's actions and accomplishments."

"Or failures." Haamiah said sadly. "Paul, please understand, none of us want to see him fail, we have all worked hard to keep him close, protect him, pray for him to rise above Lucifer's influence, but …"

The silent room resonated with their deep held concerns. "We are not to question." Gabriel said with a reverberating shout. "So, how can we assist?"

"We must have solidarity in this, my brothers. It is Bennett's final test and will determine his fall or salvation. I need your prayers and petitions for him."

"And what of Vibrant Light?" Lucas asked thoughtfully.

Miriam stood at Paul's side. "Vivi can take care of herself. Her soul is also a muscle with memory and it will do God's will, whether she knows it or not. But mostly, she is a human woman who will watch over and care for her man. She will be fine."

The meeting ended and the sound of fluttering wings shushed with each angel's exit. When all was quiet Miriam sat with a thump onto her chair. "Vivi," she said with a groan.

"Yes, Vivi. Let's hope you're right about Vivi."

* * *

Rafe's good-doing efforts were much more difficult than he expected. After speaking with Dr. Smythe, he penned an elegant letter to the prominent Doctor Edmond Rooker in New York City.

The boy, the youngest son of an associate, is only twelve years old and in a dire situation. I'm told that you are the only physician able to help him. I invite you to come to Denver at your earliest convenience to see him. Of course, all of your expenses will be paid and you will be a welcome guest in my own home during your stay. I look forward to hearing from you.

Sincerely,

Raphael Forester

Over the weeks while he awaited word by return post, Rafe often asked Manuel about young Bennie Collier.

"He wasn't in school today. With the snow, we won't see him again, probably until spring. Dr. Smythe says it's too hard for him. He's in too much pain." Manuel sat at the dinner table, pushing food around his plate with his fork. "I told my teacher that I'd take his school work to him every day, if I can borrow one of the horses, if that's all right with you."

Pride brewed in Rafe's chest and he smiled. "I'll meet you at school tomorrow and you can ride with me. Then after, we'll buy you a horse of your own."

Several of the affluent men in Denver had purchased automobiles, but Rafe preferred being seated in the saddle, or taking a carriage or sleigh during the winter when his family accompanied him around town. He didn't trust the machines, they smelled, were noisy, and appeared useless when the snow arrived anyway. He also hated the electric lights he'd had installed in the house, opting for the warm glow of candle or lamp light. Vivi teased him often, saying that he was not a man of modern conveniences, but she liked him that way.

Things moved smoothly at the river's confluence, but dragged along slowly at the mine. He refused to permit his men to dig east,

264

convinced that it was worthless. Rafe had finally made the critical decision, if the elusive vein of gold didn't come to him by January, he would close the mine for good. Billings was pleased.

On a blustery November afternoon, a letter arrived from New York City. It was simple and to the point.

My dear Mr. Forester. I can't in all good conscience leave my patients and come to Denver. I suggest that you advise your associate to bring the boy to me.

Anger boiled in Rafe's belly and he left in a stomp for the telegraph office, wondering why he'd bothered wasting time with a letter at all. Immediacy was what he needed, Manuel gave daily reports on the sick boy's condition and even though Rafe had never seen young Bennie Collier, the images of a child in so much pain cost him many sleepless nights.

WHERE IS YOUR COMPASSION? STOP. THIS BOY NEEDS CARE NOW. STOP. UNABLE TO TRAVEL TO NEW YORK. STOP. WILL DOUBLE YOUR FEES. STOP. COME TO DENVER.

RAFE FORESTER

A response came within hours.

NOT A MATTER OF FEES. STOP. HAVE SPOKEN TO DR SMYTHE. STOP. DENVER HOSPITAL ILL EQUIPPED. STOP. COMING TO DENVER WOULD REQUIRE BRINGING STAFF AND EQUIPMENT.

EDMOND ROOKER

Rafe paced his office for hours. Why was the man so damn uncooperative? For the first time since he stood at the gallows awaiting a strangling death so many years ago, Rafe found himself praying. Not for himself and his soul, but for young Bennie Collier. Dr. Smythe told of the dangers ahead, how the poor child's organs could become compromised by his condition. Rafe feared the boy might die an agonizing, unnecessary death. He actually knelt at his big leather chair and bowed his head, speaking his own words to a God he'd never really bothered with unless it seemed all was lost for himself. Would God listen to such a man?

Walking to the telegraph office he was thoughtful. This was no longer about making peace with Collier. It wasn't about keeping himself comfortable. What he wanted now had nothing to do with anyone but a very sick boy.

BRING AS MUCH STAFF AND EQUIPMENT AS YOU NEED. STOP. WILL GLADLY PAY HANDSOMLY FOR ALL YOU REQUIRE. STOP. I FEAR THIS CHLD WILL DIE WITHOUT YOUR HELP.

RAFAEL FORESTER

The return message arrived before Rafe left for home that evening. THREE ASSISTANTS AND I ARRIVE ON SUNDAY NOVEMBER 29. STOP. YOUR COMPASSION HAS TOUCHED ME DEEPLY. STOP. UNSURE IF I CAN HELP BUT ALL EFFORTS WILL BE MADE.

DR EDMOND ROOKER

On the morning of November twenty-ninth, Rafe met the elderly Dr. Rooker and his assistants at the station and drove them in his best enclosed sleigh all the way to Collier's home. The large house stood on a hill just behind the Denver Lumber mill. It was well appointed and comfortable, but far from town. Concerns didn't reach Rafe's mind until he walked his guests up to the door. He hadn't spoken to Morgan once since the trouble at the river and had no idea if the man would even let him in.

A lovely woman, plump and pink with auburn hair and twinkling blue eyes opened the door.

"Mrs. Collier?" Rafe asked, his voice raspy and throat tight. She nodded and curiously eyed the gentlemen on her porch. "I'm Rafe Forester, ma'am, and this is Dr. Edmond Rooker. He's come to Denver to take a look at Bennie."

Morgan came to the door, blinked with surprise and to Rafe's great relief, invited them all inside. He offered whisky or hot tea to help warm them against the chill, and then listened to everything Rooker said. After asking his wife to take the gentlemen to Bennie, he stood alone in his parlor with Rafe. His face was blank of emotion except for his eyes, which spoke volumes.

"You wanted peace, but this? This is too much."

"No it ain't," Rafe shook his head and fingered his hat. "It isn't about making amends, Morgan. It's about your boy. I just wanted to help your boy. I know taking him to New York would be too hard and," Rafe shrugged, "just easier to bring the doctor to you."

"It's too much. I can never repay you."

"Nothing to repay. You're a friend, Morgan." He turned to leave and Collier followed him out into the snow. "Let me know what the doctor says. He thinks he can do the operation here in Denver, brought his help and tools." Rafe loosened his horse from the carriage. "Send word and I'll come get—"

"I'll bring them down into town for you, no need to come back out here."

Rafe nodded, mounted and sighed then looked up at the dull grey sky. "Hope this man can do what he thinks he can do."

"Thank you, Rafe. Thank you, my friend."

* * *

After that day, time and events seemed to move elegantly for Rafe. He felt part and parcel in the fabric of life for the first time in his whole life. Everything had meaning, each nuance of weather and season and the beating of his heart helped him flow with this new rhythm of his days and nights, thoughts and yes, even prayers.

Intensive surgery was performed on Collier's boy at the beginning of December. Rooker and his assistants intended to remain in Denver until February, when they would determine if more operations would be needed, but they assured Rafe that the prognosis was very good. True to his word, Rafe took in the New York doctors and Vivi made sure they were comfortable and welcome in their home, going so far as to place several small gifts under the family Christmas tree for them. Often Manuel could be found, late at night, sitting in the parlor near the crackling fireplace and talking with the knowledgeable men.

"He will make a fine doctor someday, Mr. Forester," Dr. Rooker said one evening. "It's a shame he's Apache."

Rafe glared. "What's that got to do with anything?"

The good doctor sighed. "Here in the west it might not matter much, but in New York?" He sipped whisky and sat near the hearth. "But I can tell he'll be an excellent doctor. If he chooses to follow that path, I will sponsor him at the best medical schools in the east. It won't be easy, but I'll be sure every opportunity is open to young Manuel."

"Life has never been easy for my son, Doctor. Trust me, he doesn't expect anything to be easy."

For Christmas, Rafe had spent a good sum of money on a warm, fur-lined coat for Melody, but when he donned the gifts Vivi had chosen for him, the maid made her distaste known with a hiss.

"Oh my Lord, how garish!" she said under her breath.

Vivi smoothed the beautiful new black velvet jacket over Rafe's chest and watched as he tucked the new black hat on his head. Rafe grinned, ignoring Melody and thanked his wife with a passionate kiss.

"You always look so handsome in velvet." Vivi beamed.

* * *

New Year's Eve, and Rafe and Vivi happily hosted a party at their home. Their guests included Collier and his wife, the mayor, the Sheriff's family, and several of his foremen and managers from both his logging company and the mine. The house buzzed with joy and pleasantries, whisky flowed freely and Vivi had arranged special delicacies for the meal. Rafe wanted to bring in 1908 with happiness and friends, but just after the strike of midnight and as several of his guests prepared to leave, there came a loud pounding at the front door.

Rafe chuckled. "Probably the neighbors, celebrating a little too much." He pulled the door open to a desperate, tattered man holding his obviously broken arm and gasping for air.

"The mine ... the mine ... cave in ... men trapped!"

Rafe heard nothing more, not the gasps of his guests, nor Vivi's cries for him to stay away from the mine. He ran through thick snow to his stables and as though he were racing from a posse, rode hard and fast into the mountains. He never noticed the men right behind him, all his party guests wearing fancy vests and starched collars, all riding fast to keep up and help.

Howls of fear and panic reached them as they turned the final bend through the slippery pass, and what lay ahead was nothing short of total disaster. They jumped in, grabbed picks and iron bars, wedged their weight under massive rocks and choked in the heavy clouds of dust. Only twenty men were outside the mine and Rafe's mind went mad with numbers. How many were digging on that New Year's Eve night? Mayfield, who'd been celebrating at the house, was now all business, shouting orders to men who'd probably never even entered a mine before, much less dug for the lives of trapped victims.

"How many are in there?" shouted Rafe.

"Ten, maybe twelve. Men who wanted another day's wages." Rafe blinked and Mayfield stepped closer, spoke quieter. "It ain't like we all don't know you're plans for shutting this mine down."

By dawn, they'd opened the mouth of the mine and begun moving deeper and deeper into the cluttered shafts. The earth constantly shifted, dropping clouds of dirt down on them, burning their eyes, noses, and throats. Beside Rafe huffed and puffed the old New York doctor, at his other side, Morgan Collier. Another rumble shook under their feet.

"Collier, Rooker, get the fuck outta here. You'll be needed outside more."

The doctor took his exit, but Collier stayed close. "Let's split," he suggested. "Maybe we can hear someone calling."

Rafe nodded and tied a handkerchief over his nose and mouth and headed to his left. His lungs ached but his mind was sharp and steady.

"I told you to dig east, Bennett." Lucifer's voice vibrated around him.

"Get the fuck away from me."

Laughter.

"Either help me find these men or—"

"Or what? Are you threatening me?"

Rafe ignored Lucifer, frantic to find at least one breathing man in the rubble. Over the next twenty hours they dug, rescuing two badly wounded men and dragging out the broken but breathing bodies of five. Rafe slept by the bonfire and woke early, leading three freshly rested men back inside. They searched through another entire day, called out in hopes of hearing response, and held their breath every time the earth vibrated around them. Lucifer continued to speak but his words became unrecognizable babble to Rafe, his mind locked on to the task at hand, his heart refused to be deterred. By sunset on January third, the last body was pulled from the buckled mine.

"That's it," groaned Mayfield. "Everyone's accounted for."

Three wounded men, and one succumbed to his wounds soon after rescue. Nine twisted, bloodied dead bodies were brought out of hell into the light. Rafe dropped to his knees on the muddy ground near the constantly blazing fire. He'd seen men killed, witnessed Indian massacres, done murder with his gun and his own hands, but he had never seen anything like this. This was his fault, he knew it.

Over the next few days men struggled to dig graves in the frozen earth and Rafe attended funeral after funeral. In all ten cases, he served as pallbearer, helping to carry the coffins of good men from church to final resting place. He spend his nights at his office, arranging financial support for the dead men's families, and he found a few moments every day to visit the two wounded men and young Bennie Collier at the hospital. Every moment was filled, and there was one more funeral to attend.

On the night before the final burial, Rafe suddenly felt the full brunt of the tragedy. Pain crushed down on his chest and he lowered his head and sobbed. In his study, late that night, only Vivi knew the agony he suffered for she sat with him, held his head to her breast and whispered comfort.

"This is not your fault, Rafe. Mines collapse. People die, my love."

He pulled away, his eyes aching and vision blurred with tears. Did he remember ever crying? Even as a child? Roughly pushing the wetness from his face he huffed and paced. "Yes, this is my fault. I could've closed that damn mine years ago. I should have. Men are dead, Vivi. Dead because I wanted fucking gold!"

"Men are dead because they chose to be miners, Rafe. Please don't imagine you carry this all alone. Those men took responsibility too. You ran a safe mine. Mayfair told me how careful you were, how much you demanded of him to assure the men's safety. This is not your fault."

"Those men are as dead as they would be if I'd put a bullet through their heads. I killed those men for no reason. No reason."

Vivi sighed. "Yes, they're dead but —"

"Leave me alone for a while, Vivi. I need some time to think. Go to bed. You're tired."

"You're tired too."

"Go, please Vivi. Go."

"Rafe, you went into that damn mine. Did … did …"

He stood and held her shoulders, lowering his head to face her directly. He could feel her fear, her compassion and her strength. He knew how to comfort her, even if nothing would comfort him. "Lucifer has no power over me, darlin'. None. I know that now."

She nodded and sniffled then moved into his warm embrace.

"Vivi, I just need some time to mourn. I knew these men, knew their names, their families. I need to be alone to grieve their loss tonight … before we bury Michael Price tomorrow. I just need to be alone for a while. I'm gonna sit in here tonight and think, maybe even pray for them all."

She stepped back and watched his face, searching his eyes for confirmation then finally wiped her tears. "I love you so much, Rafe."

"Yeah? Well maybe someday you'll tell me why. Now go on to bed. I'm fine."

* * *

The mine collapse had affected everyone in Denver in some way. Many knew, or were somehow related, to the victims. Dr. Rooker's plans to return to New York were delayed due to the severity of the wounded men's injuries. He and Dr. Smythe, elderly men of a similar age, had become like old friends, outworking each other and ending their days with a whisky at the saloon. Collier actively reached out to take on many of Rafe's displaced miners, offering them work at his mill or as axmen. Father Montgomery had grown ill from the emotional pressure and sadness. Women talked quieter, gamblers took fewer risks, and no one looked directly into Rafe's eyes without offering condolences.

Rafe knew nothing of how to cope with such grief and responsibility. He was like a lost child, suddenly disciplined for wrongdoing and completely surprised that the threat of punishment was real. The punishment wasn't prison or the noose. It was the shocking, agonizing pain of loss. It wasn't Denver, or the miners, or even their families, that chastised him. It was his own heart, reminding him again and again that the mine should have been closed, that his selfish greed for gold killed innocent men who trusted him. Only his flaws could have brought such a disastrous turn of events.

But even within these thoughts was the constant buzz for solutions, ways to be a better man, make the better choice and take care of those around him.

Just past midnight his study door opened and someone walked in. Rafe turned from his thoughts and the moonlit view of snow-covered Denver outside his window expecting Vivi. What he saw was Melody, naked as the day she was born and wrapped in the shabby, cheap shawl he'd purchased for her years ago. Like always, he held his face expressionless and waited for her to burn her own trail into hell.

"I love you, Rafe," she whispered. "I have always loved you, and I know that you've always loved me." In the dim room he could see the tremble of her fingers gripping the fabric at her neck. She stepped closer and slowly rounded his desk.

He watched her eyes, calculating what she'd say and do, and he carefully controlled his growing distain as she released the shawl and stood before him.

"Well, well, would you look at that," said Lucifer. "Ripe for the picking, still young and pretty with a fertile womb your barren wife does not possess."

Rafe's breath came harder, hissing with a rasp as he clenched his teeth and narrowed his eyes.

"So close you can smell her wet desire. A woman to be toyed with and tossed aside. No one will ever know, Bennett, because you'll put that bullet through her head and bury her in that useless mine of yours. She's feverish for you, desperate to open her mouth and take you in, open her legs and permit you whatever you want."

Melody stood still, her knees touching his and her full breasts heaving as she took his hand and placed it at her nipple. Her flesh seemed to radiate heat and her heartbeat felt like a thumping pulse in the room around him. "You have always wanted to love me, Rafe. You've always wanted to take me. Please take me."

The heat of her breast in his hand throbbed though his body and directly to his manhood and for the span of a breath, he leaned into comfort she offered, but that moment passed into a crash of anger. With both hands he pushed her back and onto the floor. Melody scrambled to her knees.

"Please, I love you. Let me comfort you in ways your wife never could."

Rafe stood, his nostrils flared and rage quickly growing out of control.

Lucifer stood at Melody's side with a maniacal grin. "Take it. It's yours to have. Rafe Bennett can have anything he wants and you most certainly want this soft morsel."

Rafe's breath came like fire from his lungs, hard and fast, making his heart thud painfully.

The Devil continued. "You're pissed about that mine, about never finding that vein of gold. Take it out on her, she won't mind. Break her. Make her bleed. Look at her, she's asking for it. You'll feel better, Bennett, I promise."

"Get out of here," Rafe hissed, his eyes on the woman reaching out to him. She gripped his belt and with the swipe of his hand, he roughly pushed her away again. "Get out of here."

"Are you talking to me?" Lucifer said with a casual chuckle. "Since when are you so private when you fuck? I'll stick around and watch if you don't mind."

Rafe didn't focus on Lucifer's words, he only saw the ugliness of Melody's approach, now on her hands and knees, crying in whimpering sobs. "You love me, Rafe. I know you do." She looked up, her face soaked and hair mussed. "Please, love me once, just once. Let me comfort you and have this one time with you. I swear I will never ask again."

Lucifer leaned back against Rafe's desk and looked at his fingernails. "Oh come now, Bennett. You're embarrassing yourself. Take the girl already."

Rafe reached for the shawl and threw it at Melody then knelt close to her face. Fighting growing compassion for the girl, he spoke quietly but with impact. "Get out of my house. You're dismissed. Stay away from me and my family. There's no place here for you."

"Where … where can I go?" she gasped.

"The saloon's always got a place for whores, woman. Get out."

She crumbled into a heap and Lucifer gave a tsk-tsk before bending close to the maid's ear. "You know what to do," the Devil hissed like a snake.

"Get out." Rafe repeated.

"You know what to do, Melody Chase. Go and do it."

Melody stood, wrapped the shawl around herself and walked out with as much dignity as the mortified girl could muster. The moment she left his study the air suddenly lightened, his heartbeat smoothed and his breath once again regained its normal cadence. "You both stay away from me." Rafe said to no one at all. "Forever."

Exhaustion overtook him, weakening his knees but he steadied himself and went to bed where he slept until late morning. There was one more funeral to attend. Then it would be finished and he could focus on the rest of his life.

CHAPTER 33

He gave no explanation for dismissing Melody, and Vivi asked no questions. Days passed and the little maid seemed to have completely disappeared. Rafe believed her shame would keep her away for good.

He'd taken his family to visit young Bennie in the hospital, then to the hotel for lunch. The relentless winter snow temporarily stopped and an unseasonable warm breeze had come to Denver so they walked home, the children ahead and Rafe holding Vivi close under his arm.

"This summer, I thought we might build a new orphanage."

Vivi looked up at him. "Is the building in such disrepair?"

"No, it's just so small, no place for the little ones to play or study."

"And in your mind, all orphans will become doctors and lawyers?"

Rafe grinned. "In my mind all orphans should be adopted. Can't fix everything, darlin'."

"Rafe Bennett!" The shout came from behind and even though Rafe's heart skipped a beat, he was careful not to allow the slightest hitch in his step. They were only yards from his front gate.

"Rafe Bennett! Turn around with your hands in the air!"

"Walk away, Vivi," he said, slowly, carefully freeing her from beneath his arm.

"No," she whispered. "I've been with you through it all. I'll not walk away now."

"Turn around, Bennett!"

"Vivi, please walk away."

"I'll stand by you, Father."

The sound of Manuel's voice broke his heart. "No son, I need you to take care of Louise." And he shouted louder. "Let my children get inside!"

"Turn around, Rafe Bennett! Get your fucking hands up!"

Hands in the air, he slowly turned to see four men, four rifles aimed at his chest and Melody Chase standing behind them. Rafe grinned and tilted his head.

"Gentlemen, I think you've made a mistake."

"Rafe Bennett, we're taking you to trial for murder and theft then we're gonna watch you hang. Lady, get that pistol from him and toss it over here."

Vivi glared. "Get it yourself."

"Looks like we're taking two outlaws in today." One of the men laughed, looking back at the gathering crowd.

Denver was baffled, shouting "You got the wrong man! That's Rafe Forester! He's no outlaw!"

"Take that pistol from your man or I promise you, lady, someone's gonna get real dead, real fast."

Vivi stomped her foot and shouted. "He is not Rafe Bennett!"

"He Rafe Bennett or not?" The man wearing the silver star turned to Melody and she boldly shouted her response.

"He's Rafe Bennett. He told me himself."

"Fine, you go up to him and take his pistol."

Melody cowered back, shaking her head dramatically.

"I'll give you the pistol, gentlemen." Rafe called. "Just calm down, I'll set it down and kick it to you. Too many people here who could get hurt. Just relax."

As Rafe lowered his hand slowly to relinquish his weapon, the click of a rifle being cocked rang in the quiet street and sudden movement caught his eye. Before he could grab Vivi and drop over her on the ground for protection, she slipped in front of him, her arms wide. Her lovely body jerked as the bullets sliced through her strong heart. Rafe cried out and as he dropped to his knees at her side, every rifle opened fire. He tumbled onto the bloodstained snow over Vivi and with his dying breath, proclaimed his eternal love for her.

"No!" Melody screamed, ran to him and kicked Vivi's body away to make room for her own embrace. "No! Rafe, no!"

"What'd'ya think we were gonna do, lady?" The deputy asked with a snort.

With a heart wrenching howl, Melody Chase lifted Rafe's pearl handled pistol and shot her own brains out.

It was never proven that Rafael Forester was the outlaw Rafe Bennett, and those who knew him would never consider the possibility. As the people dispersed, already mourning the good man they knew and loved, no one saw the Angels standing guard over Rafe and Vivi.

EPILOGUE

When Rafe's eyes slowly opened he knew he wasn't alive, knew it because nothing hurt. Nothing ached, not his body blasted full of bullets, not even his heart. His first focus was his hands, quiet in his lap and shackled with chains, just like the times he was captured in the hands of the law. Was he imagining this? He had to be dreaming, because the chains were highly polished sparkling silver, so bright they made him squint.

He straightened in the chair. A white chair. Odd, everything around him was white, so white the room seemed to have no beginning and no end. He cleared his throat and looked left and right then again down at himself. His black velvet jacket was white. His britches, white. Boots, white. He reached up and the shining chains clanged as he brought down his hat and that too, was white. Rafe was so baffled, all he could do was chuckle.

"Something funny, Mr. Forester?"

His eyes shot up. A man stood right in front of him. Where'd he come from? This man seemed massive, not quite human. His hair was wild and yellow as the sun, his eyes, flaming hot blue. His demeanor, nothing like Lucifer.

"I'm thinkin' you ain't Peter."

"I'm not."

Thumping pounded where his heart should be and Rafe licked his lips nervously. "My children? Louise?"

The man casually leaned back against the white wall and smiled kindly. "Louise has married Manuel."

"My daughter is ten years old!"

"Your daughter is twenty-two. Time works differently here, Mr. Forester."

Rafe thought hard on that. "Where's here? Not heaven, right?"

"It's not heaven."

"It's not hell," Rafe said with a snort.

"No, it's not hell."

"My children are all right?"

"In New York, doing quite well."

"Why am I here?"

The man paced slowly, his eyes never leaving Rafe's. "Judgment is being made, Mr. Forester."

"What's all the debate about?" Rafe felt bold, after all nothing could be changed. "I deserve hell, I earned it. Burn me."

"Belligerence doesn't go over so well here, Mr. Forester."

"Fine, fine." Rafe tried to stand and do his own pacing but found he could not. More chains than he could see rattled and rang, filling the space with unbearable noise. When he stilled, it silenced and Rafe sighed. "Who are you?"

"My name is Paul."

"Listen, Paul … I do know what I've done and who I am—"

"Do you, Mr. Forester?"

Rafe figured it was futile to correct the man and point out that his real name was Bennett, so he continued. "Yes, I do. I know my sins, know them all. Yes, I tried to do better, but it wasn't enough. I didn't have time, maybe forever wasn't enough time. I dunno. I know I belong in hell … but Vivi." Rafe was surprised to feel hot tears drip from his dead eyes. "Vivi, you have to put her in heaven. She's good and compassionate, she's strong and true and … please make sure Vivi doesn't suffer for any of my sins. I belong in hell, but Vivi doesn't."

"Vivi is being judged as you are."

"No! Tell them Vivi belongs in heaven!"

"Mr. Forester, this is not my decision."

Rafe's fists tightened and loosened, jingling the chains quietly. "Will they be fair with her?"

"You don't ask if they'll be fair with you?"

Rafe grinned sadly. "I know what I am. Know I ain't worth nothin', but Vivi's worthy heaven, I know it. Tell them I'll make a deal. Drop me into Lucifer's hands this minute, but give Vivi salvation."

Rafe had no clue why he sat in judgment in the light instead of among the flames of hell. Desperately he looked around for Vivi. Could she be nearby? Could he say his farewell to the woman who gave him everything?

Silence and time moved fast then slow, the chair grew uncomfortable and Rafe itched to run as far and fast as he could. He watched Paul while Paul watched him for what seemed like an eternity.

And he observed Paul's expression as a messenger delivered the verdict. Rafe understood that it was decided. He slowly stood, the power of the chains no longer holding him down. Rafe humbly held his hat in his hand, and then he whispered.

"I take what you give me, Lord, but I beg all forgiveness for Vivi." He blinked back tears, the memories of his whole life, good and bad, sliding like a speeding train across his mind. "I'm ready," Rafe said and looked directly into Paul's compassionate eyes.

The End

COMING SOON

The Devil's Boundaries
Book Two of the Cowboy and Angels Saga

SNEAK PEEK
The Devil's Boundaries

Chapter 1

Winter, 2013, sixty miles outside Phoenix, Arizona. Four o'clock on a Sunday afternoon. It was supposed to be his day off but that never happened. Rafe Forester snorted and shook his head as he locked the pharmacy door and walked the halls. Empty. Everyone else was off at home or in the communal lounge watching the Broncos/Cowboys game on television. Staff and inmates alike. Inmates? And for the thousandth time, Rafe wondered what the hell he'd created.

Reaching into his cluttered office, he took the stack of mail from his desk and headed outside for his car. Arizona high country. He loved it and he hated it, but it was home, where he'd grown up and learned about right and wrong. The ranch had evolved several times since Rafe inherited it at twenty-five. At forty-five, this version was his livelihood, his blessing, and his curse. For fifteen years now, it had been his life.

A dusting of snow covered the desert and clung to the rusted surface of his old Chevy Blazer. Mail. He was in no hurry to open it. Nothing but bills he couldn't pay no doubt. The one letter he'd been waiting for arrived Thursday and it didn't hold the answer he hoped for, the answer he needed. Back to the drawing board. Again. If it was even possible.

He opened the driver's door and tossed the envelopes onto the dashboard, but before he climbed inside for the twenty minute ride to the old ranch house he occupied alone, he turned and took a deep breath. Bitter winter cold seared the inside of his lungs and he choked for a moment before lighting a cigarette. It was the only habit he couldn't break. Odd. He'd conquered uppers, downers, vodka, pain pills, and ultimately, heroin. Nicotine? He had no choice but to concede defeat. Maybe his ability to fight against addiction had drawn its line. Could be worse, could be better. Could be chocolate. And he grinned at the memory of Charlene. Now that was a different life and a whole lifetime ago.

Standing in the Arizona desolation as the pale winter sun kissed the horizon, it was hard to believe he was the same man. Once he was a famous New York neurosurgeon married to Charlene Alston, a gorgeous socialite who loved chocolate, especially poured over his hard and ready cock. He was once healthy and wealthy and never happy. It only took sixteen months from the first unnecessary prescription to a full blown hidden addiction. Rafe didn't even realize it was happening until he almost lost a patient. Neurosurgery wasn't something a man could do while under the influence of anything. The incident changed everything, it changed his soul and he turned his back to the craziness in search of survival. The decision cost him his practice, his marriage, his penthouse apartment and his sanity for at least a year.

When he woke sober and straight, he was on the broken down family ranch and facing the biggest epiphany of his life. Like a bolt of lightning he knew exactly what he was meant to do, and he knew without a doubt that it wasn't going to be easy. That was fifteen years ago. It hadn't gotten harder, but it sure as hell hadn't gotten easier either.

He started like any rational person, with business plans and research, the search for investors and efforts to befriend every local and state politician he could get face to face with. Most of it was useless. The only way Rafe could get started was to do it with his own hands and what was left in his own pockets. Five years wasted to learn that stupid lesson.

He grunted and lit another cigarette. It dangled in his lips as he raised his collar and plunged both hands into his pockets in a desperate effort to avoid frostbite. Five years wasted, and how many lives lost? More than he was willing to imagine. The number of people he'd helped save? That he knew and knew intimately, by name in most cases. He turned a glance at the shabby compound, his charity clinic situated on the land originally owned by his great grandfather, Dr. Manuel Forester, who purchased the property and moved there in his old age. The place he'd put his heart and soul into was likely to close before the end of the year of a miracle didn't come along.

The ranch/clinic had taken in alcoholics and drug addicts for both traditional treatment and a strict Native American style rehab that kicked ass, putting the patient through some of the most challenging physical, emotional, and spiritual tests they'd ever know. And it worked. He'd also taken in battered wives with kids and set them up in better situations for a safer future. He had taken in mentally and physically handicapped people, helped train, or retrain them, and sent them off to be self-sufficient in the world. He'd sat in his examining room across from broken legs and broken hearts alike and done whatever he could to ease the pain, but there was no one to help with Rafe's pain. Losing the clinic would be like losing his life.

Another groan and he dropped the cigarette, crushing it under his boot. He didn't like to admit it, but just maybe he'd been going about this all wrong. Maybe he'd been too headstrong, too unyielding.

Rafe wouldn't stand for limitations. He wanted any and every technique available to help find the right road for a patient. He didn't want anyone telling him how to do things; not the medical experts, not the government and most definitely, not the pharmaceutical industry. It was the reason funding was hard to find. Major investors and government subsidies liked to have control. There was no way he could, in all good conscience, accept that. Independent grant funding was all he was left to, and therein lay the real problem.

Those grants required a clear explanation of what he'd do with the money. It was too hard to explain, too diverse, too all encompassing, too unfocused, too scattered, and too difficult to track success rates – at least according to the refusal letters. Year after year he kept trying. Year after year, the same rejections.

The Mayfair Havilland Grant out of Chicago had always been Rafe's best hope, always been the one he worked hardest to acquire, and always been the first to deny him. He took his quarterly shot, actually reworking his proposal four times a year for ten solid years. Mayfair Havilland was a private grant from the multimillionaire Thomas Reed

Havilland. Havilland was a man who held special interest in helping doctors reach unbelievable goals with more than traditional medical practices. He supported aboriginal healing facilities on reservations all over the country as well as most traditional rehab facilities utilizing the interesting practices.

Havilland was a promising avenue for Rafe's clinic, no matter how hard he had to work to earn it, but that avenue came to an abrupt close. On Thursday a letter came from the Mayfair Havilland Foundation. Rafe hoped for a check, feared another rejection, but found something even more devastating. Inside was nothing but a small newspaper clipping from the obituary section of the Chicago Tribune. Tom Havilland had died suddenly and it could take years for things to be shuffled out regarding his grant intentions for the next four quarters.

Yeah, Rafe was screwed. Big time. The grant was his last hope. He'd planned to go in person to plead his case this time, a briefcase full of photos, personal and professional endorsements, a wing and a prayer. Now all he had was a plane ticket to Chicago he hoped to cash out to help pay for the next few weeks of operations.

He looked at the clinic, a compound of three buildings plus a corral, stables and bunkhouses. The medical building was ill equipped and falling apart. The stable only stood because the patients worked to maintain it. The horses, once more than thirty, were being sold off one by one to cover the cost of food and maintenance. They were down to three, Rafe's favorite sorrel sold for a good price just last week.

Inside the big building were sixty three patients at various levels of recovery, three volunteer nurses, one on-staff volunteer physician, an Arapaho medicine woman and a Lakota medicine man.

Suddenly Rafe felt like he was letting down the whole world. He needed a deep breath and a shot of good luck to get back up again after this. He closed his eyes tight and prayed with all his heart. He was concerned for Kelly Billings. The poor girl had three kids in foster care and a slowly receding alcohol issue. If she couldn't prove sobriety, she'd never get her kids back and might most likely spend more time looking for a bottle than an AA meeting. He was concerned for young Roger Falk, who was an ex-patient volunteering his free time to help earn a medical scholarship. And, Rafe was concerned for himself. How much further could he go with this?

His stomach growled and he rolled his neck. As he moved to climb into the old Blazer, the sweep of headlights in the growing darkness caught his attention. It was a quarter mile away and not hesitating after turning into the main gate. Obviously, whoever was driving the nice sedan knew where they were and was looking for him. He straightened as the shiny black car slowed and stopped.

"The offices are closed 'til tomorrow morning," he called as the driver's door opened but his breath nearly choked him when he saw her. The woman was elegant, wrapped in a beautiful white wool coat from her cashmere emerald scarf to the arch of her tan suede boots. She looked like someone he'd have known casually in Manhattan, but not like anyone he'd ever encounter at his ranch. Ah well, maybe she was lost after all. What the hell, of course she was lost. No one that beautiful ever came looking for him. "Need directions?" he grinned then actually looked into her eyes. Rafe gulped. He had never seen golden eyes like that in his life. "Please let her be so lost it'll take a week for me to give her directions," he whispered as she walked toward him.

"Um," she smiled, her long, silky black hair swayed as she walked closer. "I hope I'm not lost. I'm looking for Doctor Rafael Forester. Do you know where I might find him? I tried his house first, then came here hoping to catch him."

Rafe leaned back against his ugly car and lit another cigarette, casually eyeing her from head to toe and hoping he looked cool. "I'm Dr. Forester. Who might you be?"

She shivered and pushed her collar higher with leather covered hands. "My name is Vivian Light. I am, well, I was Thomas Reed Havilland's grant endowment director."

"Ah well, then you know me pretty damn well I'm guessing. Sorry about your boss, Ms. Light. But," he drew in and billowed smoke with steamy breath, "I hope you didn't come here looking for a job. Looks like we're out of business in a few short weeks." Bitterness wasn't his forte and being less than charming with this beautiful woman was pretty tough. The problem was, her being pretty and all didn't help his cause one bit. He tipped his Stetson and climbed into his Blazer.

"Dr. Forester, trust me," she blocked his door, standing close and leaning down to talk face to face with him. "I completely understand your frustration and concerns, and yes, I do know you very well. I've been championing your cause for years and I was positive that Mr. Havilland had turned a deaf ear to me every time."

Rafe looked up, tried not to gulp as he fell into those remarkable golden eyes. "He had turned a deaf ear, ma'am. But thanks for your efforts." He reached around her for the handle.

"Wait!" she shuffled even closer.

Now, this presented a dilemma. Should he push her away, take her home and enjoy her, or give her a listen. Common sense prevailed and he groaned. "At least climb in out of the wind."

She scurried around and slid into the passenger seat just as the heater kicked on. Rafe turned, propped his arm on the back of her seat and sighed. He understood she probably just wanted to make her apologies and wish him well. He was used to that kinda thing, so why not let this beauty do what she came to do?

She pulled her gloves off and fumbled in her pocket. "Dr. Forester," she said softly. "Mr. Havilland knew about your past troubles."

"I never made it a secret, Ms. Light. Believe me, I know. A fallen doctor is like a crumbled god. Most holier-than-thou money people like to give to the pure of heart, spirit, and body. It just ain't me." He grinned and marveled at the soft returned smile that brightened her eyes.

"That didn't matter to Tom Havilland."

"Tell me, Ms.—"

"Vivi," she interrupted. "Please, call me Vivi."

"All right, tell me, Vivi, what did matter to Tom Havilland?"

"To do things right. And," she handed Rafe an envelope, "he finally did. This was tucked with a letter on my desk the day before he died. He explained that he too had been watching and hoping for you for a very long time, that he had heard everything I had told him about this clinic. His endorsement was behind the many small grants you've received so far. Mr. Havilland had pulled together several large endowments within his organizations and many others to begin this foundation for you, Dr. Forester. For the work you do." Her eyes sparkled. "Open it."

Rafe tore the envelope opened with shaking hands and flicked on the dome light to read the figure on the check. All those zeros! He looked past her at the broken down ranch. "And they say there are no more miracles, Vivi."

"Well," she sighed softly and placed her warm palm over his hand. "It was his intention to advise you to keep everything on the ranch, to make all the improvements, start paying your staff, and keep on doing the good work you do."

"He said that?"

Vivi nodded. "In his letter to me, and," she slid her gloves on and reached for the handle. "Now that I've tracked you down, I suppose my work here is done."

"Ma'am," Rafe reached around and automatically locked all the car doors with a quiet click. "You don't come around here and do something like this then just disappear, you know."

"What does a woman without a job to go back to, do after delivering her final endowment check, Mr. Forester?"

"She lets me buy her dinner."

* * *

Young Elite Guardian angel Jonathan laughed, kicked up his heels and shouted, "Score!" as the old Blazer drove down the road.

Paul leaned back against the corral post beside Lucifer.

"You're never going to make it easy for me to get his soul, are you Paul?" Lucifer sighed and brushed imaginary dust from his sleeve.

Paul turned and raised a brow.

The two powerful angel's eyes met — the leader of the forces for God and the fallen brother — and slowly they dissolved into the darkness.

"Until we meet again, my brother," Lucifer's sigh drifted on the icy Arizona wind.

Watch for
The Devil's Boundaries
by Deborah Riley-Magnus

OTHER BOOKS by DEBORAH RILEY-MAGNUS

FICTION

The Orphans: Book One, Lost Race Trilogy

Cold in California: Book One, Twice Baked Vampire Series

Monkey Jump: Book Two, Twice Baked Vampire Series

COMING SOON

Metatron's Daughters: Book Two, Lost Race Trilogy

Amsterdamned: Book Three, The Twice Baked Vampire Series

NON-FICTION

Write Brain Left Brain
Bridging the Gap between Creative Writer and Marketing Author

Cross Marketing Magic
Developing New Avenues for Advanced Book Marketing

Author Marketing Playbook #1
*Using Your Words for Marketing, Hooking the RIGHT Buyers,
and Growing Audience*

Author Marketing Playbook #2
*The Charity Effect, Being Socially Networked, and
Keeping Your Marketing Momentum Alive*

About the Author

Deborah Riley-Magnus is an author and an Author Success Coach. Her fiction is creative and magical. A fascination with the battle between good and evil plays out in fantastical worlds built for her specific stories, worlds that deliver childlike curiosity, dark explorations of human nature, and the struggle to remain strong in the face of danger and loss.

Deborah lives in beautiful Pittsburgh, Pennsylvania, and writes in her quiet home office overlooking the sparkling city with three rivers. Seeing that view has spurred fantasies of mystical Native American peoples who lived long those rivers, the constant "what if," and the occasional shifting vision of dragon tails whipping around the glass castle spires atop the PPG building. Are there trolls under the million bridges? Does a monster dwell in the fourth river beneath the Allegheny, Monongahela, and Ohio rivers? Does the ghost of a little girl really sing in the hundred-year-old hallway behind her as she writes? This is where real fantasy comes from. And it makes this author smile.

Blog http://rileymagnus.wordpress.com/
Teach http://theauthorsuccesscoach.com/
Fiction http://drmagnusfantasy.com/
Tweet http://twitter.com/rileymagnus
Facebook http://www.facebook.com/deborah.rileymagnus

www.ingramcontent.com/pod-product-compliance
Lightning Source LLC
Chambersburg PA
CBHW061943170626
46813CB00006B/2519